A Secret
Never Told

SHELLEY NOBLE

A Secret Never Told

A Tom Doherty Associates Book · New York

A SECRET NEVER TOLD

Copyright © 2021 by Shelley Freydont

A Forge Book
Published by Tom Doherty Associates
120 Broadway
New York, NY 10271

www.tor-forge.com

Forge® is a registered trademark of Macmillan Publishing Group, LLC.

The Library of Congress Cataloging-in-Publication Data is available
upon request.

ISBN 978-1-250-75045-7 (hardcover)
ISBN 978-1-250-76693-9 (ebook)

Our books may be purchased in bulk for promotional, educational, or business
use. Please contact your local bookseller or the Macmillan Corporate and
Premium Sales Department at 1-800-221-7945, extension 5442,
or by email at MacmillanSpecialMarkets@macmillan.com.

First Edition: November 2021

Printed in the United States of America

0 9 8 7 6 5 4 3 2 1

To Lois, with many thanks

A Secret
Never Told

1

Philomena Amesbury, Countess of Dunbridge, sat on the veranda of the Manhattan Beach Hotel, sipping a glass of champagne and looking out at the dark ocean. To her right, the rowdy display of lights from Coney Island beckoned the masses.

But on the veranda of this jewel of beach hotels, the diners were enjoying a quiet decorum—some more quiet than others, depending on their losses and wins at the Brighton Beach track that afternoon.

Phil and her friend Bev Reynolds had been here for nearly a week. Bev, who had had two horses running, spent her mornings at the stable, then joined Phil for a day of sunbathing and dipping their feet in the ocean. They'd spent one day discovering the wonders of nearby Coney Island amusement parks. They'd drunk lemonade and hiked up their skirts to ride the Steeplechase, a mechanical wooden racehorse ride. Neither of them won. They'd screamed delightedly as they rose to dizzying heights for a trip on the revolving airships. They'd even managed to cling to the Human Roulette Wheel as it revolved faster and faster, throwing off passengers without regard to gentlemen's hats or ladies' skirts.

They attended the races at the Brighton Beach track. At night, they rubbed elbows with members of the Jockey Club and danced with dashing men in the moonlight to the hotel orchestra.

And yet Phil felt an overwhelming, enervating sense of . . . ennui.

There, she'd admitted it. The fact of the matter was, the Countess of Dunbridge was bored.

Sea bathing, horse racing, even amusement parks didn't hold a candle to uncovering dastardly plots and chasing villains. And there had been very little of that lately. She hadn't had a big challenge in months. And not a major one since New Year's Eve. But that had been 1907. Now it was June, and 1908 had so far been very unproductive.

Her thoughts were interrupted by a boisterous crowd carrying one of their members on their shoulders bursting through the doors of the veranda restaurant.

They gained more than a few disapproving looks. This was not the behavior considered de rigueur by the exclusive Manhattan Beach Hotel. But it was also the hotel of choice of the Brooklyn Jockey Club, whose largesse was important to the hotel's success, and so a little leeway was accorded.

Bev Reynolds led the way, looking resplendent in a teal-blue gown, trimmed with silver spangles and sporting a train of black tulle. The ocean air had wound her blond hair into tight curls, barely restrained by a sequined bandeau.

Since they'd both given their maids a holiday, Phil had opted for a fitted silver sheath made from one of the new stretch fabrics and an organza midlength jacket, both designed for easy dressing. She didn't mind "living rough," as Bev delightedly called anything that didn't include "a retinue of people telling you what to do and when to do it."

Bev saw Phil, held out both hands in greeting, and made a beeline for the table. "A celebration and a wake," she proclaimed.

"A celebration of Devil's Delight winning me an obscenely large purse this afternoon. And black," she added, twirling to show off her train, "since the antibetting law has just passed and this will likely be the last week for gambling. Legal gambling, anyway. How will anyone make a living?"

She sighed, snatched up an empty glass, and poured herself champagne from the bottle chilling in the ice bucket. "I'll be forced to take the horses to Texas and Arizona and those other places out there." Places she dismissed with a flick of her fingers and a shudder.

She turned to her motley entourage, most of whom stood barely over five feet tall, being jockeys and not exotic entertainers from the Coney Island amusements a few blocks away. They crowded round the table; waiters appeared immediately with trays of champagne.

Bobby Mullins, Bev's stable manager—formerly her deceased husband's right-hand man, now Bev's—stepped forward.

Stocky and medium height, Bobby was a former boxing champion, reformed denizen of the city's underworld, and unapologetic lover of chorus girls. He dragged his derby from his head, unleashing a mass of untamable orange-red hair that, Phil noticed, was now laced with silver.

"To Miz Reynolds!" he exclaimed, and lifted his glass.

"To Miz Reynolds," they all agreed, and drank her health.

"To Holly Farm Stables," Bev returned. "And to all of you."

They drank again. Glasses were hurriedly refilled.

"To Devil's Delight," yelled one of the crowd.

"Devil's Delight!"

"And Johnny D!"

The little man, who still sat astride a set of brawnier shoulders than his, bowed to his fellow revelers and waved to the other astonished diners.

"And to Madame Zhora!" Johnny added.

"Madame Zhora!" they chanted.

"Okay, you lot," Bobby said. "Off you go. They've got a fine dinner waiting over at the Pabst for you. Curfew is extended until midnight, but don't forget, there's another big race tomorrow."

With a final cheer, they emptied their glasses and took themselves off, noisier, if possible, than when they entered.

The restaurant sighed into quiet conversation.

"Sit down, Bobby, and have some more champagne," Bev said.

Bobby chewed the inside of his cheek, looking like he wished he could join his men in a boisterous dinner and evening on the town, but he sat.

"Congratulations," Phil said, rousing some enthusiasm. "Devil's Delight was certainly a delight today. And Juan"—the Johnny they'd just been toasting—"rode him perfectly. Kudos to you all. But who on earth is Madame Zhora?"

Bobby scratched his head, unleashing even more unruly wires of hair. "She has a place over at Steeplechase Park. The boys go to her to have their fortunes told. You know, predict how they'll do in the coming races. If they're gonna be rich or find themselves a wife."

"Really?" Phil asked. "What happens if she predicts a loss?"

"Gawd, your-ness."

After a year of knowing her, Bobby still had never figured out exactly how to address her. And she was too entertained by his attempts to correct him.

"She don't never give them a bad fortune. She tells 'em they're gonna win, make lots of money, and marry a beautiful wife. In return, I drop her the occasional betting tip. Everybody's happy."

Phil laughed. "Well, in that case . . ."

A bellboy paused at their table. "Telephone call for Lady Dunbridge."

A ripple of excitement coursed through Phil that had nothing to do with winning horses. At last . . .

"I'm Lady Dunbridge." *Dowager,* if Phil was truthful, but she saw no reason to announce it—ever. It wasn't her fault that the earl dropped dead shortly after her twenty-sixth birthday.

Bev frowned. "I hope it isn't bad news."

"Oh." Phil hadn't thought of that. Preswick and Lily? She'd left them both in the city to have a few days off. What if something had happened to one of them? They might be servants, but she didn't know what she would do without them. And here she'd been selfishly hoping for a murder.

"Surely not. Excuse me." She hurried after the bellboy.

She returned a few minutes later. Not grieving, thank heaven. And not excited, but perplexed. She sat down and reached for her champagne.

"Who was it?" demanded Bev.

Bobby's eyebrows made question marks over his eyes.

"It was Godfrey Bennington."

"Godfrey Bennington—the aeroplane enthusiast?"

Phil nodded.

"The richer-than–J. P. Morgan Godfrey Bennington? The Godfrey Bennington who has the ear of every major politician and industrialist in the country? That—?"

Phil nodded. "That one."

"What did he want?"

"He needs me in the city—immediately."

Bobby groaned. "Oh, your lady-ness, what are you up to this time?"

"Absolutely nothing." *At least not yet.* She couldn't wait.

"You think it's a . . ." Bev looked around at the other diners and leaned closer. "A case?"

"No, of course not. Just because I happened to be a friend of a friend of his when that poor young man was killed, and just happened to be able to help in the ensuing inquiries, that's no reason to think that *he* thinks . . . Though he did say it was urgent."

What could he possibly want? Did this mean that he was part of the "team," that of her as-yet-unknown employer, who paid for her suite of rooms at the Plaza Hotel, kept her in ready cash, and required only that she do what any self-respecting modern countess would do: prevent criminals from getting away with murder?

She knew Godfrey was appreciative of her part in extricating his friends from a volatile and rather scandalous murder, but they had never discussed her actual role in solving the case, nor why she was able to do so. In fact, she'd gotten the distinct feeling that he was glad to see the back of her.

She was fairly certain he had no idea of the extent of her involvement. She was very discreet. Something she had learned—but rarely practiced—in the ballrooms of England, but had made a strict habit of—thus far—in the New World.

"He's sending his automobile to take me back to the city in the morning. I suppose I must go."

"Maybe he wants to take you flying," Bev said hopefully.

"Immediately?"

"A sudden whim?"

"I don't believe men like Godfrey have sudden whims."

"Maybe it's a government matter. He does something with the War Department, doesn't he?"

"I believe he mentioned that."

"Something top secret," Bev continued, her eyes growing round.

"I hardly think . . ."

"A spy ring . . ." Bev sucked in her breath, amazed at the possibilities she imagined.

It was possible, Phil thought. And to be honest, the idea sent a ripple of excitement through her that even the Loop the Loop hadn't managed.

"But how did he know where you were and that you didn't bring your own auto?"

How indeed, Phil wondered.

Godfrey's black Daimler was waiting at the door of the hotel the next morning at the ungodly hour of nine o'clock. Though Phil had made a point to make an early night, it was still an hour with which she normally chose not to familiarize herself.

Nonetheless, a thrill of excitement shot through her as she climbed into the back seat and the chauffeur shut the door.

She immediately fell into speculation. Urgent, he'd said. Her mind raced ahead, trying to imagine what her assignment might be. Had Godfrey requested her for some War Department investigation, something concerning his passion, the new aeroplanes? Or was it a personal matter that required total discretion to prevent a scandal? Godfrey Bennington was a power unto himself; she was flattered but a little dismayed that he should call on her to help him.

But she couldn't deny this was the most alive she'd felt in months.

The scenery whirred past her without notice, and by the time they crossed the bridge into Manhattan, she had conjured everything from aeroplane hijacking to a plot against the president.

Which showed just how unchallenging her life had been lately.

The teaming traffic of Chinatown recalled her to the fact that it was summer in the city, insufferably hot away from the ocean, and that she was a little worse for wear from doing her own toilette every day. Well, Godfrey would just have to wait. A bath, a change of clothes, and Lily's talented way with hair, and she would be ready for anything.

If her servants were even at home. In her haste to pack she'd forgotten to telephone them with her change of plans. What if they were away on an excursion of their own?

Traffic slowed to a crawl. Phil pressed her handkerchief to her nose; the smell of garbage, automobile fumes, and horse droppings made it impossible to take a deep breath. She tapped her foot on the floorboard of the Daimler. Of course traffic was always horrendous when one was in a hurry.

By the time the driver finally turned onto Fifty-ninth Street and pulled up in front of the Plaza's main entrance, Phil was fairly humming with anticipation.

The doorman, dressed in the beige-and-gold livery of the hotel, was there to open the passenger door.

"Welcome home, Lady Dunbridge," he said, and motioned the bellman to take care of the luggage.

Phil practically ran across the hotel lobby to where Egbert the elevator operator greeted her with a smile and carried her up to the fifth floor.

She *did* run down the hall, rummaging through her purse for her keys.

Preswick, the dear man, opened the door before she even managed to extract them.

"Welcome home, my lady."

Dressed in his usual impeccable uniform of black suit and starched collar, her attenuated, septuagenarian butler had never looked so wonderful.

Beside him, Lily, petite and looking younger and even more attentive than usual, curtseyed low enough to be meeting royalty. She, too, was perfectly uniformed, her dark hair brushed to a shine and pulled back into a tight bun, not a hair out of place.

Perhaps they had missed her, too?

"You're here!" Phil exclaimed.

"Yes, my lady." Preswick relieved her of her driving coat and hat and handed them to Lily.

"I'm glad to be home," Phil said. "I've missed you both terribly."

"Yes, my lady. Mr. Bennington is waiting for you in the parlor."

"Oh," Phil said, taken aback. "Oh." He certainly hadn't wasted any time; it was barely ten thirty. It *must* be serious.

Phil took a quick look at herself in the hall mirror and tucked a stray tress behind her ear, while Lily shook out her lawn skirt. It would have to do.

Phil hurried to meet her guest.

Godfrey was sitting in a club chair, a copy of *The Wall Street*

Journal opened before him and a cup of steaming coffee at his elbow.

He looked up when she entered and moved gracefully to his feet. He was tall, large-boned, and barrel-chested, and he always surprised her with his agility. He was dressed impeccably in a summer suit, his mane of pure white hair brushed back in a leonine-like sweep from a high forehead.

It was times like this that good breeding and years of training came in handy. She surreptitiously pushed the same stray tress behind her ear.

"Ah, Lady Dunbridge, Philomena. I knew I could count on you."

"But of course." She gestured for him to sit, motioned to Preswick to pour her a cup of coffee, and sat on the settee across from her guest. "Now, tell me, Godfrey. How may I be of service?"

"Well, the truth of the matter is we have a situation."

"I understand." Phil leaned forward and gave him her rapt attention.

"Dr. Erik Vogeler, an Austrian psychoanalyst, has been in Washington presenting a paper to the joint meeting of the Department about the importance of psychology in warfare."

"Are we going to war?" Phil asked, alarmed. This *was* serious. "I know the Germans and Austrians are making moves that concern King Edward, but even if there is a war, how would that affect the Americans?"

Godfrey smiled slightly. "It's a changing world. A smaller world. Anything is possible." He paused. "But nothing imminent. And nothing that can't be contained by the appropriate use of a fleet of aeroplanes, which will be much more agile than the zeppelins of Germany. If it comes to that."

"And how it that going? Your procurement of aeroplanes?" Surely he hadn't summoned her to discuss German warfare and aeronautics.

"We've finally signed an agreement with the Wright brothers. But as always, the project is moving at glacial speed. Things are potentially volatile in Europe. I'm not sure we should be frittering our time away on some cockeyed theories—" He broke off, looking slightly disgruntled, then merely nodded in a way to make her think he wasn't at liberty to say.

"Oh dear." *What cockeyed theories could an Austrian psycho-analyst possibly be presenting to the United States government? Something sinister, to be sure.*

"I was hoping to send the Vogelers back to London, where they are living at the moment, but he's scheduled to deliver a lecture at the Pantheon Club at the end of the week. There will be many highly respected intelligentsia as well as other dignitaries in attendance. And some very powerful, and rich, men who aren't in complete agreement on what's best for Europe's future. And what affects Europe will ultimately affect us.

"I'll just say that his talks with the Department have been highly confidential, so we feel that it is incumbent upon us to limit his interaction with certain, shall we say, less than patriotic citizens."

"Traitors?" *Good heavens! What next?*

Godfrey ignored her question. "The upshot is, the whole family has been invited to stay at Union House, a government guest-house just up Fifth Avenue at Sixty-second Street, while they're in the city."

"And you were designated to keep an eye on them?" Phil was having a hard time containing her bewilderment. This sounded quite serious. At the government level. How could she possibly help?

"Well, I wouldn't put it quite like that. But we've all been in residence at Union House for a week and—"

"You're staying there, also?"

Godfrey nodded, at his most uncommunicative.

He must be playing bodyguard. Phil's pulse raced with curiosity and anticipation.

"The fact is . . ."

She leaned forward. "Yes?"

"Well, I'll get right to the point. I'm having a little dinner party for them tonight and I'm in desperate need of a hostess."

2

"A hostess," Phil repeated, dismayed. "You summoned me back to town to greet your dinner guests?"

"Well, yes," Godfrey said.

"Of course, I'm happy to oblige," Phil said, pulling herself together. "And flattered, but even in summer, there must be any number of society ladies who would be delighted to hostess for you." *And would crawl over each other in order to gain such a plum even if they had to drop their duties in Newport, Tuxedo, or Saratoga to do it.*

Ergo . . . There must be more to it than just a dearth of suitable hostesses.

"But none as charming as you."

She lifted both eyebrows at him and waited for him to get to the point.

"And none so competent."

"Ah." Now they came to it.

"There is a bit more to it than that."

"Then perhaps you should explain."

"Let me just preface by saying that I'm expecting nothing untoward, and there would be absolutely no danger to anyone."

Interesting, thought Phil. The mere fact that he was mentioning danger piqued her curiosity.

She took a sip of coffee and gave him her full attention.

"Unfortunately, while they were in Washington, there seems to have been an attempt on the doctor's life."

"Seems to have been?"

"He and his wife were attacked by a ruffian in the park as they walked back to their hotel one night after visiting the theater. If you want my opinion, it was merely an opportunistic thief. Normally they would have been accompanied by Dr. Vogeler's assistant, but he'd come down with some stomach malady. And they refused to accept a government escort when they were out and about."

"And was the doctor hurt?"

"No, nothing to speak of. The culprit ran off without even robbing them."

"It does seem like a crime of convenience. And rather half-hearted, at that. Why would they think that someone would purposely attack a psychoanalyst?" Phil frowned as an idea took shape. "Because of his 'theories,' perhaps?" Phil didn't really expect Godfrey to elaborate, and he didn't.

"They've been in Manhattan for several days now, the whole family and their servants. He's spent the entire time sequestered in his rooms preparing his lecture. She's spent hours at the Metropolitan Museum; evidently she's an art enthusiast and an amateur painter. The children, two of them, are left in care of the nanny, who is constantly taking them in and out of the house all day long. And absolutely nothing out of the ordinary has occurred.

"Since the assistant is still in Washington recovering from his malaise, the Department has sent one of their aides-de-camp to fill in as his secretary until he can rejoin the family."

And to keep an eye on the good doctor? Phil wondered.

"I suggested this dinner as a polite gesture. I was thinking maybe twenty like-minded people of their choice."

It sounded ghastly. "I'd be delighted to be your hostess this evening. What do I need to do?"

"As it turns out, nothing at all, my dear Philomena. They only invited four other people. Friends from a time when they were all working together in London. We'll dine at the Arsenal restaurant. It's right across the street from Union House, just inside the park grounds. They'll take care of everything. You just need to, um . . ."

"Manage the guests?"

"As you say." Godfrey reached into his vest pocket and drew out a slip of paper. "I've listed their names for your perusal."

Phil took the list. "Dr. Dietrich Lutz. Dr. Elisabeth Weiss. Chumley Griswold. And Dr. Pietro Salvos. Oh dear, a lot of doctors and not enough ladies."

"Oh, and, also the aide-de-camp, Francis Kellogg. He seems a nice enough fellow and he knows which fork to use, so I invited him to join us, just as a courtesy to the Department, you understand."

She did indeed. An extra pair of eyes and security if something "untoward" did occur.

"A definite paucity of ladies," said Phil. "Though I suppose it doesn't matter since they'll all be reminiscing and talking shop all evening. Shall I bone up on my knowledge of psychology before tonight?"

"Just come and be your inimitable self."

"And is there anything I should know about our guests?"

"Let's see. Lutz has a practice on the Upper West Side. Weiss is a lecturer at Barnard College. It's the women's college, an adjunct of Columbia University."

"Interesting. And Chumley Griswold? He's not a doctor?"

"As far as I know, having done a little background check. . . ."

She had no doubt they had all been vetted thoroughly.

"He studied chemistry but never finished his course of studies. He now seems to make his living as a party hypnotist and magician."

"Well, we won't lack for interesting anecdotes. And Dr. Salvos?"

Godfrey's lips tightened.

"Is there something wrong with Dr. Salvos?"

"Not that I know of. He immigrated here two years ago and runs a free clinic on the Lower East Side."

"An altruistic soul, perhaps," Phil suggested.

"Or a political dissident."

Phil smiled. "I can hardly wait." Even if Dr. Salvos didn't turn out to be a dangerous anarchist, there were bound to be some amusing arguments. Reunions had a way of bringing out the best and the worst of the attendees, especially when the characters were so out of the ordinary.

Godfrey stood suddenly. "Well, I'd best be going. I'll have my driver pick you up at six? That will give you a chance to meet the family and have a drink before we go. Dinner will be at eight, since the family keeps early hours, night and day."

Phil accompanied him to where Preswick was waiting by the door with Godfrey's hat.

"Oh, there is one other thing."

"Yes," Phil said, expectantly.

"Did I mention the two children?"

"I believe so."

"I thought perhaps you could lend Lily for the evening. They're a precocious pair, not to mention they leave wreckage where ever they go. I shudder every time they enter the parlor. We've many priceless objets d'art on display there. The nanny has her hands full even when their mother is present, but without her steadying presence . . ."

"I'm sure Lily would be glad to take the strain off the poor woman. Children can be a handful when traveling."

Phil actually knew nothing about children and it was beginning to look like she never would. Something that didn't bother her in the least.

"I'm more concerned for the furniture and collectibles."

"Ah, I'll tell her to be on the watch."

He left on that, and Phil turned to Preswick. "I hope you were listening. What do you make of it all?"

"I think you will probably have a better time at dinner than Lily will have with the nanny."

"Very true. I'd better go break the news."

"I like children," Lily said, as she put the finishing touches on Phil's hair later that afternoon. "Are we investigating?"

"Not as yet," Phil said. "Though as always . . ."

"Keep my eyes and ears open. Do they suspect the nanny of something?"

"They don't suspect anyone of anything."

"Sounds suspicious to me."

"It did to me, too," Phil said, smiling at Lily in her dressing mirror.

They'd come a long way, her little household, since arriving in America a year ago. And sometimes Phil couldn't believe her good fortune. Preswick, who should be retired and living on a comfortable pension, had insisted on coming with her. Lily, whom they had literally snatched from the arms of customs agents as she attempted to stow away on the ship and hired on the spot, had been trained by a somewhat disgruntled Preswick on the crossing. Phil hadn't even known her name.

As a matter of fact, she still didn't know her name. Phil had merely started calling her Lily because of her fair skin, an exotic contrast to her dark, dark hair.

It had all worked out excellently.

A year later, they lived in luxurious apartments in the Plaza and had stumbled into a lucrative and exciting detective way of life.

"Perhaps you should take your pistol," Lily said, adding the last ivory-tipped pin to Phil's hair, and slicing perilously close to Phil's scalp. It was a very sharp hairpin, rather longer than the rest and always placed last and in the same position for a quick and smooth extraction if ever it was needed as a weapon.

Phil had learned so much about the world since moving to America. That hairpin would have been a handy instrument among some of the men of the peerage she'd known, though perhaps one less lethal would have done the trick.

Lily handed Phil a gilt hand mirror, and she dutifully checked every angle of her new hair style. "Lovely, as always, Lily. You have turned into a first-class coiffeuse."

"Thank you, madam." Lily curtseyed smoothly, a sure sign that she was pleased by the compliment. Lily's curtseys could communicate her mood better than any facial expression, only to be surpassed by the angry roll of her r's when she was upset.

Lily's remarkable personality and Preswick's new interest in life were inspirations to Phil. And she would never again take anyone in her household for granted.

She felt a rush of warmth and affection for her servants—something her mother had warned her continuously not to do. It was one of the many rules she had no intention of obeying in her new life in America. As for Preswick and Lily, they were more family to her now than the one she'd firmly left behind in England.

Phil stood, letting the silk dressing kimono slide from her shoulders, and stepped into the champagne crepe de chine dinner gown that had been shipped from Paris well in time for the summer season. The currently fashionable Directoire style, with narrow skirt and high empire waist, suited her figure and comfort exactly.

As she turned to have Lily do up the buttons that ran down the back, the paillettes of pearls along the neckline glowed in the lamplight and set off the highlights of titian red in her hair. Monsieur Doucet had outdone himself.

Lily draped a wrap of the lightest rose gauze over Phil's shoulders.

"Excellent," Phil said. "I must say that this long-distance gown ordering by telegram is working out extremely well."

"And no mal de mer," Lily added drily.

"And no dealing with Americans in Paris," Phil added. "I think it must be the wave of the future. Certainly of *our* future."

On the stroke of six, Phil and Lily were sitting in the back of Godfrey's black Daimler, Phil looking like a gilded garden rose and Lily scrubbed to a shine in a crisp black uniform and white apron.

"There's Just a Friend," Lily said, as they turned the corner to Fifth Avenue. Lily wiggled her fingers at the young newspaper boy. He stood at the same corner every day, had designated himself Phil's bodyguard, and went by his self-styled soubriquet of Just a Friend.

Phil knew his name but had been sworn to secrecy, something she took seriously since he'd already saved her from danger more than once. He nodded seriously as the auto drove by, letting them know he was on the job.

They arrived at Union House two blocks later.

Lily rolled her eyes.

"I know," Phil said under her breath. "But it was very thoughtful of Mr. Bennington to send his auto. You wouldn't want my gauze to wilt on the walk over."

Lily stifled an un–lady's maid–like snort.

The driver opened the door for them and trotted up the steps to ring the bell. The door opened almost immediately and a very starched butler, surely a military man, bade them enter.

They were shown to the parlor, a spotless room with bay windows that looked across the street to the park, and showcased several Ming vases and Meissen figurines on the tables throughout.

A disaster in the making, Phil thought. "Best to keep the children upstairs while we're gone," Phil whispered to Lily.

"Ah, excellent, you look lovely," Godfrey said, crossing the Aubusson carpet to meet them. "And you've brought the inimitable Lily." An acknowledgment that was sure to please the often prickly Lily, who stood slightly subserviently behind Phil.

"I'm sure she will be of assistance to the nanny. It always helps to have an extra pair of hands." And eyes, she added to herself, in case any mischief was on the menu.

Lily bobbed a curtsey. Phil didn't have to look to see her expression; she had no doubt Lily was playing eager-to-please lady's maid.

"Shall I send you up to them, Lily? Or shall I fetch them to the drawing room?"

"Oh, bring them here," Phil said. "I confess to some curiosity to see these prodigies."

Godfrey buzzed and the butler appeared. "Collins, ask Mrs. Vogeler if it would be convenient to present her children to the countess."

The butler bowed so crisply he could have been in the inspection lane at the changing of the guards, if Americans changed their guards.

"Cocktail?"

"Please."

Godfrey poured Phil a drink while Lily took up her position inconspicuously near the wall.

It was only a few minutes before Mrs. Vogeler entered the room in a rustle of skirts, followed by a rather bedraggled middle-aged woman with two children in tow.

"Ah, Mrs. Vogeler," Godfrey said.

Mrs. Vogeler held out both hands to Godfrey and glided forward, leaving the nanny to restrain the two children, who had every intention of following their mother. "Good evening, Godfrey.

Erik got involved in his work and lost track of the time. I've asked that secretary to hurry him up, but the man seems incapable of being useful."

"Hopefully, Dr. Vogeler's assistant will be well enough to join you soon," Godfrey said. He took her hands briefly. "Let me introduce you to the Countess of Dunbridge."

Mrs. Vogeler turned her smile toward Phil. She was plump with blue eyes that looked a little large for her face. Blond hair was pulled back into a simple chignon, and she wore a taffeta gown of light green. Fashionable enough, if bereft of adornment, though her jeweled necklace might tempt the most discerning of thieves.

"Lady Dunbridge, may I present Anna Vogeler, Dr. Vogeler's wife, and a scientist in her own right."

"How do you do, welcome to Manhattan," Phil said, smoothly taking over her hostess duties.

"Thank you. I told Godfrey that we had no need to drag you away from your own responsibilities. We're quite capable of managing on our own. But I'm delighted that you're joining us for dinner."

"I've brought my maid, Lily. I thought your nanny might like some companionship and help with the children." Phil turned to cast a smile on the two younger Vogelers, which meant she didn't miss the look that passed between the two children, a look that she had shared with her sisters on many occasions. It didn't bode well for the nanny.

"Children," Anna said, motioning the two forward. "Theresa and Erik Jr., I want to present you to the Countess of Dunbridge."

They stepped forward, both blond and blue-eyed. Theresa, thin and taller than her brother, and Erik, not quite grown out of his baby fat, executed curtsey and bow ably.

"Cole, you may take the children away now. And . . . What is your maid's name?"

"Lily," Phil said.

"Really, how odd."

Lily curtseyed without hesitation, while Phil felt the heat of resentment for her.

At the door Master Erik pulled away from the nanny.

"Mr. Bennington said there's a zoo across the street. I want to go."

"We will discuss it later," Mrs. Vogeler said. Nanny Cole slipped in front of her young charge. A useless attempt to intercede, since Erik merely ducked under her arm.

"But I want to go to the zoo."

"Why don't you make a list of the things you want to see this week?" Godfrey suggested.

"Godfrey, do not encourage him. Erik Senior will want to join them in all their folly. And there's work to do."

The door opened. "Did someone say folly?"

"Papa!" both children squealed, and they both rushed to him, talking at once. "Mr. Bennington said we may go to the zoo. They have a buffalo."

"Did he? Then we all must go!"

"Cole," snapped Anna.

The nanny pulled both children away and herded them out of the room. "And see that you explain the household rules to Lady Dunbridge's maid."

The doctor turned to the others as the door shut behind him. "My fault," he said good-naturedly as he came into the room. "And you're absolutely right. One should relegate one's conversations about buffalos to the nursery."

Godfrey once again made the introductions, while Phil marveled at how closely this Dr. Vogeler resembled his children not only in looks but his freewheeling personality.

Phil could see Anna being the only voice of reason in that household. No wonder she felt it necessary to keep a tight rein where she could.

Godfrey was mixing the Vogelers drinks when the door opened again, and a tall man, wearing a serviceable tuxedo, entered the room with military aplomb.

"Ah, Francis," Erik said. "Everything in order?"

"Yes, sir. Today's notes are transcribed and locked in the safe with the others."

"Good, come and have a drink and meet our lovely hostess."

"Thank you, sir, but I'll wait until later if that's amenable." He strode farther into the room and shook hands with Godfrey with a "Good to see you again, sir." And turned to Phil.

The breath fled from her lungs.

"Lady Dunbridge, this is Dr. Vogeler's secretary on loan from the War Department. Lieutenant Francis Kellogg."

"Lady Dunbridge," he said without missing a beat, and bowed over her hand.

Not even a flicker of recognition, not a twitch, a blink, or infinitesimal squeeze of her fingers.

She, on the other hand, had to fight every instinct not to stare at him, or so much as glance at Godfrey for an explanation.

Lieutenant Francis Kellogg was totally nondescript, from his tuxedo to his demeanor. Even his hair, neither blond nor brown, was unremarkable, exactly the same color of the Corn Flakes from which he no doubt had derived his current name. It would match his usual sense of humor.

The transformation was remarkable. Or perhaps not. She was never quite sure what he really looked like. But she knew him. Even without the residual scent of his exotic pipe tobacco or the telltale twinkle of conspiracy in his eye.

Mr. X. Unless this Mr. X was a doppelgänger of the one she knew. *Oh, heavens, could there possibly be more than one?* It was one thing to allow a mysterious stranger with a penchant for solving crime into your life—and bed. But two . . . ? The mind revolted.

He had turned slightly to address a question from Godfrey.

And Phil turned to Mrs. Vogeler. "Have you been enjoying your stay here?"

"I've spent every day at the Metropolitan Museum," she said, suddenly animated. "I must say, their exhibition of Greek sculptures is quite extensive. And the German Expressionist paintings on loan from Berlin are beyond compare."

"Godfrey said you're a painter as well as a scientist."

"Yes, it's a hobby merely."

And while Anna Vogeler discoursed on composition and the relation of form to content, Phil concentrated on not searching the room for her erstwhile confederate in investigation.

Why was he here and why hadn't he warned her? Was it possible he really worked for the military?

For some reason that notion depressed her. He'd always been mysterious, elusive; a creature of the shadows, living on the cusp of danger, balanced between good and evil. But was he really just a cog in Godfrey's government machinery, assigned to play bodyguard to the good-natured doctor? Aide-de-camp by day, dark avenger at night?

Had the two men been working together the entire time since she'd met them? And if they had, where did that leave her?

3

"Shall we go?" Godfrey asked, his voice finally penetrating her surprise.

"Certainly."

"It's a short walk to the Arsenal, Godfrey assures me," Erik Vogeler said affably. "I'm sure Anna has been standing for hours contemplating the fine works of art at the Metropolitan, but I confess that I would enjoy stretching my legs after a day at my desk. You ladies don't mind, do you? Will your lovely gowns survive the trek?"

"Don't be ridiculous," said Anna.

"It sounds like a delightful idea," seconded Phil. She smiled at the bubbly doctor, while thinking, *Not wise for someone attacked in a park a mere week ago.* She did notice that not one look passed between Godfrey and Francis Kellogg throughout the entire exchange. Well, they might not be concerned, but she intended to keep her eyes and ears open.

They set off down the steps of Union House, Godfrey and Phil leading the way, followed by the Vogelers, with Francis Kellogg bringing up the rear.

Oh, how she wanted to turn around and see if he was studying the area for possible attackers. For surely that was his reason for being here. The attack on Dr. Vogeler in Washington had been taken more seriously than Godfrey had let on.

They crossed the street and half a block later they entered the park grounds. It was dark beneath the trees; only an occasional lamp lit their way down the wide path, its edges disappearing into deep shadows.

Everyone, except the quiet secretary, was extolling the evening air when they rounded a curve and a massive castle rose before them, earning a collective gasp of first surprise, then amazement.

Phil had seen the Arsenal building in daylight from the street, a heavy brick building with identical octagonal turrets at either end and flanking the entranceway. It was, by day, a massive stronghold, fortunately rid of its weaponry, and now the home of the Central Park menagerie.

But at night, with a slice of moon and the clouds hanging low behind it, it looked downright Gothic.

"Not to worry," Godfrey said. "It isn't haunted."

He'd barely gotten out the word before a ghostly creature sprang from the darkness, wings stretched wide, blocking their progress.

Anna gasped. Phil's foot stuttered.

Godfrey automatically stepped between his guests and the apparition. Francis Kellogg was by his side at the same instance, having moved as quietly and secretively as their assailant.

"Thank God I caught you in time!" said the creature in a melodious feminine voice. "I was afraid I was too late." She swept the air in a final dramatic gesture before the wings settled into what Phil realized was merely a summer cape of some translucent shimmering fabric.

Erik Vogeler laughed heartily. "Georgie! Is it really you? How fortuitous." He strode forward to kiss her on both cheeks.

Francis Kellogg melted into the back of the group and Godfrey stepped aside.

"I wouldn't think of missing it. For you," she intoned, stepping farther into the lighted path. "It was imperative."

Anna slipped up to Godfrey. "I'm so terribly sorry, Godfrey. She was not invited. I don't know how she found out about the evening."

"No matter," Godfrey said. "I'll just have the restaurant set an extra place."

Anna turned to the newcomer. "Georgina, we had no idea you were living in New York."

"I don't doubt it, my dear Anna."

"Well, we're certainly glad you have found us. Though I don't know who told you dinner was fancy dress."

Georgina was swathed in chiffon over a black underdress that reflected purple every time she moved, which was constantly. A tiara was nestled in her unwieldy bouffant hairstyle.

She trilled a laugh. "Dear Anna, one doesn't expect you to dress at all. Isn't that the same old rag you wore at the international Delphi conference two years ago?"

Anna's smile tightened slightly. "Fortunately, I was invited for my ideas, not my entertainment value. Come, let me introduce you to our hosts. Godfrey Bennington and Lady Dunbridge, may I present Georgina Nash?"

"Ah, Mr. Bennington, I've read all about you and your flirtation with the skies."

Godfrey shook hands.

"And Lady Dunbridge . . . I don't know whether to curtsey or genuflect."

Phil extended her hand.

Georgina Nash shook it.

Godfrey did not look amused. "Shall we continue to the restaurant?"

"Ah, a man in charge," Georgina said, and took his arm. "Come along, Rose," Georgina called into the shrubbery.

The bushes rustled and a younger woman stepped out, yanking her shawl from a clawing vine.

"Oh, for goodness sake. Why do you let your sister treat you so?" Anna took the newcomer's arm. "Rose, you poor dear. Shall we save introductions until we're at the restaurant?"

"Two places," Godfrey amended, and after a brief glance at Phil, he spirited Georgina toward the building where they were to dine, leaving Phil to bring the others.

The Vogelers escorted Rose between them, which gave Phil the opportunity to fall in step with the recalcitrant secretary.

"Later," he said under his breath. And louder, "May I escort you, Lady Dunbridge?" And they brought up the rear.

"The restaurant is just around the side," Godfrey said to the group. "A charming place and a delightful respite from the heat."

And hopefully away from the lingering odors of the incumbent animals of the menagerie.

They turned right along the walk where it converged with another walk to create a courtyard at the entrance of the restaurant. It was a rustic but charming wooden outbuilding, situated on a small lawn and surrounded by a hand-hewn ornamental wooden fence. Along one side, tables were laid out beneath a covered porch, where lanterns cast a festive light and spilled out into the dark.

The maître d' and his staff were lined up at the door to greet them and offer them glasses of champagne.

Rose didn't take a glass, merely continued into the room.

Erik Vogeler's eyes followed her, a slight, distracted smile on his lips. Rose seemed oblivious to him—and to everyone.

She was younger than the others, dressed in a pale-pink gown that turned her complexion what one might call "deathly" pale. Light-brown hair was pulled back from her face into what should have been a chignon, but tendrils of fine strands had escaped and curled around her thin face, lifting gracefully with every turn of her head.

Botticelli came to mind.

Fascinating, Phil thought. Dr. Vogeler certainly thought so. He hadn't taken his eyes off her since she'd appeared out of the trees. Considering his profession, he might merely see her as a fascinating study in whatever it was psychoanalysts studied. But for all Phil didn't know about that particular science, she did know about men's attraction to women, and she guessed that Erik Vogeler, the man, was enamored by this otherworldly creature.

And Phil also noticed, that though Anna didn't falter in her conversation, she was extremely aware of exactly what was going on.

As they stepped out to the porch where they would be dining, Phil heard Anna say, "Do not make a mockery of this evening, Georgina."

Seeing Phil, she added, "Georgie and Chumley used to keep us laughing night after night. Georgie with her imitations of the professors or the latest theater idols or even the pitiful creatures on the street." Anna tittered. "But not always suitable for polite company. I used to tell her she should take up acting instead of psychology."

"So you did," Georgina said, and lifted her glass.

"Chumley was studying chemistry," Anna continued. "He was the only one of the 'pure' scientists we allowed in the group. He concocted quite an array of colorful smoke and pyrotechnics to accompany their antics."

"Did someone say Chumley?" A little man appeared in the doorway to the porch, glass in hand. "And behold. You have him."

"Chumley," Anna said. "As always, you have perfect timing."

"Ah, the formidable Anna." He stepped into the room and made his way toward them with small mincing shuffles as precise as a windup toy.

A rosy red face spread upward into a completely bald pate fringed by red hair that hung limply past his shirt collar to his shoulders. Phil could imagine him entertaining a gathering of partygoers, possibly pulling handkerchiefs out of the air while he encouraged them to act like cows and chickens and other barnyard inhabitants.

Since Erik Vogeler was still smiling distractedly at Rose Nash, who had wandered away from the group, it was left to Anna to do the introductions.

"Mr. Godfrey Bennington and Lady Dunbridge, may I present Chumley Griswold?"

Greetings were exchanged. Chumley was effusive, Godfrey precise, Phil wondering where Mr. Kellogg had gotten to.

"I was just telling Lady Dunbridge about how you and Georgie used to entertain us with your theatrical antics."

"Ah, yes, we were some team, Georgie and I, good days gone forever." He flicked a look in Rose's direction. "Like this poor handkerchief." He flourished a handkerchief that had somehow appeared in his hand. He gave it a snap and it changed into confetti that drifted to the floor.

Anna clapped her hands. "And nothing has changed."

"Ah, but much has changed."

"Which is why I came," Georgina said. "Erik, I must speak with you."

"But of course," Erik said at the same time his wife said, "It will have to wait."

"But he's in grave danger."

He certainly is, Phil thought. Stuck in the middle of two warring women, while mesmerized by another. She didn't envy the good doctor. He would certainly lose skin before that battle was over.

"It came first as a kind of premonition." Georgina continued.

"Something dark, amorphous. Twice this week a vision has come to me. Danger all around you. I see it surrounding you now." She sculpted the air with lace-gloved fingers as if outlining a cloud of miasma. "And I knew I must warn you, Erik. Someone wants to do you harm."

Beside Phil, Godfrey stiffened.

"Yes, well, we'll talk about it later, shall we?" said Anna. "Come, Chumley, and tell us what you've been doing for the last seven years."

A moment later, two more guests stepped down onto the porch. Phil turned to Godfrey, but he had slipped away.

"Ah, at last," Anna said, sounding relieved. "Dietrich, Elisabeth, come meet our hosts."

They were handed champagne and they made their way over. The gentleman was tall, large-boned, and wore a spotless tuxedo and a neat mustache. The woman was dressed in a similar outfit and could have been mistaken for a man except for the bun wound tightly at her nape and the fact that instead of trousers, she wore a narrow split skirt of deep black.

Phil would have to ask her where she purchased it.

The woman who must be Elisabeth Weiss hurried over. "Are we late? I had to beg a lift from Dietrich, since I was, as usual, running short of funds. My classes ran late and I didn't feel like hoofing it across the park in this heat."

"Not at all," Anna said. "Lady Dunbridge, may I present Dr. Lutz? And Dr. Weiss?"

Dietrich immediately excused himself to clasp Dr. Vogeler on the shoulder. "We're dining early, I see," he said in a deep baritone. "Resting up for the big guns at the Pantheon Club?"

"Hello, Dietrich. I can trust you to be one of the audience at my lecture?"

"I wouldn't miss the chance of heckling you for the world."

"I'll leave you in the dust, my friend."

Elisabeth Weiss groaned. "Forgive us, Lady Dunbridge. Those two haven't missed an opportunity to argue in the ten or so years I've known them. But it rarely gets violent."

"Indeed?" Phil said.

"Yes, Dietrich is an unrepentant Freudian, Erik a faithful Jungian with Pavlovian tendencies. Ne'er the twain shall meet."

"And which school do you belong to?" Phil asked.

"Barnard. Oh, you mean of psychoanalysis. Neither. I learned quite early that I wasn't made for digging around in the muck of people's emotions. I teach philosophy at Barnard College. I introduce young women to critical thinking before they're convinced not to do so for fear of hysteria, insanity, and sexual repression."

Phil laughed. "I do beg your pardon."

"Please don't. And forgive me for rambling on. What brings you to New York?"

"Refusing to be repressed."

"Touché and welcome. Are you staying long?"

"Oh, yes," Phil said. "I've moved here permanently."

"Oh, dear," Elisabeth said. "Not your stay, forgive me, but what's *he* doing here?"

The last of the guests had arrived. And Phil thought, At last, someone who looked like she imagined a psychoanalyst would look. Tall, with dark hair slicked down from a side part. Mustache and goatee lending erudition to his passionate dark eyes.

The entire party went suddenly silent as Pietro Salvos walked to the edge of the porch and stood surveying the others.

"I was invited, I came." He lifted his chin.

Further conversation—of lack thereof—was interrupted by the maître d' announcing dinner.

They all took their places on their own volition in a loud and haphazard way, and Phil was glad she hadn't bothered to plan the seating. She thought she would be forgiven for momentarily thinking of Coney Island and the Human Roulette Wheel.

In the confusion of the moment, no one had noticed that one of their party was missing.

"Where is Rose?" Georgina said to others.

They all looked around the room. Rose wasn't in sight.

"Ah, there she is." Georgina gestured across the porch and into the night where Rose hovered outside the open windows just above the ground.

Phil swallowed a cry of surprise, then realized the girl hadn't levitated but was merely balancing on the wooden fence railing that surrounded the restaurant.

"Rose," Georgina called. "Come in to dinner."

Rose Nash spread out her arms and Phil half expected her to fly to the table.

"Rose!"

The girl lifted in the air, then dropped to the ground. Moments later she appeared in the doorway.

"Unnerving, isn't it," Elisabeth said quietly. "You'd hardly know that she was a brilliant young scholar. Brilliant. Then one day, voilà. What you see. Georgie took her away after that. I don't think any of us have seen either of them since. It pains me to see she hasn't improved."

Sitting down to dinner did nothing to veer the ideological combatants into polite conversation. They might have become less combative . . . evidently not even passionate scientists would yell at each other down a row of crystal and silver. But it didn't keep them from poking a fork at their neighbors, or scowling over the epergne at the person opposite.

". . . now that cocaine has been found to be addictive . . ."

". . . never as efficacious as . . ."

"Hogwash, always your talk therapy, you should come into the twentieth century with the rest of us. . . ."

". . . addiction or insanity? Some would say . . ."

". . . this new experimental drug . . ."

". . . repetitive and constant . . ."

"Did you hear about the Telepathic Society's experiment in . . ."

". . . bunch of fools . . ."

"Why can't you just admit . . ."

Only the Nash sisters sat silent, Georgie with an air of slight disdain, and something else . . . calculation? Beside her, Rose ate her dinner and stared off into the distance.

By the dessert course, Phil was nursing a headache. Godfrey looked a little worse for wear. Only Francis Kellogg seemed unfazed, following the conversation politely, just as if he wasn't doing a little analyzing for himself.

As soon as the last course was cleared, they left the restaurant, but it appeared the gentlemen had no intention of ending the evening. They merely recongregated on the far side of the court-yard, near a copse of trees, where they lit up cigars.

Elisabeth, Georgina, and Anna joined the conversation, and Elisabeth went so far as to light a cigarillo.

Rose wandered off in the opposite direction and sat on a bench on the other side of the courtyard, and Phil followed her in case she decided to stray farther.

Across the way, the argument grew louder and more pas-sionate.

Suddenly one voice, Pietro Salvos's heavily accented Italian, rose above the rest.

"You're a swine, Erik."

"Now, Pietro," Anna said. "No reason to open old wounds now."

"No? Isn't that why you invited me here? To enjoy my humil-iation?"

"No one has done that," Elisabeth said. "Come, let Dietrich and I give you a ride home."

She took his arm, but he pulled away. "Do not patronize me."

"Let him have his say," Erik said.

"No," Georgina said, in a voice so commanding that for a sec-ond, they all fell silent. "I've sat here all night listening to you. You hypocrites."

"You're just jealous, Georgie," countered Dietrich. "You just couldn't cut it, face it."

"You think I would choose to be like any of you?" She spat, actually spat, on the ground.

"Good Lord," Elisabeth said.

For once in her life, Phil had no idea of how to diffuse the situation. One rarely encountered expectorating females at a din-ner party. She looked for Godfrey but he was still inside. Francis Kellogg was nowhere to be seen.

"Like you, Pietro?" asked Georgina. "A cheat and a fool. Or Di-etrich, molesting women and calling it a cure."

"That is a lie. If you were a man . . ."

"I would have killed you long ago," Georgina answered.

"And you, Elisabeth. Neither woman nor man, fish nor fowl, cloistered away from the world. You should have made a stand."

Elisabeth reached out but Georgie bore on. "And the rest of

you? I know your secrets. I see what is in your minds. What you are planning. Oh, yes, I see it all. Every single thing, and I'm not afraid to tell."

"Georgie, enough," Elisabeth said. "I think maybe you've had too much champagne."

"Perhaps I have." Georgie turned in a show of fabric, her cape glistening in the lamplight, and strode across the walk toward her sister, her cape lifting in the breathless night.

"Oh, heaven, she's having us on," Chumley piped in. "Clever Georgie. Just like the old days. Brava." He began to applaud.

Georgie had just reached Phil when Anna joined the applause. "Chumley's right. Brilliant, Georgie. You're always so droll."

Georgina turned back to face Anna. "I see it all." She lifted her arm just as an explosion rent the air.

Across the sidewalk Erik Vogeler clasped his arm. Anna screamed and reached for her husband as he sank to his knees and the others crowded around him.

Good God. Phil had been standing right here and she hadn't guessed what Georgina had in mind. All night long the woman had sat quietly enjoying dinner with murder on her mind.

Phil hesitated only for a second. She whirled around, ready to fight or to pursue but only Rose still sat on the bench staring into space.

Georgina Nash lay on the pavement at Phil's feet, face up, a neat round hole right between her eyes.

4

"For a woman who saw everything, I bet she didn't see that coming," said Francis Kellogg, kneeling down by the body.

Phil swayed on her feet, then dropped to her knees beside him. She would never have his sangfroid and wasn't sure she would want it. How could the man be so unmoved?

He didn't bother to feel for a pulse. The surgical placement of the bullet and the pool of blood beneath her head put paid to any question of that.

But how? Georgina's arm was extended when the shot rang out. She couldn't have turned the revolver on herself. There had only been one report.

Still, Phil eased Georgina's skirt aside with one finger.

"Don't bother," Kellogg said. "You won't find a weapon."

"But Dr. Vogeler—" Phil began.

"Was definitely shot, a flesh wound in his upper arm."

"But where—"

"Good question. And by whom?"

"Shouldn't you be out searching for the killer?"

"Not my job currently."

"And what exactly is your job, Lieutenant Francis Kellogg? And I hope to hell that isn't your real name."

"Would you still love me if it was?"

"I don't love you now, regardless."

"Well, it isn't, and please take every precaution in not giving my precarious position away to the authorities who will no doubt be here within the hour."

"Good God. Georgie must have fainted dead away." Chumley Griswold shuffled over to them, and stopped so suddenly that he rebounded, then clapped his hand to his mouth and ran into the bushes.

"So—" Phil turned to ask Kellogg how he had gotten there so quickly, but he'd taken the opportunity to disappear.

Godfrey appeared in the doorway of the restaurant. "What was that?" He took in the situation at a glance. "Everyone, inside. Now!" He didn't wait but went back into the restaurant. It was a few minutes before he returned.

He strode over to Phil, took one look at Georgina, and let out an expletive. "Where is Griswold?"

Phil pointed to the bushes where the sounds of retching told the story.

Godfrey ran a hand over his face and knelt to examine Georgina's body.

"What happened?"

"Just what I'm trying to figure out. I—"

The sound of heavy footsteps cut off the rest of her answer. A man wearing a heavy jacket ran down the sidewalk from the street. He was stocky and thick, or maybe it was just his coat that made him look so. It was much too heavy for the summer.

He stopped beside the body. "What happened here?" he demanded, his voice a rasping baritone.

"Who are you?" Godfrey demanded.

The man didn't answer; his eyes had moved from the body to Rose, who still sat unmoving on the bench, and lingered there.

"My assistant, Ivan Thomas," called Dr. Salvos from the doorway of the restaurant. "He's been waiting on the street with my automobile."

Salvos saw Georgina and strode over to them, arriving at the same time Chumley staggered out of the bushes.

"Has she fainted?" Salvos asked.

"She's dead," Griswold choked out, and ran toward the others, who were crowded into the open doorway.

"*Al diavolo con lei!*" exclaimed Dr. Salvos. "What's the woman up to now?"

"They got her," Ivan said.

"What are you talking about?" Godfrey said.

"Shot her. Dead."

"Who?"

"Good God." Dr. Salvos said, and knelt by the body. "You mean whoever shot at Erik hit Georgina instead? Impossible."

And yet she's dead, Phil thought.

"A trick." Dr. Salvos said.

"Do not touch her," Godfrey ordered. "She is obviously quite dead."

Dr. Salvos looked skeptical; he stood, but didn't move away, just looked down at Georgina's body, pulling his goatee and muttering to himself. Rose sat immobile and unemotional, seeming oblivious to her sister's body, while Ivan paced the distance between them.

Godfrey took Phil aside. "I've had the manager call for the police and told him to ask specifically for Detective Sergeant Atkins. I don't relish having to deal with him again, but I can no longer ignore the possibility that someone is attempting to kill Dr. Vogeler. And now this. What a mess."

"I can think of none better to handle this situation discreetly," Phil agreed.

"No. But whether he gets the message is another matter. Vogeler isn't hurt badly, but I want to get him and his wife back to the house and out of harm's way."

"Yes, and I think you should take Miss Nash, too. She seems to be in shock. I'm not even certain she realizes what has happened."

"Of course."

He looked around. "Where is that aide-de-camp? Of all the times to go out for a smoke."

"He was here a minute ago," Phil said. "Perhaps he is securing the perimeter?"

"Not his job."

The same thing Mr. X had just said to her a minute before. So what was his job here? Certainly not keeping Dr. Vogeler in clean socks and underwear.

Phil took a moment to brush off her skirts while she surreptitiously looked north to the trees to see if he was there, looking for signs of a lurking assassin. If the bullet grazed Vogeler's arm before killing Georgina Nash, the killer would have to have been positioned there.

"Ah, there he is," Godfrey said.

Phil straightened up. Francis Kellogg stood at attention by the edge of the sidewalk, exactly where Erik Vogeler had been grazed by the bullet.

"You there, Kellogg. What are you doing?"

"Securing the area, sir."

"Yes, well, I want you to take Dr. and Mrs. Vogeler back to the house. A driver is waiting in back and the butler is telephoning for the local physician who attends guests at Union House when needed. A Dr. Faneuil. He will meet you there."

"Sir." Francis practically clicked his heels together and strode into the building without giving either Phil or Godfrey or even the body a second look.

Phil wondered if he had found anything that would lead them to the murderer. And if would he share what he found with her.

"Dr. Salvos," Phil said. "Would you please take Miss Nash inside and ask Mrs. Vogeler to take her to Union House."

"But of course," Salvos said, and walked around Georgina to scoop an unresisting Rose to her feet. Ivan took her other side and they gently escorted the girl inside.

Phil watched them go. How differently they all treated the younger sister from the older: one with affection, the other with contempt. No doubt there was a story there. But did it have anything to do with the murder or the attempt on Dr. Vogeler's life?

"Perhaps you should go with them," Godfrey said.

Phil smiled sympathetically. "Thank you, but I expect that between the staff and Nanny Cole and Lily they will manage quite well without me, and you'll need someone to help you keep the curious at bay." Indeed, there were several restaurant workers huddled at the side of the building. "Though perhaps the other guests might also be allowed to wait at Union House until Atkins arrives. I'm sure he will want to get statements from all of them, and they will be more comfortable there."

"Of course." He started toward the restaurant, stopped, looked back at the body.

"I'll be fine until you return. And someone must keep watch."

Godfrey nodded and hurried away.

And Phil was alone to take a closer look at the body.

Not that there was much to learn. One bullet to the forehead. Georgina had fallen straight on her back from the impact.

How could a bullet wound one man and kill another person several yards away? Highly unlikely. She'd seen shot penetrate an animal and bury itself in a tree. But from such a distance and with such accuracy? This was the work of either a skilled marksman or a bizarre coincidence.

As they said at the racetrack, What were the odds?

Very high, Phil had to admit. But as Preswick's favorite fictional detective said, "Once you eliminate the impossible, whatever remains, no matter how improbable, must be the truth."

And she was fairly certain that the bullet that had grazed Erik Vogeler's arm was the same one that had killed Georgina Nash.

This would require a methodical examination of the scene. She knew what to do. Sherlock Holmes might be their inspiration, but Dr. Gross's *Criminal Investigation* was their bible.

She began at Georgina's feet, turned around to look across the sidewalk to the approximate place where Dr. Vogeler and his guests had been standing when the shot was fired.

She walked cross the pavement, taking even strides, counting the number of steps to reach the spot where Vogeler had stood, and peered over the railed fence that separated the sidewalk from the trees. The murderer would have had to fire from somewhere within that clump of trees. He would have left evidence, no matter how slight, of his position.

The police would search the area. And make a hash of it, if they didn't find Detective Sergeant Atkins quickly. And where were the police? Surely one of the park patrolmen would have heard the shot and come to investigate.

Did Godfrey have the kind of influence to stop their involvement cold? He would certainly try to contain the damage. She'd learned that during their first murder encounter.

Atkins, however, would want a clear account of what had happened. Phil looked across the pavement, trying to recall exactly where all the dinner guests had been standing when the actual shooting occurred. She conjured up that last conversation. Dr. Vogeler had been standing against the fence just under that low-hanging pine bough. He was facing the courtyard, so that Phil could see his features in the lamplight. The others formed a semi-circle facing him: Dr. Lutz, Dr. Weiss, and Chumley on one side; Dr. Salvos, Anna, and Georgina on the other, just like stage curtains.

And though she knew it was too early in the investigative process to concern themselves with motive, from the dinner conversation alone, there were plenty to choose from.

Except they had all been in plain sight when the shot was fired.

She walked back to where Georgina lay on the ground, stepped past her, and sank onto the bench where Rose had been sitting.

Time was passing and while she waited here, the killer would be getting away. They didn't even have a viable suspect. Salvos's assistant, Ivan, was the only one Phil knew of so far who didn't have an obvious alibi.

She looked from the trees to the walkway to the street. Could he have fired, then crept away without a sound, disposed of the weapon, then run back along the sidewalk to enter from the opposite direction? He hadn't been the least winded when he arrived. And where had he ditched the weapon?

She had to admit to feeling a sudden urgency to see what he was hiding beneath that coat.

Godfrey rejoined her after a few minutes and sat down beside her on the bench.

"They're all at Union House. I've alerted Collins not to let any of them leave."

"Could he stop them if they tried to?"

"Oh, yes, and he would be supported by Cook and the kitchen boy."

"I see," Phil said. Indeed, she was getting a better understanding of the household staff.

"I have apprised the park police of the situation. They will be keeping the area clear."

"They don't want to be in on the investigation?"

"I think they were relieved to have it taken out of their hands."

For herself, Phil was itching to look in those trees for possible clues. But she knew better. She had no gloves, no tweezers. It was nigh impossible to carry investigative tools on one's person while wearing a summer frock.

By the time Atkins finally arrived, nearly an hour later, Phil was beside herself with impatience. Godfrey had gone into the restaurant to telephone the nineteenth precinct for information on the detective sergeant's whereabouts when the familiar figure of John Atkins strode down the path from Fifth Avenue.

And Phil was reminded of the first time she and Bev had met the detective sergeant.

"Just like a dime-novel cowboy," Bev had said when he'd first walked into Bev's parlor. And though he did occasionally appear at the curb in the department's Panhard et Levassor town car, and though the NYPD did have a horse brigade, they had yet to see him astride.

But as Bev had remarked, "A modern woman could but dream." Tall, broad-shouldered, well dressed, and ruggedly handsome, he was also an astute investigator, and, unfortunately, a perfect gentleman, much to their chagrin.

You would never find Detective Sergeant John Atkins taking advantage of a woman, no matter if she wanted him to or not.

He zeroed in on Phil. "Why is it that you always precede me to these crimes?"

"It was a dinner party," she said, as if that would explain it all away.

"Shouldn't you be in Brighton Beach?"

That surprised her. "Keeping tabs on my whereabouts?"

"I just happened to have business with Mrs. Reynolds's stable manager recently and he said Mrs. Reynolds had horses running there." He flashed the smile that had won their hearts—or at least their prurient interests—at their first meeting.

"Bobby isn't in trouble, is he?" Bobby had gone straight as Bev's stable manager, but he still kept his fingers on the pulse of the New York underworld and was thereby immensely helpful in Phil's investigations. But it also meant that he kept in touch with some questionable associates.

"No, I just wanted to apprise him of new anti-gambling laws. But you didn't answer my question."

Actually, she'd forgotten what it was. Oh, yes, Brighton Beach.

"I was there, but Godfrey needed a hostess for his dinner. How could I say no?" She gave him a perfect hostess smile.

"How indeed. And conveniently poised to cover up any scandal if necessary."

"Perhaps," she agreed, frowning. "It's an odd situation."

"I have no doubt."

"But here is Godfrey," she said, as Godfrey stepped from the inside the restaurant and strode toward them. "I'll let him explain." Because Phil couldn't begin to.

She started to step away, but Atkins stopped her by the expediency of grasping her elbow. It was smoothly done, but effective. "I'm certain you have been making your own observations, and I expect you to share them with me once my initial inspection is over."

"But of course," she said, resuming her progress as his hand slipped from her arm.

"Good evening, Detective Sergeant," Godfrey said.

It was a ridiculous thing to say. It wasn't a good evening. A man was wounded. A woman lay dead at their feet.

The look Atkins gave him spoke volumes.

"I took the liberty of sending for a private mortuary van. They should arrive shortly."

There was a moment of the inevitable male confrontation, a silent, subtle, but obvious battle of the wills, though Phil wouldn't lay odds on either man winning.

"I wasn't certain when you would arrive or if they would be able to reach you, and we couldn't very well leave her here all night."

"So I was told. I was at the theater when I received a message that I was to come here immediately at the request of Mr. Bennington. I came straightaway."

"Thank you. I believe the manner of death is self-explanatory," Godfrey said superfluously, but it got them over the moment of tension. They'd been here before. Standing over a body, each man determined to follow his own procedure, and Phil wishing they would just get on with it.

Georgina no longer looked as if she'd merely fainted. Her skin had taken on a waxy patina in the lamplight, her expression frozen in time.

"Mrs. Vogeler asked that we cover her," Godfrey said. "I assured her we would as soon as you finished your initial inspection."

Phil would be relieved when they did finally cover her face. It seemed such an ignominious way to leave the world. And she suddenly felt sad for the flamboyant woman, lying alone on the pavement. Unliked, unmourned, and deserted by her friends in favor of the comforts of Union House. It wasn't a kind way to be remembered.

Phil stood back while Atkins bent over the body. He looked at the wound a long time, then stood and turned, surveying the area. He stopped when he got to the place where Phil had looked for signs of the killer. Where Mr. X had undoubtedly done the same.

And she was thrust into the same frustrating situation. Again.

Atkins expected her to cooperate with him; Mr. X, he of the Francis persona, would expect her to work for him; and Godfrey would trust her to prevent any information leaking out to the public.

Three, no, four investigators if one counted herself, and she did, working separately and uncooperatively toward the same goal.

There would be no communicating with the others, much less working together as equals. All three men knew their own territory, would fight for it to the death, she had no doubt. She'd watched them in action before.

John Atkins and Godfrey at least showed a modicum of respect toward each other.

As for Mr. X, he never cooperated with anyone, as far as she knew. Phil didn't believe Atkins or Bennington had ever met him. At least not as himself.

She'd certainly been careful not to mention him to Godfrey or the detective sergeant, though she was sure Mr. X knew all about them.

But of course, John Atkins didn't live in the shadows like her sometimes associate did. She wasn't certain about Godfrey.

Had he requested "Francis" as a replacement? Or had someone else sent him for different reasons? And if so, was it pure chance that Dr. Vogeler's longtime assistant had succumbed to food poisoning? Or had someone helped him along in order to make room for a spy in their midst?

Three men, with different methods, different agendas, possibly, and not willing to share information. Especially not with Phil.

Which one would be able to get the job done?

Well, Phil thought. *When in doubt, rely on yourself.* And fortunately she'd already set up Lily in the household.

5

The detective sergeant ended his perusal of the body and stood facing them. "This woman was a member of your party?"

"Yes," Godfrey said. "It was just a small dinner party to welcome Dr. Vogeler, who is the government's guest while in the States."

"You think this may be a military matter?"

"Certainly not. It must be some random act of violence by a criminal or a madman with no clear aim in mind. But with a terrible unfortunate outcome."

Godfrey hadn't wasted any time in drawing a line in the investigation, warning Atkins not to encroach. It would only make the detective sergeant that more determined to get to the truth.

"And that is Dr. Vogeler?" Atkins said, nodding toward the body and extracting a black notebook from his jacket pocket

Amazing, Phil thought. The man even kept an incident book in the pocket of his tuxedo.

"No," said Godfrey. "This is Dr. Georgina Nash."

"A surfeit of doctors this evening," Atkins commented as he wrote.

"Dr. Vogeler is giving a lecture at the Pantheon Club in a few days. A small number of his colleagues were invited."

"Any witnesses?"

Phil looked away. If he thought there was a surfeit of doctors, what would he call the number of witnesses?

"Not what you would call witnesses. No one actually saw the miscreant and no one seems to know where the shot came from— only the direction. They were all standing there on the pavement when the shot was fired."

"These doctors. Are they working on anything that would make them targets of an assassin?"

Godfrey barely hesitated. "Not Dr. Nash or any of the others that I know of. As for Dr. Vogeler, I'm not at liberty to say."

"Godfrey," Phil said.

"There was a possible attempt on his life while he was in D.C., but we supposed it was the typical theft of unsuspecting tourists. These intellectual types tend to be self-centered and unrealistic about their importance. I'm sorry to say we didn't take the attack as seriously as we perhaps should have."

"But Dr. Vogeler wasn't shot."

"He was. The bullet grazed his arm and continued across the way to kill Dr. Nash."

Atkins looked from Godfrey to Phil.

She nodded. "As strange as it sounds. There was only one shot."

Atkins rubbed his chin; looked from the trees where the group had been standing and back to the body.

"So they were all standing over there by the fence."

"Yes," Phil said. "Except for Dr. Nash's sister, Rose, who was sitting on the bench, there. I was standing about here. I had come over to check on her. She had a tendency to wander off during the evening."

"Mentally deficient," Godfrey replied, not mincing words. "An accident of some sort."

"And you, Mr. Bennington? Where were you?"

"In the restaurant, where I was consulting with the manager. I came out as soon as I heard the shot."

"You knew what it was?"

"I work for the War Department, Detective Sergeant."

"So do hundreds of political appointees who have never touched a weapon," Atkins added.

"I'm one of the ones who has."

Here they were again, already at loggerheads, Godfrey intent on keeping the situation under wraps, Atkins already determined to get to the truth, with Mr. X lurking on the edges waiting to do whatever he was supposed to do.

And where had *he* been at the time of the shooting? He'd appeared at her side quickly enough.

"Oh, do call a truce, gentlemen," Phil said. "A man is wounded. A woman lies dead. And time is passing."

"Duly chastised," Godfrey said, with an appropriate smile. "I will furnish you with the guest list."

"And I will be discreet as always," Atkins said, pointedly ignoring Phil.

"And now that we've gotten that out of the way," she said, "shall we proceed?"

"So, you, Mr. Bennington, didn't witness any part of the shooting."

"No."

"Where are the others? You didn't let them leave?"

"I did not," Godfrey said. "But I didn't know when or even if you would be located. The restaurant needed to start closing up and since I saw no reason to keep them from it, I thought it best to have everyone wait at Union House, the guesthouse where the Vogelers are staying. It's right across the street. You can question them there if you think it necessary."

"I do." Atkins turned to Phil. "I suppose it's up to you to tell me what you saw before the shot was fired."

"Certainly," she said. "As I said, Rose was on the bench, I had come over to check on her. Everyone else was grouped over there by the fence. They were having a rather animated discussion of various subjects and then it turned rather personal, though I really wasn't listening. At the end Dr. Nash left the group to come toward her sister. Then Mr. Griswold began applauding, saying she was having them on like the old days. Everyone turned toward her, Mrs. Vogeler laughed, said something like 'Bravo, Georgie. You're so droll.'

"Dr. Nash turned back to the group and raised her arm just as the shot was fired. It all happened so fast. At first I thought she had fired the pistol." Phil held out her hands. "How is it possible that she's dead?"

"That is what I plan to find out. Once the shot was fired, what happened?"

Godfrey gestured across the pathway. "I came out of the restaurant, realized that Dr. Vogeler had been injured. I was concerned about getting him out of harm's way. I didn't realize Dr. Nash was dead until Phil told me when I came back outside."

Atkins gave Phil an appraising look.

"I thought she had fainted. Everyone had gathered around Dr. Vogeler and I was going to join them when something made me turn back to Dr. Nash. And then I realized . . ." She swallowed.

"I understand. And no one else came to her aid?"

Phil shook her head. "They all went inside, they were terribly concerned about Dr. Vogeler. Oh, but Dr. Salvos's driver had been waiting by his automobile on the avenue. And he ran down the path behind us when he heard the shot."

She looked down at Georgina's face, trying to remember. The blood that had pooled beneath her head had finally stopped spreading. The hole in her forehead looked like a dot painted on her skin.

"Dr. Salvos came out of the restaurant, and the driver, Ivan, I think is his name, said, 'They got her.'"

"Who?"

"He didn't say. I asked Dr. Salvos to take Rose, Miss Nash, inside, and they both accompanied her."

"She didn't react to the fact that her sister had just been shot?"

Phil shook her head. "No. Nothing. It was almost as if she weren't here at all. Then Godfrey sent them all to Union House."

"Where this Dr. Salvos went to treat Dr. Vogeler's injury?" Atkins asked.

"No," Godfrey said. "I telephoned to the staff butler, Collins, to ask Dr. Faneuil to meet them there."

"You invited a number of doctors to dinner and yet had to send for an additional doctor to treat a simple graze?"

"Yes. The guest list consisted of several psychoanalysts, a chemist, and a professor of philosophy."

Atkins made a barely audible noise that Phil was certain was a suppressed laugh. It *was* rather ridiculous. A full table of doctors, and not one could attend to a minor injury. Not of the body, anyway.

"Is there anyone else who might have seen anything? The kitchen staff?"

"I doubt if they could have seen anything from the restaurant."

Phil didn't offer up the final guest, and she breathed a sigh of relief when Godfrey did.

"The secretary," Godfrey said. "Actually," Godfrey continued, "he's one of our men. Vogeler's assistant was taken ill while in Washington. We assigned a man to accompany Vogeler until he was back on his feet and could rejoin them here."

"And this replacement's name?"

"Lieutenant Francis Kellogg."

"And where was he during all of this?"

Godfrey shook his head. "Haven't the foggiest."

"Not with the man he was supposed to be assisting?" Atkins looked at Phil.

Phil looked down at the body. She wished they would at least cover her face.

"I didn't really notice him. Though he was here a moment after. Before I knelt down to see if she was still alive."

"Did you see where he came from?"

"No." That much was the truth.

"And the alacrity with which he appeared would preclude him from having stood on the other side of this area in that stand of trees and shooting Dr. Nash?"

"Really, Atkins," Godfrey exploded. "He is one of our own men. He didn't even know he would draw this assignment."

Atkins just continued to write.

There was nothing to preclude army officers from committing murder. Even if Francis Kellogg was a military man, which she doubted.

"Excuse me for a moment." Atkins walked away and into the restaurant without another word, leaving Godfrey and Phil looking at each other.

He reappeared carrying an electric torch, which he must have borrowed from the kitchen, and strode over to Georgina's body, where he examined the wound at length. Then he shone the light on the surrounding sidewalk and shrubbery.

When he appeared satisfied, he returned to the body, stood just above the doctor's head, his feet on either side of her tiara, and pointed the torch straight ahead. The beam of light hit the leaves of the trees across the way where the killer must have lain in wait.

"She fell straight back," he said more than asked, not taking his eyes from the beam of light.

"Yes," Phil answered.

"And you were standing where you are now?"

"Yes."

"And the group was standing between the trees and the victim."

"Yes. Near the edge."

He walked across the pavement until he was standing straight across from Phil.

"Here?"

"Yes."

"Can you remember who was standing where?"

Phil looked across the pavement. Tried to picture the scene. "Dr. Vogeler was standing against the rail facing the group. I could see his face."

"So no one was standing directly between him and the victim."

"Not exactly." She closed her eyes. "They were close but not static. There were quite a lot of gesticulations and movement. Turning back and forth to whoever was talking at the moment. Sometimes blocking Dr. Vogeler from my view, but for the most part I could see him."

Atkins turned to Godfrey. "I suppose you would object to bringing your guests back to recreate their positions."

"In the strongest possible way. I would love to see the back of them. Hopefully we can persuade Dr. Vogeler to cancel his lecture and return early to England."

Atkins nodded. "Then I suppose I will have to depend on her ladyship to remember what she can. Vogeler was standing here?"

"A little to your left," Phil said. "Just a half step. I remember that the needles of that pine tree looked like a parasol over his head."

Atkins stepped to the side.

"That's it."

He turned suddenly, aiming the beam straight ahead. It shone on the front of Phil's skirt. It was only a light but Phil started violently. And saw immediately that something was wrong.

Atkins held the torch at elbow level. If the killer had been standing and aimed straight, the bullet would have hit Georgina Nash, who was slightly shorter than Phil, right above the knees. Atkins crouched down shone the torch again.

He tried another angle, then another, until the beam caught Phil in the eye, and she turned away in reaction.

Had Georgina been the intended victim after all? Because she was trying to warn Dr. Vogeler of some danger? She had forgotten to tell Atkins that.

Godfrey cleared his throat. "The man knows his job, I'll say that for him."

Atkins turned away from them and shone the torch into the trees. Clicked it off and returned to where they were standing.

"It's too dark to make a decent search tonight. I'm going to ask the park police sergeant to station some men around the perimeter until I can get a closer look in the morning."

"Very well," Godfrey said, just as a vehicle pulled up at the other side of the restaurant.

"That will be the mortuary van," Godfrey said.

Indeed, two men carried a stretcher around the side of the building. After a brief discussion, the body was transferred to the stretcher and carried away. And Georgina Nash was gone, just like that.

It seemed so cruel that she wouldn't be laid out at home so her sister could mourn her properly. If Rose was even able to understand that Georgina was dead.

"You are free to return to the others," Atkins said. "I shouldn't be here much longer. Please see that everyone remains at Union House until I can join you. Lady Dunbridge will accompany you."

"Of course. I have to pick up Lily anyway."

He raised both eyebrows at that.

"She's helping the nanny with the Vogeler children tonight. They seem to be quite a handful."

Godfrey left Atkins with the address of Union House, and the two of them walked down the path to the street, Phil's hand resting lightly in the crook of his elbow, to join the other well-dressed couples walking home after an evening out.

"I'm sorry you came all the way back to town to have this happen," said Godfrey, as they waited for a carriage to pass.

"Don't be. To tell you the truth, Godfrey, I was bored to tears.

And though I'm extremely sorry for Dr. Nash's demise, I'll willingly help in any way I can."

His expression was one of resolve, not gratefulness. "I honestly didn't think there was any danger."

"No," she agreed. But concerned enough to replace the ill secretary with a person of Mr. X's—*Francis Kellogg*. She'd better get used to calling him that—abilities. And in the light of what had happened, it seemed even more certain that the food poisoning suffered by the assistant had not been coincidental.

Did Godfrey know who was staying beneath his roof? Phil wouldn't be surprised to find that the military were used to keeping secrets not only from the public but from each other.

Which put the problem in a whole new light. She paused on the sidewalk. "What's to become of her sister? I wonder if there is a relative to take over her care."

"I'll get someone on that first thing tomorrow. Perhaps Anna Vogeler is aware of someone. I imagine Dr. Faneuil has sedated her and put her to bed." He sighed. "Suddenly we have a full house."

"I truly apologize," Godfrey said. "But, by God, I'm glad you agreed to come. Any other hostess would have fainted dead away and required smelling salts."

Really, intelligent men could be so dense. Phil could have named several women who would have dealt with this crisis admirably. After all, women were trained to deal with the most horrendous things, from lapses of etiquette to outright brawls.

And though murder didn't usually occur at a dinner party, Phil was coming to learn, it wasn't unheard of.

"Don't give it another thought," she told him. "I'm only glad I can be of service." She stressed the last word slightly, seeing if he took the bait. He didn't. Either he'd been expecting something like this or else he had no idea of how ready and capable she was to investigate.

They passed a man leaning against one of the new affordable Fords. Ivan, Dr. Salvos's driver.

He straightened and pulled the cap from his head.

"Is Dr. Salvos inside?" Phil asked.

"He is."

"Would you like to sit in the kitchen? I'm sure—" Phil stopped herself. She'd been about to say that the police would like to talk to him, but he might bolt. He looked like he'd rather be anywhere but here. "If you'd like a cup of coffee," she finished.

He nodded sharply. "Thank you, but I'll wait here."

"Very well." She nodded and accompanied Godfrey up the stairs.

"That was Salvos's driver?" Godfrey asked.

"Yes."

"We'll leave him to Atkins. Let us go see how our guests are faring and hope that the detective sergeant comes to relieve us shortly."

Collins greeted them stoically, visibly unfazed by the raucous exchange of voices coming from the drawing room.

"Into the breach, as they say," Phil said.

"Yes, my lady," the butler said, relieving her of her wrap.

"I think perhaps coffee would be in order."

"Yes, my lady. Right away."

Godfrey led her into the parlor, where they were met by a tableau that in any other circumstances might be forgiven for evoking an illustration from an issue of *Punch*.

As soon as Phil and Godfrey stepped into the room, Dietrich Lutz jumped up from the couch and headed toward them.

"Bennington, I for one resent these strong-arm tactics. I am not one of your enlisted men, and I demand to be released."

"I am not holding you," Godfrey said. "But you are all witnesses to a murder and will have to give your statements to the police when they arrive."

"This is an unnecessary imposition. I have an important meeting first thing tomorrow morning."

"Actually *this* morning, old man," said Chumley Griswold, taking his pocket watch out and checking the time. "With any luck you'll make it home in time to shave and change out of your evening attire."

"I've had enough. I will be glad to talk to the police at my office tomorrow afternoon. Though I don't know what they can possibly ask. None of us saw what happened."

"Subliminally, my dear Dietrich." Chumley let the watch dangle until it began to swing in a slight arc. "Heaven knows what you might have seen in your subconscious."

"I don't find you amusing, Chumley."

Chumley shrugged and pocketed his watch.

"Sit down, Dietrich," Dr. Salvos said from where he stood by the mantel. "Have some respect for Georgie."

"The woman was a charlatan. Insufferable in life, insufferable in death."

"And you are a pig."

Chumley snorted out a laugh, sounding so like the barnyard animal that Phil was afraid Dietrich might take it as an offense. That's all they needed, two hotheaded dinner guests dueling at dawn in the back garden.

"You didn't even like her, Pietro," Chumley continued blithely.

"Only because of what she did to young Rose."

"Gentlemen," Godfrey interceded. "This will go more quickly if we all remain calm. I'm sure the detective sergeant will join us as quickly as possible."

"I think," said Phil, "if Collins can manage coffee, I will go upstairs and check on Anna and her husband and see how Lily fared with the children."

Godfrey nodded; he obviously hadn't thought about the Vogelers. No doubt he was more concerned on planning a strategy for containing the rumors.

As for Phil, she was more interested in finding out the state of Dr. Vogeler's injury, the state of Rose's mind, and the whereabouts of her elusive confederate, "Francis Kellogg," who she noticed was not in the room.

Collins directed Phil to the Vogelers' quarters, a suite of rooms at the back of the house, and Phil wondered if this had been for quiet or for security reasons.

She knocked softly and the door opened. Lily stood on the other side.

She bobbed an infinitesimal curtsey and opened the door wider.

Anna Vogeler sat bolt upright in a straight-back chair next to the bed where her husband lay. She rose slightly and turned her head.

"Lady Dunbridge. I thought perhaps you were the doctor." Anna looked almost as pale as her husband. "He's seeing to Rose, but he promised to check back in on Erik before he left."

"I don't want to bother you," Phil said, but came farther into the room. "I just came to make sure you have everything you need. Though I see Lily has brought you tea."

"Oh, yes. I had to send my own maid to see to Rose who was quite incapable of helping herself. Poor, poor girl. Lily offered to assist the doctor with his ministrations." She smiled slightly. "Since I was also incapable. Normally I am a rational woman but . . . not when it's my own husband. Lily stepped in. She's a marvel, Lady Dunbridge."

"Yes, she is," Phil said, thinking, *And clever to manage a way to get a closer look at the situation.* No doubt she would be able to tell them the severity of the wound and the angle of the bullet trajectory.

The Dunbridge household had made good use of the fallow months to study up on crime-scene investigation.

"You've trained her well."

"Not I," Phil said. "My butler, Preswick. Another one who is indispensable." Though sometimes she wondered if it hadn't been Lily training them since the day they'd found her on the docks.

"I'm sorry." Anna sat down suddenly and lifted her hand to her forehead.

Lily reached for the *sacque dramatique,* a useful bag that held all the essential items they might need while out visiting, shopping, or catching criminals. Smelling salts, handkerchiefs, sewing scissors, plasters, pencil, notebook, and lockpicks.

Lily hurried across the room to Anna. "Madam," she said, then swept the salts neatly below Anna's nose and returned to her place in the corner.

Anna shuddered. There was a knock on the door and Lily jumped up to attend.

"Dr. Faneuil," Anna said. "Come in."

A small dapper man with thinning white hair came into the room.

"Lady Dunbridge, this is Dr. Faneuil. Lady Dunbridge has kindly come to inquire about Dr. Vogeler's condition."

He bowed, dipping his head just enough to show deference.

"How is the patient?" Phil asked.

"Nothing to worry about. Merely a flesh wound. He's been put to bed with a sleeping draught. That's why he lies so still. Please don't be alarmed."

Phil had no intention of being alarmed.

"I'll be going if I'm no longer needed. I've given a sedative to the young woman, the victim's sister, I believe. I understand there is no family now that her sister is deceased. I presume she is under the care of a physician?"

"I'm afraid I don't know," Anna said.

"I'm afraid I don't know either," Phil said. "I just met her tonight."

"Ah. In that case, I'll talk to Mr. Bennington before I leave. If he can keep her here overnight, I'll make arrangements to have her committed to Bellevue when I come to check on Dr. Vogeler in the morning. Good night." He turned to leave.

Anna jumped from her chair. "Wait, Doctor! Committed? Bellevue? Isn't that the psychiatric hospital?"

"Yes, it is. One of the best charity wards in the country."

"It's an asylum! You can't send her there."

"I'm afraid that if no family steps forward to make that decision, I will have no choice. The young lady is quite mad."

6

For a moment Phil just stared at him. It had been obvious from the start that Rose Nash was not quite in this world. But mad? Had her sister's death pushed Rose over the brink?

"She is certainly not mad," Anna said, so calmly that Phil turned to look at her. Consequently, she was in time to see Anna's face change from concern to calculation. "You mean she's acting incoherently brought on by the shock."

"Possibly." The doctor's voice was also measured. If he was the attending doctor for Union House, he had no doubt already been made aware of the situation and the occupations of the guests. And though he appeared very cool, there was just a hint of disdain in his voice that told Phil just how little he thought of the new "science" of psychoanalysis.

"However, whether it is recent or of an earlier date, temporary or permanent, we won't be able to ascertain until she is evaluated by a psychiatric doctor. I'm going to recommend to Godfrey Bennington that she be removed there.

"After that, if her family wishes to transfer her elsewhere that will be their decision. I'll return in the morning to examine her and oversee the transfer. She should sleep until then. Good night."

He nodded to both of them, then strode out of the room.

For a full minute Anna just stared at the door.

"Idiot," Anna said, rousing herself. "We'll just see about that." She started toward the door. Stopped. "Lily, would you please ascertain that the doctor has left? I won't be responsible for my speech if he is still downstairs."

Lily shot up from her chair, managing to curtsey while still getting to her feet, and headed for the door.

"I apologize, Lady Dunbridge. I didn't mean to give orders to your servant. I hope she isn't too upset by the situation. But she seems so . . . efficient."

"She is." *In more ways than you can imagine.* "And at your disposal as long as needed," Phil said. "She doesn't succumb to circumstances and . . . she knows how to be discreet."

With that, they were met with a bloodcurdling scream from outside the door.

Phil was closer and she reached the landing first, just in time to see Lily running back up the stairs. Standing in the middle of the landing was the source of the scream, a young woman who must be Anna Vogeler's maid.

She kept screaming until Anna grabbed her, shook her, and, finding that didn't work, slapped her soundly across the cheek.

"Now, what is it?"

The girl made choking noises, jabbed her finger in the direction of an open door down the hallway, and wailed. "She sat up! Like she'd risen from the dead. She's—She's—Oh, madam, it isn't natural."

Downstairs, the drawing-room door opened, and Godfrey and John Atkins ran into the foyer, followed by the dinner guests, their voices rising with agitation. The whole house had been alerted to whatever was happening.

Phil didn't wait any longer but ran down the hall to Rose's bedroom. She stopped cold in the doorway. Rose Nash, wearing a borrowed white nightdress, sat bolt upright in the large four-poster bed. Her eyes were open in a wide, unnatural stare.

The hairs on Phil's arms and neck rose as one.

Anna burst into the room, followed by Lily, dragging Anna's recalcitrant lady's maid by the arm. She immediately broke into new hysterics, which Lily remedied by telling her to put herself to bed, and shoved her out the door.

Anna crossed to the bed and sat down on the edge. Rose's stare didn't waver. She didn't react when Anna took her hand.

"Well, whatever that doctor gave her to help her sleep obviously missed the mark." Anna gently lowered Rose's hand back to the bed. And still Rose sat rigid and unaware.

Phil became aware of Lily inching closer to the bed and John Atkins and Godfrey stepping into the room.

"Lily?" she said quietly; she didn't want to upset whatever state Rose Nash was exhibiting.

Lily shook her head minutely and stayed where she was.

Rose began to thrash. "I can't find the ducks. I did it! Where are the ducks? I did it."

"No, Rose," Anna said from across the bed. "It was some stranger. You were sitting on the bench. Remember?"

"Of course she didn't kill Georgie!" cried Dr. Salvos, who broke through the group that had congregated in the doorway. He hurried to the bedside. "She is not the villain here. The villain is dead."

Rose flung both arms out. "I did it! Diditdiditditditdidi—"

She screamed. And kept screaming.

"Rose!" Anna reached for her, but Salvos pushed her away.

"Leave her alone! All of you. She isn't awake. You'll only frighten her."

It was hard to hear him over Rose's screaming.

Lily stared, dumbfounded. So did Phil. What unearthly thing had possessed the young women? Perhaps she was mad, as Dr. Faneuil had stated.

"You're the one," Anna cried. "Get away from her!"

Pietro turned to the others, effectively putting himself between Rose and them.

And suddenly, as if someone had turned off a light, Rose's eyes closed, she fell silent then slumped forward. Lily rushed around the bed to lower her to the pillow.

"She will sleep normally now," Salvos said. "It is a condition. She had these episodes as a child."

"Nightmares?" Atkins asked.

"Perhaps. No one knows for certain. Something amiss in the brain. She doesn't sleep, she is not awake. Stuck somewhere in between, we think."

Phil couldn't prevent the shiver that went through her.

Atkins came to stand next to Phil and Godfrey.

"She did it? Did I hear her correctly?"

"I heard her, too," Godfrey said. "Everyone did."

"Nonsense," Salvos said. "She doesn't realize what she said. She won't remember any of this when she truly awakens."

"Conveniently," Godfrey said.

"How do you know this?" Atkins asked.

"It is a condition."

"Incubus," proclaimed Dietrich Lutz from the doorway.

"Oh, do shut up, all of you." Elisabeth Weiss pushed Lutz aside and strode over to the bed. "This calls for a woman, mere mortals that we are." She moved Dr. Salvos aside and felt for Rose's pulse, checked her eyes.

She reached for the bottle on the bedside table, opened it, and took a sniff. Returned it to the table.

She turned back, not to Anna or the others, but to Godfrey. "Laudanum. She seems comfortable enough now, though I would leave someone with her during the night in case she wakens again."

"And if she does?"

"If she becomes irrational, another dose shouldn't hurt her."

"Very well, I'll get one of the staff—"

"I can stay with her," Lily blurted. "Sir," she added as an afterthought, as well as a sharp, bobbed curtsey that made Atkins snort.

Let him snort, Phil thought.

"Thank you, but that really isn't necessary." Godfrey smiled benevolently.

"I'm a very good nurse," Lily answered.

"Is she?" Godfrey asked Phil.

"Yes, indeed." Though Phil fortunately had never as yet had to test the veracity of her statement. They'd all been remarkably healthy since arriving in Manhattan. "It will relieve Anna's maid, who seems very distraught."

Godfrey frowned. "How will you manage?"

"Women have been dressing and undressing themselves for centuries," Elisabeth Weiss said, coming to join them. "I imagine Lady Dunbridge can survive without her for one night."

"Of course," Phil said. "Besides, it's almost morning."

"I'll arrange something more permanent for her in the morning," Godfrey said. "Now, perhaps we could all go back downstairs, where I'm sure Detective Sergeant Atkins will get your details as quickly as possible so you can get to your beds."

The group turned as one and moved down the hall toward the stairs.

"I'll be with my husband," Anna announced, and followed the others out.

Phil was sure she could hear Atkins grinding his teeth beside her.

"You won't get anything useful out of them tonight, Detective Sergeant," Phil said. "They couldn't agree on the smallest thing the entire evening. It might be better to question them alone and after food and spirits have worn off."

"I was just thinking the same thing," Atkins said. "Away from . . . everyone else."

Phil didn't reply. She'd understood the words he didn't say: *Away from meddlesome countesses.* Fortunately, she had no intention of letting him have his way.

He ushered her toward the door, and Phil just managed to see Lily reaching for her ankle and the stiletto resting there.

Downstairs the dinner guests had reverted to anger and arguing, smoke filling the air around them. Only Elisabeth Weiss lounged back in a chair, smoking her cigarillo, as at ease as any gentleman at his club.

"Don't be alarmed," Elisabeth said, as Atkins looked over the room. "Put two scientists together and you will have an argument. It's the nature of the animal." She lifted the cigarillo to her lips, then expelled a cloud of smoke.

Dietrich stormed over to Atkins. "I'll be damned if—"

"Oh, do be quiet, Dietrich," Chumley Griswold said, following him over. "You're not the only one here who works for a living."

Dietrich snorted. "Bilking old ladies out of their money by sleight of hand."

"Oh, I assure you, there's more to it than that."

"You—"

"Gentlemen," Elisabeth interrupted. "Just give the detective sergeant your addresses so that we can leave. I, being someone who actually *does* work for my living, have an early class in the morning."

Atkins quietly slipped his notebook from his pocket.

"My practice is on the Upper West Side." Dr. Lutz gave his address.

Chumley lived on Park Avenue, just a few streets away. He gave his address loudly and smugly. "Not only is my practice larger than yours, Dietrich, my house is grander."

"Thank you, Mr. Griswold." Atkins turned to Pietro Salvos.

He gave an address on Orchard Street.

"And your driver?"

"Ivan. He also helps in my practice."

"Last name?"

"Thomas. Ivan Thomas."

"Thank you, I will speak with him also."

Pietro gave him a sharp nod. "Yes, but what I wanted to say is, I think I should stay."

"Here?" Atkins asked.

"Yes. You deal with the criminal element every day. But there is no element more devious than those in the world of psychology."

"What are you saying exactly?" Atkins asked in his blandest voice.

"Any one of us could have killed Vogeler."

"But Dr. Vogeler isn't dead," Atkins pointed out.

"But he should be."

"Oh, Pietro," Elisabeth Weiss said, exasperated. "Your verb tenses are atrocious. Why don't you spend some time perfecting your English instead of poking around in people's brains?"

"What did you mean, Dr. Salvos?" Atkins poised his pen above his notebook, as effective an intimidation as Phil had ever seen.

"Just that . . ." He frowned at Dr. Weiss.

Elisabeth flicked her ash into a cigarette dish, then ground out the end of her cigarillo. "He just meant to say that it's common knowledge that there have been attempts on Erik's life. God only knows why. Except that Erik has always had an exaggerated concept of his own importance. So naturally, when a shot was fired, we automatically assumed it was meant for Erik. The fact that it missed its mark is not the fault of Dr. Salvos's mangled syntax."

Atkins tilted his head slightly. He was listening to more than her words.

"I wouldn't worry, Dr. Salvos. Miss Nash is in capable hands. Good night."

Dietrich slapped Salvos on the back. "Give it up, Pete old boy. It's too late for Rose anyway."

Pietro shot him a look of pure hatred but let himself be led away.

The three men were almost at the door when Chumley suddenly whirled around in a gesture that rivaled Georgie Nash's sweeping entrance from the trees earlier. Phil could see how they might have been partners in comic antics in their youth.

"I know! You are all invited to my house to see my work in situ. A wake for dear old Georgie."

"Really, Chumley . . . ," Dietrich began.

"I'm serious," Chumley said. "Perhaps Georgie will contact us from the grave and tell the detective sergeant who killed her."

"Rubbish."

"It's been known to happen. Souls whose work is unfinished. No? I also do a little table turning on the side, and read the tarot." He smiled coyly at Dietrich. "It's very popular. So popular that I've virtually given up science completely. And I have plenty of room for everyone." His voice traveled upward as if he was wishing them all a happy new year. "You'll all come, of course. You wouldn't want to slight poor Georgie, not even you, Pietro. And bring Ivan. No reason the poor boy can't have a little fun. I'm sure you must work him to the bone."

Pietro clenched his fists at his side but merely said, "If you insist."

"I do. I do. You all must come, Lady Dunbridge, Mr. Bennington. Detective Sergeant. And the Vogelers. You must relay the invitation to the Vogelers. We must have them."

He reached into his pocket and handed them each a card, engraved on ivory paper, thick, expensive, the script looking as elegant as any English peer's. "The address is there. Shall we say . . . Wednesday evening. Eight o'clock? Until then." He swept through the door, which Dietrich was still holding open.

Dietrich glared as he passed. "Are you coming, Elisabeth?"

"Wait just a minute, I have still to leave my address with the detective sergeant."

She stood in front of Atkins as dutiful as any schoolgirl.

And Atkins just as dutifully wrote it all down, though Phil couldn't keep from noticing that he was fighting a smile.

"I'll be in my offices most of the day. I lecture at Barnard College. You may have heard of it. It's right across the street from Columbia."

Atkins looked up. He was definitely intrigued by this woman; so was Phil.

"So close, yet so far away," she continued in a winsome voice. "They've managed to keep us at bay thus far. But we're getting closer. It won't last forever. No more than denying us the vote, or locking us away in asylums whenever we become inconvenient or 'hysterical' over the way we are treated. There will be women at Columbia University sooner than you might think. Good evening, Detective Sergeant. Thank you for a mostly lovely evening, Bennington." She stopped at Phil. "A pleasure to meet you, Lady Dunbridge." She tapped her finger to her temple. "We women . . ."

She didn't finish what she was going to say. But Phil thought she understood, *must stand together.* Did that mean she wanted to find out who murdered Georgina Nash? That she knew more than she admitted? Or was she merely finagling a date for afternoon tea?

Phil wasn't clear, but one thing she knew for sure: Detective Sergeant Atkins wouldn't be the only one paying a visit to Elisabeth Weiss.

Atkins closed his notebook. "That is all of the guests?"

"Yes," said Godfrey, going to the drinks table. "All but the Vogelers, and you're welcome to question them tomorrow." He held up the brandy decanter. "Philomena, Atkins?"

They both demurred.

Godfrey poured himself a brandy.

"And the secretary?" Atkins asked.

Phil had hoped he'd forgotten about the elusive Kellogg. But of course he wouldn't.

"Oh, yes," Godfrey said. "Lieutenant Kellogg."

Atkins took out his notebook again. "Where is he now?"

"I imagine he's gone up to bed," Godfrey said. "I sent him back with the family after the incident. I needed someone with a cool head to oversee things until I was able to return."

Atkins looked up from writing long enough to lift an eyebrow. "An attempt on his charge's life? A murder, two screaming women, and he takes himself off to bed?"

"Dr. Vogeler is an energetic being and a demanding one. Kellogg isn't a viable suspect. As I said. He was temporarily assigned to the position by our office only a few days ago when the permanent assistant was taken ill. When he has recovered enough to join the doctor, Kellogg will go back to his regular post."

"Which is?"

"He's currently assigned to the hospitality division."

"You're kidding?"

"Absolutely not. Visiting dignitaries are usually assigned an aide-de-camp to arrange schedules, handle anything that needs to be done, from missing laundry to—"

"Murder?" Atkins supplied.

"I suppose. Even murder, though I can't remember it coming to that. Not lately anyway."

"Nonetheless, I'll want to question him in the morning."

"Certainly."

"And what was the nature of Dr. Vogeler's visit in Washington?" asked Atkins, ignoring what Godfrey no doubt thought was a dismissal.

"Government business."

"And the New York Police Department's and mine when he comes here and a resident is murdered on my turf."

"Actually, the grounds around the Arsenal are under jurisdiction of the Central Park Police," Godfrey pointed out.

"Who are perfectly capable of chastising ladies illegally picking the flowers, stopping a runaway carriage horse, or nabbing the occasional pickpocket—if they bother to show up for duty at all. I'm assuming you knew that, or you wouldn't have called me."

Phil stifled a yawn. He was getting a second wind. She was ready for bed. It had been a long day.

"Do you believe Dr. Nash's murder was somehow connected to Dr. Vogeler's 'government business'?" If Atkins's tone became any drier, his words would be delivered in sand.

"Possibly, but before you ask, I'm not at liberty to discuss the subject of these meetings."

Atkins's eyebrows rose. "With due respect, that gives me little to work with."

"Mainly just some ideas about conditioned reflexes and faster reaction times on the battlefield. Soldiers get conditioned fast enough in the field. Kill or be killed. And that's all I can say."

Godfrey downed the brandy and replaced the glass. "Aeroplanes. That's where the future lies. Now, if that is all, perhaps we could continue this tomorrow. Lady Dunbridge, allow me to see you home."

"No need of that," Atkins said. "I'd be happy to drop her on my way back to the station."

"Yes, Godfrey, if the detective sergeant doesn't mind, I'm perfectly fine to let him escort me home. There's no reason for you to go out again," Phil said, taking his arm. "And frankly, I'll feel less anxious about Lily staying with you in residence."

"I assure you, she is quite safe," Godfrey said. "But I of course will accede to your wishes, my dear." He bowed over her hand. "I do appreciate your efforts to make this a . . ."

"Memorable evening?" she finished for him. "Until tomorrow then."

"Quite." He walked them to the door while Phil mentally recited the addresses she'd heard, using a little nursery ditty by which to remember them. As they walked down the steps, she was so busy concentrating on not forgetting that she didn't notice the Western Union boy, whose bicycle was careering down the sidewalk.

Atkins grabbed her arm and pulled her back as the cyclist screeched to a stop at the steps of Union House, let his bike drop to the sidewalk, and ran up the steps.

"A telegram!" Phil turned around to watch, but Atkins took her elbow and hurried her down the sidewalk

"Nothing that can't wait until tomorrow, and I want to be out of sight before Bennington realizes I don't have an automobile at my disposal."

"We're walking?" she asked incredulously.

"Yes, it's a lovely night." He smiled at her in the light of the streetlamp. "And we won't have to worry about the driver listening in."

"Ears," she said. "Just a Friend told me he never uses the telephone because the telephone girls have 'ears' and aren't above selling information they hear to the highest bidder."

"He's right, though I doubt if he's ever gotten much chance to even see a telephone, much less use one."

"No," she said, suddenly tired and wishing she could do more for her stalwart, self-designated protector.

"Are you going to question me tonight?" Phil cracked an involuntary yarn.

"Tomorrow will be soon enough."

"Then I have a question," she said.

"I doubt if you'll stop at one, but go ahead."

"When Rose was screaming and Salvos said she had a condition, Dietrich Lutz said, 'Incubus.' It sounded like an accusation. What does it mean?"

"I'm sorry to disappoint you, but I have no idea."

"And—"

"You've used your one question and we've arrived at the Plaza."

"You can be very annoying."

"So you've told me many times. I won't see you inside," he said formally.

"Worried about your reputation?" she asked, but her heart wasn't in it.

"Always. Good night, Lady Dunbridge." He tipped his hat. "Oh, and if you're thinking about an early-morning promenade through the park, just know that I'm having a guard posted at the scene to keep the area secure."

"I wouldn't expect less. Good night." She didn't stamp her foot until she was inside and waiting for the elevator to her apartment.

7

The problem with leaving one's lady's maid to serve another, Phil thought as she stood in front of her bedroom mirror, was getting out of the dress said maid had put her into hours before.

She twisted so that she could see the row of tiny buttons down the back. She could reach the buttons with one hand, but couldn't hold the buttonhole steady long enough to ease the button through without stretching the delicate fabric.

Maybe she could slip it down over her hips to the floor; the new fashions were much less constricting than those of the year before. She wiggled her arms out of the off-the-shoulder straps and eased the fabric down to her waist before it stuck. She tried to inch the back of the dress around to her front in order to get a better grip of the buttons. That effort only managed to tangle the fabric.

It was definitely time to rethink her next order from Paris.

Well, something had to be done, and she couldn't very well awaken Preswick to help her. He would be horrified.

Maybe over her head. She hiked up the skirt and managed to lift it up to her shoulders, far enough to toss the skirt over her head—where it stuck on her tiara.

"Damnation!"

"Perhaps you could use a little assistance?"

Phil yelped in surprise. "How long have you been here?"

"I was waiting for you."

"You could have made yourself known a little sooner."

"I was enjoying watching you."

The skirt was extricated from her tiara and fell softly down her back. Deft fingers went to work on the tiny buttons, and the gown slipped to the floor.

Phil turned to face Lieutenant Francis Kellogg.

"Francis" let out an appreciative groan. "I don't have much time. There's been a change."

"What are you doing here?"

"I would think that was obvious." He wrapped the ribbon closing her camisole around his finger.

"I mean in Manhattan, disguised as Francis Kellogg. And really, what a ridiculous name, it reminds one of the cereal." She sucked in breath as he moved closer. "It isn't your real name?"

"No." He tugged at the ribbon and the bow fell away. At the same time, he turned off the lamp with this free hand. "I've been called back to Washington. I'm to leave immediately. Well, as soon as I'm finished here."

"Did you know this was going to happen?" she asked as he walked her backward in the dark.

"This or the murder?"

"The murder."

"It was a surprise to me."

"So you're not here because of the threats to Dr. Vogeler's life."

He walked her backward until she was standing against the four-poster bed.

"Does Godfrey know—"

"God, no. And please do not enlighten him."

"Atkins is already suspicious. He plans to question you in the morning."

He pushed her backward and she landed with a bounce on her satin comforter.

"I won't be here in the morning."

He never was. "Does Godfrey know you're leaving?"

"He may by now."

"The telegram," she said.

He leaned over her, his hands braced on either side of her shoulders.

She was seized by an unexpected and unsettling dread. "Be careful."

He laughed softly and his fingers brushed her hair. "You can't be careful in this business. You just have to be smarter and faster than the other guy."

"But—"

He ended the rest of her question with a kiss. And by the time she thought to ask her next question, he had already slipped into the night.

She lay staring at the ceiling, tracing the pattern of the ornamental medallion and wondering what besides murder was going on.

It was becoming more and more obvious that, if it was not the War Department, whoever it was had enough influence to substitute the usual rotation of aides-de-camp in order to put Mr. X—Francis—in position. And since Phil had yet to be enlightened as to who her employer actually was, she was in a bit of a quandary as to know where her duty lay. With Godfrey or with Mr. X—

Francis, she reminded herself. She really must think of him as Francis or risk giving him away.

Francis . . . Her eyelids grew heavy; there was nothing like a champagne dinner, a murder, a traumatized young woman, and a walk home with the delectable Detective Sergeant Atkins topped off with a visit by the most infuriating, elusive, passionate colleague to make a countess want to sleep like the dead.

But there was work to do.

As soon as the sky began to turn to gray, Phil dressed in a split-skirt walking suit. Not an ideal outfit for a morning call, but it was too early for a morning call. It was too early for anything but heading for bed after a late night out on the town—or for an early-morning walk in the park.

She tore off the page of partial numbers and street names she'd hastily scribbled down on her return the night before and slipped it into her dressing-table drawer. She wrote a quick note to Preswick and sneaked down the hall toward the front door. She could hear Preswick in the kitchen, and it wouldn't be long before he went to awaken Lily, only to find Lily gone. There was no time for explanations at the present moment. She left the note on the hall table and slipped out the door.

Phil had no doubt that there would be a guard at the restaurant as Atkins had promised. Still, she needed to get a look at the area where the killer had waited before it was trampled by unsuspecting visitors or lead-footed patrolmen. If she was lucky she might even beat Atkins to the scene.

It wasn't just curiosity. With her colleagues uncooperative

with each other, she felt it imperative to learn the facts for herself. Someone needed to coordinate their efforts. And she was—if not exactly happy—willing to oblige.

Just a Friend was already at his spot on the sidewalk when she crossed the street to the entrance to the park.

"Hey, where ya going?" The young newsie tucked his papers under his arm and ran to catch up with her.

Phil slowed. "Good morning, you're up early." Had he grown taller over the winter? He was certainly carrying a little more weight, thanks largely to Preswick's generous heart.

"Naw, I always get here before daybreak. So's nobody tries to steal my spot. It's a vicious business, paper selling."

"Well, I hope you sell lots of papers today."

"But where're you goin', *my* lady?"

Phil stopped to grin at him. His way of saying *my lady* was completely proprietary, as if she was his and his alone.

And she was. She owed him and his newsie friends her life. Her little family of Fifty-eighth Street Irregulars, who all went by soubriquets like Big Nose Mike and Snowball McGee or Shuck-work Caruthers.

"I'm just going for a short walk in the park," Phil said.

"You shouldn't go in there without an escort. 'Specially this time of day. All sorts of lowlifes sleep there. And those park coppers aren't worth a plug nickel."

"I'll be fine. I'm not going far. And I'll stay right on the drive."

"I don't know." He looked back at his corner.

"Go back to your papers. If someone steals your corner, who's gonna be my lookout man?"

He grinned at her lapse into slang.

"Now hurry."

He hesitated only for second, then raced back to his corner. Phil continued on her way, walking briskly, partly for exercise and just a bit with skittishness. Fortunately the drive was wide and the early sun was already creating mosaics on the pavement as its rays found their way through the heavy foliage.

She passed the zoo and arrived at the far side of the Arsenal a few minutes later, only to find one of the "plug nickel" park police guarding the copse of trees where she'd planned to search.

A small setback for a woman on a mission. She looked quickly around, then grabbed her purse with both hands, and ran up to him, saying breathlessly, "That man just tried to steal my purse!"

"What man? Where?" asked the officer, looking up and down the drive and finding no one in sight.

"He ran between those buildings there." She pointed, and said more shrilly, "There he is, I insist you arrest him."

The policeman shifted from one foot to the other. "All right, but you wait here. And hold on to your purse."

"I will, officer," Phil promised, clutching the purse so hard she was afraid he might see the outline of her pistol inside. "Now hurry, please."

He trotted off. As soon as he rounded the corner of one of the zoo buildings, Phil threw her leg over the fence and slipped into the underbrush. She didn't think she had much time. The officer didn't appear to be the most enthusiastic of pursuers. Which was just as well, since she truly hoped he didn't find some innocent person to arrest.

She didn't move at first, just took in the scene, determined not to disturb anything. She had no illusions about her experience as an investigator. Even in the dark, with a torch, John Atkins was more than capable of finding anything left behind, which of course there would be. Criminals always left something of themselves behind; it just wasn't always easy to find.

But she'd had her little successes.

She carefully stepped away from the walkway. The killer had to have been waiting in the trees. It wasn't an ideal place to hide, at least not in the daylight. She could see vehicles driving through the park. She could hear the traffic from Fifth Avenue. And straight ahead, through the lower-hanging branches, was the section of pavement where they had congregated after dinner.

She checked the surrounding ground and, not seeing any footprints or disturbance, she crept forward until she had a clear view of where the group stood that night.

And ran straight into John Atkins.

"I was about to give you up," he said.

"You knew I'd be here?"

"I do believe I've learned not to underestimate you. What have you done to my patrolman?"

"Sent him after a nonexistent thief. Please don't let him arrest anyone for stealing my purse." She held it up. "Safe and sound. Have you found anything?"

"A mildewed newspaper, a knit cap that has been here at least since the fall. Nothing else so far."

"There must be something," she said, slipping past him. "Dr. Locard says—"

"I know what Dr. Locard says. And if the killer left something behind, I'll find it."

"Two sets of eyes are better than one, Detective Sergeant." Even though his were a delicious lake blue.

He just returned her look with one of exasperated humor. How did the man manage to look this good when he couldn't have gotten any sleep last night?

But he was freshly shaven and wearing a light summer suit. He was also carrying a canvas bag.

"Why aren't you arguing with me about interfering?"

"Because I know once your interest is piqued, you won't give up."

"Does that mean that you'll let me help with your investigations?"

"It means that you're incredibly annoying. But I could use an extra pair of hands just now. And since you sent that poor officer off on a wild goose chase, you can do the job." He shoved the canvas bag at her.

"What do I do with this?"

"You hold it while I collect all the trash that has accumulated over God knows how long." He smiled his most devastating smile at her. Fortunately he seemed to have no idea of his effect on the female populace of Manhattan.

Or if he did, was his attitude merely a means of staving off droves of smitten women? Did he consider her one of those who needed staving off? The thought was lowering. She prided herself on her sangfroid, whether it came to a murder suspect or a lover. She refused, absolutely refused, to be smitten with any man.

Though Phil had to admit he had a somewhat disconcerting effect even on her.

"Or you can pick up that mildewed newspaper and I'll hold the bag."

She snapped the bag open and held it out. He scooped up the soggy newspaper and tossed it into the bag. He followed it with the woolen cap.

Phil wrinkled her nose. Holding the bag and its contents away from her clothes, she followed him through the trees and soon began picking up the odd piece of detritus herself.

The shrubbery was thick in places, and though the actual area wasn't very large, it was dense enough to be able to conceal someone at night. Certainly dense enough to snag the weave of her split skirt.

Even watching carefully where she stepped, the fabric managed to catch on branches and thorns several times as she searched for more things to put in the bag. More than once, her hair caught in low-lying branches and she had to yank it free.

After a few minutes, her hands were dirty, her suit was smudged, and her person had become home to several twigs and leaves. Pieces of hair, which she'd had to dress on her own that morning, were hanging in her eyes.

Atkins, on the other hand, moved through the trees with the ease of a gentleman at the opera, managing not to even wrinkle his trouser crease.

Men could sometimes be very annoying.

A few feet later, they came into a small clear space, just large enough for a killer to wait for his prey.

Atkins held up his hand, telling her not to move. They were standing very close to each other, almost touching.

"Here?" Phil asked. "This is where he stood?"

Atkins nodded. He was staring out between the branches. With the sun shining, it was amazing to Phil that no one had seen him even in the dark.

Atkins lifted his hand, ran his fingers along a branch about shoulder level. Phil had to stand on tiptoe to see what he was doing.

"How tall is Erik Vogeler?"

Phil thought. "Not more than half a head taller than I am."

He looked her over, then turned away and ran his hand over a lower branch. Shook his head. Held his arm out as if it were a gun and pointed it through various places in between the branches. Put his arm down finally.

"How on earth did the bullet find its way to Georgina Nash?" she wondered out loud.

Not getting a response, she continued, "He would have to choose his moment well. Erik Vogeler must have turned away or stepped to the side, just as he aimed. So he only managed to graze his arm instead of hitting his torso. The way they were gesticulating throughout the conversation, it might have hit any of the others standing so close. It must have been terribly difficult to . . . um . . . what do they call it? To get a bead on his victim."

Atkins dipped his chin. "There are times, Lady Dunbridge, when you make my blood run cold."

She huffed out an uncountess-like sigh. "But it bypassed them all and ended up across the sidewalk in Georgina Nash's forehead. What are the odds?"

"Hmm" was the only encouragement she got.

"The ultimate irony," she added.

"Perhaps."

"You don't think it was just some crazy person who struck out violently without intention, do you?"

He was silent.

"A potential robbery?"

Nothing from the infuriating detective sergeant.

"Atkins," she cajoled. "Who could it have been? I mean, after having seen and heard these psychologists at dinner and afterward, I can almost imagine one of them losing his temper and striking out in anger or pure exasperation. No one agreed on anything. It was a heated evening.

"But this didn't grow out of the heat of the moment. All the combatants were in full view . . . for the most part. Godfrey was inside, Ivan came running from the avenue. But everyone else was still here when the shot was fired. The maître d' vouched for Godfrey. Not that he'd—"

A look from Atkins stopped her midword.

"Well, he would never."

"Wouldn't he?"

"Actually, I can't be certain. Maybe if it was a matter of national security that couldn't be dealt with through normal channels." She grimaced. "You think Godfrey hired an assassin to get rid of an annoying houseguest?"

"Probably not. And he wouldn't be so obvious, if he did. What about the secretary? What ails Vogeler's regular assistant?"

Phil shrugged. She was thinking desperately on how to keep too much light being shed on Francis Kellogg, aka Mr. X. If she didn't believe Godfrey could be a cold-blooded killer, she wasn't so sure about Mr. X. Sometimes she wasn't even sure they were working for the same people or even on the same side.

And since Godfrey didn't seem to know that he wasn't who he was supposed to be, she would try to stay out of it.

"Why aren't you answering me? You're usually quite ready to give an opinion."

Phil pursed her lips, an expression used quite often by Phil and her sister's long-suffering governess.

"I was thinking."

"Who else is traveling with them?"

"Let's see, the nanny, Mrs. Cole, and Anna's maid. I don't know if Dr. Vogeler has a manservant; I suppose he would, though perhaps his assistant also assists him in dressing. From what I gleaned from the conversation, scientists don't make a lot of money. That they need to have a sponsor, or a university position. Or a family able to support them. And psychoanalysts are just being recognized by the scientific community and the competition is, as I recall someone saying, 'cutthroat.'"

"I see. Are either Dr. Vogeler or his wife from wealthy families?"

Phil looked at him in surprise. Then said haughtily, "I wouldn't know."

Atkins snorted. "Too well bred to ask?"

"One doesn't. Though she was wearing an impressive diamond necklace last night."

"Hmm. What about Ivan?" Atkins asked. "Would he have had time to fire the shot, climb out to the street, and run around to the park entrance?"

"Getting rid of the weapon on the way?" Phil thought back. "I guess it's possible. He would have had to drop the weapon somewhere and come back for it." She sighed.

"Which he could have done any time while you were in the house."

"True," she agreed. "But now that I think about it, he was wearing a heavy jacket even though it was a warm summer night. He could have merely hidden a pistol inside it."

"And something larger?"

"Larger, good heavens, like a rifle?"

"I'll have a better idea of the weapon, once Godfrey's 'private' mortician releases the bullet to the police."

Phil held her peace while she waited for his chagrin at having Godfrey interfere in his investigation to pass.

Really, these men. If only they would cooperate, investigations— not to mention life in general—would be so much more efficient.

Atkins knelt down, perusing the ground. Phil turned in the opposite direction and continued her own search. As she moved, she caught glimpses of Fifth Avenue and found a narrow space in the shrubs where someone could have slipped back to the street.

She glanced over her shoulder: Atkins was still studying the ground. She started to go back; she was suddenly feeling the need of a cup of coffee and a large breakfast. She pulled her split skirt tight and continued on, eyes glued to the ground and the low-growing bushes.

She discovered some scuff marks where the earth had been disarranged by several animals or perhaps a fleeing murderer. It was impossible to tell. There was not one discernible individual footprint that Phil could ascertain. Not even broken branches, as if he'd crashed through the shrubbery in his haste to get away.

When Atkins came up behind her, she pointed out the scuff marks. His expression didn't look promising.

They continued slowly through the brush, Atkins leading the way, Phil, a step behind, holding her skirt close. Each of them searched the ground and the surrounding brush as they carefully picked their way toward the avenue. They were mere steps away when Phil's skirt caught on a hawthorn and refused to give even after several sharp tugs. Phil knelt down to tug it free.

And found something besides her skirt caught by the long sharp thorns.

"Wait!" she cried.

Atkins froze.

"What is it?"

"I found something." Phil reached for it, but Atkins stopped her.

He knelt down beside her, looked at it from all angles. Stood and extracted a pair of tweezers from his pants pockets. Knelt down again. It took some maneuvering before the small scrap of fabric was completely extracted and Atkins stood, holding it between the tweezers' pincers.

Phil peered closely at it. White cloth, torn, but she could see something was embroidered on it. Initials? Or a symbol, but it was impossible to determine since the tear had cut the embroidery in half.

"That hasn't been here since last fall," Phil pointed out. "Do you think it was torn from the killer as he ran away?"

"Possibly."

"A handkerchief?" Phil hypothesized out loud. "Unusual. A close-weave linen? Or cotton, perhaps. Well, never mind, Preswick will know."

Atkins slipped the remnant into a small paper sack he took from the same pocket as his tweezers. "We do have our own experts at the station."

Phil couldn't stop her eyes from rolling upward, but forbore commenting. The detective sergeant was a little sensitive about the state of the police department since Roosevelt had left and his reforms had largely followed him. They would get the answers they needed much faster by consulting her butler.

"Awfully sloppy to leave behind this much incriminating evidence," she said.

"Incriminating . . . or convenient," he said.

"Convenient? Oh, I see. You think it was left there on purpose?"

"Perhaps."

"A setup," she said, not being able to contain her excitement.

It received the look it deserved.

"I don't suppose you're going to let me see what it is?"

"I will. In good time."

"Really?"

"Yes. But I suggest we hurry, because I believe your park policeman has returned empty-handed." Indeed, she could see bits
of the officer, who stood at the edge of the trees, fists on hips and
looking in all directions.

Atkins took the canvas bag, stepped over the rail to the sidewalk, and reached back to help her over. She climbed over with
more haste than grace.

"It's still too early for a morning call," Phil said, brushing her
skirt. "And I must change before rescuing Lily from Union House.
Shall we adjourn to the Plaza? I for one could do with a hearty
breakfast. Which they do wonderfully. Besides I want to see what
we collected this morning."

Not to mention that Preswick still didn't know what had happened last night. By now, he must be beside himself with worry,
and she didn't relish facing him alone.

She looked over to John Atkins. She didn't think Preswick
would scold her in front of the detective sergeant. He had no com-
punction when they didn't have an audience.

"I'm certain Preswick will be glad to take notes while we eat.
And I can give you my impressions of the guests at last night's
dinner, so you might as well—Was that a growl, Detective Sergeant? No? Good. It's much too early to be exasperated. As for
myself, I am feeling quite exhilarated."

8

If the Plaza's doorman was surprised to see Lady Dunbridge returning to the hotel resembling someone who had spent the early hours not at the last strains of the ball but rummaging through discarded trash in Central Park, he didn't show it. He didn't even blink when he realized she was accompanied by the well-dressed man, whom he must have figured out over the last few months was a policeman.

He merely bowed and said good morning, managing to include Atkins in his greeting without really "seeing" him. The Plaza was, among other things, very discreet.

As for Preswick, he had spent fifty years ignoring the foibles of his employers. He, too, merely bowed as if he'd been expecting them and let them into the apartment. But she could tell it was taking him an effort.

"Preswick, my dear," Phil began. "Everything is fine. Lily is fine. I'll tell all in a few quick minutes but I must tidy myself."

Someone stifled a snort; she wasn't sure which of her male companions it was. Perhaps both.

"Will you please make the detective sergeant comfortable, see to whatever needs he has, though he looks annoyingly unfazed by our outing. And do take that bag into the kitchen where the detective sergeant can pick it up later."

Preswick bowed and relieved the detective sergeant of the bag before he could resist.

"And then order us both some breakfast. I'm famished and I'm sure the detective sergeant must be, too."

"Thank you," Atkins said stiffly. "But I've already breakfasted."

"A hard roll from a street vendor, no doubt."

His expression told it all.

"No one will be ready to receive guests—or policemen," she added as an afterthought, "at Union House for another hour or so." She gave him her best dazzling smile. "And you can interrogate me over eggs and ham."

She left them to decide things between themselves.

She had reached her bedroom when she heard Preswick say, "If you'd like to wash your hands . . ." She closed her door.

One look in the mirror, and Phil cursed herself for letting Lily stay at Union House overnight. She had to admit to being a little anxious about how she was faring.

She quickly changed into a kimono of light green, appliqued with large pink peonies. She splashed water onto her face and all the other places that counted and sat down at her dressing table.

There her confidence faltered. One might say, if one was being polite, that tendrils wisped around her face.

Actually they looked like Medusa might look if Medusa were a well-bred lady who had gone abrawling. She managed to shove the tresses back into the mass of waves and curls, and secured them with pins. She'd just have to choose a flattering hat to hide the worst of it until she could get to Union House and excuse herself to have Lily work her magic.

But for breakfast, and John Atkins, she would have to make do. She pulled a few wayward pieces of park leaves from her chignon and went to confront her day—and her butler.

Preswick had prepared the round table at the turret window. Though she noticed only one place was set.

Not only was the man infuriating, he was stubborn.

Atkins stood at the window. Phil could swear there was a slight blush to his cheek. He was most certainly seeing this as an act of impropriety, though Phil didn't see why. He was a gentleman in every sense of the word. It was why he was always sent on the cases that involved, as they said in England, "members of the ton."

When Phil had left her homeland, she'd determined to leave pomp and ceremony behind. America was a modern country with modern ideas and independent women. She intended to be one. So far she was doing pretty well.

She joined him at the window. "Are you really refusing to . . . break bread with me?" Silly, but his uptight notions of propriety were inspiring her toward the biblical.

"I'm on duty," he said gruffly. So why was he fighting a smile? The man was sometimes an enigma.

"Well, at least accept a cup of coffee. Come, sit down. You can ask questions and I'll answer between bites."

He reached for his breast pocket, but she stopped him.

"Preswick will stay to take notes. Don't worry, he's very thorough. And besides, I haven't had time to bring him up to date on all that's happened." She lowered her voice. "He's very concerned about Lily."

"I've already apprised him of Lily's fate," Atkins said. "And of the murder. And though I can't prevent him from taking notes, I'll take my own, thank you."

"Suit yourself."

He moved behind her and held her chair; she had to admit she admired his ability to adhere to civility when he probably wanted to brain her.

They waited for Preswick to serve her, pour them both coffee, then take his place near the food trolley, pencil and paper in hand and coffeepot at the ready.

Phil slathered a piece of toast with marmalade and smiled across the table at Atkins before taking a feral bite out of her toast.

A few bites later, when her hunger was somewhat muted, she took a sip of coffee and said, "Now, where would you like me to start?"

"How about the beginning?"

"That's the odd thing." She speared a piece of ham and contemplated the bite. She told him about receiving the telegram from Godfrey asking her to return to the city. "Needless to say, I was intrigued."

"And you walked blithely into a murder."

"At the time, I didn't know there was going to be one. He needed a hostess for the dinner which he was giving for the Vogelers and a few of their friends."

"That was it? He needed you to play hostess? Did he at least hint at anything else?"

"Not until later, when he did explain that there had been a possible attempt on Erik Vogeler's life earlier. He dismissed the seriousness of the threat, saying that psychoanalysts tend to exaggerate." She shrugged slightly. "I guess he was wrong."

"But Erik Vogeler isn't dead."

Phil sighed and pushed her plate away. Preswick whisked it away. "No, but Georgina Nash is."

Atkins and Phil sat across from each other, not speaking, while Preswick refilled their cups and returned to his post, pencil poised over his paper.

The detective sergeant's mouth twitched. Lord, but the man was impatient.

"Let's see . . ." She told him about Georgina Nash jumping out of the bushes and warning Dr. Vogeler that he was in danger. Then Rose followed her out . . . "Looking like the famed *sonnambula*."

Phil shuddered just thinking about the unworldly vision that Rose Nash had made. "Rose may not be mad, but she's certainly odd, even before the murder of her sister. Evidently she was brilliant before whatever tragedy—which no one has explained as yet—made her the way she is now.

"And they're all doctors," Atkins asked.

"Most of them, old friends from university, who've reconnected over the years at various conferences across Europe. And yet it seems everyone had lost touch with the sisters. They weren't even invited, but somehow found out about the dinner and made a surprise appearance. And I must say it was quite a surprise.

"They all spent the evening passionately arguing about repression and hysteria and the like. I confess, I didn't understand half of it.

"After dinner, the discussion became quite heated, until finally, Georgina turned on the group as a whole, claiming that she knew their secrets, and wasn't afraid to tell them. Nothing specific, but threatening, almost as if she was able to . . ." Phil trailed off; she didn't know quite how to explain it.

"Read men's minds?" he finished.

"No more than most women can," Phil said. "But watching her in action, I could understand how people hunted down the presumed witches of this world. It was uncanny."

Atkins glanced up from his notes. "Can you remember exactly what was said?"

Phil shook her head. "I had gone to check on Rose. And quite frankly, it wasn't the kind of conversation that begged attention. These kind of games are common in ballrooms throughout Europe and, I expect, the United States, too. Laughter turns to innuendo, whispers start, then rumors fly, everyone gets in on the fun, until suddenly it becomes large enough to destroy a person's reputation or worse. And without anyone ever knowing the exact details."

Atkins visibly shuddered.

"Not useful in police work, perhaps, but can be devastatingly powerful in society."

"I'm not unaware," he said. "Can you be a little more specific?"

Phil thought back. "She called Dr. Salvos a cheat, alluding to some scandal in the past, and accused Dr. Lutz of using medicine to take advantage of women. Dr. Weiss of being . . . unfeminine?

"Then she turned and walked away. Chumley Griswold laughed, and said she was having them on, and began applauding.

"Anna called something like, 'Georgie, you're so droll.' And they all began applauding. The shot rang out. And Georgie slumped to the ground. I thought she'd fainted.

"I thought she'd fainted," Phil whispered, as the truth finally hit her and her breakfast rebelled. A woman was dead at Phil's feet with her own sister sitting not six feet away. And they had all been applauding.

Phil shook herself.

"Preswick?"

"Yes, my lady."

"Purchase some books on psychology and psychoanalysis. And hypnosis."

"Hypnosis?" Atkins asked, surprised.

"Chumley Griswold, a chemist, now makes his living hypnotizing people at parties, performing tarot-card readings and similar parlor tricks."

"I don't see a need for you to study any of this."

"It's interesting, don't you think? I was surprised how little I actually knew. I see articles in the newspaper all the time—this new psychoanalysis is very much the thing in some circles—but I skip right over them." *To read the society and crime pages,* she had to admit. "I went to a séance once. It was supposed to be great fun but it was silly and hurtful. Taking advantage of grieving people trying to communicate with the dead. I don't believe I've ever had a relative whom I wished to see beyond the grave." *Or in person, for that matter.*

She realized that she was no longer being listened to. John Atkins was looking over her head. Amused at something behind her? There was only the wall behind her.

She was considering asking him if he was all right, when he suddenly looked her straight in the eye.

"What does this have to do with the War Department?"

Taken off guard at the sudden turn, Phil floundered for a moment.

"If you think I'm in Godfrey's confidence, I'm not. The only weapons used at dinner were subtle and not-so-subtle backstabbings . . . until the shooting."

"And after the shot was fired?" Atkins prodded.

"Godfrey came out of the restaurant and ushered everyone inside. Ivan ran in from the street where he had been waiting with Dr. Salvos's car."

"And the sister?"

"She just sat there until Dr. Salvos and Ivan took her away. Then you came and you know the rest. Now, if we're finished, we can take a look at the evidence we found."

"Shall I fetch the canvas bag, my lady?"

"Not necessary, Preswick," Atkins said. "Actually, if you don't mind putting it out in the garbage?"

Phil's eyes narrowed. Even more so when she caught the twinkle in his eye. He hadn't been looking for evidence. He'd been teaching her a lesson in humility.

She was not amused. There was a murder to solve.

He cleared his throat. "We still have one person, at least, unaccounted for."

"Oh?" Her attention was yanked back to the one line of questioning she had been dreading: how to mention Francis Kellogg without saying too much or too little, or betraying a nervous titter, a too-nonchalant gesture. John Atkins would be aware of the smallest misstep.

"The substitute secretary," Now he reached into his pocket and brought out his own notebook. Opened it. "Francis Kellogg."

"I'm not sure. I didn't pay much attention to him. He wasn't really a part of the group. Godfrey only invited him to be polite."

"Or to be on hand if trouble did break out."

Phil let that pass. "He did reach Georgina almost immediately."

"Did you see him coming?"

"What?"

"Where did he come from? He must have been somewhere close to arrive so quickly."

She willed her heart to stop pounding. Where *had* he come from? He wasn't there and then he was. Like he usually did things. *Don't think about that,* she told herself.

"I couldn't say. He was just there. Almost immediately," she added. "He couldn't have come from the trees that quickly even if he burst through the crowd and ran straight across the walk."

She made herself stop talking.

"Then I suppose we can discount him, and the sister, also."

Phil slowly let out the breath she'd been holding. She didn't know anything for certain. "Now, can we take a look at the scrap of material we found today?"

She quickly apprised Preswick about their search.

Preswick put down his notebook, removed the coffee cups, ran the crumb knife over the table, and whipped out a clean napkin to cover the tablecloth while Atkins reached into his pocket for the paper evidence bag.

Atkins placed the bag on the clean napkin, thoroughly cleaned his own hands on another, and slid the scrap onto the table. Phil and Preswick leaned closer.

"If I might, Detective Sergeant." Preswick produce a clean pair of white gloves, exchanged them for the ones he'd been wearing, and gingerly unrolled the sides of the fabric until the partial figuration was on display.

Atkins eyebrows rose.

"A good butler always has an extra pair of clean gloves handy, Detective Sergeant," Phil said.

Especially for handling evidence. A habit that Preswick's had adopted from Sir Arthur Conan Doyle.

"Uh-huh," Atkins said, and leaned over to get a better look.

Since Preswick was holding the fabric open, Phil reached around him for the notebook and pencil and quickly drew a rendition of what she saw.

A curved black line about a centimeter thick, which could be part of a circle. An initial? "O," perhaps. There were three more shorter lines curving from the main curve at equal distances.

"What do you think it is, Preswick?"

Transferring the edges to one hand, he reached into his trouser pocket and pulled out a jeweler's loupe. Whether he needed to identify the smallest drop of gravy on the best napkins or a clue to murder, Preswick was always prepared.

"It has the initial appearance of linen. Very fine."

"A monogrammed handkerchief?" Atkins asked.

"Perhaps," Preswick said.

"The detective inspector thinks it was planted at the scene to throw suspicion on someone in particular," Phil said. "It was caught by a thorn of a hawthorn bush."

"I would have to agree with the detective sergeant. Though fine, the fabric is too tightly woven to be torn by a branch. It would even take a sharp edge and considerable force to tear it. Most likely a clumsy attempt at misdirection, would you not agree, Detective Sergeant?"

"I would," Atkins said. "And if you ever decide you want to go to work for the New York Police Department, Preswick, just say the word."

"Thank you, sir, but I'm quite content with her ladyship."

"I have no doubt."

"Well," Phil said, interrupting this seditious attempt to steal her butler. "If they were going to implicate someone, you'd think they would leave something with a full initial on it. And save us some work."

"Me," Atkins said. "Save *me* some work. You will stay out of it."

"Which moves this from any possibility of a spontaneous malfeasance," Phil said, ignoring him, "into the realm of planned intent."

Atkins's head snapped up and he shot her a fulminating look, and again that twitch of his lips. What was wrong with the man?

"Or a crime of passion, perhaps smoldering for years before finally bursting into flames again," Phil said enthusiastically.

"You've been reading Lily's dime novels."

"What? You don't think repressed passions can lead to violence? The psychoanalysts certainly do."

Atkins's lips quivered. "Of course I do. I beg your pardon."

"A planted clue, implicating someone, perhaps exacting revenge on the victim as well as the supposed perpetrator," Phil elaborated, growing to her subject.

"We won't know more until we find the other half."

The royal we, or was he including her?

Atkins stood, slipped his notebook into his pocket. "Thank you for the coffee." Again that weird little half smile. What was he plotting?

"I'll show the detective sergeant to the door," Phil said. They walked to the entryway in silence but when they reached the door, she stopped him.

"You know everyone is going to balk at your questions."

"They always do," he said pleasantly.

"You'll do much better if you take me along."

"Probably, but this is a police matter." His lips quirked.

It was galling.

"Detective Sergeant Atkins, why do you keep smiling?"

"I have no idea. Lack of sleep, perhaps. Or maybe . . ." He broke into a full grin. It was dazzling. "Pardon me, but . . ."

He reached toward her cheek. . . .

Heavens, she thought.

But his finger bypassed her face to tug at her hair. "It could be this." He held up what appeared to be a twig. One that she had obviously missed in her hasty toilette.

"It's been distracting me for the last hour."

"I do my best to amuse," she said, feeling uncharacteristically deflated.

"And you do, in a way that will one day drive me to Bedlam."

"Oh, I hope not. But speaking of Bedlam, I think we'd better get over to Union House before Dr. Faneuil sends Rose Nash there."

"I agree," he said. " However, I will be going to Union House . . . alone."

Fine, Phil thought. She'd give him a twenty-minute head start. That was only fair. She already had one piece of information that he didn't. The identity of the nondescript aide-de-camp *cum* secretary. And that piece should keep her at least one step ahead of the detective sergeant.

9

A half hour later Phil was ringing the doorbell at Union House. She had changed into a walking dress of navy-blue dotted swiss. And having not been able to do much to salvage her hair, had pulled a white-and-yellow cloche over the whole embarrassing mess.

Collins showed her into a dark paneled library, where Godfrey stood at a bow window that looked out to the street. His hands were clasped behind his back and the sun streaked across his thick white hair before illuminating a spot on the carpet.

He turned sharply when Collins announce her.

Like a lion sensing an attack, Phil thought.

"Philomena," he said, coming toward her and forcing, but not quite achieving, a smile. "I suspect you've come to retrieve your maid. She was a godsend. And Cook and the housekeeper took good care of her."

"Thank you. I'm glad she could be of help. And how are things this morning?"

"Fine, just fine." He hesitated, then gestured her over to a small settee near the fireplace, now enclosed in a decorative screen picturing an English fox hunt.

As soon as she was seated, he sat in a chair facing her. She could tell only good breeding prevailed. He wished her elsewhere.

"I'm surprised that Detective Sergeant Atkins isn't here," Phil said. "Or is he upstairs questioning the patients?"

"Not as yet."

So Atkins hadn't come straight here. Had he gone back to the park without her? To continue his search? Had he seen something she hadn't and intended to keep from her? Well, she'd see about that.

"How are the patients this morning?"

Godfrey looked surprised. "Fine; they seem fine. Actually, I haven't heard from the Vogelers. It's been a busy morning. The housekeeper checked in on Miss Nash and Lily. Who she's taken a shine to, by the way; said Lily was well trained for one so young. She even had the cook send up some breakfast, since Lily refused to leave her patient."

"She's a clever girl," Phil said, wondering for the umpteenth time just how old Lily was.

The mantel clock chimed, and Godfrey automatically checked his watch against it. "I expect Atkins any minute. Actually, I'm surprised he's this late."

"Perhaps he's pursuing other lines of investigation," Phil said. "While we're waiting, why don't you tell me what happened last night after I left?"

"Last night?"

Phil laughed. "Oh, come, Godfrey. The telegram? The one that was delivered as I was leaving? If Atkins really hasn't been here this morning, I can only surmise that it is the telegram that has put you into such a brown study."

"I wondered if you had seen that."

"Tell me, if it isn't confidential."

"I suppose it can't hurt to tell you. Kellogg has been recalled to Washington. Effective immediately. No explanation. No authorization. I don't know why they sent him if they were just going to recall him."

"How extraordinary. Are they planning to replace him?"

"I have no idea. I've placed a call to them; as of yet no one has seen fit to return it. Bureaucrats have their own sense of time. Slow and slower."

"Maybe the assistant has recovered and is on his way here."

"Perhaps, but someone should have informed me of the change in plans. I have business to attend to, none of which includes playing host to the Vogelers."

Phil nodded sympathetically. Godfrey wanted to be out plotting sieges, planning the future of aeroplanes, and getting the Wright brothers to sign on the dotted line, not playing nursemaid to a psychoanalyst and his family. "I will be glad to help in any way I can."

"If it isn't too much inconvenience."

Inconvenience? Wild horses couldn't drag her away. Not with a murder to be solved and her elusive colleague "recalled" and Godfrey Bennington involved. It could be a matter of national security.

"Of course not. I would be delighted."

The door opened, and the butler announced Detective Sergeant Atkins, who strode in like a man on a mission. Where had he been for the last half hour?

"Atkins," Godfrey said, by way of greeting. They shook hands and Godfrey gestured for him to sit. Godfrey remained standing.

"I'll try to be quick, as usual, but I'll need to speak with the staff, the Vogelers, and the secretary, Francis Kellogg."

"The staff have been instructed to cooperate," Godfrey said. "I'll call for Mrs. Vogeler, but I'm afraid you won't be able to talk with Mr. Kellogg."

"And why is that? Surely he has a few minutes to spare to aid the investigation."

Phil concentrated on not looking like she already knew the answer.

"Kellogg's been recalled to Washington. He's already gone."

"What? And you let him leave?"

"I only received the telegram after you left last night. At that late hour, I saw no reason not to wait until the morning to deliver the message. But when the butler went up to give him his orders first thing this morning, he had already cleared out."

"A rather precipitate leaving. Did he also receive a telegram?"

"Not according to Collins. And he's been in service here since it opened. A retired military man."

"And you're certain Kellogg didn't see the telegram last night?" Atkins asked.

"He did not. Being a methodical man, I read it and locked it in my desk drawer overnight."

Being a suspicious man, Phil thought, not that a simple desk lock would stop Mr. X.

"I can ask that he give an affidavit of what he witnessed when he arrives in Washington," Godfrey continued.

"Yes, if you could arrange that. And if someone would ask

Mrs. Vogeler to come down? Perhaps there is somewhere where I could question her?"

"Yes, of course. You'll have privacy in the morning room. I'll have Collins ask her to meet you there."

"Thank you, but before you do, could you please enlighten me as to why the army feels the need to replace the doctor's assistant with a man of their own?"

Godfrey hesitated, as if wondering how much to confide. "The fellow, Alan Toussaint, fell ill while in Washington. Some stomach ailment. So as a courtesy we loaned Vogeler a replacement until Toussaint recovered and could return to duties."

"Anything else I should know?"

Godfrey said nothing.

"I can hardly investigate when you're purposely keeping me from information I need."

Still nothing from Godfrey.

Atkins waited.

For the longest moment Phil had the impression they had both turned to stone.

"Godfrey, please," she ventured. "You know we are both completely trustworthy."

She got a sharp look from Atkins for her trouble, while Godfrey consulted the carpet and her statement trembled in the air between the two men.

Finally, Godfrey pulled up an additional chair and sat down. "Very well, I'll tell you something. But it must not leave this room."

Both Phil and Atkins leaned forward. With a tempting morsel like that they needed no encouragement.

"For the last year or so we've been hearing about experiments—overseas, mind you—that are using various mind-controlling techniques to enhance the performance of enlisted men.

"Dr. Vogeler claims his methods can train men to follow orders without question by creating a habitual, methodical, primal reaction to those orders. Bah. Why would you want a soldier who couldn't think for himself?

"The concept of psychology in warfare is nothing new," he continued. "Armies have been sending rumors in advance of an attack for centuries. Exaggerating the size and power of armies, creating fear and distrust of the enemies' own leaders and each other.

"But what he is proposing would change the face of how our own soldiers approach war. If it works. Which I doubt. If we accepted his program, men would become mindless killing machines. Reprehensible."

He didn't have to tell them where he thought the future of warfare lay. Aeroplanes.

"Nonetheless, it was decided that he should be invited to present his theories to the Secretary and his cabinet. Vogeler had the endorsement of our counterparts in London and they wanted our opinion, since other countries had been talking to him and others of his ilk.

"We agreed to hear what he had to say. It is good diplomacy to be coordinated with allied nations. And to be truthful, the Department wanted to be in a good position if things moved in that direction."

"Are you talking about a bidding war?" Atkins said thoughtfully.

"Possibly. Which, if the program actually works, could give the owner an important edge. So Vogeler and his entourage were invited to D.C. The plan was to present his program there, then continue to Manhattan to present another paper to members of the Psychology Society.

"While in Washington, he gave his spiel; the family did some sightseeing and Mrs. Vogeler visited the museums; his assistant fell ill; and there was an attempt on the doctor's life."

"Which was?"

"Attacked in the park as he and his wife were returning from the theater."

"An attempted robbery?" Akins suggested.

"That was the general consensus, but we didn't feel we could take chances. And yet we didn't want to give him a military escort and excite any untoward attention. And with his assistant unable to perform his duties, we saw the opportunity to replace him with a government man for their sojourn in New York, which was only supposed to be a few days."

"And now this second attempt and the murder of Dr. Nash. It

will look bad in international circles. Not to mention it's a damn inconvenient time for me. Sorry, Philomena, a slip of the tongue."

She waved him off. "Don't mind me."

Godfrey's eyebrows dipped pensively and he rested his elbows on his knee, looking at the carpet. "The Vogelers are Austrian. As you probably know, the king has been involved in a series of important talks with the German kaiser."

"I read about the talks in the *Times*," Phil said. "But what do they have to do with Dr. Vogeler?"

"Nothing, per se. But there are certain aspects of Austro-German relations that are not appreciated by the king. And considering the coincidence of an Austrian psychologist presenting to the War Department in England and the United States, certain of my superiors are suddenly skittish about Vogeler's motivations."

Godfrey had alluded to his "superiors" before in their acquaintance, but it was never clear to Phil exactly what his position was in the government.

"They think he's acting for a foreign government?" Atkins asked.

"But he was recommended by the British government," Phil said.

Godfrey sighed. "Yes, but not all men in the government agree on what is best for England—or, I might add, the United States."

Phil glanced at Atkins, who appeared to understand, while Phil felt at sea.

"There is a fight, unseen by others, going on in the closer circles. Some men in power in the government and in the financial market see a very different future for England and Europe than the rest of us. Some, you might say, border on the . . ." He swallowed, as if he was having a hard time getting out the word.

Atkins did it for him. "The traitorous?"

"As you say."

"Traitors?" Phil exclaimed.

"Staying in power is not an easy task. Keeping your allies in power is even harder. And to some men, power is everything. Above family, above duty, above country, even above what is right."

Phil might not be conversant in politics—until recently she had considered them particularly boring—but she understood power and the craving of it. You learned that in society very quickly.

"Oh, good heavens. Do you think some well-meaning patriot is trying to kill Dr. Vogeler?" Phil asked.

"Or some other party who wants to prevent him from selling to us."

"Vogeler must have some impressive methods," Atkins said.

"He does, and not ones I'm in favor of. It entails first breaking down the normal behavior of our men."

"Torture?" Atkins asked.

"Not physical, but breaking down the process of rational behavior and replacing it with less thought and faster reaction times. Something called conditioned response training."

"The methodology of this scientist Pavlov?" Atkins asked.

Godfrey's eyes widened ever so slightly in surprise.

"I've never heard of him," Phil admitted.

"He's had some success in altering the behavior of salivating dogs," Atkins enlightened her.

"And he's a Russian," Godfrey said, as if that explained everything. "They're officially our ally but . . . well, allies come and go. And the news coming out of Russia is, well . . . confidential," he added.

"Russians and Germans and Austrians aside," Atkins began, "you think someone is actually trying to kill Dr. Vogeler because of this program."

"A hired assassin?" Phil blurted out. She hadn't even considered that.

"It's possible," Godfrey said.

Atkins coughed out a breath of disbelief. "Considering what a poor shot he is to have missed that badly, I have to question the good sense of the people who hired him."

"True." Godfrey leaned back and templed his fingers.

"Was it one of your people?" Atkins asked.

Phil stilled.

Godfrey stood abruptly. "How can you suggest such a thing?"

Another deadlocked look between the two men.

"I'm merely asking the question."

"Well, it's nothing I'm privy to. This was supposed to be a small dinner party, some sightseeing, a lecture, and then I would put the Vogelers on a ship back to England.

"This is not a secure house. We don't even keep a complete staff. A housekeeper whose job is *not* to wait on the doctor and his wife hand and foot; a butler who carries out the minimal of duties when someone is in residence; and a cook and kitchen staff adequate to make breakfast and serve coffee and hors d'oeuvre if the need arises. We keep a minimal security detail. I was asked to accompany them to Manhattan and serve as ad hoc host while they were here."

"Seems an odd duty for someone of your . . ." Atkins searched for the word. "Authority."

"They needed someone who could think on their feet. They don't want anyone killing him on our watch. But they especially don't want anyone killing him in Washington." Godfrey stood abruptly. "I shouldn't have said that. I apologize. Philomena, if you could entertain the detective sergeant until I return? I'll see about that call from Washington, and send Mrs. Vogeler to be interviewed."

"Of course."

He strode out of the room.

"Afraid I'll search his desk while he's gone?" Atkins wondered aloud.

"You know not. Godfrey wouldn't be so rude as to leave you cooling your heels by yourself. After all, I am his temporary hostess. But would you?"

"Would I what?"

"Search his desk?"

Phil knew *she* would. She was dying to do it now, but the detective sergeant was curtailed by rules and regulations that few in the department beside him actually followed.

He answered with a scowl. "Temporary," he said.

"What?"

"You said 'temporary hostess.' You and Francis Kellogg, both temporary. Too many movable parts to this puzzle for my liking." He stopped, tilted his head.

Phil had heard it, too; the distant ring of a telephone.

A few minutes later, the door opened and Godfrey entered, not like a man who had discharged a duty, but one who was fighting to control his temper.

He went straight over to the call bell, pressed it with undue force. The butler appeared. "Collins, coffee."

Collins shut the door without a word.

Then he continued past Phil and Atkins to the bow window. Stood there for nearly a minute, looking out.

Phil and Atkins waited until, finally, he turned to face them.

"That was the personnel division returning my call."

Phil glanced at Atkins. They both knew something untoward was about to be imparted. But it also seemed that Godfrey was loathe to impart it.

"However—I must ask you—"

Atkins straightened slightly in his seat. "I know. Total confidentiality and, as I always assure you, I won't divulge anything that isn't necessary for bringing a murderer to justice. Both I and Lady Dunbridge can be trusted to use the utmost discretion."

A slight nod on Godfrey's part.

"They said they had never heard of Francis Kellogg. I explained to them about his assignment and about the telegram recalling him.

"At which point they told me they hadn't sent him, they had no one on the roster by that name, and they hadn't recalled him. Although they did finally manage to find the paperwork that requested a man of secretarial skills for the Vogeler visit. And informed me that the order had been cancelled before the paperwork was completed."

"My goodness," said Phil. "By whom?"

"That's just it. They only have 'cancelled,' stamped across the paperwork. I might chalk it up to bureaucratic incompetency, but the man was here—"

"And now he's gone," Atkins pointed out, as he reached in his pocket for his notebook. "Is it possible that he was part of some plot to kill Dr. Vogeler?"

The question hung in the air.

Godfrey finally jolted to life. "By God, if he is, I will find him and have him court-martialed!"

Phil held her peace. Her head was reeling. Mr. X, an assassin?

He was certainly capable. And if he was . . . She couldn't make herself go further down that road.

If Mr. X wasn't really with the War Department, wasn't sent by the personnel division, who had sent him? Someone or some group who had the power to override an internal request and substitute their own man. It had to be someone higher up in the government, surely.

But not Godfrey. It was becoming clearer with every passing minute that Godfrey was not in league with Mr. X. Unless he was playing a very deep game. And she knew he was capable of that.

She thought over the cases she and Mr. X had been involved in together. The subsequent arrests that were made that didn't always seem to be a part of her own murder investigation.

"Which makes this Kellogg fellow my most obvious suspect," Atkins said.

Phil bit her tongue not to intercede as a thrill ran through her. Not Mr. X, it had to be someone else. Did that mean they still had an assassin in their midst?

"Well, that is a quandary," she said aloud, earning her a tight smile from Godfrey, and a mere tightening of the lips from the detective sergeant.

"Is there anything else?" Atkins said.

"Actually, there is. Now Alan Toussaint is missing."

"The ailing assistant?" asked Phil, wondering what turn this case would take next. It hadn't been a full day since Georgina Nash had been murdered.

"Not so ill as you thought," Atkins said. "Unless . . ."

He trailed off but Phil had gotten the gist of his statement. *Unless it had all been planned. Or the assistant had been "taken care of."*

"No one realized he was gone until last night. He didn't bother to check out of the hotel. He could have left any time yesterday—or even earlier."

"Which potentially leaves him without an alibi," said Atkins. "Please inform me as soon as you have news, or if he shows up here."

"And Francis Kellogg?"

"I'll send out an alert for him. Can you give me a more accurate description?"

That almost undid Phil.

Godfrey shrugged. "Decent height."

"Could you be a little more specific?" Atkins asked.

"It's hard to say, not six feet. He had a slight stoop, the kind secretaries and clerks get from leaning over a desk all day."

And the kind, Phil thought, *that a master impersonator used to conceal his true height.*

"Light-brown hair."

"Eye color?"

Godfrey shook his head. Both he and Atkins looked at Phil.

"I'm sorry. I didn't notice." And there had been so many eye colors in the past: gray, blue, brown, hazel. Last night she'd been so busy trying *not* to look at him that she really hadn't noticed.

Collins returned with the coffee tray, and Phil thought they were all glad for a respite from this convoluted turn of events.

They were studiously sipping at an excellent brew when they heard a commotion outside.

"Now what?" Godfrey exclaimed.

"Maybe that's Alan Toussaint," Phil suggested.

The door opened and Dr. Faneuil strode in.

"Bennington, what is this? First, I'm told that I can't see either of my patients. Patients whom I got out of bed last night to attend. And that my services are no longer required. Is this your doing?"

Godfrey had only half risen from his chair when Anna Vogeler swept in. "I apologize, Godfrey. My dear husband refuses to be fussed over, even by me. And I insist that Rose be left to my care. I won't have her going to an institution to be poked and prodded and all manner of things. I owe it to Georgina."

The doctor stretched to his toes, the cords of his neck standing out like wires above his stiff collar. "That is an insult, madam. Bellevue has one of the most respected psychiatric departments in the world. You have a very fragile young lady upstairs, and if you refuse to let her be evaluated, I won't be held responsible."

"Dr. Faneuil, my husband is a top psychoanalyst."

"And not qualified under law to practice medicine in the state of New York. Or anywhere else, as far as I know."

"We are both trained to treat problems of the mind. We know Rose and we know her history. We have dealt with these setbacks before. I won't have her suffer more trauma than this tragic death has already wrought."

"Then it will be on your heads. I officially withdraw from the case." He nodded sharply. "Bennington."

"I'll see you out."

The two men strode out the door, leaving Anna Vogeler standing in the middle of the room.

Anna turned to Phil. "Lady Dunbridge, how do you do? Please forgive me for my bad manners. I'm just so upset. But he doesn't understand. Rose is very special and she needs personalized treatment. These old-fashioned doctors are just incapable of embracing new ideas.

"I know he's out there trying to convince Godfrey otherwise. You'll support me in this, won't you? Poor Rose would be irrevocably damaged, more so than she already is, to have strange doctors prodding her with questions and performing awful treatments."

Fortunately, Phil was spared answering by Godfrey's return.

"I'm so sorry, Godfrey," Anna said. "But it was fortunate that I was on my way down to see you when the doctor arrived. I'm sure he means well, but I just couldn't allow for Rose to undergo any more than she already has. She will do well enough in Erik's capable hands, and mine. If this is too much of an inconvenience, we can move to a hotel for the duration of our business here."

"That won't be necessary," Godfrey told her. "Union House is at your disposal."

Phil imagined him chewing on nails to get the words out.

"Thank you. You are so kind. Hopefully, Rose will be able to travel as soon as Dr. Vogeler's lecture is presented."

Phil couldn't stop an involuntary glance at Atkins.

"I'm afraid it may be longer than that," he said.

Anna looked blank, then said, "We have hope that she will rally soon."

Phil was fairly certain that was not what Atkins meant. Which she had no doubt Anna Vogeler would be learning soon.

Anna turned to go. Turned back to Godfrey. "By the way, have you seen Francis Kellogg? I can't find him anywhere and Erik insists on going on with his lecture. But he relies on Alan to help him prepare slides and charts and such. Alan is so devoted to Erik. But this Kellogg . . . I suppose he does his best, but no one seems to have seen him."

She pronounced "Alan" in the French manner.

"I'm afraid, Mrs. Vogeler, that Kellogg was recalled to Washington late last night. An emergency, evidently."

"Recalled? Is Alan on his way? Is he here?" She actually looked around the room as if he might be sitting in one of the wing chairs.

"No. Not as yet."

"But they have sent a replacement?"

"I'm afraid not. Dr. Vogeler will just have to make do. Perhaps one of his colleagues would be willing to fill in. Dr. Lutz or Salvos, perhaps."

"No! Absolutely not. Lutz is a Freudian. And Salvos is not to be trusted. I don't like to speak ill of our former colleagues. But he was disgraced on the Continent, his theories debunked when it was learned his process was faked. He was banished from the university and is not respected among his former peers. Why do you think he's is living in obscurity in America?"

And why invite him to dinner, if you despise him so avidly? Phil wondered.

"In fact, I've taken the liberty of informing your butler that he is not to be admitted to this house while Rose is here. Neither he nor his assistant—as he calls him—Ivan. Rose is petrified of him."

"Of Dr. Salvos or of Ivan?" Phil ventured, earning her a sharp look from John Atkins.

"Ivan. As you might have noticed, he has deep psychological scarring. He had once been an assistant to Pietro in his laboratory. And when he returned from the Boer War, Pietro took him back. I suppose Pietro felt responsible for him. But not the wisest decision, considering everything else."

Phil didn't know if Anna was purposely dropping tidbits to stoke curiosity, but Phil's was stoked. Dr. Salvos and his assistant would be one of the first stops on her list of witnesses to be interviewed.

"Perhaps Monsieur Toussaint is on his way here as we speak," Phil said, jumping into the fray.

Surprisingly, Anna Vogeler took both Phil's hands in hers. "Oh, I hope you're right, Lady Dunbridge. I fear for my husband. But he will not be thwarted. He is so devoted to his work. But I can't help but worry. You know how it is to be the wife of an important man."

Indeed Phil did. It was something she'd been trying to forget since becoming a widow.

"I regret I mustn't tarry. Thank you for coming." Anna started toward the door.

"Mrs. Vogeler." Atkins tone of voice would have stopped Phil in her tracks. But Anna didn't seem to hear him. "Mrs. Vogeler, if you wish to leave town anytime soon, you will answer my questions now." Atkins hadn't raised his voice, but Anna turned abruptly and looked at him wide-eyed.

"But why? I've told you I saw nothing. And neither did my husband."

"Nonetheless . . . You can tell me again. You can also tell me if you know of anyone who might have reason to wish your husband dead."

It was an impertinent question, even for a police officer. Atkins's voice was smooth as silk, but Phil knew he was fuming. She, herself, was a little put off by Anna Vogeler's willful ignorance.

"Good heavens, psychologists are terribly competitive and territorial, but they wouldn't actually resort to physical murder. Besides, they were all at dinner. Why aren't you out arresting Francis Kellogg? It's evident that he had no business here. He was completely incompetent. Now he could be out there anywhere, plotting against my husband," Anna continued, her voice climbing higher in agitation. "He may try again. Oh, Godfrey. How could you have put him in our midst?"

"Investigations sometimes take weeks, even months," Atkins said without inflection.

It took a moment for Anna to understand him and she deflated. "Oh, very well. You're very persistent, Detective Sergeant."

He nodded, a gesture somewhere between acknowledgment and agreement.

She turned to Phil. "Lady Dunbridge, could I please impose on your generosity for the use of Lily during Erik's lecture? I don't want to leave Rose alone and my maid is useless around the girl."

"Certainly."

"Thank you. Now, Detective Sergeant, if we must . . ."

Godfrey practically lunged for the bell. "I'll have Collins show you to the morning room."

10

Drats, Phil thought. Now she would have to go through the tedious process of questioning Anna herself. She knew as well as
anyone, except perhaps the detective sergeant, that women were
much more likely to confide in other women, to the point of in-
discretion.

Godfrey returned, looking beleaguered. "She was so amenable in Washington. But after the first attempt and now this, she's
become downright tigerish. Oh, I do beg your pardon."

"It's quite all right, Godfrey," Phil said. "The whole situation
is extraordinary."

"Hmm," said Godfrey, not inviting any questions.

She asked anyway. "You mean to let him present his lecture?"

Godfrey blew out air. "He was invited by the Pantheon Club.
It is out of my hands."

"Do you expect more trouble?"

"With what I'm learning about this group, I'd be surprised if
there isn't."

So would Phil, and the sooner she did something about stopping it, the better. "I know you're busy. It's past noon, and I must
really retrieve Lily and get her home before Preswick comes looking for us both."

"Of course. I'll—"

"You needn't call Collins. I'll fetch her myself. Poor man must
be out of breath with all these comings and goings."

Besides, she wanted to see for herself just how fragile Rose
Nash really was and why Anna Vogeler was so anxious not to let
the doctor examine her.

She did take a tiny detour and stood outside the door of what
she presumed to be the morning room, but heard not a sound.

Admitting temporary defeat, Phil made her way upstairs and
knocked lightly on the door to Rose Nash's room before stepping

inside. The room was dark, the curtains pulled tightly together; a potent sweetness hung in the air.

Laudanum, most likely.

One small lamp was lit by the bed and screened from the occupant, who looked very pale in the weak light.

Lily was slumped in a chair by the bed, her head resting on her chin. A magazine was open on her lap. As Phil tiptoed closer, she noticed several other magazines on the floor at her feet.

Lily must have been reading to the girl all night.

Phil touched Lily's shoulder. She awoke with a start. Looked around. Saw Phil and sprang to her feet. The magazine slid to the floor.

"My lady?" Lily said, in an uncharacteristically small voice. "Thank goodness you've come."

"Lily? What is the matter? You should have had the butler telephone me."

"No, it—" Lily cast her a furtive look and glanced toward the open door of the dressing room.

Phil followed her gaze. Raised her eyebrows at Lily, then walked toward the window, attempting to catch a glimpse of anyone who might be in the other room. Listening?

Phil said, "Why is it so dark in here? Is Miss Nash still asleep? It must be close to noon."

"They gave her another dose near sunrise."

"Who did?"

"Mrs. Vogeler. She said it was very important that she not wake and become agitated. And Dr. Vogeler came in several times to check on her. I thought he should be in bed, but I didn't tell him so. Mr. Preswick wouldn't approve."

"I dare say he wouldn't, but we've both done our duties to the Vogelers for now. It's time for you to be home. We have work to do."

"Did you get any sleep last night?" Phil ventured, as she and Lily crossed Fifth Avenue to the park side of the street.

"Yes, my lady. Enough," Lily said, clutching the magazines she'd been reading to her chest.

Phil frowned. Lily saved her "my lady"s for public or when she was flustered or angry. She didn't appear to be either at the moment.

"Lily, is something the matter? Are you angry with me for leaving you at Union House all night? Because if that is the case, you don't have to go back."

"But I do."

"Then tell me what is upsetting you?"

"They're going to put her in an asylum."

"No," Phil said. "Dr. Faneuil wanted to take her to the hospital to be examined. But Mrs. Vogeler has dismissed him. Though I must say, I think that was a mistake. The girl does not look at all well."

Lily shook her head. "Mrs. Vogeler told me that we must be very careful with Miss Nash because she had a trauma. I'm not sure what that is, but it's very bad and she can be pushed over the edge. . . ." Her voice became almost a whisper. "That means insanity, doesn't it?"

"No," Phil assured her. Actually, she had no idea. Rose Nash did not seem to follow the usual rules of decorum, flitting around the park like a sprite, climbing onto fence rails in the middle of a dinner party.

Even Phil at her most outrageous hadn't acted that peculiarly. And Phil had had a husband who would have gladly sent her to an asylum just to free himself of the bother of having a wife. She couldn't stop an involuntary shudder.

"It would be ter-r-r-rible," Lily said.

"Yes, it would," Phil agreed, surprised at the vehemence in Lily's voice. She rarely rolled her r's anymore, a habit she'd had when they first met her whenever she was extremely upset. She'd been doing it less lately and Phil had hoped that she was beginning to feel more at ease in her new home.

"The Vogelers intend to treat Rose themselves. Evidently she was their patient before."

"Before what?"

"I'm not sure." It was something Phil should find out.

They fell into silence. Neither of them wanted to dwell on what an asylum would mean to anyone, much less an innocent young woman like Rose Nash.

By tacit agreement, they began walking at a brisker pace and had just passed a delivery wagon when a figure jumped out from between two trucks, barring their way.

The image of Georgina Nash jumping out from the trees flashed in Phil's mind. She reached to push Lily behind her, but Lily had dropped to a crouch, pulled back her skirt, and was reaching for her ankle.

She bounded up so quickly that Phil didn't have time to stop her. She was still clutching her magazines in one hand, but in the other, her stiletto glinted in the sunlight.

By then, Phil had recognized their assailant. "Lily, no!"

Phil could feel her maid shaking beside her, more with rage, Phil thought, than fear. Lily never ceased to astonish her.

"Ivan," Phil said.

Ivan put up both hands. "I want to talk. Not hurt you. You must help me," he said, staring at the point of the stiletto, and his mouth twisting grotesquely between each burst of words.

"Put it away, Lily," Phil said, not taking her eyes off Ivan. His eyes were wild, but his body shrunk back as if in pain.

Slowly Lily lowered the stiletto. From the corner of her eye, Phil saw her hide it behind her skirt.

Phil took a breath while Lily stood her ground and Ivan's watchful eyes switched from Phil to Lily with the precision of a metronome.

"Now, Ivan. What do you have to say?"

Ivan exhaled, the tension sloughing off him almost visibly. He wasn't a bad-looking man, though his face was deeply lined and scarred on both sides, the result of battle, most likely. She'd thought him older last night in the park. But in the daylight, he appeared to be not more than thirty.

He still wore his heavy coat as if it were winter instead of a sweltering summer day. He wasn't large and lumbering, as she had previously thought, just incredibly overdressed.

He darted a look around, his head moving in staccato tics that reminded Phil of the wood pigeons on her father's estates when there was a cat nearby. "They won't let me in to see Rose. They won't let Pietro in." His fists clenched. "You must help her!"

"She's being well cared for." Phil said, watching his oddly delicate fingers open and close beneath his drooping coat sleeves. "I'm sure—Where *is* Dr. Salvos?"

"Seeing patients," Ivan said. "He's—"

The next words were drowned out by the backfiring of a passing truck.

Phil and Lily jumped in surprise. Ivan's arms flung outward. He let out a howl and launched himself in their direction.

He hit the space between them, but with his arms rigidly out to the side, they had no recourse for escape. Both women stumbled back under the impact.

Being smaller, Lily was thrown to the sidewalk. Phil tripped on her own skirt and heard fabric rip. Her knees gave out and she fell to the side, taking Ivan with her. His coat smothered her face and she fought to stave off the force of his weight.

She heard a distant war whoop in a high soprano. Her ears must be ringing. But the whoop grew louder and closer.

Ivan jumped to his feet, his victims forgotten. He whirled around. Ready to attack.

Beside Phil, Lily scrambled to her feet, still holding her magazines under one arm and the stiletto in her free hand.

"Lily, don't!" Phil frantically untangled her skirts and pushed to her feet, grabbing Lily by the bow of her apron to prevent her from fighting back. That's when she recognized the small figure running from the corner: Just a Friend, clutching his papers under his arm and shaking his free fist in the air.

"Hey, you, leave them ladies alone!"

Ivan took a step back and turned, only to find a small whirlwind barreling toward him. He swung back to Phil and Lily; raw power thrummed around him.

"Ivan, please—" Phil began, holding Lily with one hand and her other one out in a useless attempt at warding him off.

But he didn't attack again, just uttered a string of unintelligible sounds, then leapt, not toward Phil and Lily or his attacker, but between the parked trucks, disappearing just as Just a Friend reached them.

Not content with scaring him away, the newsboy shoved his papers at Lily and followed Ivan between the trucks.

"Be careful!" Phil cried, which was silly on her part, since Just a Friend had been making his living on these streets for longer than she'd been in America.

A burst of horns and curses rose from the street. Phil cringed. "Just a Friend! Come back!"

A few seconds later he returned, red in the face and huffing out air. "Lost him." He retrieved his papers from Lily, who was now clutching Just a Friend's papers as well as her magazines.

Phil was relieved to see that the stiletto had disappeared. She took a breath to collect herself. After all, she was the countess, and her two companions were under her protection. Though sometimes it did seem the other way around.

"Well, we *are* having an exciting day," Phil exclaimed, trying to calm her frayed nerves. "Thank you for your quick action," Phil told him. "Both of you," she added to Lily.

"Who was that guy?" Just a Friend demanded.

"A gentleman we met last night," Phil said.

"You oughta be more careful of your associates, 'cause that ain't no gentleman, if you ask me."

"No, he doesn't appear to be," Phil agreed, though until that truck backfired, she'd begun to think that beneath his thuggish appearance, she sensed a better-behaved man. Everything after that proved her wrong. Maybe it was all that the psychoanalysis talk over dinner last night that made her think there was more to Ivan than met the eye.

"Excellent work, Just a Friend. Once again you've saved our bacon."

He grinned and doffed his cap; Phil dropped a dime into it.

"Now, I think it's time for us to go home."

The three of them turned south and walked to the Plaza, Just a Friend leading the way.

"An invigorating morning," Phil said to Preswick as he let Lily and her into the apartment.

"Yes, my lady." His demeanor was unruffled as always but his eyes cut to Lily for the merest second. "Has something more happened?"

"We were attacked on our way home!" Lily said.

Preswick looked to Phil for confirmation.

"Well, in retrospect I believe it was more like being accosted. At first. Then he seemed to go quite berserk." Phil turned to Lily. "You're all right?"

Lily lifted her chin. "Yes, madam. If Just a Friend hadn't come, I would have—"

"Yes, my dear, I know you would have. Fortunately, you didn't have to."

"He chased him away," Lily added.

"Yes, but time is passing and I think after we tidy ourselves, we might have some lunch and begin to piece this case together."

"I thought you might, my lady," Preswick said. "I took the liberty of setting up the study in the usual manner."

"Excellent," Phil said. "Though . . . Lily, would you like to rest for a while?"

"I'm not tired." Lily stood a little straighter. She might not be tired, but she was pale and definitely feeling some strong emotion. Phil didn't blame her. She was feeling quite undone, herself. And her dress was a mess.

"In that case, we'll convene our council of investigation. Preswick, sandwiches and lemonade, lots of it."

Preswick bowed and went to call down for lunch to be delivered.

One of the many great things about the Plaza, Phil thought. Food that was prepared in a subterranean kitchen and delivered to your rooms, arriving faster and hotter than ever it did at Dunbridge Castle or any of her other residences in England.

"Lily, why don't you change out of that uniform into something . . . that isn't a uniform. . . ." Phil pulled off her cloche hat; several strands of hair escaped to her shoulders.

Lily looked doubtful.

"I'll tidy myself today. You run along, we'll reconvene in the study. It's time we took this appalling situation into our own hands."

"Yes, madam," Lily said on an expulsion of air. "I won't be but a minute." And still clutching her bundle of magazines, she hurried down the hall to her room.

Phil did what she could to her own appearance, then feeling

quite recovered, other than a slight exhilaration left over from the encounter, she retrieved the list of addresses from her dressing-table drawer and went directly to the study, where a square table and three straight-backed chairs were placed in the middle of the room. At the moment, the table was free of clutter and wore a sheen of wax that attested to Preswick's industry while she had been out that morning.

He had set up the large easel board that served as a repository for maps, clues, and information. It was, as yet, empty except for a new map that had replaced the one from their last investigation.

Phil was visited by a familiar energizing thrill. That board would soon be filled with their own evidence as well as the gleaning of bits from John Atkins's investigation, which would eventually lead them to a killer. How Mr. X's mission dovetailed with theirs was yet to be known, his mind being on other things last night.

No matter; it would all come together. And as much as she felt for poor Rose Nash, she couldn't deny the excitement that coursed through her.

She reached for her notebook, which had been placed on the sideboard, and took her first note.

By the time Lily returned, looking fresh and quite lovely in a peach cotton shirtwaist and deep-green skirt—and still holding her bundle of magazines—Phil had written several pages.

The sight of Lily made her pause. She looked like any other young woman on the cusp of life, if more exotically beautiful than most. There really was no reason for her to always wear the stark black-and-white maid's uniform. Many lady's maids wore their own clothes to serve their mistresses. But Preswick and Lily had both balked at the idea.

After several attempts to stretch the established rules, and only causing seismic upsets, Phil had given up. It was interesting that servants would cling to customs long after their mistress had given them up. Perhaps it was more assuring to know where your place was in the world. So things had remained the same.

Preswick arrived with a tray of sandwiches, a large pitcher of lemonade, and a bucket filled with ice.

While he poured out the lemonade, Phil piled her plate with

sandwiches. It hadn't been that long since breakfast, but investigation and ruffians always gave her an appetite, and she didn't want Lily to be shy about eating.

Lily took a plate and sat down in her usual seat and placed the plate and her magazines on the table, then took a notebook similar to Phil's from her skirt pocket.

Phil lifted an eyebrow. "Well, now that the excitement has died down . . . I took a few notes during the night."

Preswick, who had eschewed the sandwiches, announcing that he'd already partaken of lunch, crossed over to the desk and collected one of the folders that were stacked there.

"These are my additional notes from the conversation earlier this morning." He drew several sheets of paper written in even copperplate.

Even Preswick's jottings were impeccable.

He placed one of the sheets on the table. It was a sketch of the embroidery on the torn fabric, much more accurate than the one she'd attempted.

"Excellent, you two. We seem to have a plethora of information already." Phil turned to a fresh page in her own notebook. "Let's start at the beginning, since all three of us have different bits of information."

Phil began with Godfrey's telephone call, catching Lily up on what had transpired at the restaurant; the unusual murder and the strange behavior, or lack thereof, from Rose Nash. "She seemed quite unaware that her sister was dead at her feet. Rose seems to be . . . a little unusual."

"Cook says she's gone around the bend," Lily said.

Preswick cleared his throat.

Lily straightened up. "I'm just reporting what she said."

"And what do you think, Lily?" Phil asked.

Lily shrugged. "I just don't want them to lock her up. Dr. Faneuil said we were like two beautiful flowers, a Lily and a Rose." She lowered her eyes. "She's not hurting anybody. They shouldn't lock her up."

"No," Phil agreed. "She's Mrs. Vogeler's patient at the moment. Evidently she suffers from a fragile psyche due to some tragedy, which we must look into."

She and Preswick caught Lily up on the things she and Atkins and Preswick had discussed that morning.

"Now, for the cast of players."

Preswick tore off the page of his notebook and began a fresh sheet.

"The Vogelers, traveling with the children's nanny, Mrs. Vogeler's maid, and usually with Dr. Vogler's assistant, Alan Toussaint, who was taken ill in Washington and was replaced temporarily with"—she only hesitated a mere moment—"an aide-de-camp to serve as secretary assigned by the War Department as a courtesy."

She hated not being able to tell them the identity of the secretary, but she understood Mr. X's insistence on secrecy.

And what you didn't know, you couldn't accidently give away. Not that she thought the three of them would ever be so foolish, not even under torture, if it came to that.

"My lady?" said Preswick.

"Yes, well. He was suddenly recalled to Washington and has already left. No one mentioned a valet."

"Dr. Vogeler doesn't have one," Lily said. "That Mr. Kellogg had to help him out of his coat." Lily giggled. "Like the cereal."

"Just so," Phil said. Leave it to the man to make a spectacle of the whole affair. "Then there are the dinner guests."

Preswick pinned his latest page of notes to the board and started a new sheet.

"Colleagues of one sort or another, and all friends from before. I found it impossible to remember who was a Freudian, who was a Jungian, or what difference it mattered. But here is a partial list of their addresses. I remembered the best I could, but some of them are vague." If Atkins would share information, she wouldn't have to proceed in this half-cocked fashion. And if Mr. X didn't pop in and out like a mole in the garden, dropping clues and leaving without explaining, her investigations would go so much more efficiently.

And if they all three coordinated their efforts half as well as she and Lily and Preswick did . . . Well, forget that. Men liked being in charge, so she would just have to let them think they were and get on with her own solutions.

"So, besides the Vogelers, Godfrey, and I, there was Dr. Elisabeth Weiss. She teaches philosophy at a women's college on the Upper West Side.

"Dr. Dietrich Lutz has a private practice, also on the Upper West Side. He has a somewhat overbearing demeanor in general, and especially toward Dr. Nash.

"Chumley Griswold, an odd-looking creature. He's a chemist, but seems to make his living by entertaining at parties, hypnotizing guests and doing magic tricks. He lives on Park Avenue. I didn't hear him state his exact address, but he offered to give a wake in Dr. Nash's honor and handed out his card." She produced the card from the pages of her notebook.

"A very affluent neighborhood," Preswick said, and added the address to the pins he'd placed in the map at each mention of the guest addresses.

"Let's see. Dr. Salvos, who evidently was disgraced earlier in his career but who still agreed to come to dinner. He lives on Orchard Street. I couldn't hear the numbers of the address, and I have no idea where Orchard Street is."

Preswick's hand hovered over the map. "I believe that is downtown in the immigrant section of town. Ah, there." He placed another pin in the map.

"Dr. Salvos also has a driver or assistant, Ivan, who waited on the street with his automobile.

"He's the one who attacked us," Lily said.

"Indeed," Preswick said, looking to Phil for confirmation.

"I think he meant to ask for our help. Mrs. Vogeler has forbidden him and Dr. Salvos to enter the house. But suddenly he turned vicious. At least I think . . ." Phil looked at Lily for her opinion.

"After the backfire."

"That's right," Phil agreed. "Interesting."

"And our young newsie gave chase?" Preswick said.

He had taken to the boy, making sure he had a warmer coat for the winter, and Phil knew that the extra sandwiches from lunch would soon find their way to Just a Friend's stomach.

"Yes," Phil said. "He was a fierce protector. But not the most careful. Ivan is a grown man, large and strong. He obviously can't be trusted to contain his temper."

It was a discussion they'd had often, usually after Just a Friend had performed some act of bravery that put him in jeopardy. Bobby Mullins had offered to give him a job and lodging at Holly Farm, but the boy was determined to keep his papers and his job as Phil's protector.

"So they were all mean to each other," Lily reminded Phil, earning a stern look from Preswick.

"Actually they were all polite to each other on the surface, saying things half-jokingly but with an undercurrent of malice, in that way people who have known each other for a long time will do.

"And the strangest thing was that the Nash sisters weren't even invited. Godfrey had to have two extra places set. We should find out who told them about the dinner, and then perhaps we can figure out where they live.

"It was strange. When the shot was fired, everyone immediately crowded around Dr. Vogeler, thinking he was the intended victim. But it was Georgina Nash who lay dead. The bullet had hit her forehead, directly between her eyes.

"If someone had meant to kill her, it would have been a perfect shot."

11

"Perhaps it was," Preswick said.

"That's what the detective sergeant and I considered," Phil said. "It would be very clever. But if one of them was involved, how was it done? They were all in plain sight. None of them could have fired the shot."

"A hired killer?" Preswick suggested.

"Perhaps, but for what reason?" Phil wondered aloud. "Because he was a Jungian instead of a Freudian. Or was it the other way around?"

"A vendetta, perhaps," suggested Preswick. "The doctor must have many competitors among the psychoanalysts."

"Enough to kill? Perhaps a disgruntled employee," Phil said. "The maid or nanny?"

"Or the assistant," Lily said. "Maybe he faked his illness and sneaked to New York to kill Dr. Vogeler."

"Possibly," Phil said. She really should curtail Lily's reading of dime novels. Her imagination was livelier than ever. "But no more guessing. Hypotheses, we need hypotheses. And to form one, we need evidence. Lily, tell us what happened at the house last night."

Lily nibbled her lip. "Let's see. The maid came into the children's room to tell Nanny she was going to tidy up the dressing room while she waited for Mrs. Vogeler's return. That was not too long after you all left. The nanny, Mrs. Cole, put the children to bed." She rolled her eyes. "It took a long time. Then she had her tea and fell asleep in their dressing room.

"I don't think either of them left the house. I didn't fall asleep. Just sat in the chair in the children's room until everyone was roused by the commotion downstairs."

"What happened then?" Phil poised her pencil over her notebook. Preswick did the same.

"The maid ran out of Mrs. Vogeler's room. Nanny managed to rouse herself to come out and look over the bannister. But then she came back and said she would stay with the children and I was to ask Mrs. Vogeler if I was needed.

"So I did. She and that Mr. Kellogg were holding up Dr. Vogeler. He kept saying he was all right, but they were fussing over him like he was on his last leg." She glanced at Preswick. "I mean like he was seriously injured. Which he wasn't.

"They practically carried him past me and took him to a room down the hall. A different room from the one Mrs. Vogeler was using," she added.

"Mr. Kellogg asked me to help the doctor when he arrived. I don't know why. There were a bunch of staff people standing around downstairs.

"So I helped. Not that it took much. It was just a narrow little cut across his arm. About here." She pointed to her own arm, midway between the shoulder and elbow.

"And what of Mr. Kellogg?" Phil asked.

Lily's forehead puckered. "He left the room as soon as they brought Dr. Vogeler in. I guess he was waiting for Dr. Faneuil downstairs."

More likely packing his bags and doing a scarper, thought Phil. But she was fairly certain he wasn't the killer. She hadn't lied when she told Atkins that he'd appeared at her elbow almost immediately. She hadn't told Atkins about the outrageous comment he'd made.

Besides, he would never have missed a target less than ten feet away and still hit Georgie Nash right between the eyes instead.

Of course, it was a perfect shot if he'd aimed for her in the first place.

Which brought Phil right back to the same conclusion. The bullet was meant for Georgie.

"What happened after that?" Phil asked.

"Mrs. Vogeler asked me to stay with Dr. Vogeler, so I sat in the chair where I was when you came back. Then that silly maid screamed and . . ."

They quickly filled Preswick in on the details where their stories crossed.

He actually almost frowned.

"And after I left?" Phil asked.

"I stayed with Rose all night."

"And nothing else happened during the night?"

"Nothing interesting. Rose woke a few times. Dr. and Mrs. Vogeler both came in to check on her at various times. The rest of the time I slept in the chair."

"You were surrounded by your dime novels when I came this morning. How clever of you to bring them to read to the children."

"I didn't," Lily said.

"You sent to Preswick for them?"

"No, my lady. They came this morning . . . for me. . . . Mr. Collins brought them up. He said they'd been delivered."

"How odd. But who would do such a thing?"

"Mr. Kellogg. It must have been him, because he came last night to look in on Rose. I'd been reading something the housekeeper gave me. It was really boring, but she said it might help soothe Rose. She'd been restless, though I don't see how with all the medicine Mrs. Vogeler kept dosing her with.

"I must have nodded off, because the book fell out of my hands and I woke up, and then I saw him. He was standing at the bedside. He picked up the book and said it was a wonder that it hadn't put us both into a coma.

"He told me he'd get me something more interesting to read. But I should take better care of my books. That they were important things and a person should not let them fall on the floor or let anyone lift them. That's slang for 'steal.' Funny that a gentleman like him would know such a thing."

"Well," Phil said, marveling. "Perhaps Mr. Kellogg is a fan of dime novels, too."

"He must be. Because they're really good ones."

"How nice of him." But strange. Impossible? He'd been waiting for Phil when she returned home last night. "When was this?"

"Early this morning, before even the maids were up. I wanted to thank him, but when I asked Cook when she brought me tea, she said he'd been sent back to Washington, that he'd already packed up and gone."

"How odd."

"And they're brand new. As soon as I started reading them, I realized the pages hadn't even been opened. I checked, because Mr. Preswick says to observe everything." Lily touched the stack of dime novels gently.

So he'd stayed long enough to buy a stack of dime novels and have them sent to Union House for Lily? What on earth for? Unless . . .

Maybe he'd left a message inside one. "May I see them?"

Lily handed them over.

There were four in all. Each with a distinctive four-color cover. Flimsy, printed on cheap paper, especially popular among working-class readers. Men read of the exploits of the Wild West; shop girls found love within the pages of stories about women like them. And Lily learned slang and no telling what else from her favorite private detectives.

Was it good for her to be reading these tales of derring-do? She'd just pulled a stiletto on Ivan without a thought.

Perhaps Phil should take more responsibility for her learning, though Phil was the last person to dictate what someone should read, think, or do. She, for one, wouldn't listen to that advice.

She picked up the first magazine. Nick Carter, "The Silent Partner: or Crime's Carnival." Phil wished her own disappearing partner would not be so silent. Was he making a joke? She turned the pages, found nothing. Put it down and picked up the next.

"The Secret Service: The Bradys and 'Mr. Magic.'" A cavernous dungeon was depicted on the cover. Mr. Magic, wearing a long, star-decorated cloak, was definitely the villain in this story.

It was hard to tell if Mr. X was playing with her or sending her some kind of message. Or if none of it meant anything at all.

But the Secret Service? Phil was a little vague on whether it actually existed or not. Something else she should learn about.

Nothing was left inside the second book. She picked up the next.

Another Nick Carter. This one titled "A Dangerous Woman."

He was definitely having a joke at her expense. Not one but two women on the cover appeared to be assaulting the unfortunate Mr. Carter. But considering one was old and haggard and the other young and pretty, Phil guessed which one was trying to save him from the other.

Her head was beginning to swim as she picked up the fourth and final novel.

"Three Nick Carters?" Phil exclaimed.

"He's my favorite, madam. But how did Mr. Kellogg know?"

"I have no idea," Phil said truthfully. Of course, "Mr. Kellogg" knew lot of things he had no right to know.

"Though, I must say, he is rather impressive, this Mr. Carter," Phil said, studying the cover. Carter in his blue suit taking on two men, against a backdrop of a Ferris wheel and colorful pennants. "Four Scraps of Paper." Phil looked more closely. And read the second title printed beneath the title: "Or, Nick Carter's Coney Island Search."

No coincidence that she'd just returned from Coney Island. Had he been there to overhear Godfrey's telephone call?

Mr. X. Mr. Magic, indeed. Phil riffled quickly through the pages. No underlining, nothing written in the margins, not even a dog-eared page.

Had it just been an affection gesture by their elusive partner in investigation? It wasn't outside the realm of possibility. He was constantly surprising her.

But surely they meant something. Silent partner. Secret Service . . .

"There's something strange about them, isn't there?" Lily asked. "I'd never even met him, but he knew who I was, and my name, and he said he knew I'd like these. And Rose might like them, too."

Preswick's subtle change of expression was all too perceptive. The man was too smart by half. Had he already guessed that they weren't working on this case alone?

"Well," Phil said, avoiding his eye and handing the novels back to Lily. "We must make a start somewhere. What do you say we take a drive downtown to this Orchard Street? Perhaps we can find out why Dr. Salvos and Ivan are so eager to see Rose. And why Anna Vogeler is so determined to keep them away."

Phil, Lily, and Preswick separated long enough to change into what Preswick called their "mufti." Civilian clothes of various types from expensive to drab. Today was a drab mufti day. Phil dressed in an unadorned skirt and blouse, Lily in a gingham working-girl dress, and Preswick in a worn summer suit. Where these outfits came from, Phil had never inquired.

They decided to take a taxi downtown, though Phil had wanted to call for her Daimler, which had languished in a nearby garage most of the summer. But Preswick convinced her that the area they were visiting would be ripe for theft or looting for parts, so she'd given in.

They were deluged by a brief afternoon shower on the ride downtown that only left the air hotter and more humid, and left the three of them feeling a bit soggy. By the time the taxi let them off at Delancey and Orchard, the sun was already beating down, turning the puddles into pockets of steam.

For several moments, all they could do was stand on the corner and gape. It was one of the poorest neighborhoods Phil had ever seen.

Rows of dilapidated tenements lined both sides of the street. Windows were flung open. Laundry hung from lines stretched from building to building, not drying in the humidity but capturing every soot particle that hung in the air.

Children were crowded onto tiny fire-escape platforms playing and roughhousing and sticking their heads and sometimes whole torsos out between the bars as they called to friends on the street.

Finally Preswick said, "I believe it's this way."

They walked south on a street jammed with people going about whatever business they had. Women trudging with baskets, trying to avoid the puddles and detritus that filled the ground. Children darting in and out of wagons and carts, oblivious of the filth beneath their bare feet.

And the smell. Between horse droppings and unwashed bodies and rotting food, it was nearly impossible for Phil to take a full breath, and yet the denizens of Orchard Street went about their lives as if not even noticing the heat or the odor.

This was as far from Fifth Avenue as Dorset Street was from Kensington.

It took much searching and several inquiries to find Dr. Salvos's residence. It was a nondescript brick building among all the other nondescript brick buildings. They only recognized it when they saw a sign hammered onto the front façade: CLINIC. P SALVOS.

"My lady, perhaps I should go in. There is no telling what kinds of diseases we might find."

"I will go, too, my lady," Lily seconded.

"We'll all go," Phil said. "And do you think the two of you could forego calling me 'my lady' while we're here?"

"Yes, my—" Preswick clamped his lips down on the last word. Lily merely nodded.

"Then let us proceed."

A woman, holding a child whose only clean part was the bandage around his forearm, passed them on her way out. "Dr. Salvos is a godsend, I wish I could pay him in more than soup, but he is too generous." She looked from Phil to Preswick to Lily. "Is this the patient?" She took Lily's chin in her free hand. "Don't be afraid. Dr. Salvos will make it better. Won't he, Nardo?" The child nodded and held up his bandaged arm. "She's such a pretty thing," the woman said, and let go of Lily's chin. "So pretty." And she hurried down the street.

They went inside to find a large antechamber filled with people waiting to see the doctor. Some stood; some sat in the few chairs lining the walls. A few were using the unoccupied desktop to relieve their weary legs. Children wailed in their mothers' arms, while others ran or crawled without restraint. Some sat quietly staring straight ahead; Phil thought they must be Dr. Salvos's patients. But who saw to all the others?

"They seem quite busy," Phil said. "I hope he'll speak to us."

At that moment, Dr. Salvos came out of a back, holding a metal dinner pail before him.

The waiting room erupted in questions and pleas.

"I am closed for lunch for half an hour. Be patient, please."

He caught sight of Phil. She rushed forward through the disappointed crowd before he could get away.

"Dr. Salvos, I see that you are busy, but I really must speak with you."

He sighed with resignation. "This way."

The crowd began to complain, vociferously.

"She's my sister," Dr. Salvos yelled above the din. They all quieted down, the yells and angry faces transformed to smiles and welcomes.

The three of them followed the doctor down the hall and into a smaller room, where he placed the lunch pail on a rough wooden table and gestured to the chair across from him for Phil to sit.

"These two are your servants, I suppose. We don't have servants here, so please sit down where you will." He motioned to several stools next to a tall bench that might have been an examining table.

A dry sink was pushed against one wall between a chest with various instruments spread out on top and a dented metal cabinet, scratched as if from years of wear and secured with a heavy lock.

"Drugs," Dr. Salvos said, when he saw Phil looking at it. "When it is filled, it is worth much money. They are given without payment to my patients. But some are desperate or greedy enough that they would steal them to sell on the street for a profit. So, yes, I own a revolver. Those who would steal, I would gladly shoot." He got a bowl and spoon down from one of the shelves and sat down across from Phil.

"I only have half an hour, and I'm already running behind time, since my assistant isn't here and things are bit unorganized. I was about to have my lunch, if you don't mind watching me eat."

"Soup," Phil said. "Please enjoy it while it's still hot."

"You must have met Mrs. Collaci on her way out. Those boys of hers." He poured the contents of the pail into the bowl.

"She had wonderful things to say about you. You take care of physical injuries also?"

Dr. Salvos didn't reply. He was too busy shoveling soup into his mouth, though the soup looked close to water and didn't smell that wonderful.

A few spoonfuls later, he paused and looked over his spoon. "Injuries, diseases. Whatever I can do. You were expecting a fancy office, perhaps?"

Phil hadn't known what to expect. It certainly wasn't this.

"But you are a psychoanalyst."

"Psychologist. There is a difference."

Any other time, Phil might have asked him to enlighten her, but at the moment she had more important things she needed to know.

"I don't know why you are here, Lady Dunbridge. I ask myself what would bring a countess to this squalor and hardship, unless you want to donate money to our poor clinic. And I rather doubt that.

"Detective Atkins has already been here. Asking his questions. Neither I nor Ivan have anything to do with the Vogelers or the Nashes, not anymore. I didn't even know the sisters were in America. So you've wasted your time, if you are looking for someone to blame."

"Actually, I'm here about Ivan," Phil said, unsettled by his accusation.

"He knows nothing about it."

"He accosted my maid and me on our way back home from Union House just a few hours ago."

"Ah, so that is where he's got to."

"You didn't send him?"

"No. That is one of the reasons you see me at such disarray. He usually sees to the waiting room for me. He keeps thing organized and moving quickly. If you insist on his being arrested, these people will be turned away. Do you want that on your conscience, Lady Dunbridge?"

"Good heavens. I just thought you should be aware. He didn't hurt us, he just wanted our help. But not everyone will be as understanding as Lily and I. I wanted you to know so perhaps you would see to it that he doesn't get himself in trouble."

Salvos put down his spoon. Most of the soup was gone except some not very appetizing dregs at the bottom of the bowl.

"In that case, I thank you. I will speak with him. There are so many here with so many hardships and very little means of helping themselves. Ivan sometimes helps me with difficult cases. He was not always as you see him. He was my student assistant back in London. He would have become a fine doctor. But as you see. Alas."

"Does he have physical disabilities as well as . . . the other?"

"A few, nothing major. His affliction you cannot see. It causes him to sometimes be dogged by depression and respond from fear or anger instead of rationally. The world does not look or act the same for him and thousands of others as it does for us."

"Could he be dangerous?"

"To himself, unfortunately, yes. To others? I have not seen him do so. But why do you ask me this? Detective Atkins has already done so. He seemed satisfied with my answers. Oh, I do not fool myself. I know they will have to find someone to arrest. And if they don't find some vagrant, they will come for Ivan."

"Why?" blurted Lily.

The doctor smiled at her. The first smile Phil had seen; it certainly softened his harsh features.

"Because it is easier than accusing someone with power and money."

"And who would that someone be?" Phil asked.

"I don't know, nor do I care. Georgie has met the devil. It is out of our hands."

"Don't you want to know the truth?"

"The truth." He lifted the bowl to his lips and drained what was left of the soup, then put it down with a thud and wiped his mouth. "I used to think I knew what the truth was. I was an arrogant fellow in those days. Now, the truth eludes me. Is truth these desperate people all around us? The mother whose children cry inconsolably from hunger or pain or afflictions we cannot see and which will mercifully take them from us and their pain all too soon? Those same diseases are cured just a few blocks away, but not here.

"It is a truth that men come back from battle suffering from a terrible unseen malaise. At least those who have lost a limb or an eye or walk with a limp are pitied by others, instead of ignored or ridiculed. That is a truth."

He pushed his chair back suddenly and took his bowl to the dry sink.

The whole place was old and probably riddled with weeks if not months of illness. And the people of Orchard Street came here for help. It was enough to make Phil cry.

She didn't; countesses didn't cry. But she did feel a hot wave of guilt for her life, so frivolous and wasteful most of the time.

Well, she couldn't cure diseases—she didn't even know how to ease a splinter—but she was capable of catching criminals, and she would do just that.

"Dr. Salvos, I just want to help."

"Help? How on earth can you help? Are you a surgeon?"

"No, but I want to find out who killed Georgina Nash. Don't you want that person to come to justice?"

"I gave up on justice long ago. Neither I nor Ivan seek retribution."

"Then why is he so intent on seeing Rose; is it because of you?"

Suddenly resigned, he sat down again. "I have to get back to work but I will tell you. Ivan and Rose were young lovers. Before he left for battle and returned as you see him, he was a charity student. He'd lost his parents at an early age and had been sent to the orphanage."

Lily, who had found a basket of fabric strips, began rolling them into usable rolls.

"He was accepted into the university and was placed under my tutelage. *Dio,* he was a handsome fellow then. Not like now. He met Rose because Georgina was a member of our group. They became very close. He fell deeply in love. Everyone fell in love with Rose.

"Ah, but she, too, was different then. Beautiful and brilliant. And perhaps a little cruel. Ivan worked so hard to get ahead. To be worthy. He cleaned the laboratories at night to earn extra money so that he could send her posies and candy and other nonsense. At last, one day, he got up the courage to ask her to marry him.

"Foolish boy. I tried to convince him to wait. I hoped he would grow out of it. Anyone could see she carried passion only for her work, even then.

"She turned him down. He was broken-hearted. One day, not long after that, he didn't come in to assist me, and we found out later that he had signed into the army and been sent to fight in the Boer War.

"He returned as you see him now. Worse, actually. He begged me for his position back, but I was no longer employed myself. I did what I could. Gave him a corner to sleep in until I was thrown out of my rooms because I could not pay the rent.

"Anna took it upon herself to rehabilitate him. I think she must have known in her heart what Erik had done to me and wanted to atone for his betrayal. She worked with Ivan so that he could better live his life. He made great strides, went long periods without the uncontrollable rage or debilitating fear. I was thankful for her help, she didn't ask for anything in return."

"And Rose?" Phil asked.

Salvo huffed out a breath. "Rose was kind when they inevitably met, but she was obviously afraid of him. I couldn't afford to keep us both, and yet I couldn't throw him out on the street. We worked our way to New York on a freighter. He was strong, driven by an inner rage. I was not so, and sometimes he had to finish my work so I wouldn't be punished. We met some others who told us to come to Orchard Street. In New York we would find work, and we have been here since." He laughed softly, bitterly. "So much work.

"We were all so sure of ourselves in those days, convinced that we alone knew how to unlock the secrets of the psyche. And now I only can unlock that medicine cabinet over there, and half the time it's empty."

Salvos wanted to see the back of them, but Phil needed to know one more thing. She chose her words carefully. "I don't mean to pry but"—but she was going to regardless—"they said you were disgraced. But you used the word 'betrayal.' There is a difference."

"A difference without distinction—at least for me."

"I don't understand," Phil said.

"Erik and I were working separately on . . . well, it doesn't matter. It's quite complicated, adapting certain neuron stimuli . . . We were both up for a coveted position on the faculty. We both

turned in our research papers, and then I was called into the offices of the jury. It seems that they'd received an anonymous
letter that my research was faulty, that I had not used proper pro-
cedures and had changed the outcome. That I had cheated. I was
not given a chance to defend myself. Erik was given the position.
And I was dismissed from the university completely. A lie from
an anonymous letter."

"And would no one support you?

"In that place? Everyone there walked the tightrope. The competition was so intense that everyone watched the other for the
slightest misstep. And when that person failed, they were eager
to fill the vacuum.

"Elisabeth and Chumley were in different schools. But Lutz
and Vogeler. They were like those runners in a race crouched at
the starting line to get a quicker start. To fill my shoes. Vogeler
won, and to his discredit, a few months later, he published his
own research, taken directly from mine. He is the cheat and the
scoundrel. And Anna is so blind to his faults she supported him.

"Her family is very wealthy. That money helped Erik push me
out of the institute and usurp my position. Poor woman, she is
the smarter of the two, and yet she gave up everything to forward
his work. I hope to heaven the scales are never lifted from her eyes.
It will be a devastating disappointment.

"Now you know our entire story, even though Ivan's wasn't
mine to tell. You can leave us both in peace now. Ivan did not
kill Georgie. I did not kill her. You must look elsewhere for your
murderer."

They were dismissed.

Preswick and Lily rose to their feet. Lily had finished with the
fabric strips, and rolls of clean bandages sat side by side in the
basket.

"Thank you, Miss Lily. That was a big help."

And Lily curtseyed.

Phil wanted to hug her. This gaunt man and his watery soup,
whether wronged falsely or not, still deserved respect.

He walked them to the door, through the antechamber that was
once again filled with patients, but who now were calmly waiting

their turn. And Phil saw the reason for the sudden calm. Behind the desk sat a young man, dark hair neatly slicked back, above a worn but clean suit and vest.

Without his cumbersome jacket, Phil hardly recognized him. And with one look at his eyes, she was certain he didn't remember her.

12

Phil, Lily, and Preswick returned to the Plaza to find the evening editions of the newspapers and a stack of books from Brentano's waiting for them.

Phil immediately dismissed the other two with a "Do with yourselves what you like." She was going to take a long bath, order something substantial for dinner, and eat it on the chaise in the parlor while she read about God only knows.

"Oh, and Lily, I'd like to take another look at the dime novels Mr. . . . Kellogg left you, if I may. I'll be very careful with them."

Lily hurried off to retrieve them from her room.

"Shall I order you dinner, my lady?"

"Yes, for a half hour from now. The kaleidoscope shifts in this matter, Preswick. A clue, several motives. A beginning at last."

Two hours later, having just polished off a lovely beef pie, Phil lay stretched out on the chaise longue sipping a second glass of burgundy and pondering the information learned today. If Pietro's version of his dismissal was the correct one, it would shed an entirely new light on Erik Vogeler and on those who might wish to see him elsewhere . . . permanently.

There had been no mention of Georgina's murder in the evening editions of the paper. Godfrey had somehow seen to that, but it had only been a few hours, and journalists were tenacious creatures. It couldn't go unnoticed for long.

Phil picked up the top book, a tome titled *The Psychopathology of Everyday Life,* by Sigmund Freud, who had been mentioned more than once during dinner. Most of it went right over her head and it didn't take long before the words began to swim before her eyes.

She glanced over to where the bright covers of the dime novels beckoned to her.

Nick Carter's "Four Scraps of Paper," with its Coney Island

setting, was on top. It was hard to believe that just a few days ago, she'd been riding the same amusements that were pictured on the cover without a thought of murder in her mind.

And bored, she reminded herself. *Well, maybe just a few pages.*

Unlike Dr. Freud's erudition, the escapades of Nick Carter immediately engaged her. And she was so deeply immersed in the quick-witted detective's adventure that she actually jumped when the clock struck midnight.

Already a new day, and still no closer to finding the killer. Someone must have seen something, the smallest oddity that would help lead them to an arrest.

But for tonight, Phil must be content to remain in the dark.

The morning editions were much more informative than the previous evening's, though the details were still vague, thanks, no doubt, to Godfrey's clout among the Arsenal staff. One small paragraph in the *Times* stated that a woman had been shot outside a Central Park restaurant Monday night, a possible victim of a foiled robbery. The lead line was followed by several paragraphs on the disintegration of the park's services and decrying the lack of care put into such an important landmark and place of entertainment for the city.

Fortunately, no one was mentioned by name, which was a good thing, or Phil would have Martha Rive, the newly promoted news editor at the *Times* who had been pivotal in Phil's last big case, pounding down Phil's door for the "inside scoop."

The murder of two gangsters in Coney Island and an article on the illegal selling of opium and morphine received much more page space. Unfruitful, at best.

Still, there was little time to spare.

"I intend to call on Anna Vogeler this morning. See if she can shed some light on the things Dr. Salvos told us yesterday. Perhaps I'll suggest a visit to the museum. Just the two of us."

She opened the *Times* to the arts pages and the gallery and museum offerings. "She seems very taken with the Met, and it's close by. I wonder what exhibits are being displayed. One should at least be able to converse halfway knowledgeably about art while one is fishing for information. Discreetly, of course."

"Yes, my lady." Preswick filled her cup.

Phil searched the page. "Ah, the exhibition of German Expressionists that should have opened last week at the Metropolitan has been postponed until winter. Thanks heavens for that. I've always found them a heavy-handed bunch."

She went back to her search. Something niggled at her thoughts. Hadn't Anna said she'd seen that exhibit and enjoyed it very much? How many German Expressionist exhibits could there be?

One was too many for Phil's taste. Maybe a nice landscape display. Or . . . "Perhaps a simple morning call would suffice."

"Yes, my lady."

It was decided that Lily should accompany her to Union House to read to Rose Nash for a couple of hours. They struck off in good time, as Phil pointed out, "Before the lady has a chance to escape to the museum."

Just a Friend saw them cross the street. He tossed a coin to another newsie several yards away and hurried to catch up.

"He's keeping my place safe," he said, and marched ahead of them, frowning at anyone who got too close. They arrived a couple of minutes later at the door of Union House, and he hurried back to his post.

Collins answered the door almost immediately, and informed them that Mr. Bennington was in business meetings and would not return until that afternoon. Mrs. Vogeler had taken the children to the zoo. Dr. Vogeler was upstairs, preparing for his lecture with orders not to be disturbed.

"Thank you, Collins. Lily has come to read to Miss Nash for a couple of hours. If you would inform the housekeeper that she is here, I'll see her upstairs, and get her settled."

Collins would; he bowed himself away, and Phil and Lily went upstairs to Rose Nash's room.

Nothing had changed since the night before. The draperies were still drawn. Not even a lamp was turned on.

But Phil could see a shadow huddled by the bed.

"Who is it?" Dr. Vogeler stood abruptly.

Well, well, Phil thought. Instead of preparing his lecture, he'd been sitting by Rose Nash's bedside.

"Ah, Lady Dunbridge, I was just checking on our patient." His voice sounded gruff, as if he had a sore throat. He strode over to them, moving like a phantom, until he came suddenly into a sliver of light where the sun sneaked past the heavy velvet curtains.

His eye were red-rimmed, and Phil was taken aback for a moment to think he might be grief-stricken. Over Georgie Nash . . . or her sister?

"Lily offered to read to Miss Nash this morning," Phil said. "Your wife said she was comforted by it last night." Though Phil didn't see how the hair-raising adventures of Nick Carter could possibly calm one down. They certainly had excited Phil.

"Ah, yes, of course. That would be acceptable. If you will excuse me. I must get back to my work." He hurried away without waiting for her answer.

As soon as he was gone, she and Lily both tiptoed toward the bed. The girl seemed to barely be breathing.

"It's not right," Lily whispered, "to keep her asleep like this."

No, it isn't, Phil thought. But neither of them knew the extenuating circumstances. And it was odd that Rose had bounded awake from under such a stupor. The few times Phil had been administered laudanum, she'd slept for hours, unaware of anything. There was definitely something out of the usual here. It was as if Rose was fighting the drugs meant to help her.

"Madam?" Lily began walking toward the dressing-room door and Phil realized she wanted Phil to follow her.

As soon as they were inside Lily shut the door and turned on the light.

They were in a large, square room paneled in dark wood. There was a massive wardrobe, generous cupboards, and a row of shelves, all bare but for one. This was a government guesthouse whose guests never stopped for long and didn't bring much with them. The dressing table likewise was unused. The only sign that someone had actually used the room at all was an octagonal table that held several brown glass vials of what Phil presumed to be tonics and sedatives for Rose.

The gown Rose Nash was wearing the night of her sister's murder was hanging limp from a solitary wire coat hanger. A pair of silver shoes sat beneath it.

Phil picked one of them up, held it to the light of the narrow window. Grass-stained and caked with earth and leaves. Of course, she'd been standing in the trees behind her sister when they first made their appearance.

Phil returned the shoe and felt the fabric of the dress, paying close attention along the seams. One never knew what one might find, and she didn't think Atkins had been allowed to investigate this room or question Rose, though no doubt he'd tried.

Lily pulled out a drawer. "Madam?"

Phil stopped her own search to see what she'd found.

The drawer held a clean pair of folded stockings and linens—kudos to the government staff—and a small beaded purse.

In for a penny . . . Phil thought. She carefully lifted the purse, but her attention was arrested by what was concealed beneath it: another vial of dark liquid.

Phil reached into her skirt pocket and pulled out a handkerchief. One never knew when the police would actually start using fingerprinting consistently in investigation. She opened the little jar and sniffed, quickly screwed the top back on. Laudanum.

Lily moved closer. "That's the vial that Dr. Faneuil left. I knew something was fishy."

They turned simultaneously to the little table and the vials it held.

"Then what are these others? They must be giving her something else," Phil said, her mind racing. Perhaps they've already started the treatment they planned for Rose. "Keep an ear out," she told Lily.

Lily opened the door a mere crack and peered out.

Phil uncorked the first bottle. Not laudanum, but a more astringent odor that made Phil's eyes water. And completely unfamiliar. She returned it to the table and sniffed the second. Something sweet and unpleasant. Phil didn't recognize it, either. Nor could she place the largely unscented contents of the third bottle.

"I wish we could take a sample."

Lily looked around. "I can—"

"No, absolutely not. I will find time to talk to Mrs. Vogeler and ask her outright, though I do wish the woman would stay put. There's been a murder, after all. You are not to do anything untoward."

"I am not afr-r-r-raid."

"I know, my dear, I saw you in action with Ivan, but please don't put yourself in harm's way. Or in a situation that would have you arrested. I don't know what I would do without you."

Lily looked up sharply, and Phil swore her eyes filled with tears.

Phil looked away. It wasn't like her to gush so, or Lily to react with anything but sangfroid.

It must be the heavily perfumed air.

"But she doesn't want to take it," Lily said. "She's fighting it. She wakes up and begs me to take her home. But we don't know where she lives."

"Have you tried to get her to tell you?"

"Yes, but she just keeps talking about ducks and stuff like that. Maybe she lives in the country. Or near the park. Maybe she could take us there."

"Perhaps," Phil said. And they might learn something important if they had access to the Nashes' living quarters.

"But if no one is there, she can't live on her own, can she? She'll have to go to the asylum."

Phil wanted to say she would never let the that happen, but she wouldn't lie to Lily. She would have no influence over what happened to Rose. "I hope not. Mrs. Vogeler seems intent on treating her."

"But how can they? She wakes up suddenly and asks me if she killed her sister. I just tell her no, but what if . . .'"

"She didn't kill her sister," Phil assured her. "She was sitting on the bench when it happened. I saw her, myself. Detective Sergeant Atkins traced the trajectory of the bullet from the bushes behind Dr. Vogeler. Far away from where Rose sat. Why does she think she killed Georgina?"

"She doesn't say. She can't stay awake for long. But what if she wakes up and someone else hears her? Though . . .'"

"What, Lily?"

"What if she's not always asleep when they come in?"

"She's pretending?"

"Maybe. Once, it was near morning, she'd been raving like she does, and the door opened. Rose collapsed back on the bed and Mrs. Vogeler came in. She lifted her up and dosed her again. Rose didn't stir, not at all. Mrs. Vogeler said, 'Don't worry, dear girl, we'll help you soon. It's going to be all right,' or something like that. Like she knew that Rose could hear her. It was creepy."

"I've heard that people who are unconscious or in a coma might be able to hear what people are saying around them. That's why you're reading to her. You said it calmed her, didn't you?"

"Yes, she gets quiet when I read."

"Do you think maybe you could rouse Rose while I'm here?"

"I can try."

Phil followed her out of the dressing room, turning once to make sure everything was as they had found it. She didn't know why she was acting so furtively. But since they had no suspects as yet, it paid to treat everyone as suspicious.

They crossed quickly to the bed.

"Rose, it's Lily. I've come to read. I brought more Nick Carter stories."

There was no response from the sleeping girl, not a sigh or a twitch, nothing to show that she may have heard.

Lily moved closer, shook Rose's shoulder. "Rose, I've brought someone to help."

Without warning the girl's eyes popped open, wide, unseeing. Staring straight ahead like the gruesome, painted eyes on memorial portraits.

Just as sharply, her hand struck out at Lily.

Phil reacted just as sharply to stop her, but Lily had taken it in both of hers.

"My bag! My bag." Rose sank back, turned her head, saw Phil, and gasped. It seemed for an ungodly moment that she had stopped breathing, then with a ragged inhale, she closed her eyes.

"Madam?"

Phil was already hurrying to the dressing room and pulling out her handkerchief. She hadn't even searched Rose's purse in her haste to identify the liquids in the vials.

She turned on the light, opened the drawer, and took the purse out in one smooth movement. She quickly opened the clasp to find very little: a hankie, a compact, a small change purse, but no change. She squeezed the purse itself. Ran her fingers along the lining and found a narrow slit near the seam. Carefully, she slid the tip of her finger inside. Felt the edge of a little rectangle of cardboard—and heard the outer door to the bedroom open.

She quickly shoved the purse back into the drawer and hurried out to come face-to-face with Mrs. Vogeler's maid.

"Oh, there you are," Phil said, taking the offense. "I was looking for some fresh water for Miss Nash. It's very important to give the invalid liquids."

"The ewer is right on the side table," the maid said.

"Yes, but I wasn't certain the water had been changed this morning. I thought there might be water laid on in the dressing room."

The blasted girl didn't answer. Hysterical one night, surly the next day. Thank heaven Phil had Lily and Preswick.

"Please refill the ewer immediately." Phil gave the maid her iciest dowager stare.

It worked. The girl scurried over to the bed, tossed a look at the sleeping Rose, and carried the water ewer out of the room.

Lily rolled her eyes. "Stupid, that one."

"She'll be back any minute." Phil started to return to the dressing room, but a small, imploring voice stopped her.

"Lily? Is she gone? I need my purse. Please."

Rose saw Phil and shrunk back.

"Don't be afraid," soothed Lily. "This is Lady Dunbridge. She saved me. She wants to help you. Rose, listen to me."

But Rose had closed her eyes and once again lay as if dead.

Lily's head snapped toward Phil. "That maid never comes in when I'm here. She was spying."

"I'm sure she was, so don't give her any reason to keep at it. Or to tell the Vogelers."

She drew Lily aside. "Something is hidden in the lining of her purse. See if you can find out what it is, but only once you're certain the maid isn't anywhere nearby. Will you be all right here alone?"

Lily nodded.

"Then I think it's time I made a visit to the zoo."

Phil left her card with Collins, as any morning visitor would do.

She walked down the steps, feeling ill at ease. There was something not quite right there, either with Rose's relationship with the Vogelers or with Rose's real or feigned sedated self. And if feigned, how was she doing it? And more to the point, why?

Phil crossed the street and walked the half block to where they'd entered the park for dinner only two nights before.

As she retraced her steps down the wide walk, she peered into the greenery, trying to reconstruct the events of the night of the dinner party. It had been dark, and they had been conversing on various subjects, not paying attention, when Georgie Nash had jumped out at them. *Just about here.*

Phil whirled around, garnering a few strange looks from a couple walking past her. It had all happened so fast. Lily would have had her stiletto in hand if she'd been here, but the only quickly acting person among them was Dr. Vogeler. What had he said? "Georgina, is it really you? We had no idea you were in town." Something like that.

No one knew where the Nash sisters lived. Maybe they were just visiting. She sighed. They might never find out where Rose called home.

A group of colleagues . . . dare she say friends . . . reunited for Dr. Vogeler's dinner. And not one thought to ask them where they lived? They'd been close once, back in Europe. They'd moved on since then, several of them to New York, as it turned out. Most of them seemed to be aware of where the others were practicing and what they were doing, except for the Nash sisters. No one even seemed curious as to their circumstances, and yet there were still undercurrents of intense emotions between them. And animosity from at least one of them. Though she had to give Pietro Salvos credit; he had contained it for most of dinner.

Phil reluctantly pulled herself from speculation and continued on her errand. She would need to speak with Detective Sergeant

Atkins before things progressed much further. It was ineffective for them to carry on separate investigations when cooperation would be so much more efficient. Though she doubted she would have any better luck with him than she'd had with Mr. X over the subject.

Men, she thought.

So, until they accepted her, she would have to question Anna Vogeler about Georgina and her sister on her own.

The area in front of the park entrance was crowded. Being a weekday, it was mostly populated by nursemaids and perambulators, mothers or nannies. They strolled or sat on the benches, gossiping or just resting, happy of the occasional breeze, as it was not only a respite from the heat but also from the odor of the zoo.

Their charges, feeling no such need of rest, chased each other between the pedestrians. There was a small line waiting to pay for tickets at the zoo entrance, but most were just as content to walk the grounds for free.

An ice-cream cart was set up nearby, tempting young and old with waffle cones filled with domes of frozen delight. A balloon man, his colorful wares riding sticks in a cloud above his head, shooed away children who crowded round him, stretching and jumping as they tried to snag one of the treasured toys.

Hawkers sold maps of the park, "parasols guaranteed to last" (at least long enough to see you through the menagerie), cups of sweetened lemonade, and other delights. A park custodian shuffled along, jabbing at trash with a pointed stick and depositing the captured offenders into a gunnysack slung crosswise over his shoulder. A row of shoeshine boys, young and adult alike, lined the sidewalk, mostly at their leisure as the rush for morning shines had passed hours before.

Phil saw the Vogeler children first, holding Nanny Cole by each hand and pulling her toward the balloon man.

But where was their mother?

Phil scanned the crowd, looked up and down the path. Then she saw her standing on the far side beside the railing several yards away. Her head turned right and left, as if she was expecting someone.

And she was.

Chumley Griswold shuffled up the sidewalk toward her, though he didn't seem to notice her. Coincidence? They hardly seemed like people who would meet clandestinely in the park. Or anywhere, for that matter.

Nonetheless, Phil eased forward, keeping her eye trained on Chumley. He stopped at Anna. She took a last look around and said something to him. Not a "fancy meeting you here," greeting, not even particularly friendly.

Phil crept along her own side of the wide sidewalk, trying to get closer to them, but still not able to hear even a snatch of conversation.

But here came the balloon man. She could fall in step behind him and slip across to the other side of the path without being seen.

She took a step, her foot hit something hard, and she tripped, nearly losing her balance. There was a clatter and the sound of rolling. A shoeshine boy, a tall lanky man, jumped up from his work, grabbed his box, and scooped up the brushes and tins that had fallen to the ground. He didn't even look up, just growled at her before returning to his customer.

The balloon man was gone. She'd missed her opportunity. And then she had a suspicious thought. She'd made sure her path was clear before she'd moved. She'd trained herself to do that in her study of crime-scene investigations. That box hadn't been in her path at all.

She looked over to the shoeshine "boy." Of course. He'd used this disguise before. He often wore disguises even when they weren't necessary. The truth was, she suspected that he just liked dressing up.

Phil inhaled deeply. She smelled tobacco, followed by a pervasive odor of zoo animal, but she didn't recognize the exotic aroma of his usual pipe tobacco. He'd also tricked her that way before.

She eased closer, careful not to look at him. She could see Chumley gesticulating, opening and closing his fingers in a steady rhythm. Anna seemed to be only half listening, in a hurry to get away.

Phil leaned over just enough to address the shoeshine boy without being overheard.

"You seem to be repeating yourself."

He ignored her, except for a more violent buffing of the gentleman's shoes.

"Are you going to tell me what you're doing here, so we don't work at cross-purposes?" Phil had to quickly turn her face aside when Anna, without warning, scanned the area, fortunately passing over Phil without seeming to recognize her.

The shoeshine boy gave a final slap to the shoes and stood up, the gentleman paid, and the "boy" turned to her. "You want your shoes shined, lady?"

Phil opened her mouth. Shut it again. It wasn't Mr. X. She knew the instant he faced her.

"Sorry, no, I don't." In the surprise of nonrecognition, she'd taken her eye off Anna and Chumley. She was in luck: they hadn't moved. But three yards away from them, the trash picker was leaning against the iron fence, resting on his elbows, his stick balanced on its point on the walk. The epitome of a very slow moving, slow-witted trash collector taking a break.

He yawned; his jaw dropped and his mouth made several comical grimaces like a cow chewing cud. Phil looked on in amazement. He had perfected the role, and she would be mightily impressed if she weren't so annoyed. Then his mouth snapped shut, incorporating a dip his head in Phil's direction.

Damn the man. He was supposed to be in Washington. Leave it to him to be in the most ridiculous disguise in broad daylight in a crowd. He enjoyed the risk. If he didn't watch out, he'd be in jail for murder.

She looked away, perusing the walk as if deciding in which direction to go. Willing him to stay put until she made her way over for a little chat.

She strolled unhurriedly across the width of the walk, smiling at something she pretended to see, looking anywhere but at him.

When she finally managed to make it to the rail where he was standing, near enough to have a conversation without appearing to, she glanced his way to make sure he was still there—he had a terrible habit of disappearing just when she needed to talk.

"What are you doing here?" she asked, studying a dandelion

that had sprung up in the grass just on the other side of the iron railing.

"Trying to make the world a cleaner place," he said, reaching into his pocket and pulling out a small package.

She couldn't see exactly what it was without turning toward him, but her pulse raced with excitement. Instructions? A list of suspects? She looked toward the ticket booth and sidled a step closer to him. Looked back just in time to see him to unwrap what appeared to be waxed paper and lift out a thick sandwich of meat and cheese.

He took a bite.

Phil felt like chewing nails.

And to make it worse, she'd moved to a place where he was blocking her view of Anna and Griswold.

"They think you murdered Georgie Nash or are part of a conspiracy to overthrow the government. The War Department never heard of Francis Kellogg. They have men waiting to grab you when you step off the train in Washington."

"Good thing I'm not going to Washington—at least not as Francis," he said, and drew his arm across his mouth.

Phil had to hand it to him, she'd never seen him break character. If he ever got tired of doing whatever it was he did, he could have a second career as a stage actor.

Or perhaps investigating was his second career.

Phil tried to wedge herself against the rail to catch a glimpse of the couple they were both following. She was just in time to see Anna open her purse and take out a flat, brown packet. She handed it to Chumley, who slipped it inside his jacket.

Without a word, Anna turned and walked away. Phil ducked her chin just as she strode past them. Chumley turned in the opposite direction.

"So what is this all about?" Phil asked.

"That's what I expect you to find out." He crammed the remnants of his sandwich in his pocket and picked up his trash stick.

"Wait," she said.

"Can't. I have a hypnotist to follow. Oh, and kindly refrain from harassing Anna Vogeler for a few minutes. I don't want her to think that you've been following her."

Phil stared in consternation as he moseyed off down the path after Chumley, who was shuffling quickly toward the Fifty-ninth Street exit.

Phil considered following them, but her view of the two men was impeded by the balloon man, who'd stopped in her path and was immediately surrounded by boisterous children.

And when Phil finally steered herself clear, Chumley and Mr. X had both disappeared.

13

Phil stared at the space where they had been. Had he just told her to follow Anna Vogeler?

She had every intention of following her.

Anna had joined Nanny Cole, who was holding up tickets for the zoo. Without a backward look, Anna scooted the children ahead of her and they all walked through the entrance.

Without further deliberation, Phil went to buy herself a ticket, where she waited somewhat impatiently in line, and thought about what she'd just seen: Anna handing a packet to Chumley. Perhaps he'd merely left something behind at the restaurant and Anna agreed to return it.

But no hellos, no small talk, no thank-yous? Anna had practically shoved her package toward him. He'd taken it without even looking at it, and they'd turned away without a goodbye. No, their meeting had to be something more than a dropped cuff link.

And Phil intended to find out what.

It took several minutes to get her tickets and she decided to go directly inside.

She had no sooner stepped through the brick entrance of the zoo proper than she realized it would be no easy feat to question Anna while trying to make herself heard over the roars, squawks, and trumpeting of exotic animals mixed with the squeals and shouts of excited, demanding children.

Not to mention the odor.

Perhaps she could persuade Anna to join her in a tête-a-tête at one of the tables set up near the sidewalk lemonade stands, hopefully a safe distance from the zoo and sheltered by the trees.

The Central Park zoo was rather small and haphazardly put together, Phil thought. Still, it was hard not to be distracted when she found herself in front of an octagonal water pool, where she stopped to peer through the high mesh fence.

Inside its confines, a man with a bucket of fish was feeding several sleek, attentive sea lions, and Phil thanked her stars that Mr. X had opted for trash picking instead of fish feeding; she could smell the man's bucket of fish from where she stood. She wondered briefly if he had a wife.

For a moment, Phil forget completely about the conjugal closeness of fishmen or the murderous intentions of psychoanalysts to enjoy the antics of these playful creatures.

Nonetheless, she had business to attend to. She drew her eyes away and searched the crowd.

Anna and her children were standing on the far side, among the crowd of other adults and children, standing on tiptoe, pressed against the honeycombs of the fence, to get a better look as the sea lions happily snatched their lunch from the air.

Nanny Cole saw her first and touched Anna's sleeve. Anna turned around.

Phil toodled her fingers in greeting. She watched Anna's expression of surprise change to calculation; a slight nod and a smile invited Phil to join them.

Phil didn't hesitate.

"Ah, Lady Dunbridge. Did you need to see me?"

"I was just dropping Lily off to read to Miss Nash and Collins informed me you had brought the children here. I thought I might tempt you away for a lemonade. The zoo is delightful, but the heat can be daunting."

"We want lemonade, too, Mama," Erik Junior said.

"It's hot here," Theresa added. "We want lemonade."

"And so you shall have it, my dears. Nanny will take you, but don't you want to see the buffalo first? Papa will want to hear all about it when you get back to Union House."

"Oh, yes," Master Erik practically shouted. "Black Diamond. They put him in a circus, but he used to roam the plains. . . ." The boy's voice turned downright oratorical.

"Yes, dear, you are quite correct."

"I want to see Black Diamond," Theresa parroted.

Phil smiled and silently willed the nanny to take them away.

"Cole," Anna said.

"Come along, children," Nanny Cole said, scuttling them away.

"And ice cream, too," Master Erik called out as a parting salvo.

"I'm so lucky to have children with inquisitive minds," Anna said, taking Phil's arm as if they were old friends. "Even if it includes ice cream and lemonade."

"It must be . . . lovely," Phil answered.

"You don't have children of you own?"

"The earl unfortunately died before we were so blessed." Phil repressed a shudder at the thought of any little earls in his image running around the dark passages of Dunbridge Castle.

"I'm sorry for your loss."

No need for that, Phil thought, but merely said, "Thank you."

She wasn't fooled by the question; it wasn't designed to show sympathy but to put a little distance between the two women. A claim of slight superiority because of their motherhood—or lack of it. A kind of "psychology" Phil had seen before, though wasted on Phil. And unless Anna Vogeler had been living in a remote land away from all forms of news from England, she would have known of the earl's reputation. And most likely Phil's, too.

They reached the entrance and headed for the outdoor café. They found a free table, covered with a white cloth, where they were served two frosty glasses of lemonade.

Anna put her purse on the tabletop; Phil kept hers in her lap.

Handy things, a lady's purse, with their secret compartments and hidden inner linings. Even the smaller ones of the last few seasons managed to fit packets and pieces of cardboard as well as a satisfying array of necessities, from lip rouge to love letters, sewing kits to pearl-handled derringers, like the one that was nestled in her handbag at this very moment.

"I must tell you," Phil began, "I saw Ivan, Dr. Salvos's driver, yesterday. He was waiting outside Union House when I picked up Lily. I was worried that he might have accosted you and the children."

"Poor Ivan," Anna said, not bothering to look around. She sipped her lemonade. "He was once Pietro's protégé, if you will, but after the scandal, Pietro disappeared in disgrace and Ivan found himself out of a position."

Not exactly the way Pietro Salvos had told it, but no one ever told the entire truth.

"Erik would have offered him something, but he was no longer fit enough to be useful. The war, you see. Oh, not so much physical; he has his arms and legs. But men come back from war with more scars than those visible to the eye. Scars deep inside that keep them from being productive citizens, loving sons and husbands. They call it Soldiers' Heart. Simpletons. It can drive a man into violence or push him into the hell of insanity. There is no heart involved."

"You seem well informed," Phil said. "Was that your field of study?"

Anna's eyebrows rose ever so slightly.

Phil hurried on. "I believe someone mentioned that you had been a practicing physician before your marriage."

"Yes," Anna said. "Part of my study. My theory is if you take those broken psyches and retrain them, they will be stronger and more efficient than ever. Think of it. Men who might have been indecisive or meek or noncompetitive can be put back together again, better, more useful and . . . And most importantly, these men could enjoy fulfilled, happier lives," she added, almost as an afterthought, it seemed to Phil.

"Men, of course, are disgusted that such a study would be taken on by a woman. They refuse to even acknowledge this syndrome, preferring to call men who suffer from it weak and cowardly, while they quietly shake in their spit-polished boots and pray it doesn't happen to them."

She shuddered. "Forgive me, Lady Dunbridge. I don't usually bore on and on like this. I can't imagine why I am now. Perhaps because of your keen interest, and it is—it was—a particular interest of mine."

"But no longer?"

"Yes, of course, but as you see, I am kept quite busy with my husband and my children."

"Pardon me if this is impertinent, but do you miss your work?"

"I still dabble a bit. But nothing acknowledged by academia. Not surprising, since it a man's sphere." She laughed, a thin sound. "At least according to them. I am, after all, a woman, whose mind isn't capable of understanding the higher concepts of science, and whose place is still at home dropping children every year until she becomes too old or dies in the constant demand of maternity. An archaic attitude, considering this is the twentieth century, but sometimes the most scientific of men are the last to grasp the actual science of things."

Now she gave Phil a genuine smile. "I confess, I'm a bit of a nuisance to them, and they're forever giving me sly looks and making innuendos about the next addition to the family. Between you and me . . . my husband, though brilliant in his field, is more than eager to please them. He's waiting blithely for me to drop again, thinking another child will make me content and please his colleagues, while taking pressure off of him. Fortunately, I was fitted for a Dutch cap. He doesn't even notice, poor man. You wouldn't give me away, would you, Lady Dunbridge?"

"Oh, dear no. Glass houses and all that."

"I felt you would understand." Anna's mood changed suddenly and she leaned over the little table. "But tell me, haven't they found that secretary yet? He's still out there. What if he comes after Erik again? They haven't even ordered extra policemen to secure the hall where he is to lecture. Anyone could walk in and he would be open game."

"I'm certain Detective Sergeant Atkins is doing all he can to investigate. But it's difficult. Is there anyone else who might have reason to harm your husband? Someone who wasn't invited?"

"No. Many are jealous. But they are arguers, they pound the table, tear their hair, and yell to be heard. But shoot someone? No."

Phil remained silent, waiting for her to say more. To reason out more than she had said so far. A scientist surely would conjecture beyond the most obvious. Was Anna so incurious as to who might bear a grudge against her husband?

Or even if he was the intended victim at all. He had gotten off with a minor wound. Georgina Nash had lost her life.

"It must be that Lieutenant Kellogg who disappeared. I never understood why they sent him. He was totally useless. Always hanging about and not really helping. I was certain he was just waiting to steal my jewelry."

Phil fought the urge to laugh. More likely he was finding opportunities to search for signs of . . . wrongdoing? Dishonesty? Disloyalty?

"I was a little concerned about leaving my maid to sit with Miss Nash. Not because of anyone attempting to attack Dr. Vogeler again, but because Miss Nash seems erratic, at best."

"Ah, Rose. She had such a unique understanding of the human mind, could present arguments that would make the most confirmed skeptic believe, through sheer intelligence, not the disgusting trappings of a fake charlatan."

"Charlatan? Are you referring to Dr. Salvos?" *Or Chumley Griswold.*

"Doctor. *Pfft.* They would have stripped him of his credentials if he hadn't disappeared. Immigrated to America, where he lives by doing who knows what? I was surprised that Erik wanted to see him. Though he always felt bad for what happened. I, for one, don't see how he could feel sorry for Pietro. He got no more than he deserved. There is no place for cutting corners and fudging facts in science. It takes long and steady study. It can't be rushed. Whether he outright cheated on the results or was just plain careless, I suppose we'll never know."

"Is that why you won't allow him to see Miss Nash?"

"He's not to be trusted. He hated Georgina. I have to wonder at his intentions toward her sister." She sighed, and opened her purse as if to pay.

Phil held up her hand. "Please, I invited you." And without giving Anna time to take her leave, asked, "What about Georgina?"

"What about her?"

"No one knew she was coming to dinner. She wasn't on the guest list. Yet your friends seemed to accept her, though, I must say, they were rather rough toward her."

"No worse than any English ballroom, I imagine," Anna retorted.

"Perhaps not," Phil agreed. Though she'd never seen a lady gunned down in a ballroom.

"Georgina always managed to put herself in the center of things even when she wasn't wanted. We were friends once. I didn't respect her as a scientist—most of us didn't—but I detested her for what she did to Rose."

"Good heavens. What did she do?"

"She ruined the girl's life."

"But how? Is that why Dr. Salvos hated her?"

"Salvos," Anna said dismissively. "He accused her of turning Rose against Ivan. Of course, Rose needed no such persuasion. Ivan was a dim satellite in her bright orbit." She frowned slightly. "You are very inquisitive."

"Sorry, it's just so tragic. But it's also fascinating. The way people's minds work. I never thought about it before, the strange assortments of friends one has. And what makes them do the things they do. I sometimes marvel at some of the people in my circle. I, of course, can only marvel," Phil effused. "But psychologists, to actually study such things, then help people understand themselves? Why, I'm quite bowled over."

"It is fascinating. And to answer your question . . . it isn't Pietro who wants to see Rose. It's Ivan. Poor boy. He was infatuated with Rose from the first day he saw her. She, of course, had no time for him. He never had a chance. She was destined for great things. He was a poor apprentice, fated to live in the shadow of others." Anna sighed. "It is tragic that he's lost so much of himself, and yet he clings to his remembrance of love."

"You don't think he's capable of still loving?"

"Perhaps, but his is an obsessive love, dangerous and possibly hurtful. You think I'm being unkind, keeping Rose from him, but he can't be trusted not to hurt her, or worse, when she fails to live up to what he wants."

"Good heavens. And you can predict these things through . . . how?"

"A combination of various methods. Study of subjects suffering similar conditions, facts presented over time in groups of subjects. This is a common but misunderstood malady. They call it neurasthenia, a weakness of the nerves. It has nothing to do with nerves. It is their mind, their psyche, that is broken."

"And Pietro was also studying this condition?"

"Oh, no, Pietro is a romantic. We should have been able to predict Ivan's downfall just from his personality type. He should never have been given such a position to begin with. But hindsight, as they say . . . I imagine Pietro's only interest in Rose now is to help the young lovers. Only they aren't lovers, and they never will be."

"And what about Rose?" Phil asked, knowing she was wandering into a possibly taboo subject. Rose, no more than Ivan, appeared to be in her right mind.

"Rose could never return Ivan's misplaced love. He has nothing to recommend him. And she . . ." Anna suddenly looked around as if expecting her children. Willfully, Phil thought, misunderstanding Phil's question and ending any more discussion of Rose Nash and Ivan.

"And Mr. Griswold?" Phil persisted, watching for the smallest hint of acknowledgment of their meeting a few minutes before.

"Chumley was the life of the party, and still is by all accounts."

"But you're no longer friends?"

There was a brief and, Phil thought, telltale hesitation.

"The group hasn't been friends for years. We've all gone our separate ways. It seems that most of them have come to the United States. Several others are in Europe, but if they wanted to kill my husband, they didn't have to travel all the way to New York to do it."

Nicely done, Phil thought: she'd managed not to answer Phil's question about Chumley while seeming to do so. It might be a psychologist's technique, but Phil had learned a thing or two about evasion in the parlors of some of England's most conniving peeresses.

She would get her answers, no matter how these psychologists tried to play with her. And she would bring a killer to justice.

Any further conversation was interrupted by two excited children, chased after by a huffing Nanny Cole. They were both licking ice creams. Master Erik downed the last bite of his and demanded lemonade from his mother. Theresa seemed to have fed most of hers to the front of her pinafore.

"Back, back, you little imps. Lady Dunbridge will think you are heathens."

"I'm a buffalo!" cried her son, who made clunky movements around the table.

"I'm a buffalo, too." Theresa joined him in his antics, spilling the rest of her ice cream down her front.

"You are certainly dirty enough to be buffalos." Anna laughed and motioned Nanny Cole to move them away. "It happens every time they go to the park. Cole, please take these gremlins back to Union House and give them both baths."

"You, too, Mama, you, too." Both children continued to jump and cajole until Anna excused herself.

"I'm afraid I must see to my maternal duties now. Thank you for the lemonade and our chat." She was pulled away by two pairs of sticky hands.

Phil finished her lemonade in peace, thinking what an ordeal Anna Vogeler's "imaginative" children must be. And thanking her stars that she hadn't been put to that particular test.

She hadn't learned much in their short conversation. If Anna Vogeler could only come up with the aide-de-camp as suspect, she couldn't have thought much about it. Or at least hadn't been willing to speculate in Phil's presence.

Chumley Griswold meeting Anna in the park. Pietro Salvos working in a free clinic in the tenements. Ivan a ruined man. So far any of them could have wished Erik Vogeler dead.

Phil just couldn't see a way through as yet. Never mind, there was always a surplus of information before you could begin distilling it into the few facts that would lead to success.

After all, as Mr. Holmes said, "It is a capital mistake to theorize before one has data. Insensibly, one begins to twist facts to suit theories instead of theories to suit facts." And Dr. Gross in his handbook *Criminal Investigation* would certainly concur.

What she needed at the moment was another perspective.

It was just past two o'clock. If she hurried she could just fit in one more interview before evening.

She turned her steps toward the Plaza—keeping an eye out for trash pickers, hypnotists, and unbalanced doctor's assistants—to change into something suitably academic.

14

An hour later, Phil, wearing an olive-green skirt and ecru linen blouse, complete with starched collar and black ribbon tie, looked in her mirror to attach a straw boater firmly on her head. Satisfied with her ensemble, she set off for the hallowed halls of Barnard College for women in its new location on Broadway and 119th Street.

Preswick had ascertained Elisabeth Weiss's lecture schedule, and Phil would have just enough time to waylay her before she left for the day. Preswick agreed to pick Lily up and take a taxi home. Phil wouldn't take the chance of Ivan attacking them on the street.

Phil took her own taxi uptown.

She was brimming with questions. To Phil's mind, Elisabeth Weiss was the most perceptive of the group. And, from what Phil had observed, the least emotionally involved. A perfect witness, and someone who, unless Phil missed her guess, had a wealth of inside knowledge about the others. If only she would be willing to share what she knew with Phil.

She just hoped John Atkins didn't have the same thing in mind, and they would find themselves *face à face* at Dr. Weiss's door.

The taxi took her up Broadway, with its new "wave of the future" apartment buildings and brownstones with their own garages, something that would certainly be convenient when in a hurry. Phil had hardly used her own auto in the last months due to the convenience of the line of cabs waiting at the Plaza door.

They drove through the Seventies and the Eighties, and Phil was beginning to wonder if they would leave town altogether when the taxi stopped at the gates of a cluster of stately buildings.

One glance at the iron sign told her she had arrived at Columbia University. Barnard College should be right across the street.

Phil paid the driver and crossed the thoroughfare to the women's campus.

Barnard consisted of an expanse of land with a solitary but impressive U-shaped edifice of red brick, detailed in limestone and terra-cotta. Ionic columns supported a long portico across the façade of the main entrance.

Fortunately, Phil was spared the trouble of finding an information desk by a serious-looking young woman who was walking briskly down the sidewalk toward her.

"Professor Weiss? She's in Milbank Hall. That way." She pointed to the rectangular building that rose several stories behind her.

Phil thanked her and walked up the sidewalk toward the building. Classes must be letting out, because she had to fight the stream of young women hurrying out the door.

She was just stepping into the building when she saw Dr. Weiss striding down the hall in the opposite direction.

Phil caught up to her at the door to her office.

"Ah, Lady Dunbridge. Detective Sergeant Atkins advised me that you might be paying me a visit."

"Did he?" Phil said drily.

The professor was dressed in a simple tweed skirt and cotton blouse. Her hair was pulled back in a tight bun at the nape of her neck. She was somber, serious, without a hint of the irony that she'd worn the night before.

"Yes, evidently you have a certain reputation."

Phil gave her a slight smile.

"Don't worry. I can't stand a woman who *doesn't* have a reputation. If we all behaved properly, I wouldn't be teaching here; there wouldn't even be a college for women; and there certainly wouldn't be a future when women are accepted to the grand university across the street."

"You think they will be?" Phil asked.

"Oh, yes. If I were Georgina Nash, I would say that I predict it. But alas, poor Georgie." She smiled suddenly, but a little sadly. "I knew her well."

She collected herself and unlocked the door, gesturing for Phil to enter before following her in and dropping a heavy tome she'd been carrying onto her desk.

"I'm very sorry about your friend."

"Thank you." Dr. Weiss turned to face Phil. "And now that you have expressed your condolences, tell me, Lady Dunbridge. What exactly is your interest in this case?"

Phil blinked at her directness, then quickly gathered her wits. "A guest was murdered at a dinner party I was hosting. Isn't that enough?"

"I believe the common reaction to that by a hostess would be to pretend it didn't happen."

"I'm afraid my reactions are rarely common," Phil said, with a bit of a bite. She knew Dr. Weiss was just trying to get a rise from her, and it had worked. Phil smiled. "But if you must know, I'm an insufferable snoop. I can't help myself."

"Well, at least you're honest. I find that refreshing. Not many people are."

Phil among them, Phil thought wryly. But it couldn't be helped; that was part and parcel of her new vocation.

"Since you came all this way, and I have a feeling you won't give up easily . . ." Dr. Weiss held up her hand. "I'm quite willing to indulge you if I can, but could we please do it away from campus? There's a nice little tavern around the corner; I'm finished for the day and ready for a drink. They frown upon the habit on the campus proper. And if you're lucky, Dietrich will make an appearance, as he often does about this time of day, for a post-patient and preprandial drink with like minds," she elucidated. "Shall we?"

They walked two blocks and turned onto a side street, where McLaughlin's Tavern, a stucco cottage, was wedged between an apartment building and a warehouse.

Dr. Weiss pulled open the heavy oak door and noise billowed out. It was crowded and dark inside, and Elisabeth had to yell over the din to be heard. "The students, but there's a nice little snug behind for the professors. Mostly male, but the good thing about that is they usually leave me alone."

"The oddity in the hallowed halls?" asked Phil as they pushed into the room.

"As you say."

They wove their way through the throng and the cigarette

smoke and through another door, into a smaller room filled with heavy, dark-wooden tables, a bar with a row of stools, and a couple of banquettes, one of which had a sign pinned to the beam next to it. PROF WEISS'S OFFICE.

"A little joke." Dr. Weiss gestured for Phil to sit down on the closest bench.

Phil wondered what the joke was.

Dr. Weiss slid onto the bench facing the door. "To see who enters and to scare off any would-be interlopers," she said. "I suggest the whiskey. It's Irish. The beer is cheap. They wouldn't know a wine list if it was written in Greek."

She raised her hand in the air, lifted two fingers, and put them down again. "I'm a regular. Though not to worry, I'm never impaired."

Once their drinks were delivered, Elisabeth pulled out a white handkerchief and wiped the rim of her glass, then tossed the linen square to Phil, who did the same.

"Now, what would you like to know?"

Phil handed the handkerchief back. "First, just let me say that if Detective Sergeant Atkins would see his way to including me in his interviews, you wouldn't have to cover the same territory twice."

"Oh, if I do, I'll certainly be disappointed."

Phil recognized a challenge, no matter how subtle. And she flattered herself that she might pick up more information on the personal interactions of the group than Atkins would be able to do.

"He caught me between my ethics class and senior seminar. He's very thorough, that man."

"He is," Phil agreed. "And?"

"I gave him the facts as I know them." Another curve of her lips, which just hinted at a smile. "I assume you want the gossip."

"Do you mind if I take notes?" Phil asked, reaching into her purse for her notebook.

Dr. Weiss glanced around the room.

"Just tell your colleagues, if they ask, that you were doing an interview on female professors for the *Times*."

"And what will I say when there is no article?"

"Oh, I think I can manage one. I have a friend there. I daresay she might be interested."

"On the society pages?"

"Actually, she was recently promoted to the news." And when Phil offered to give Martha Rive an exclusive once this murder was solved, she wouldn't mind squeezing the story on Barnard College into a column or two.

"In that case, fire away," Dr. Weiss said, and polished off her whiskey. Her hand went up; two more glasses appeared on the table. Phil sipped her first drink and asked her first question.

"The people who were at dinner last night were all friends at one time?"

"More or less. We all made the rounds of symposiums and lectures when we were in London. It was years ago; we became very close. But let me warn you at the outset. I haven't kept in touch with any of them, except Dietrich, mainly because he lives and practices just a few blocks from here. We drink at the same watering hole and occasionally share a cab, me out of financial necessity, and he because it allows him to be magnanimous. Though I assure you I always pay my half of the fare." Dr. Weiss laughed. "Actually he owns an automobile, but he's too cheap to drive it unless there is someone to impress. I am not one of them."

Interesting, thought Phil, and wrote: *DL. Needs money?*

"And quite frankly, I'm much less interested in digging around in the muck of the individual mind than I am in changing the collective attitude toward women. Please, don't feel the need to comment or write that down."

Phil stopped writing. "It would make an excellent quote."

"But too seditious."

Phil nodded. "In case you're wondering, I wholeheartedly back your view."

"I thought you might. Anyway," Dr. Weiss continued, "as I told the detective sergeant, we all parted ways several years ago. I turned my eye toward teaching. Chumley, who was never the greatest student, moved into the cheap-parlor-tricks business. I knew he had moved to New York, but we don't run in the same circles. I have a different life now."

"And Pietro Salvos? The Vogelers said he was disgraced." Phil saw no reason to tell Elisabeth Weiss that she'd already spoken to the man himself.

"Indeed he was, thoroughly. I was there for his undoing. I think that's what turned me away from the practice of psychiatry. He was eviscerated by his peers and by the head of the institute. He was accused of fixing the results of his studies. His accuser never was named, which we all thought totally unfair. He could have had a thriving practice but for that one stupid mistake. His reputation and career were ruined; he was dismissed from his post. No other university or reputable institution would touch him.

"The academic world is an unforgiving one. The world of practical application is a competitive and jealous business. And those on the fringe, as the psychoanalysts are now, are the worse. He became a pariah. He swore he had faithfully recorded his data, but it didn't matter. Some were genuinely outraged, but many were just happy to have one less person in competition for a small pool of positions and stipends.

"Our little group stood by him . . . at first. Then slowly we, too, turned way. He left London, and the first I heard of him again was at the Vogelers' dinner. Frankly, I couldn't believe he'd come. To face everyone who used to be his friends and colleagues. But perhaps . . ." She stopped to take a sip of her drink. "Even after all these years, I still have a hard time believing he cheated. It goes against all we believed in. Of course, Erik and Anna have flourished in certain circles."

"Why do you say 'of course'?" Phil asked.

"Mere speculation. I don't follow them except for noticing his publication in scientific journals, or a newspaper article about his lectures. If you ask me—and now we wander into opinion, mine—Erik is a good-natured man with a passionate belief in the practical applications of psychoanalysis, but not very deep, himself, if you know what I mean. He was given the position Pietro lost, but I think his success is largely due to Anna's unflagging work on his behalf. And her family's money. She was a psychologist in her own right, and a having a good amount of success in the study of trauma. But even in those days, she had begun to relinquish her own practice to bask in the glow of Erik's success."

"And the Nash sisters?"

"They were the biggest surprise of all. I had no idea where they were. Georgie and I had been close at one time. She was already a practicing psychologist when I knew her, and supporting Rose while she finished at the university."

She laughed softly. "Georgie was a classic example of a psyche in rebellion. By day, a hard worker, always shoulder to the wheel, so to speak. By night, the life of the party. Determinedly entertaining. She and Chumley always made us laugh. Chumley was amusing. with his pyrotechnical tricks. But Georgie was truly funny . . . with a vengeance, if you will."

"And Rose?" Phil asked.

"Ah, Rose, she was the bright star in our firmament. Younger than the rest of us by years. But already exceeding every one of us. Now, there was a mind."

"Do you know what happened to her?"

Dr. Weiss shrugged. "No one knows for sure. Georgie arrived at their laboratory one morning to find Rose as you've seen her now. She searched the lab for anything Rose might have been working on during the night, some formula that she had taken by mistake. But she found nothing. Georgie blamed herself. Though I don't see how she could be guilty, certainly not of negligence. She might have been a less than excellent psychologist, but she was devoted to her sister."

"Are you saying Rose might have taken some kind of drug?"

"It's possible; many practitioners are experimenting with drugs. There are new discoveries every day. Some may unlock the door to understanding diseases of the mind that have been hopelessly untreatable for centuries."

Phil thought of the drugs on the dressing table at Union House. Were they merely sedatives, or something to help Rose return to normal?

"Is that what *you* think happened?" Phil pressed.

"I guess it's possible, though sometimes these geniuses just snap for no apparent reason. But a good scientist doesn't indulge in doubts and guesses." She smiled suddenly. It lightened her face until she was almost mischievous. "At least we don't admit to it.

"I don't even know why we were all invited to dinner."

"And yet you went."

She shrugged. "Who doesn't like a free dinner? Which, by the way, was excellent. Call it curiosity. Call it an attempt to reconnect. To reminisce. It couldn't have been further from either of those. Georgie was like a caricature, Rose like some otherworldly creature. I hardly recognized them. And I have to say, that was something I would have preferred not to tell the detective sergeant. I resented having to explain it to him, even though . . . especially because he was sympathetic. It's hard enough to carve out a place for yourself in the hallowed halls of male intelligentsia without making fools of ourselves, or having some other woman making us fools."

"You resent Georgina for being foolish?" Phil asked, turning the page of her notebook and thinking that Dr. Weiss's air of eccentricity might have put her in that same category in men's eyes.

"That night? Initially. Then I realized that she was merely playing with us. That used to be Chumley's role, back in our younger days. Leading us on and shocking us no end. Now, he's become merely eccentric. But Georgie . . . I didn't see it right away, and I'm not certain now. That Georgie's strange appearance was intended to be more than mere entertainment. I think everyone felt it. You saw the way they treated her at dinner."

"As cruel as any lady's drawing room," Phil said.

"Indeed. Women face all sort of abuse. Especially in the sciences, where men still believe they are equipped with the only minds capable of understanding higher concepts and numbers. You learn to ignore it. Or not to care. I've learned to ignore it. They've learned to tolerate me." She paused to take a quick look around, then leaned closer. "I can postulate rings around quite of a few of them. It's a delicate balance to keep them from turning on me."

"But you don't seem to me like a woman who backs down or acts subservient," Phil said.

"Not in the least; that is certain death. I merely act like one of them, and if we stay here any longer I'll light up a cheroot. They used to laugh; now they barely notice."

"A learned response?" Phil said, using one of the few terms she managed to remember from the dinner conversation.

"Exactly. It's served me in good stead. But Georgina invited

abuse. She always did. Always on the attack. Lashing out before
they did. Though, really, who could blame her? She had made it
on her own. Fought for everything thing she could scratch from
the powers that be. She had to protect her own reputation, as well
as Rose's. Though who am I to judge? I never had to debase myself as Georgina had to do, but then I didn't have her burden to
bear.

"And behold, Dietrich has arrived like clockwork. I wonder
what the iconic Dr. Freud would say about that? I have no doubt
that Dietrich has his own theories about what happened to Rose
and to Georgina. It must be so lovely to question everyone you
meet and never feel the need to question yourself. Yoo-hoo, Dietrich, over here."

She fanned her fingers in the same way she'd summoned their
drinks from the bartender. Dietrich made his way over to the
table.

"Well, this is a surprise," Dietrich said, bowing slightly to Phil.

"You remember Lady Dunbridge?"

"I do indeed. And what brings you to our enclave of erudition?"

"Lady Dunbridge is writing an article for the newspaper."

"Really?" Dietrich said.

"A little hobby of mine," Phil said.

Dietrich cut a sharp look at Dr. Weiss. "I don't think we should
be discussing the details of Georgie's demise for the news. It could
be bad for everyone's reputation. And bring undue notoriety to
your college and my practice."

"She's doing an article on women in education. Sit down and
have a drink with us, Dietrich." Elisabeth moved over to make
room for him. "You can give us your opinion."

The bartender arrived shortly thereafter with a dark, foamy
glass of beer. It didn't take long for the conversation to devolve
from the future of education to who was most likely to have killed
Georgina Nash.

Dietrich, as Elisabeth had predicted, was full of theories about
who the murderer might be.

Anna Vogeler. "She should have put as much energy into her
own work as she did her husband's career and procreating offspring."

Erik Vogeler. "He should have stuck with Freud instead of being seduced by that upstart Jung, dabbling in areas he obviously didn't understand. He'd do better to spend more time figuring out what he actually believes."

Elisabeth shot an amused look at Phil.

"Now, Pietro Salvos. There is a prime example of someone who cracked under pressure and tried to take the easy, and dishonest, way out."

And Chumley. "Once a clown, always a clown," Dietrich proclaimed, and closed the case on who might have wanted Georgie dead.

About the victim herself, he was less forthcoming. "Who knows? None of us have had contact with her. We don't even know what she's been up to these last years. She may have kept unsavory company. Jumping out of trees the way I was told she did before we arrived. As if she were a common psychopath, not a physician. We may never know. But certainly, none of us killed her."

Rose he dismissed with a wave of his hand.

Further than that, he refused to speculate, preferring to talk about his own theories, and soon the two women made their excuses and left him to pontificate to the now solely male clientele at McLaughlin's Tavern.

15

"Dietrich is a pompous ass," Elisabeth said. (Somewhere during the second whiskey they had agreed to call each other by their first names.) "I forget just how pompous until I see him with a new audience. Already old-fashioned and out of step. But like so many men enamored by their own situation, he will adhere to those theories long after Dr. Freud has moved on to newer theories, leaving his devout followers to argue over things he no longer even believes."

"But you put up with him."

"The devil you know. Besides, I've gotten used to him. He's the quintessential Freudian. Repressed, Oedipal, and narcissistic. But, if you're wondering . . . not so much so that he would resort to murder. Besides, he was standing right next to me when the shot was fired."

Elisabeth stopped in the middle of the sidewalk. "I don't know why you're really delving into this so deeply. I suspect you are more than you let on." She held up her hand. "Do not worry. I don't intend to delve into your psyche to figure out why. I gave all that up long ago. But I would give you some advice."

Phil, who had stopped to face her, was thrown a little off her game. "And I would take it . . . probably."

"Everyone was in plain sight when Georgie was killed. It doesn't mean that one of us wasn't behind her murder."

"And do you have someone in mind?"

"I do not. I could say at least I didn't do it. Though I wouldn't expect you to believe me. In fact, I would be disappointed if you did. But I'll also say that unless it was some unsavory acquaintance of Georgie's, which seems doubtful, I would look at one of us as the moving force. I suppose we all were annoyed by her at one time or another. But enough to kill? Who knows? Most of us haven't even seen her in years, if we can be believed, which you would also be a fool to do."

"I don't intend to rule anyone out at this point."

"Then you *are* investigating," she said, her voice tinged with subdued triumph.

"Yes, and I would hope you would keep that to yourself."

"Working with Detective Sergeant Atkins?"

"Yes, though he doesn't know it."

Elisabeth laughed out loud. "Poor man. I will tell you this. You would do better to disregard the obvious. Everyone in that group—except, perhaps, Chumley—has studied the inner workings of people's minds and psyches. They can be devious. If they planned a murder, they wouldn't be found holding a smoking pistol."

"You're not suggesting some sort of mind control?" Phil asked.

"I'm not suggesting anything, except to keep an open mind. My rooms are down this street. There's a taxi stand on Broadway."

"One last thing," Phil said. "No one seems to know where the Nashes lived or if they have family."

"Like I said, no one even knew they were in town. Their parents are long dead. Georgie, being several years older, has taken care of Rose since she was a child. Good luck."

"Will I see you at Chumley Griswold's wake tomorrow?" Phil asked.

"But of course. I wish I hadn't seen any of them. But now that I have, I can't stay away."

On the ride back to the Plaza, Phil thought about what Elisabeth said as they stood on the street, that she would do better to disregard the obvious. Which made her think of Preswick's favorite detective, Sherlock Holmes, saying, "There's nothing more deceptive than the obvious fact."

And what if the obvious facts weren't even the actual facts?

A puzzle within a puzzle? Or a puzzle completely outside its box? Everyone had expected Erik Vogeler to be the target, and yet Georgina Nash was dead.

Unfortunately, the picture seemed no clearer than it had been before. Phil wondered if Atkins was having any better luck.

By the time she reached her apartments, Phil was tired and hungry, and the effects of the whiskey had begun to wear off, leaving her with a dull headache.

"Good evening, my lady," Preswick said, and took her purse. "Mr. Bennington telephoned with his apologies. He's held up in meetings out on Long Island and won't return until later this evening."

"Aeroplane business."

"Yes, my lady. And Mrs.—"

"Just as well. I've had a tiring day." She stopped at the hall mirror to unpin her hat. She looked ghastly. Maybe an early night would be in order. "Could you ring for some dinner? I'm famished."

"There are sandwiches and tea cakes in the parlor."

"Excellent. You anticipated me."

"Yes, my lady, and Mrs.—"

"Phil! Did you miss me?" Bev Reynolds appeared in the archway to the parlor, gin and tonic in hand.

"—Reynolds is in the parlor," Preswick continued without a hiccup.

Phil dropped her hat on the foyer table. "Bev, I thought you were going directly to Sheepshead Bay for the next races."

"I was, but most of the boys have taken the two-year-olds back to the farm and the others won't arrive in Sheepshead until tomorrow. Bobby and some of the jockeys are staying in Coney Island for some fun. I meant to stay, too, but to tell you the truth, I was bored without you—and dying of curiosity."

"You drove all the way back to town because you were bored? It's wretchedly hot and everyone who can be is out of town."

"Spill, Phil. I want to know what Godfrey Bennington wanted. And what you're up to. I've been scanning the newspapers, but I came up with nothing but some poor woman getting shot in Central Park during an attempted robbery. So you can't be—" Bev sucked in a breath. "No-o-o. She wasn't even dead when you received your telegram."

"Well, I'm . . ." Phil hadn't even managed to move out of the foyer when Preswick, who *had* managed that feat, reappeared at her elbow with a gin and tonic, a drink that was having a rebirth that summer.

"Investigating. I knew it! But how is she involved with God-frey Bennington? Not something with the War Department. Is it? My goodness. Is that why you're being so mum?"

"I'm not being mum," Phil said. "I'd tell you, but you haven't let me get in a word edgewise. Preswick, I think I will opt for cof-fee instead of gin."

Preswick bowed and left them.

Phil went straight into the parlor, where she put down her drink and picked up one of the delicate tea sandwiches that Monsieur Lapparraque did so well. Not terribly substantial, but delicious.

"Shall I call Marty?" Bev continued, following her into the room. "She'd die for a story like this."

"No! Absolutely not," Phil said.

"My lips are sealed. But I can help. What do you want me to do?"

"To begin with, sit down."

Bev's face fell.

"Just for now there is nothing to do. That's pretty much what I'm doing. Godfrey needed me to be his hostess for a dinner party. Pure and simple."

Well, not so simple, perhaps, but she had no intention of giving away what might turn out to be government secrets to anyone—especially to Bev, who was an ebullient partner in action but some-what indiscreet when secrecy was required.

"How were the races yesterday?" Phil asked.

She let Bev ramble on while she assuaged her hunger, which also went a long way to relieving her headache.

By the time Preswick entered with coffeepot and cups, she was feeling more like herself.

Bev wrinkled her nose. "Coffee?"

"I've spent my afternoon in an Irish pub," Phil told her. "I need my wits about me."

Preswick poured out the coffee and Phil gratefully took the cup.

Bev drained her glass and reached for Phil's untouched one.

"This hits the spot," Phil said, just as the mantel clock struck six. "Preswick, I think Lily has spent enough time reading to the invalid today. Please ring Union House and have them send her home. But request them to put her in a taxi just in case Ivan has been skulking around again. I don't want to take a chance of any more run-ins. Mrs. Vogeler says he suffers from trauma from battle and he might be dangerous."

"I believe that the condition is not an uncommon plight with soldiers," Preswick said. "It can be quite devastating. I'll fetch Lily myself."

He left the room just as the front door burst open and Lily ran in. "I got it!" She skidded to a stop in front of the archway, saw that Phil had company, and attempted a curtsey as she turned the corner.

The affect had Phil holding her breath and Bev, after a startled intake of breath, laughing out loud. "Oh, how I've missed everyone."

"S-sorry, my lady," Lily said.

"Oh, don't mind me," Bev said. "What did you find? We're all agog with wonder."

Lily glanced at Phil and, when Phil nodded, gulped in a breath.

"Right after you left, that nosy maid came in again and wouldn't leave until Mrs. Vogeler returned. When she did, they sent for me to help Nanny Cole with those children. They went to the zoo." She wrinkled her nose.

Preswick cleared his throat before Lily could inform them of what she thought about the children—or the zoo.

"Well, we'd just gotten them in the bath when they called me back again. Rose—Miss Nash had had another episode, though . . . Anyway, I couldn't get away until now, but—"

"Next time," Phil said. "If there is a next time, call us to pick you up. I don't want you walking alone."

"Oh, I wasn't alone. Just a Friend hadn't left for the day and he walked me all the way to the door of the hotel, then the doorman chased him away."

Phil didn't point out that Just a Friend would hardly be an impediment to Ivan. She would just make sure that Lily was not left on her own again.

"But I got it!" Lily reached into her apron pocket and lifted out what appeared to be a business card.

"This was what was hidden in Rose's purse lining?" Phil asked, taking the card from Lily.

Bev scooted over to breathe over her shoulder.

"'The Oddity Shop,'" Phil read. "'Arcana, Amulets, Hypnotism, Panaceas.'" It was printed in a medieval script and decorated with a symbol: a full circle with a series of half arcs radiating from the circumference.

"It's like a sun with eyelashes," Lily said. "But why did Rose hide it?"

"I don't know," Phil said. "Perhaps so it wouldn't fall out accidently?" Or in case someone searched her purse. Rose's purse had been unusually empty for a young lady's. Phil had thought so at the time.

But she was beginning to see a larger picture. Or in this case, a completed picture. If she wasn't mistaken . . .

Phil looked up at Preswick. He flicked a glance at Bev.

"True blue," Bev said. "Cross my heart." And put the actions to the words.

Preswick turned on his heel and left the room. He returned moments later with a sheet of paper. He moved the sandwiches off the table, wiped it off with his handkerchief, then put the paper down.

"What is it?" Bev asked, barely above a whisper.

"A sketch of the clue found at the scene of the crime. Only half of this design was embroidered on a handkerchief."

"And this is the complete symbol." Phil placed the card next to the scrap.

"It is," Lily whispered. "It is the same. Look, Mr. Preswick."

"Indeed," Preswick said.

"But what was it doing in Rose's purse?" Phil said.

"Oh my," Bev said. She sat up straighter. "Who is Rose? A clue to what? Are you going to tell me what the crime is, now?"

"Yes, but it will have to wait."

"Why? What are you planning?"

"I have a sudden desire to have my fortune read."

"Not at The Oddity Shop."

"At The Oddity Shop."

"You're not," Bev wailed. "Look at the address."

"Mermaid Avenue. Coney Island. I know. It's unfortunate you that you already left. I could have telephoned your hotel and asked you to go investigate. Preswick, call round to the garage and have them send over the Daimler immediately. You and Lily change into your mufti, you're both coming, too. This may be the clue that we needed to break the case."

"I'll come, too," Bev said. "And you can fill me in on the crime and all the suspects and motives on the way."

"But you just drove all the way back from Coney Island."

"Which is just why I won't be left out now. Besides, my Packard is parked right downstairs. And I know the way to Mermaid Street."

16

It was after seven when the lights of Coney Island finally appeared on the horizon. Phil had spent the ride filling in Bev—at the top of her lungs—on the who, what, and where of the murder. And speculating about what they might find when they got to The Oddity Shop.

"I hope I haven't brought you on a wild goose chase," Phil called over the roar of the engine. "The shop may be closed."

"I doubt it," Bev called back. "The parks don't close before midnight and I imagine everyone else stays open to take advantage of the last-minute rush to buy things."

Bev turned onto Surf Avenue, the wide main thoroughfare that ran along the entrances to the individual parks and hotels. To one side of them, a forest of iron and steel pleasure rides and attractions rose like a magical kingdom; on the other, shops and eateries and vendors of every sort beckoned to the crowd. And what a crowd. The sidewalk and street teemed with revelers of all ages.

They'd gone less than two blocks when Bev slammed on the brakes, and a horde of people—dressed in work clothes or beach clothes, carrying bags and parasols, and all excited—rushed across the street in both directions.

"Train must have just gotten in," Bev said, and drummed her fingernails on the steering wheel.

"Is Mermaid Avenue nearby?" Phil asked, feeling suddenly anxious to get the job done.

"It runs parallel to this one," Bev said. "I'll turn off Surf as soon as I can."

Phil looked over her shoulder to Preswick and Lily. Lily's head was cocked back, her mouth opened in amazement as she turned from one side of the street to the other. It looked like a pleasure outing was in the cards for her little family. Maybe they could bring Just a Friend along with them.

Preswick was also looking, but straight ahead. "I believe there is a cross street up ahead, my lady," he called over the engine.

Bev saw an opening in the crowd and the Packard shot forward. Half a block later they turned onto Sixteenth Street.

The crowd was less dense here, but was still migrating toward the amusement parks and their many allures.

This street was lined with brick houses and wooden bunga-lows, small hotels and eateries not in the best state of repair. A few shops offered cheap souvenirs. Sign upon sign advertised what was inside the stores and what waited in the major attrac-tions nearby.

At the end of the block, they turned onto Mermaid Avenue, and any semblance of family entertainment vanished. The souvenir stores were replaced by everyday needs: butchers, bakeries, hard-ware stores, and tobacconists.

Wooden houses and brick apartment buildings squeezed to-gether as if holding each other up. Electric lines draped from pole to pole along the sidewalk, some sagging precariously close to the heads of passersby. Open bars spilled customers onto the street, who in turn spilled their beers over each other.

"This is what I was afraid of," Bev said. "Not the most salu-brious of neighborhoods. Though not the worst, either, I guess."

Phil was thinking the same thing, and for the life of her she couldn't begin to imagine why Rose Nash had hidden the Odd-ity Shop card in her purse lining. Not as a souvenir, surely. Phil doubted if a tourist would venture here.

They slowed down when they neared Seventeenth Street. The surroundings, if anything, seemed even less inviting: a jumble of buildings, saloons, tenements, and questionable hotels.

Bev pulled to the side and exchanged looks with Phil. "Shall I make the turn and slowly cruise down the street, while you look for the shop?"

"It's there," Lily said, and pointed between them down the street. "Next to the hotel on the corner."

Phil saw the hotel. Next to it, separated from it by what might be a narrow alley, was a three-story brick building. And next to it, a bungalow that reminded Phil of the one in the Nick Carter story, but appearing uninhabited.

She looked back at the brick building. The first-floor storefront must be The Oddity Shop, though how Lily could know this in the waning light was impressive. For herself, she needed a closer look.

"Everyone stay here; I don't want to call attention by driving a yellow auto slowly in front of it."

"We'll all go," Bev said.

"No, you need to guard the Packard." Phil started to get out.

"My lady, wait," Preswick said. "I will go and inquire."

"About getting hypnotized," Lily suggested helpfully. She wasn't at all humbled by the stern look he shot her.

"I will do the inquiring," Phil said. "But thank you. I'll be careful."

Preswick sat back, his face expressionless. Though, after their long history together, Phil had come to recognize the meaning of every one of his blank butler looks, and this was his disgruntled face. The dear man.

Phil got out and, opening the clasp of her handbag to be closer to her pistol, she lifted her skirts and picked her way to the shop window.

Gold lettering arched across the top of the glass, but it was so old and flaking that Phil could barely make out the words. But the symbol below was large and clear enough to see. A large gold circle with radiating arcs. The same sign as the one on the torn linen in the park, and on the card they'd found in Rose's purse, which was now residing in Phil's.

And beneath that: OCCULT AND ARCANA INTERESTS. HYPNOTISM AND TAROT. POTIONS OF ALL KINDS. And in the lowest corner of the glass: PROPRIETOR C. GRISWOLD.

Phil stared. C. . . . Chumley? Chumley Griswold? It had to be. But how was it possible that Chumley Griswold owned this derelict shop? The dapper, eccentric man with his supposedly sumptuous brownstone and his successful career as entertainer to the upper class?

The window was darkened with a green baize half curtain secreting the things inside. There was a dusty book of magic and a pack of tarot cards spread across the window display shelf, and a heavy necklace of questionable metal with a large pendant with scribbling engraved on it. Surely worthless, or it wouldn't have been left in the window.

And if it was true that no one knew of the Nashes' whereabouts, how did it happen that Rose Nash had Chumley's card?

Phil was aware that coincidence sometimes played a part in the real world, but she didn't believe it in this circumstance.

Besides, she didn't have time for coincidences. She needed a lead. Chumley Griswold had to be involved. At least with the Nashes. Unfortunately, she couldn't very well walk in and confront him.

A chill ran up the back of her neck and she whirled around. Bev waved encouragingly from the Packard. No one else seemed to be paying Phil any mind, but she was getting a creeping feeling that she was being watched.

Merely nerves, she told herself, and pulled her bag closer.

She stepped toward the door and peered in the glass. The shop looked totally deserted. She tried the door handle. Locked. Then she noticed the sheet of paper taped on the glass: BACK AT EIGHT.

A good thirty minutes before he or whoever worked here returned. She took a few more seconds to look around and, seeing nothing of any use, returned to the others.

"No one was there, but it's Chumley Griswold's shop."

Bev chewed her bottom lip, thinking. "He's the one that . . ."

"The party-entertaining ex-chemist," Phil supplied.

"Let's see, he's the weird-looking one with the hair?" Bev added.

Phil nodded. "He won't be back until eight. If you don't mind waiting."

"I don't, but I think we should go get Bobby. He's probably just leaving the stables now. We have plenty of time to get there and back."

"If you think it's necessary," Phil said.

"Oh, I do," said Bev. She lifted her chin, and Phil saw the four hulking men—Phil could hardly call them gentlemen—who were making a beeline toward the Packard.

Bev gunned the motor and the Packard shot away, leaving the four men staring after them.

Phil breathed a sigh of relief. Having Bobby Mullins with them seemed like an excellent idea.

"If he isn't at the track," Bev said, "he's probably at the hotel. They're staying at the Pabst. It's right across the street. Convenient, even though it does have a dance hall attached to it. But, Lord, there isn't a place in Coney Island that isn't a temptation."

Bev turned back onto to Surf Avenue, maneuvering around pedestrians and other vehicles with ease. The sea air was bracing, even though Phil couldn't actually see the water, since the view was blocked by souvenir stores, arcades, and the exotic façades of Steeplechase, Luna Park, and Dreamland. As they drove past each fanciful gateway, she caught glimpses of towers and giant wheels, serpentines and mountains, thrill rides and sideshows. And everywhere, people.

They inched their way forward, while street vendors enticed the crowd with edible delights, and men and boys hawked tickets, running in between the traffic to ply their goods.

Along the street, every façade was covered with colorful promises. THE LAST DAYS OF POMPEII. THE INEXHAUSTIBLE COW. TRIP TO THE NORTH POLE. WILD MEN OF BORNEO. One more fantastic than the other, until Lily was practically hanging out of the auto in excitement.

"Look! Look!" Lily cried, as they passed a man in a top hat walking on stilts. A signboard hung about his neck, a picture of a wurst sandwich printed the front.

Phil smiled back at her. "Very exciting, isn't it?" A trip to Coney Island was definitely in the cards.

"No. I mean that poster back there. The girl on it was Rose. At least, it looked just like her."

Phil nodded. Every third poster had a picture of a beautiful young girl. "Was she an acrobat? Or a dancing girl?"

Lily had corkscrewed herself around to catch a last glimpse of a clue she must have conjured in her desire to help her new . . . dare Phil say . . . friend? Lily had certainly taken a liking to Rose Nash.

She snapped back to the front. "It looked just like her." She huffed out a sigh and leaned back against the seat. "It really did."

A few minutes later, the Packard finally shot past a building advertising the reenactment of the Galveston flood and onto an even wider avenue that ended suddenly at the water and an incredible view of the ocean.

Phil breathed in the air before the avenue jibed at a sharp angle past a grand hotel. A few minutes later they arrived at the horse entrance of the racetrack.

Bobby and several stable boys were just exiting. Phil saw his carrot-red hair even though it was partially concealed by a cloth cap.

He stopped. The others stopped behind him; they all pulled off their caps and waited while Bobby came over to the car, attempting to smooth down his wiry hair that even copious amounts of brilliantine couldn't tame in the ocean air.

"Miz Reynolds. I thought you was going back to the city."

"I did, but something's come up. I hate to spoil your evening, but I need to borrow you for a little while."

"Whatever it is, I'm your man." Bobby glanced over to Phil, and she wondered how he would address her today. He never seemed to remember the right order of words. "Good evening, Miz Countess, and, um, Miss Lily, and you, too, Mr. Preswick." He leaned in confidentially. "I just don't want to get too far from the boys. They know how to have fun and sometimes too much, if you know what I mean."

"It's only for an hour, probably," Bev said. "Just down the street."

Bobby scratched his head, unleashing a sprig of hair.

"On Seventeenth and Mermaid Avenue."

"Miz Reynolds, there ain't nothin' you need to do down that way. You go any farther and you're in bad territory."

"That's why we need you." Bev shrugged her shoulders in excitement. "We're on a mission."

"Aw, Miz Reynolds." He'd addressed Bev but he shot a sideward glance at Phil. "What have you two gone and gotten yourselves into now?"

"We'll tell you all about it on the drive over," Bev said. "The sign said he'll be back at eight."

"Who?"

"We'll tell you that, too."

He tugged at his collarless work shirt. "I better change first."

"No need. We don't mind a little *eau de stable,* do we, Phil?"

"Not at all," Phil agreed. "Climb in, we don't want to be late."

Bobby looked skeptical. Though he had trimmed down from

working at the stable, he'd also acquired muscle, and it was a tight squeeze. Preswick moved next to Lily, who made herself as small as possible. Bobby stuffed his cap onto his head and climbed in.

"I gotta bad feeling about this," Bobby said, as Bev pulled to a stop near, but not too near, The Oddity Shop. "Hey, you, beat it!" He shook his fist at a boy who'd come up to check out the Packard.

"This is not the kind of place you want to come to, Miz Reynolds. You don't even want to know what goes on in the neighborhoods around here."

"What does go on?" asked Phil.

"If it's illegal, it goes on."

"So why would someone have a shop here? Especially one in the arcane arts?"

"Beats me," Bobby said, scanning the street. "I'm not even sure what that is," he admitted. "Like crystal balls, and hocus-pocus stuff?"

He said all this while constantly taking in his surroundings, something he'd been doing since they'd arrived. Even the people on the streets seemed to be in a hurry to get inside.

Though Phil could still see the sun as it moved closer to the rooftops, none of its light seemed to penetrate the street, and dusk descended.

She glanced at her lapel watch. Almost eight.

"If you don't mind me asking," Bobby said, "what are you planning to do when this guy gets back?"

"I'm not sure," Phil admitted. "I just wanted to see what this place was and why Ro—our friend had his card in her purse. But since we're here . . ."

"You don't want to go and do anything, beggin' your pardon, stupid."

"No, but I need answers. The police are looking for the wrong man. It's imperative we find the right one. I'll just go in as a customer. Oh, damnation. If it's Chumley himself, he'll recognize me—"

"My lady, I adjure you . . ."

"Mr. Preswick and I will go in," Lily volunteered.

"None of you can go into that shop," Bobby said. "I bet you money that no one like you ever comes to that shop. They don't never come to this neighborhood and if they get lost and are lucky to leave it again, they do so rid of a few possessions."

Slowly, one by one, they all turned to look at Bobby.

"Even people like me don't go in there. They'd pick me out as a bleater, for sure; you'd have to borrow a gunnysack to carry my pieces back to the farm for burial if they didn't drop me in the river first."

Phil raised her eyes at Bev.

"An informer," Bev enlightened her.

"Well, we can't have that," Phil said. She looked across the street to the shop. "If nobody who would be interested in esoterica and parlor tricks would ever come here, why would he have a shop here? It doesn't look like it has even a modicum of security. Anyone could just break a window and grab whatever they wanted. I doubt if anyone would even notice."

"If there ain't a big killer dog waiting inside. And if he's paying for protection, then . . . Nah, who would even be interested in that stuff? It's gotta be a front." Bobby nodded, pleased with his conclusion. "And if he ain't selling hoodoo in there, what's he selling?" Bobby pulled off his cap, scratched his head, then shoved the cap back on.

"What kind of front?" Phil asked.

"Don't know. Probably best not to."

In the distance, the sun slipped behind the roofs of Coney Island. Dusk blanketed the surrounding shanties and buildings. A few unbroken streetlamps tried to dispel the gloom as shadows began to move along the street.

Phil felt Bobby lean forward, tense and aware. She glanced back at Lily and Preswick, both alert, and she wondered if she was being totally irresponsible to put them in such apparent danger.

And then she saw him, scurrying along the street, not like a man who lived on the posh Upper East Side, but more like a creature of the night.

"Gorn, is his hair red," Bobby expelled on a breath of surprise. "Redder than mine. And it's almost dark."

On his words, the final hint of sun snuffed itself out like a candle. There were a few rectangles of stingy light in the nearby houses and businesses, and a tiara of radiance in the distance, where the amusement parks were still crowded.

And in between . . . darkness.

Mermaid Avenue could have been another city, another country, another world.

Chumley was bent over, carrying something under one arm. Something heavy? He stopped at the door of his shop, looked quickly around the street.

Inside the Packard, no one moved, just slumped down in their seats as if that would keep them from being seen.

Then in one quick sleight of hand, Chumley unlocked the door and slipped inside. The door closed behind him. A minute later, a low glow made its way over the baize window curtain.

"Now what do we do?" Bev said.

"Is that who we're waiting for?" Bobby asked in a whisper.

"Partly," Phil said. "I want to see if anyone else comes." Though she couldn't imagine who. She doubted if any of his former colleagues knew about this side of Chumley Griswold.

This had to be important. And to be honest, it wasn't like she had anything else.

"Shit, duck!" Simultaneously with his warning, Bobby lunged forward, clapped his hands on the tops of Bev's and Phil's heads, and pushed them down in the seat, out of sight. Phil didn't dare look back to see if Preswick and Lily were safely tucked away.

She didn't know what or whom they were hiding from and was afraid to look. She was scrunched up, half on the floor and half on the seat. She heard Bev breathing close by, saw the top of Bobby's head, cap pulled down to his ears, appear over the seat.

His eyes clocked back and forth. "I'll be da—I'll just be," he breathed, keeping his eyes focused on something Phil couldn't see.

"What is it?"

"Who," Bobby said. "It's Louie the Lump, as I live and breathe."

"Who's that?" Phil eased up enough to peer over the dashboard and saw a skinny, hunched-over figure—wearing a shapeless suit and looking guilty of everything Phil ever imagined—go into the store.

"You don't want to know," Bobby said, not taking his eye off Louie as he slipped into Chumley's shop.

"I need to know," Phil insisted.

"Aw, Gawd. He's somebody that oughta be in jail. I thought he was in jail. He just snuffed Kid Twist Zwerbach and Cyclone Louie in front of the whole world over some dame. Pardon my French, over a lady friend."

"What do you think he would be doing here?"

"Nothing good."

"Perhaps you could elaborate," Phil suggested.

"Depends on what this Chumley fella's selling. Or maybe twisting his arm for protection money. Which don't make sense. I don't think he could even be selling anything legal outta there. Nobody would even come down this street except by mistake and they'd get out as soon as they figure out where they aren't. Maybe hooch or dope? Could be a drop-off point. I'm thinkin' they're not in there to buy books or . . . love potions, maybe?"

Phil frowned at him. He looked completely serious.

"Hell—heck, your 'ness, it's Coney Island. People'll buy anything here. And Louie was in love. Or so he said."

Further conversation about Louie the Lump's love life was cut short when the shop door opened again and Louie came out.

"That didn't take long," Bev said.

"'Cause he either got what he wanted and it's underneath his jacket, or else he got rid of what he didn't want and it ain't."

"Dare we find out?" Phil asked, reaching for the door but hoping Bobby would stop her.

Bobby didn't have to.

As they watched Louie the Lump slip into the night, another figure stepped out of the shadows and followed him into the darkness.

Phil held her breath, willing herself to see who it was and if it was someone she knew, aka Mr. X or John Atkins, but she couldn't tell, and soon they'd both disappeared around the corner.

Friend or foe, she wondered about the second man, who obviously had been waiting for Louie or watching the shop or both.

She was so intent on Louie that she almost missed a third man who came from the opposite direction, his hat pulled low over his brow, the shadows preventing a good view of his face.

Phil expected him to follow the other man after Louie the Lump, but he didn't. He stopped at the door to the shop, took a quick look around. Then he opened the door and slipped inside.

Another customer? Someone picking up what Louie had just left? Or even taking it by force? Suddenly, the possibilities seemed endless, and more sinister.

"I need a closer look," Phil said. This time Bobby stopped her by the expediency of grabbing the back of her shirtwaist.

"Beggin' your pardon," he hissed. "But you'd best leave the lookin' to me."

"Okay, but I'm coming, too."

"No, you ain't . . . your countess-ship."

"We'll all go," said Bev, and started to open her door.

"Halt!" Bobby ordered, making them all jump.

"Shh," they chorused together.

Bobby's face looked like it might erupt. He pulled his cap off his head and twisted it in both hands. Phil imagined someone's neck in those beefy fingers. At last he said, "Mr. Preswick, do you know how to drive an automobile?"

"I do not."

"Then you and Lily stay here to protect Miz Reynolds. Her lady here can go with me. But you three stay alert and be ready for a fast getaway if we give the signal."

He climbed out of the back seat, and Phil joined him on the street.

"What's the signal?" Lily demanded.

"When you see us running for our lives."

17

Phil just had time to clip her purse to the belt hook Lily had added to most of her outfits before Bobby grabbed her elbow and spirited her across the dark street.

They reached the other side just as three raucous, obviously drunk men rounded the corner. Bobby shoved her into the narrow opening between the shop building and the hotel. He slipped in front of her in an agile way that reminded her that he'd been a boxer in his younger years and might still be able to adequately take care of himself and her.

The men passed, arguing at the top of their lungs and punching each other in a cloud of beer and good humor that was bound to get out of hand before long.

They didn't slow down but wove and stumbled their way toward Surf Avenue.

"*Whew*," Phil said.

"Don't you go *whew*ing too soon," Bobby mumbled, and eased back toward the sidewalk.

He stopped at the edge of the building, holding Phil back with one arm, and eased his head past the bricks to look out.

They stood that way for an inordinate amount of time, Phil afraid to move or take a deep breath, until she was beside herself with impatience. "What's happening?"

"Shh" was all she got.

The longer they hid there, the darker the street became. If the newest "customer" didn't hurry, they wouldn't be able to see his face at all when he did finally come out.

Phil heard the door shut, but when she would have leaned forward, Bobby pushed her back. Which was a good thing, since the man walked right past them.

Bobby squeezed her arm. He didn't have to warn her. Phil had stopped breathing.

The man looked behind him, then hurried back the way he'd come. But in the brief moment he'd turned in their direction, Phil just managed to get a good look. She didn't recognize him. Smooth shaven, well featured, and well dressed, he was a far cry from the previous Louie character.

Phil scanned the street; no one stepped out of the shadows to follow this man as they had Louie the Lump. So, was this second customer merely a coincidence? As she wondered, the newcomer stepped into a taxi that must have been waiting at the side of the street.

With its lights off? Phil knew they'd been off because they nearly blinded her when they popped on again as it drove by.

Something suspicious was going on in that store, and Phil intended to find out what it was. She eased away from Bobby, who was intently watching the street, and peered down the narrow passageway that led only to deeper darkness.

She had no intention of going down that particular unknown.

But Chumley's building had two small rectangular windows several feet above their heads. They were protected by iron bars. A faint and dingy light tried to make its way out from inside. With poor effect.

But it showed her that someone—Chumley, most likely—was still in the store.

And then the lights went out, pitching them into darkness. Something rattled from behind them.

"Just rats," Bobby said, which did nothing to assuage her unease.

They pressed close to the bricks. Heard the front door open. Close. The rattling of keys, the turning of several locks, and finally the rusty creaking of a metal grate, which Phil imagined covered the front window.

Drat! Phil knew they couldn't safely pick one lock, much less several, in full view of the street. But . . . Her gaze drifted upward, where the two windows were now black rectangles, just out of reach. Maybe there was something to stand on, but she was loathe to go down that black alley to see.

She looked over to Bobby, then back up to the window.

Could he? Would he? She did a quick calculation. Their heights together were more than adequate to reach the window, though surely they were locked. And there were those inconvenient burglar bars, but she might at least be able to see inside. The windows weren't *that* far away.

Fat chance. Who ever heard of a countess, much less a dowager countess, climbing . . . Oh, but she had, years before she'd become a countess. She and Bev had been students at Madame Floret's. They'd been accidently locked in the cellar while pilfering a month's worth of fine chocolates. Phil had stood on Bev's shoulders to reach the coal chute, then climbed out and come around to let Bev out. Phil bet she could still manage it.

"Bobby."

Bobby's head swiveled toward her, followed her gaze upward. "No way you're gonna get in that window, your lady-ness."

"I need to take a look inside."

He still shook his head, but he looked up. "It's got burglar bars on it. And it's dirty, I bet. You ain't gonna see nothing in there."

"Just boost me up like you would a jockey. It will be easy. I can drop back down on my own."

Bobbly grumbled; she heard something about regret. Reluctantly, he leaned over. "Hold onto my back and put your foot in my hands," he said. "But don't expect me to pick up the pieces if you fall."

"I won't," she said blithely, something she was not feeling at all.

She pulled up her skirts. It was dark, so no immodesty was involved. Groped for his back. He slid his cupped hands under her upraised foot.

"Ready?"

"When you are."

She felt him bend his knees. She prepared to push off.

And she was springing upward. She reached to the window and grabbed onto the metal bars, scrabbling with her feet against the bricks for purchase.

There was a shudder beneath her hands, and one end of the bar swung away from the window casing.

For a perilous moment she hung from one arm.

"Come down," Bobby hissed. "I'll catch you."

Phil knew she should. But there was a chance . . . She threw her free arm up, pushed on the window with all her might. It gave, creaked, gave just a bit more, then stuck.

But she was just able to slip her hand inside and pull her body against the wall. She let go of the other end of the bars, pushed that hand inside, and clung to the sash, her feet dangling in open air.

"Bobby, stand underneath me. I need your shoulders."

"Please—Mi—"

"Hurry!"

He shot beneath her, grabbed her feet, and positioned them on his shoulders. She released one hand and heaved with all her might. The window creaked all the way open.

She scrambled over the edge, thankful for the inky night that hopefully hid her derriere and flying skirts from view. For a moment, she stuck fast, her bottom half hanging out in empty space. But she shifted and shimmied across the sill until her hands touched the floor, then she walked them away from the wall until the rest of her slid over the side and fell to the dusty floor.

She pushed to her feet, looked around, and sneezed. She went back to the window, looked down at Bobby. He was barely more than a dark shadow. But his teeth were bared.

"Can you get up, if I pull you from here?"

Bobby held up a finger, then backed away. For a second she thought he had given up. But when he was several feet away, he bent over, shot forward, running in an arch, and made it several feet up the wall. His arm darted out, and he managed to grab onto the sill.

Phil was so astounded that he started to slip back before she grabbed him by both wrists. It took both of them exerting mammoth amounts of energy and cursing before Bobby squeezed through and fell to the floor at her feet.

He stood up and shook himself.

"Now what?" asked Bobby's disembodied whisper.

"Now we'll see what we're dealing with."

"You don't dare turn on a light; what if someone sees it?"

"They won't believe their eyes." Phil reached into her purse and pulled out the rectangular case that people might be forgiven for thinking was a flask. She pressed the switch and a dull beam of light shot into the darkness.

"Well, gorn, it's one of them Ever Readys," Bobby said. "You do think of everything your . . . ness."

"One can but try," Phil said, and swept the dim light around the room.

They were in a square room that contained several sparsely filled bookshelves and several display cases, also rather bare of things to sell. It was all very dusty.

Bobby nodded, his head looking eerie in the Ever Ready's beam. "A front," he said.

She cast the light around, looked behind the cabinets for a cashbox or sales book, but found nothing. There was, however, a door at the back of the room.

Phil hurried toward it, turned the knob. "Unlocked," she exclaimed. And opened the door to a set of stairs leading upward. "Look, Bobby. What do you think is up here? A storage room? A contraband depository?" She started up the stairs.

Bobby hurried behind her. "You can't go up there. What if he comes back? We'll be trapped."

The stair creaked beneath her foot.

"At least we'll hear him coming," Phil said, and hurried up the rest of the flight. She heard Bobby groan, then his heavier footsteps following her up.

They both paused when they reached the top.

"Good heavens," Phil breathed, shining the Ever Ready around. A long, high table was set up with microscopes, beakers, Bunsen burners, bottles, mortars, and pestles. On a shelf behind it, rows of vials and jars were lined up like in an apothecary, a sight Phil remembered from science class at Madame Floret's. She and Bev had once tried to make their own whiskey in the bottles pilfered from the lab room.

Nearby a smaller table held several books, notebooks, and scattered papers. And beyond it, a glass cabinet was filled with more vials, already filled and labeled.

"It's a laboratory," Phil said, just as her flashlight went out. That was the annoying thing with this clever invention: the light just didn't last very long.

She felt her way over to the worktable. Pressed on the light again. Someone—Chumley?—was doing experiments. For his entertainments? A few colorful poofs and crackles to heighten the excitement?

But Phil rather doubted it. You could buy those kinds of tricks from various and sundry novelty stores. No, she suspected that they had just discovered the source of Chumley's purported lavish lifestyle.

"Can you tell what any of these mixtures are?" Phil whispered.

Bobby picked up one beaker, sniffed it. Started to put his finger in down the neck of the bottle.

"Don't!" Phil said. "It might be poisonous. Or a love potion."

Bobby quickly returned the beaker to the table. Picked up another and gave it a whiff.

After two more attempts, he shook his head. "Don't smell like any dope I recognize. Uh, I keep up on these things 'cause of people doping horses and stuff."

"Only natural," Phil said.

She looked over the array of vials, and for a second, she contemplated trying to steal some of the mixtures to show Mr. X or Atkins, or Godfrey. But she doubted the glass would survive the return trip out the window. She would have to be content to report it and leave it to others to do the rest.

She started to turn, but Bobby stopped her. Put a finger to his lips. Then she heard it. The snick of several locks right below them. Footsteps striding across the wooden floor.

She turned inquiring—and maybe just a little panicked—eyes to Bobby, who jerked his head toward the back of the room. They sped toward what appeared to be a cupboard. Phil's skirt caught the edge of the table and something rolled across the floor.

Bobby reached the door. It was a shallow closet filled with papers, boxes, and cleaning equipment. Bobby pushed her inside and climbed in after her.

They stood so close she could hear Bobby swallow as the footsteps came up the stairs. Stopped at the top.

Was he looking around for intruders? Had he heard them? Had he turned on the light? Phil didn't even dare turn her head to see.

Something ran across her foot and she bit back a gasp, then held her breath.

It seemed an eternity while the sounds of activity just outside the closet door kept them still as statues. Then finally the footsteps receded down the stairs. And Phil let out her breath.

Bobby's grip on her person didn't relax, and she wasn't about to move until Bobby told her to. And she thanked her lucky stars for his checkered past, and his reformation to become Bev's loyal right-hand man.

They waited until they heard the door being locked again downstairs. Waited, still listening, for any other sounds of someone still inside.

Bobby eased his elbow out of Phil's ribs and opened the cupboard door, then practically fell out of the confined space. Phil came out more slowly, every ounce of her quaking like blancmange.

Bobby didn't stop to explain, just grabbed her wrist and pulled her toward the stairs. "Stay!" he commanded, which she did, showing just how rattled they both were.

Bobby crept down the stairs, keeping close to the rail to minimize the creaking of the treads. When he reached the bottom, he looked quickly around, then motioned her to hurry.

Phil flew down the steps without a mind to the noise. She'd barely reached the floor before Bobby was pulling her toward the window.

He eased the window open, cautiously peered out, then stuck his head completely out of it and looked around.

"Come on, your ladyship, down you go."

Phil was so astonished that he'd actually managed to say "ladyship" that she didn't move at once.

"You just get your bottom half out and I'll hold your arms and lower you to the ground. You'll have a bit of a jump down. Just don't break anything, we're gonna make a run for it."

Phil nodded, lifted her skirts, and threw one leg over the windowsill. First her dinner gown getting stuck on her tiara and now her skirt hiked up to her knees in order to climb in and out of a window. Her mother would be appalled.

The sheer thought gave her strength, and she hoisted her second leg after the first.

She shimmied her feet and legs out of the window until she was balanced half in and half out, reversing the process of her entry. Bobby took her arms and she slid down the outside wall. When Bobby could reach no further without falling out after her, he let go. She dropped the last few feet to the ground without mishap.

Bobby scrambled out of the window and, hanging from forearm and elbows, he closed the window and pushed back the bars in a semblance of where they'd been, then dropped to the ground beside Phil.

They didn't hesitate but headed toward the street, Bobby leading the way.

He slowed long enough to check the street, then trundled her across the sidewalk toward the Packard.

They only made it a few feet.

A drunk appeared around the corner and staggered down the street toward them, singing at the top of his lungs as he wove first one way, then the other in a dizzy parody of a dance. When Phil hesitated, Bobby pulled her away.

She heard the Packard's engine rev up as the drunk sang, "Waltzing Matilda, wa-a-altzing . . ." He twirled past Bobby and neatly scooped Phil from Bobby's grasp. "Wa-a-a-altzing Mati-i-i-i-lda," he crooned as Bobby danced around them like the prize fighter he used to be. But the drunk was a smooth operator and danced her out of Bobby's reach.

"Waltzing—" He broke off long enough to whisper, "Don't talk to anyone about this before you talk to me." "—ilda," he screeched off-key. "You'll come a—"

Bobby made a grab for her, but somehow managed only to grab air, and the "drunk" whisked her around and down the street. "Did you touch anything?"

"No. Only the bars broke, but Bobby put them back."

"—Mathilda with me."

And suddenly she was spinning by herself, and the drunk wove away, caterwauling into the night.

The Packard screeched to a stop beside her.

Bobby threw Phil into the front seat and jumped in the back without bothering to open the door.

They sped off down an empty street. And even though Phil searched the shadows, there was no sign of the drunk.

"I just about had a heart attack when Chumley came back," Bev yelled over the engine. "I was ready to come fight for you, but Preswick's cooler head prevailed. Which is a good thing or Chumley would have seen us on his way out again. But that drunk was the final straw, even for Mr. Preswick."

"Did you discover any clues?" Lily asked.

Phil just shrugged. She looked into the back seat, where Bobby was still huffing from exertion and their narrow escape.

"I think maybe I did, Lily. But I'm not certain what it means." Phil sat back, glad to be in the fresh ocean air after the dust and chemical odor of Chumley's workshop.

John Atkins would definitely want to be apprised about this night's work. She would have to tell him about what had occurred. Well, perhaps not all of it. Not until she met with Mr. X and learned how this all fit into the murder of Georgina Nash.

"I hope you're not planning on doing this again anytime soon," Bobby said. "We got important races coming up and we're running a practice trial tomorrow. And . . ." He held up both hands. "I don't want to know the particulars of what we did tonight, or why. If I don't know, I won't crack under the third degree. Detective Sergeant Atkins is not gonna be happy about this. I got a feeling the other one ain't gonna be happy either."

The other one. Mr. X.

Phil most avidly agreed.

They dropped Bobby off outside the Pabst hotel dance hall.

He climbed out of the car much more slowly than he'd jumped in a few minutes before. He was probably feeling the strain of the evening. Phil knew she was. Muscles she hadn't used in years, or maybe ever, were screaming for a hot bath and a gin and tonic.

"Thank you, Bobby," Phil said. "You went beyond the call of duty tonight. And I appreciate it."

Bobby leaned both hands against the doorframe. "Always glad to help out where I can, but I better go check on the boys now. You ladies promise me, no more shenanigans tonight."

"Oh, Bobby," said Bev, who had sat in the car while they were scaling walls and hiding in cupboards. "Where's your sense of adventure?"

"These days, I save that for the track, Miz Reynolds. Now, I don't want to know nothing about what you're up to, or why we did what we did tonight. I just want you to promise me you won't go about doing anything else down here." He looked from Bev to Phil, then shot a commiserating look back to Preswick. "At least not without getting me first. Gawd, I don't know why you do these things, horses oughta be enough."

"We do them for Phil," Bev said. "We owe her, Bobby."

Phil try to demur, but Bobby cut her off.

"Yeah, I know we do. That's why I'm telling you don't go down here nowhere on your own. If I'm not at the track, one of the boys will know where to find me. And don't go asking questions of nobody—and I mean, nobody. You never know who you're talkin' to down here, or who's paying 'em."

He doffed his hat to Lily and Preswick, then to Bev and Phil, and with a quick look around the street—a habit Phil was certain he'd picked up during his former days of dealing with thugs, criminals, and ne'er-do-wells—he strode toward the entrance of the dance hall.

As he reached it, the door banged open and two men flew through the air and landed sprawled in the street.

"And stay out," yelled a giant of a man who stood in the doorway, massive feet apart, his thick arms crossed over the apron tied around his middle.

The men scrambled on all fours until they gained their feet, then ran off down the street.

"Evenin', Little Maurice." Bobby doffed his cap at the man, stuck it in his back pocket, and went inside.

18

By the time they arrived back at the Plaza, it was late and Phil was hoarse from recounting her adventure with Bobby over the thrum of the car engine.

Bev dropped Phil, Preswick, and Lily off, invited herself to join Phil at Chumley's soiree the coming evening, and took herself home to a much deserved sleep.

It was almost dawn before Phil was awakened by the sound of her bedroom door opening.

She automatically reached for the bedside lamp.

A hand closed over her wrist before she could complete the task.

"Oh, it *is* you," she said, on a jaw-cracking yawn. She could but try; one day she might even beat him to the light.

"You were expecting someone else?"

"No, we need to talk," she said, finally rousing herself from a deep slumber.

She heard faint rustling, then he pulled the covers back and climbed into bed. "I don't have much time."

"Truer words, but business first. What are you up to? Why are you still in New York? Atkins is halfway to believing that you murdered Georgina Nash. He probably has men out combing the city for you. What if he starts asking problematic questions?"

"You haven't told him about me."

"Of course not, but it makes it very difficult. I can't believe that I'm not obstructing the law by holding out on him. I haven't even told him about The Oddity Shop, because I never know what is okay to talk about. Did it ever occur to you—"

He cut off the rest of her sentence by the simple act of covering her mouth with his.

It worked, as it always did. She completely lost her train of thought—for a few seconds. She pushed him away.

"What if Bobby had recognized you on the street tonight? What if he cracked under the third degree?"

Mr. X cracked a laugh of his own. "Where do you pick up this stuff?"

"From Bobby. He didn't want to know anything about what Bev and I were doing so he wouldn't be able to tell the police if they questioned him."

"Bev Reynolds. I thought I recognized that Packard. What does she know?"

"So far, nothing much. Just that Godfrey needed me to hostess his dinner party—"

"Is that what he told you? That old scoundrel."

Phil gritted her teeth as much in consternation as trying to ignore what he was doing to the neckline of her nightgown. "You mean he had an ulterior motive?"

He mumbled something unintelligible and kept doing what he was doing.

"And that a woman who was a member of our party was killed by a stray gunshot and Lily is sitting with her sister who is . . . uh . . . traumatized."

He looked up. "That girl is more than traumatized." He rolled to his side and propped himself up on one elbow, suddenly all business. "How did Bobby get involved? No, I don't mean that. What the hell were *you* doing there?"

"I just wanted to see where and what The Oddity Shop was. Atkins and I found a torn piece of embroidered linen in the bushes outside the restaurant. Obviously a plant."

"Obviously. But you didn't find your way to Coney Island because of an embroidered hankie."

"No, I found a business card in Rose Nash's purse for The Oddity Shop. It had the complete design of what was only partial on the linen scrap."

"Did you, now? Rose Nash. Interesting."

"Why? What do you know?"

"About Rose Nash? Not much more than you. So you found this card and decided to stake out the place. Did you tell Atkins?"

"No. But I don't see why you can't cooperate with each other."

"Besides the fact he thinks I'm a murderer? Which, by the way,

I'm not. It just isn't done. He can catch his murderer, that's your job. Mine is something else."

"Drugs?"

"Damn."

"Was that your man who followed Louie the Lump last night?"

"Not mine. Please tell me you didn't try to break in."

"Well . . . Actually, we did break in."

"You and Bobby both? Through the window, I'm guessing."

She nodded. She wasn't sure he could see the gesture, so she added, "How could we not? The window wasn't locked and the bars were loose."

"I know," he said patiently.

"How did you know?"

"How do you think they got loose?"

She sat up. "See, this is what I mean about lack of communication. I could have saved myself and Bobby a lot of work and a near-miss run-in with a murderer, possibly two, if you had just communicated that you'd already done it."

"I've been busy—not to mention on the run."

"Why don't you go back to Washington? You'll be under government protection, won't you, until this is solved?"

"Where do you get these ideas? No, never mind; Lily's adventure novels. Now, tell me, is Chumley still going through with his 'salon'?" He drawled out the last word like a French dandy.

"Yes."

"You'll be there?"

"Of course."

"Excellent. And can you please keep Atkins distracted for a few more days?"

"What are you going to be doing?"

"Oh, this and that, starting with this." He moved closer to her. Normally at this point, her mind would click off and her baser instincts would take over, but tonight something new had crept into her feelings about her elusive partner. Worry and fear for his well-being.

"Stop thinking," he said, and did his best to make sure she did.

But when he finally sat up and reached for his clothes, the unsettled feeling rushed back in.

"If Atkins knew what you do, what you are, he wouldn't—"

"If I get caught, it will be my fault. Where's my other shoe? Ah." He stood and leaned over her, braced on his hands. "Would you miss me?"

"I daresay, though I suppose I could visit you in Sing Sing."

"Until the big finale!"

"Stop it. It isn't a joke. If he knew you were on the same side—"

"It's better that he doesn't know about me at all." He brushed his lips against hers. "Do not care about what happens to me. It is bound to happen sooner or later."

Phil's blood ran cold. "Fine. But could you plan on later, as I'm rather enjoying your company."

He flashed her a grin, and she realized it was getting light outside.

"I gotta say, things are never dull with you, Countess. Watch your back. I'll be in touch." And he walked out the door just like he belonged there. She didn't bother to follow. After months of trying to figure out how he always magically disappeared into his surroundings, suddenly she didn't want to know.

It was afternoon when Phil finally woke again, feeling surprisingly refreshed. She'd expected to be stiff in muscles that a countess didn't ordinarily exercise, unless she was training for one of the bicycle treks or health walks that had suddenly become popular with the ladies of society. Or extricating oneself from one of Mamie Fish's breakneck speed dinners.

She rang for Lily and dressed in a walking suit that was appropriate for an afternoon visit, and also was equipped with a split skirt that would be convenient if the need arose. Which she had no doubt was a distinct possibility.

Mr. X might not take his life seriously, but she did.

Preswick, as always, had the daily newspapers pressed and refolded for her perusal. Before she'd finished the front page of the *Times,* breakfast arrived.

Even after months of life at the Plaza, Phil was still amazed that breakfast cooked in the basement kitchen, sent via dumbwaiter to the floor waiter, who brought it down the hall to her apartment, could still be piping hot, when meals at Dunbridge Hall, with its own kitchen and waitstaff, couldn't manage to get anything but lukewarm food to the table.

"Ah," she said. Life in the New World was good. Everything she'd hoped for and more. She reached for the marmalade.

There was still very little news of the murder in any of the papers. Either Georgina Nash didn't warrant more than two inches of column space or Godfrey had been successful in keeping the details under wraps. Phil suspected a little of both. The front pages, however, were filled with news of Louie the Lump's capture and arrest.

Amazing how the murder of a couple of thugs fighting over a Coney Island dance-hall girl could garner more interest than the murder of a psychologist in Central Park.

She'd just finished her last piece of toast along with the last newspaper, Hearst's sensationalist *New York Journal,* when the telephone rang.

Preswick went to answer it.

He returned a minute later. "Mr. Bennington would like to speak with you, my lady."

"Yes, of course." Phil dropped her napkin to the table.

It was a short call. And to the point.

"I'm sorry I missed you yesterday. Meetings with the higher-ups."

Phil was beginning to think that Godfrey was as high up as they went, but she let it pass.

"I was hoping you could come by for a drink this afternoon and perhaps tell me anything that you've heard. The whole family has gone out for the day, including those two children, the nanny, and the maid. It will take both of them to keep the little so-and-sos in check. Say three o'clock. Is that too early? I know they're planning to return in time to dress for Griswold's exhibition tonight. It would give us a chance to—"

Pass along information about the investigation? "I'd be delighted to."

"And perhaps I could borrow Lily again tonight, and tomorrow for Dr. Vogeler's lecture, as well? I'd rather not leave Rose Nash unattended."

"But of course." Phil had no doubt Lily would agree.

"Ah, excellent. I look forward to this afternoon."

"As do I. See you then." Phil rang off. "I've been invited to Union House for cocktails this afternoon," she announced. "Which means changing into something a little less sporty. And Lily, Mr. Bennington asked if you could visit with Rose tonight and tomorrow night."

Lily nodded enthusiastically.

"I think we should try to return this card before Rose discovers it's gone. And perhaps find out why she has it at all."

"I can do that tonight," Lily said.

"I told him you would come, but Lily, only if you feel safe. I can telephone him back and say you're not available. I'm not certain we can trust anyone at Union House, except perhaps Godfrey, and sometimes I'm not certain of him."

"I'll be careful," Lily said. "Plus, we might still learn something useful from Rose."

"True," Phil said. She hoped so. Because so far there were still only two obvious suspects. Dr. Vogeler's assistant, Alan Toussaint, and the mysterious Mr. X.

At ten to three, Phil was dressed in one of the new sheath-styled frocks. A delicious combination of hyacinth blue and orchid chiffon, it opened to the knee on one side, which, if Phil was of a fanciful bent, would make her feel like one of the sea goddesses. Phil, fortunately, was no such thing, but she did think she looked rather well.

Lily topped her coiffure with an elaborate blue toque, and Phil set off on foot and alone for Union House. Considering it was mid-afternoon and Just a Friend would be at his post at the park entrance, she felt she would be perfectly safe from Ivan or anyone else who chose to accost her on the two-block walk. And it occurred to her that a tête-à-tête with Ivan Thomas might be not unuseful.

However, she arrived at the door of Union House unmolested.

Collins let her in and showed her into the parlor, where not Godfrey but John Atkins was standing at the mantel.

With his back to her, she took a moment to, one, get over her surprise and chagrin for being duped into this meeting, and, two, for appreciating the figure the detective sergeant cut in a well-tailored gray serge suit.

He turned, and his expression told her she was the last person he'd expected, and that he wasn't pleased.

Really, if he wasn't impressed by her new gown and Lily's coiffure, there was no hope for him.

But she understood. She'd hoped to get an update from Godfrey in private. And no doubt so had he. But it was imperative that she find the real murderer before John Atkins found the wrong one.

He nodded slightly. "Lady Dunbridge. I should have guessed this was more than an informal meeting with Bennington."

"As should I have."

"You didn't know?"

"Not even a hint."

"Well, I wonder what his motive is."

"I've no idea of that, either. And where is he, is the more obvious question."

"Collins said he'd been called to the telephone on government business and he would be with me—us—shortly."

She smiled while she gathered her thoughts. Should they discuss things while they were waiting for Godfrey or be content with small talk?

Atkins reached into his jacket pocket and pulled out a card that he held out for her to see. "I assume you also have one of these."

"Why would you suppose that?" she asked, thinking, *What on earth? How does he have one and how much does he know?*

Instead of handing her the card, he slipped it back into his pocket. "The man posted outside The Oddity Shop said a yellow Packard was parked on the street, an unusual occurrence in that neighborhood. Doesn't your friend Mrs. Reynolds have a yellow Packard?"

"Yes."

She pulled Rose's card from her purse.

"Where did you find that?"

"In the lining of Rose Nash's purse."

"Something I didn't have access to," he said.

She gave him a sympathetic look, which she hoped was fraught with "I told you so," "You should have asked me," "If you'd only trust me to help," and various other things left unsaid she thought he should know.

But alas, it was for naught.

His only response was "You should stay out of this. I don't know why you keep showing up in my investigations. It has to be more than pure meddling. I hope it's for a good cause and not that you're some kind of paid informer."

"That's insulting. Besides, who would I inform to?"

"That news reporter comes to mind."

"Marty? I would never. Have you seen anything other than police-report information in any of the papers?"

"No," he admitted.

"Well, there you have it."

"Nonetheless, you shouldn't have done that. It almost blew my man's position. Though I suppose I have to give you some credit for finding the embroidered scrap of linen in the park."

She knew he was being generous. He wouldn't haven't missed the clue in the park if she and her skirts hadn't gotten in his way. And he'd have figured it out if she hadn't invited him to breakfast, where they ferreted out the possibilities of what it could be.

"That was *your* man?" she asked, with admiration that she couldn't keep out of her voice.

"Not mine, per se, but I'd asked the Brooklyn department to post a man outside the building to watch who came and went. And because of it, they were able to pick up someone who has eluded us for two weeks."

"Louie the Lump," Phil said.

Atkins, who had just taken a sip of his drink, choked and broke into a coughing spasm. "How do you know these things?"

"Sheer coincidence." She wouldn't "rat out" Bobby unless absolutely necessary. "I know about Louie because his photo was in the newspapers." *Maybe.* Had there been a photo? She certainly hoped so.

His eyes narrowed. "Remarkable," he said. "Should I take you at your word?"

"By all means," Phil said, and gave him her most brilliant smile.

With that particular tension passed, she told him about Ivan accosting them on their way home from Union House the day before last.

"I should probably arrest him, but I have absolutely no evidence. I hate to do it, the poor man suffers enough as it is." He grew silent, then took a sip of his drink. "Besides, as I see it, the assistant and that damn missing secretary are still the most viable suspects. Maybe even in on it together."

"Why?" Phil blurted. "I don't know about Mr. Toussaint, but the secretary was with everyone else when the shot was fired."

"No one knows that for certain. Everyone just assumed he was there with everyone else. No one can actually swear to where he was at the moment the shot was fired. Including you."

"And who knows where this assistant really was?" she countered.

"Or where he is now?" Atkins added. "Nor does anyone seem to know where Georgina and Rose Nash lived. I've had someone searching the city records for evidence that the Nashes even live in New York. If we knew that, we might have a better idea if she was the intended victim or an innocent bystander."

"No clue in her personal effects?"

"Not even a subway token."

"None of the people at the dinner know?"

"Not one. Or so they say."

"Then how did she know to come to the dinner?" Phil asked. "Someone must have told her about it."

"That's my thinking. I've tried to talk to Miss Nash, but the little they've let me see of her has been unfruitful. She just stares ahead, seeing things the rest of us can't. If everyone hadn't vouched for her condition, I might think she was acting, though for what reason I can't imagine. At least not now. She keeps saying she wants to go home, but can't—or won't—say where home is.

"When she did rouse herself, she mumbled something about ducks and wheels, and things that make no sense. If they had come in from the country, surely there would have been a return ticket in Dr. Nash's bag. You didn't find one in Rose Nash's bag while you were searching it, did you?"

"Sorry, I didn't," Phil said. "But . . ."

"Go on."

"There was hardly anything in it. A change purse with no change. No ticket stub. As if . . ." She trailed off.

"It had been searched and removed of any incriminating evidence? Perhaps by Rose herself?"

Phil frowned at him. It was exactly what she'd been thinking, though she hadn't thought that Rose might have done it. "Do you really think she might be faking this whole thing? Perhaps she's an actress. Have you checked the theaters?"

He didn't deign to answer.

"I know, a huge undertaking."

"My captain doesn't want to have anything to do with the whole mess, says it's a federal problem and they can do the legwork. He's just letting me proceed to make it appear like he's cooperating. Godfrey Bennington is a very powerful, not to mention rich, man. Not to be ignored. Besides, it keeps me out of his way."

"He must have been pleased when you picked up Louie?"

"I think it was more consternation than anything else, and technically it was the Coney Island beat police who made the arrest. Both the Brooklyn and Manhattan divisions have looked high and low for Louie for two weeks. My guy picked him up by chance. Though it might not be chance." He narrowed his eyes at her. "Is there a connection between Chumley and Louie the Lump that I should know about?"

"I don't know what they have in common," she said, truthfully. *Well, mostly truthfully. It could be anything from extortion to drugs to protection or a myriad of other things.* "I don't suppose Louie talked when he was picked up."

"He's as slick as they come. He's counting on his friends in the system to get him off. We'll see. He's a two-bit grifter. If we're lucky, we'll get him to go down for murder—I beg your pardon."

"For what?" Phil asked.

"For falling into police jargon."

"I actually found it very . . . scintillating," she said, more teasing than flirtatious. She walked past him to make herself a drink.

"Hmmm," he said, following her over to the drinks table. "I

would have called Collins, or made you a drink, myself, except that it really isn't my place."

"Oh, pooh. I don't think Godfrey would hold it against a guest whom he's left stranded for pouring a countess a gin and tonic."

He smiled—ironically, she thought—and took the glass from her.

She watched him go about making her a drink, as comfortable at Godfrey's drinks table as he was anywhere else she'd seen him.

He looked serious but very at home, which was extremely attractive. She couldn't help but smile in sheer appreciation of that jawline, the deep-set eyes, the—

His voice, which was just as attractive, broke into her reverie. "I'm sorry, what did you say?" *I was so busy admiring your attributes that I forgot to pay attention.* And that wasn't good.

"I said that I suppose you're going to attend Chumley's display of nonsense this evening."

"I wouldn't miss it for the world," Phil said. "I find people's convoluted minds, their deep-seated secrets fascinating, don't you?"

"I suppose I can't dissuade you."

"Why on earth would you want to?" She grinned. "Are you afraid Chumley might delve into some deep, dark secrets of my own? Or yours, perhaps?"

He coughed out a breath, as if someone had just gut punched him (another phrase she'd learned from Bobby Mullins).

One look at his face and her levity drained away.

She just stared at him. Most of her secrets had already been laid bare to the world. Did the detective sergeant have dark secrets of his own? She'd always taken him at face value: honest, hardworking, compassionate, yet rational. All the things that made up a good person. Not to mention his dime-novel good looks. A secret past made him infinitely more interesting.

But no, she didn't want to think of John Atkins as having a dark past. All this psychoanalysis talk had her looking for meanings where there were no meanings but the obvious.

Honestly, life had been much simpler when ulterior motives were all about sex and scandal and power instead of repressions, Oedipal drives, and superegos. She might never look at innuendo in the same way ever again.

"Ah, I think that's Bennington now," Atkins said.

The door opened and Godfrey walked in. He was wearing navy-blue striped trousers with a dark blue blazer, and for a second Phil imagined him as a captain at the helm. Though Godfrey would be piloting an aeroplane.

"I'm sorry to keep the two of you waiting. A last-minute hitch that had to be dealt with. These aeroplane contracts. Philomena, my dear, I hope you don't mind that I invited Detective Sergeant Atkins to join us."

Phil demurred, not daring to look at either man.

"I knew you both would want to know that Alan Toussaint has reappeared. Evidently yesterday, but I was away in talks and didn't see him until this morning, as the whole family were rushing out to sightsee. But they should be back any minute. And you can question him then. I'm sure we'd all like to hear his explanation."

He said this in a way that dared Atkins to override him.

Atkins stayed mum, though they all knew he preferred to do his interrogations in private. Phil knew his bland expression hid an aggressive and precise thought process. He knew what Godfrey was doing and, for some reason, he didn't argue. He must have his reasons.

Phil had her own reasons for wanting to hear Toussaint's story. She sat back to wait for his return.

"Oh, by the way, Godfrey," Phil said. "Do you think Mr. Griswold would mind if I brought a friend tonight? Bev Reynolds just returned to town and I thought it would be interesting for her."

"Daniel Sloane's daughter? Certainly, the more the merrier. Shall I send a car for the two of you?"

"Thank you, but we'll drive ourselves, and bring Lily round to sit with Rose on our way."

"Good. At least the damn girl is awake. Maybe Lily can get her to hand over some information about herself. I can't keep her forever."

"I believe the Vogelers are planning to take her with them," Phil said.

"I can't just turn over an obviously incapable woman to strangers. They'll have to go through the proper channels."

"Which channels would that be?" Atkins asked drily.

"Yours, perhaps," Godfrey shot back without hesitating.

Atkins laughed, which surprised Phil. "Touché," he said. "Not the worst idea I've heard."

"Detective Sergeant," Phil exclaimed. "You're not planning to arrest Rose?"

He shrugged. "Why not? She's already confessed."

19

"I know you don't mean it," Phil said.

"No?" Atkins said. "If I weren't working cold here, with people not where they should be, and others not being what they seem. The most important witness living in fairyland, and no one really cooperating? Hell—pardon my language—but I can't even find the main suspect. It's like he vanished into thin air."

"Well," Phil said, her mouth suddenly dry, "perhaps Chumley Griswold can conjure him up for you tonight."

"And that's another thing—"

"Look at the time," Phil said. "I'd love to stay and let you gentlemen entertain yourselves with your speculation and witty repartee, but I really must take myself off to dress for this evening's entertainment."

They both stood so quickly that Phil suspected they were anxious to get rid of her.

"And if you're plotting something and planning on leaving me out, I suggest you rethink that idea."

She swept from the room. At least she had meant to sweep, but before she reached the door, it opened and the Vogelers all crowded in. Phil barely dodged out of the way of two sticky children as they scrambled inside, talking a mile a minute.

"Children," Dr. Vogeler said ineffectually, and followed them in, looking as sticky and unkempt as his offspring. He was followed by Nanny Cole, who was in a similar state but not appearing to enjoy it as much as her charges. And she was followed by the man who must be Alan Toussaint.

And for the second time meeting Dr. Vogeler's "assistant," Phil was struck dumb.

It was the man they'd seen at The Oddity Shop the night before. Phil had memorized his features in that one brief moment, just in case she came across him again. She hadn't, however, thought it would be this soon.

Up close, in the daylight, he was a prepossessing man, with short-cropped hair and beard. More muscular than Phil thought necessary in a psychoanalyst's assistant. He was perfectly groomed, attentive to his employer, and at his ease, certainly not like someone who would be skulking around Chumley's Coney Island shop at nightfall.

But he was.

Phil bit back her surprise and managed, "How do you do? You must be Alan Toussaint."

"Why, yes," he said in a suave French accent, but looking slightly taken aback.

"I'm Lady Dunbridge, and *you* have been quite the object of our speculations."

"Indeed, madam."

Obviously, he had no patience for meddling countesses. Phil couldn't say that she blamed him. He'd definitely been up to no good lately.

"Yes. The Vogelers were quite worried about you, first with your illness and then with your . . . disappearance from Washington."

"I didn't disappear. I merely left my hotel rooms to rejoin Dr. Vogeler."

"Ah, well, we *are* relieved. Did you just arrive?" A rather clumsy attempt at gleaning information, she had to admit. But she was impatient to see if his alibi would hold or whether he was about to lie to her about his whereabouts for the last three days. At which point she would have to figure out what she could tell to whom.

It was enough to make a countess lose her temper.

"Yes, I believe we would all like to know that," Godfrey said.

They certainly would. Though even if he had been in New York longer than he admitted, why go to all that trouble when he must have had innumerable opportunities to get rid of his employer, and without it even looking like murder.

Unless he'd really been after Georgie Nash.

But why? Something to do with the Vogelers or with the Nashes? Anna was completely solicitous of Rose, and Erik Vogeler seemed completely unmanned by the girl's unresponsiveness.

A love triangle came to mind, but Alan, Erik, and Rose? Anna, Alan, and Erik? Anna, Rose . . . Well, she wouldn't piece it together standing here, smiling at an impatient doctor's assistant.

"I arrived yesterday," he said, his French accent growing stronger as his annoyance increased.

Phil didn't see why he was being so testy if he didn't have anything to hide.

"I didn't realize I was under house arrest."

"No such thing," Godfrey said. "But common courtesy would have saved us a lot of concern over your safety."

"In that case, I apologize profusely," said Toussaint formally. "I didn't realize anyone expected me to inform them of my activities. I was feeling better, so I checked out of the hotel and came to join the Vogelers."

"There was no record of you checking out of the hotel," Godfrey persisted.

"Are you—" Toussaint cut off his words, made a slight bow. "An error on the desk clerk's part. I remember he was quite busy at the time with an arriving tour group."

Godfrey's eyes narrowed, but he didn't comment.

"And when did you arrive—exactly?" Atkins asked, stepping forward.

Toussaint's manicured eyebrows rose. "And you are?"

"Detective Sergeant John Atkins, and I'm investigating the murder of Georgina Nash."

Toussaint opened his hands in a typical Gallic gesture of dismissal. "And I need an alibi? Will a train ticket suffice?" He couldn't keep the slight smile from his full lips, and Phil decided she didn't like him one bit.

But her dislike didn't make him a murderer. It did, however, make him a purveyor of whatever Chumley was selling. She would have to tell Atkins at least that much . . . wouldn't she?

"It would be a start," Atkins said.

Which made Phil start, until she realized he was still talking to Toussaint and not her.

"If you could collect it now?"

"If you wish. Unless the maid has emptied the trash. . . ."

"Even so," Godfrey interjected. "The collection service hasn't picked up yet. And being a federal guesthouse, the refuse is always double-checked before it is surrendered."

Phil thought "surrender" was an odd choice of words, but she was gratified to see Toussaint's smile slip just a bit.

"Well, now that that's been settled," Dr. Vogeler said, "do you know if my wife has returned yet?"

Phil had noticed her absence but just assumed she'd taken herself upstairs to get away from the exuberance of the rest of her family. The doctor seemed oblivious to the fact that someone had tried to kill him, twice in the last two weeks; that someone *had* killed Georgina Nash; and that he and possibly his family members might still be in danger.

"Wasn't she with you?" Godfrey asked.

"Yes, until she saw an interesting little museum down by the seaport and deserted us. She often does," he said with a fond smile. "Art and science, a perfect marriage."

Phil had been thinking, *Ne'er the twain . . . ,* but she obviously didn't have the optimistic insights to the human spirit that the doctor had.

Nanny Cole had managed to corral the children and shooed them out of the room.

"I'll go look for that ticket," Toussaint said, and with a slight bow, followed her out.

"Looks like I must fend for myself," Dr. Vogeler said, looking after the others. "Ah well." And he left the room.

Godfrey was left staring at the door, openmouthed. "I swear, I'll send them all packing as soon as his lecture is over."

"On the condition I've found the killer," Atkins said. He smiled suddenly. "Or you could move them to the Plaza until I do."

Godfrey roared out a laugh. "Sorry, Philomena, my dear, but can you imagine?"

"No, and it's not something I wish to contemplate," she said. "If you'll excuse me. I will see you this evening." She didn't bother to attempt sweeping out of the room, which was just as well, as she heard the two of them chuckling as she shut the door.

* * *

Phil called for her Daimler to be sent round at twenty to eight.

Bev arrived at the Plaza at seven. "I came a little early. I thought we might need a fortifying cocktail."

They had two for good measure, though Phil noticed that Preswick had used a light hand on the gin. And Phil had to admit they might need clear heads tonight. She didn't know why she was expecting trouble. Probably overwrought nerves, due to the fact that now that Alan Toussaint had returned, Atkins might turn his focus on the missing secretary as the main suspect.

"Do you expect trouble?" Bev asked, breaking into Phil's thoughts.

"I don't know what to expect," Phil said. "But it seems odd that Chumley invited us all. No, 'challenged' would be a better description, to attend what is obviously a soiree, even though he called it a wake. And even odder that everyone accepted."

"And even odder," Bev said, "after our visit to his Oddity Shop."

"Definitely strange," Phil said.

"Are we going to search for clues while we're there?"

"I don't know what we'd be looking for. But if the situation arises, I may take a quick peek around. You will stay with the others and make sure no one follows me."

Bev nodded seriously. "Shall I question anybody?"

"No. We're just there to observe tonight. If there are any more dustups that might postpone Dr. Vogeler's talk and the possibility of ridding Godfrey from the responsibility of hosting him and this family, he will combust. He's in the middle of sticky aeroplane negotiations—"

"I wonder if he'd be interested in giving us a ride someday?"

"Once we solve this case, I'm sure he'd love to." In the meantime, she *had* to solve this case before Mr. X, who insisted on running around "at large," got nabbed for a murder he didn't—most likely—commit.

At ten to eight, they dropped Lily off at Union House, clutching her bundle of dime novels. Once the door closed behind her, they continued on to Chumley's residence on Park Avenue, where Phil pulled to a stop in front of a row of impressive brownstones.

"Nice neighborhood for a man who deals with the likes of Louie the Lump in a Coney Island junk shop," Bev said.

"I was thinking just that," Phil agreed. "Though maybe people like Louie are the reason he lives so well."

They climbed the steps and rang the bell. Chumley himself answered the door.

He was dressed in black trousers and a bottle-green velvet smoking jacket trimmed with black braid and closed with black frogs. A brocade smoking cap was perched at the center of his bald pate and a black tassel hung over one eyebrow.

He snapped his fingers, and a diminutive servant appeared from behind his back to relieve Phil and Bev of their driving coats.

"Welcome, my dear countess, and you've brought a friend."

Phil introduced Bev, who looked pleased and so particularly clueless that Phil could have hugged her.

They were in a central foyer. To their right, double doors closed off what was probably a parlor. Chumley led them through a double door on the left and they entered a second parlor.

"A double brownstone," Bev said under her breath. "Impressive."

The room looked like any upper-class Manhattan parlor, with dark furniture and adorned with many pillows and decorative arts. Paintings hung on the walls, delicate figurines graced the tabletops.

Rich family, indeed. Someone must be subsidizing Chumley. If not his family, then who? Phil could imagine several possibilities, most of them unsavory.

Other guests had already arrived. Elisabeth Weiss stood conversing with Dietrich Lutz. They were both wearing tuxedos and looked like a pair of erudite bookends.

Pietro Salvos, in a well-worn dark suit, was conversing with a man Phil almost didn't recognize.

With the lines in his face smoothed, Ivan Thomas looked much like any other young man. He might have even been nice-looking once. And dressed in pressed trousers and a double-breasted jacket, it was hard to imagine him hunched over and lurking in the shadows. And Phil thought she could see the man he once had been before the ravages of war had destroyed his psyche.

What had Anna said about men suffering from "soldier's heart"—the "traumatic neuroses" Phil had read about—that they could be put back together even better than before? Phil didn't see how, but whatever Anna and doctors like her could do would be welcomed.

Phil wondered if Pietro had been carrying on the work with Ivan that Anna had begun. He'd certainly given the young man a safe haven.

Phil introduced Bev to Elisabeth and Dietrich. They were offered glasses of champagne. Godfrey and the Vogelers arrived minutes later.

"Ah," Chumley said, before the Vogelers had even said their hellos. "We're all here. Let us begin. This way please."

Godfrey hesitated. "Actually, there's one more."

As if conjured, the front bell rang.

Chumley made a curious little bow and left the room. A minute later, they heard his "Ah, Detective Sergeant Atkins. How nice of you to attend our little gathering."

He appeared in the doorway, Atkins looking formidable behind him.

"This way, please," Chumley said, gesturing to the other guests.

They all moved toward the door, and Phil fell in step with Dr. Salvos.

"I'm surprised to see you here," she said quietly.

Pietro flicked his fingers. "I don't mind indulging Chumley's penchant for entertainment tonight, but I will not attend the lecture tomorrow. Chumley is a diversion, but I have no interest in what Erik Vogeler has to say. Any theory he proposes arises from a weak mind."

He gestured for her to precede him through the door to the second parlor, where a semicircle of gilt shield-back chairs were set up facing one end of the lush room.

"There is your friend sitting with Dietrich, if you want to join her." He turned to Ivan. "Shall we find a seat?"

Ivan shook his head and went to stand by the doorway.

Taking the not-so-subtle hint, Phil made her way to the empty seat next to Bev. She'd meant to stand near the back, in case she had the opportunity to slip away for a quick look around, but she saw now that it would be impossible. John Atkins stood at the back, taking everything in, including any attempt she might make to leave the room.

She sighed and sat down. They were near the center of the semi-circle, with their backs to door, and a chill ran up Phil's spine as she thought of Ivan standing there behind them.

Then she heard a curtain being drawn across the doorway, and turned to look. Ivan was now standing just inside a curtain of heavy black-velvet drape, and the tiny servant was just slipping out of sight.

Suddenly the lights dimmed; smoke arose from several places in the room, and the sweet smell of incense filled the air.

The sweet smell of incense, the sweet smell of the medicine in Rose's dressing room, the sweet smell of the potions in Chumley's loft laboratory. Phil wondered briefly if they were all being drugged as they sat waiting. It would certainly heighten their response. But somehow she couldn't imagine Chumley intoxicating his female clients over their tea and crumpets while he read their minds and hypnotized them into telling their secrets.

And where did Louie the Lump fit in? If he did fit in. Maybe he just needed a cure for his unrequited love of a dance-hall girl.

Phil was following that possibility when she realized that though the audience was sitting in darkness, a cone of light had appeared before them. It seemed to be coming from an overhead spotlight.

Someone snorted. It had to be Dietrich, who was sitting on the other side of Bev.

Chumley stepped into the light, his arms by his side. He was no longer wearing his green smoking jacket, but a full-length cloak that swept along the floor. Phil was reminded of the magician in his star-covered robes on the cover of Lily's Nick Carter story.

Abruptly he lifted his arms and opened his fingers, releasing a burst of orange-red smoke that drifted toward the ceiling before dissipating.

Almost everyone reacted, though Phil was certain many of them had seen the trick before, perhaps even knew how it was done. And yet they were all succumbing to Chumley's spell.

Phil automatically glanced at Ivan, who had shrunk back against the drape. This had not been a very good idea; the smoke must remind him of the battlefield. She leaned over to see if Pietro was worried, but he was focused solely on Chumley.

A series of flamboyant sleights of hand followed, and Phil forgot about Ivan to pay attention to what Chumley was doing.

He was entertaining, Phil had to allow him that. And he was adept at the tricks he performed.

But gradually the mood began to change, his flair for exhibitionism slipping into something more serious, more aggressive. Something that reminded her a bit of Georgie Nash's activities at the Arsenal dinner. And she remembered that the two of them had often entertained their friends, probably with something very akin to this.

"I know what you're thinking," Chumley intoned in a slightly trebly voice. "Oh dear," he giggled. "Perhaps I shouldn't say that. Poor Georgie said something similar just before someone killed her."

He threw up his arm to shield himself, the sleeves of his cloak suddenly growing wider, hiding his face and torso.

At the edge of the room, John Atkins stood at the ready.

Chumley slowly peeked over the top of his arm. "Surprise, I'm still here. Did I frighten you? Perhaps a little card trick to lighten the atmosphere. Let's see, someone to assist me. Someone with no tricks up their own sleeve. Ah, Ivan. Come up and hold the cards for me."

Everyone turned to look at Ivan, their faces cast in macabre shadows by the extreme lighting. Ivan looked startled and pressed himself even closer into the curtains, his expression frozen like a deer at the click of a rifle.

Pietro stood. "Not necessary, Chumley. I'll volunteer."

Chumley laughed delightedly. "But alas, no, my friend. No one will trust you not to cheat."

Someone gasped. It was hard to tell who it was, but other than that, the participants had become completely still.

Chumley walked through the crowd, his eyes focused and intense on Ivan. "Be a good man and come help me with this."

Ivan didn't move.

"Come, Ivan." Chumley came out to meet him. "You're the perfect one to hold the cards." He smiled around at the others as if he held the key to their lives in a deck of playing cards. "Is he not?"

No one answered.

He continued to peruse the room, more slowly now, his eyes lingering on each face, setting off a ripple of unease. Then he shrugged it away. "It's a card trick. Who doesn't love a card trick?"

He stuck out his hand as if to strike Pietro's assistant, but instead, playing cards fluttered from behind the man's head. Chumley caught them in his sleeves and deftly arranged them into a deck.

Someone started to applaud, but stopped. Most of the audience was too tense to be amused. Whatever was going on here, it was more than just an evening's entertainment or a friend's wake.

Chumley gestured toward the cleared stage. Slowly, Ivan walked past him and into the light.

"Wonderful," Chumley said. He shuffled the cards so that they arced and floated in the air. The trick won him a round of begrudging applause. A series of familiar tricks was presented, Ivan choosing a card, guessing a number, cards disappearing from Chumley's hand and reappearing in Ivan's jacket pocket.

Standard tricks.

Then, as quickly as they'd appeared, the cards disappeared again. Chumley bowed deeply to Ivan, and Ivan, head bent, returned to his place by the door.

Chumley clasped his hands together at his chest, smiled enigmatically. And Phil found herself wondering how he managed to keep his cap from falling off his hairless head.

He caught her eye and she looked away. "But I wouldn't invite you all here for a few parlor tricks alone. No. I think something a bit more—" He took a delighted, savoring inhale. "—intimate is in order. Something I'm certain Georgie would enjoy. From the grave, so to speak."

Anna Vogeler started to rise. Dietrich made a disgusted sound in his throat.

Atkins had changed position. Was he expecting something to happen?

"Ah, but then, of course, Georgie did know all."

From around the room, brilliant streams of light shot through the air, all but blinding them. Chumley swept around the interior of the semicircle, holding out his arms, the sleeves now covering his hands, the skirts of his cloak flowing out behind him. He ended back in the center spotlight. With a flourish of sleeves, he made a final turn. The lights went completely out, leaving the room in total darkness but for the one lone, small light from above.

And in that light, hanging from a chain: a gold pocket watch.

"Oh, really, Chumley" came from the darkness.

"Really, Dietrich. Do you want to volunteer?"

"I do not. Hypnotism is a scientific technique, not some cheap trick to gull the innocent."

"Afraid of what we might find out, Dietrich?"

"Empty threats. I have nothing to hide and I refuse to cluck like a chicken, which for your information isn't possible in an unwilling subject. Hypnotism is a serious business, not something to be used as a mockery."

"Oh, I'm deadly serious," Chumley said. "But if Dietrich is squeamish about having his innermost secrets on display, who will volunteer?"

No one offered themselves.

"Then it seems I must choose." Chumley walked toward Erik Vogeler, changed his mind, approached Elisabeth Weiss, but before she could demur, he shook his head and moved on.

He traversed the space, his arms and body undulating like an exotic dancer's. No longer a ridiculous little balding man with a high voice, he was a conjurer, and Phil, in spite of herself, was drawn in. Chumley chuckled, paused when he reached Dr. Salvos, but shook his head, and turned toward the others.

"Of course," he continued. "The trigger doesn't have to be a watch, as most of us are aware. It could be anything really, or nothing but the sound of my voice."

"Get on with it," Dietrich called out. "It's simple enough even for you to conduct. We all use hypnotism with our patients."

Chumley turned on him with a flourish. "But can you unlock

their innermost fears?" He raised his chin, his eyes slowly looking upward until he was looking at the darkness. "What say you,
Georgie? Shall we expose their souls?"

He turned back sharply, and he was standing in front of Erik
Vogeler. "What about you, Dr. Vogeler? Do *you* think we can unlock the secrets you hold so close? Or," he continued, without
waiting for a reply, "perhaps your beautiful wife? Wouldn't we all
just love to take a look inside her . . . um . . . mind."

"You're insulting," Erik said, standing up, but sounding more
hurt than angry. "I think we've all had enough entertainment for
tonight."

"Are you afraid to know what the lovely Anna is thinking?"
Chumley pointed his manicured finger at him, and Erik fell back
in his chair.

Across the room, Atkins edged closer to the audience. Godfrey had disappeared completely. Phil moved to the edge of her
chair.

"I know. Someone who is unknown to us. Whose secrets can't
have been told to any other person in this room." Phil braced herself as he moved toward her. She had no intention of divulging
anything, much less secrets. But though Chumley slowed as he
reached her, he passed her by and stopped in front of Bev. "Perhaps this lovely lady?"

"Me?" Bev said. "You don't know anything about me."

Chumley laughed with delight. "That's the whole point. May
I?" He held out his hand, soft, almost feminine, the fingernails
long and perfectly manicured.

Bev shrugged, appearing delighted, though she managed to cut
a look toward Phil as she took his hand.

Phil took the hint, but there was no way she going to leave Bev
to Chumley's machinations.

He led Bev to a chair that had appeared in the spotlight while
they were watching Chumley. He turned the chair around so that
it faced slightly away from the others, and Bev sat down. Which
left them all witness to the watch as it began to move, barely
noticeably at first, growing in increments until it reached a full
arc, back and forth, back and forth, though the hand that held the
chain didn't seem to move.

Phil felt herself being drawn to the watch and yanked her gaze away.

"Now, just relax, my dear. Focus on the watch."

Atkins was scanning the audience; Godfrey was still absent. Had he grown bored and left without telling anyone? He would never. Perhaps he was suffering from the same apprehension as Phil and Atkins and had gone to telephone for additional support.

More than likely he had slipped out to enjoy a cigar on the stoop.

"Let your eyes close. That's right." Chumley's voice was no longer tinny but smooth and calming.

Phil had seen this bit before. She didn't think Bev would succumb, but they hadn't discussed it before the party. Neither of them had anticipated hypnosis, definitely a failure on their part.

Phil could only sit and will Bev to stay awake while she prepared herself to be ready to spring if she didn't.

"You are in a safe place; there is nothing to fear."

Bev's eyes fluttered, closed, opened, then closed again.

"And now, the truth will out," said Chumley's disembodied voice.

Dietrich started to stand, but Elisabeth grabbed his sleeve and he sat back down.

Bev's chin dipped.

"What do you see?"

"Soldiers!" Ivan cried from the back. He looked wildly around. "Soldiers coming! Hurry! You must—" The rest was unintelligible.

Pietro jumped from his seat. "Dammit, Chumley! What have you done?" He pushed his way through the startled guests and rushed toward Ivan.

But too late to stop him. Ivan was on the attack, grabbing people out of their chairs.

Atkins threw himself into the fray. The drapes parted with a clatter of brass rings, and Godfrey appeared, blocking the exit.

Chumley stood forgotten in the middle of the spotlight, Bev still in the chair. "When I clap—"

Bev jumped up. "Never mind, get out of my way." She ran toward Phil.

Most everyone had managed to run out of Ivan's path and huddled in the various corners of the room. Only Anna stayed where she was, reaching out, saying Ivan's name, soothingly, repetitively, and for a moment it seemed he would calm. Then he howled, clapped his hands over his ears, and stumbled to the door.

Dietrich and Atkins converged and made a grab for him. With superhuman strength, Ivan shoved them away. They both landed on the floor, stunned.

Godfrey stood his ground in the doorway, but Ivan flicked him out of his path as if he were made of straw.

It was incredible to watch, and by the time Phil had recovered herself, Godfrey and Atkins were racing to the front door.

Phil followed, but they were all too late.

The door gaped open and Ivan was gone.

20

"What happened?" Bev asked. "I wasn't even under yet. What did I miss?"

"I'm not sure," Phil said, and ran after Atkins, who had pursued Ivan down the front steps.

Godfrey was standing on the landing, looking down the street. Phil stopped beside him. Atkins was nowhere to be seen.

That didn't bode well.

Pietro Salvos brushed past them and ran down the steps just as Atkins appeared several houses down on the opposite side of the street. Pietro didn't wait but rushed toward him, meeting him in the middle of the street and grabbing his arm.

"Please. He is not violent. He just got confused with all that stupid nonsense of Griswold's."

Akins shook him off and bounded up the stairs to the brownstone, not stopping to say a word. A distracted Pietro followed close behind.

"I guess he lost him," Phil said.

"Evidently," Godfrey said, and gestured her back inside.

They reached the foyer just in time to see Chumley leading Atkins down the hallway.

Pietro started to follow, but Godfrey stopped him.

Pietro held out his hands beseechingly. "Please, you must understand. He didn't mean to harm anyone, he was trying to help them."

"I've seen it before," Godfrey said, not unsympathetically. "Traumatic neurosis. But you can't guarantee he won't be pushed into violence. I've seen that, too."

"He never has before. You can't tell how long this episode will last. It may already be over. He may be lost. Or hurt." Pietro's voice broke, and Phil stood helpless, wishing there was something she could do.

A few minutes later, Atkins strode back down the hall. Ignoring Godfrey and Phil completely, he stopped at Pietro. "Do you have your auto here today?"

"Yes."

"And what make of car is it?"

"A Ford, but it is still sitting outside."

"So he is on foot."

Pietro didn't answer.

"Inside, everyone," Atkins said, and flicked his head toward the parlor, where a group of anxious, curious faces were crowded in the doorway.

"Now," Atkins added. Godfrey and Phil preceded Atkins and Pietro through the door, though she could tell Godfrey was chafing from being included in Atkins's orders. She had a feeling that no one ordered Godfrey to do anything, possibly not even his "superiors," whoever they were.

As soon as Atkins stepped inside, everyone began talking at once.

Bev took the opportunity to ease toward Phil.

"No luck finding him?"

"Unfortunately, no," Phil said, watching Pietro go over to the window and look out to the street.

Anna went to stand beside him. Phil and Bev moved closer so as not to miss any interchange between them.

"I'm sorry, Pietro," Anna said. "You know I tried to help him. I even thought I was getting through to him just now, but his neurosis is just too strong. He seems more unpredictable than ever. What if he's approached by someone in all innocence and he mistakes them for his enemy?"

"Are you saying he might attack a stranger?" Atkins asked, striding toward them.

Anna shook her head. "I can't say for certain. He may be cowering in a corner somewhere. He might attack. By mistake, of course. He may see the uniforms of your officers and believe they are enemy soldiers."

"Traitor!" exclaimed Pietro.

"No, no," Anna said. "I would never turn against him or you."

"Not you, but him!" Pietro stuck out his arm and pointed to

Erik Vogeler. Everyone in the room reared back. "You. This is your doing. Not content with destroying my life, you have to ruin all that was dear to me. A young man who should have had a bright future ahead of him is broken inside. All because—"

"Get control of yourself, man," Erik said, finally losing his good nature. "I had nothing to do with Ivan's breakdown. Nothing at all."

"I know better."

Phil and Bev both leaned forward in anticipation, but he changed course. The fire seemed to drain from him and he addressed Anna in a sad, defeated voice. "I pity you for being married to such a man. You were always smarter and more driven than he. What a waste."

Anna smiled sadly. "Pietro, that is unkind. I made my choice freely. And it was a good choice." She smiled reassuringly to her husband. "These things happen. It's no one's fault. Ivan couldn't accept that Rose didn't love him. He's not the first man to go to war because he'd been spurned by a young woman. We have to accept it."

"I could kill you, Erik."

"Okay, that's enough," Atkins said, grabbing Salvos by the arm and holding him away from the others.

"How true, Detective Sergeant," said Chumley. "Pietro, you're acting just like this was a scene from *Tosca*. It's the Italian, you know," he said confidentially to Atkins. "Very *passionato*."

"Thank you, Mr. Griswold. If you could just take Dr. Salvos over to stand with the others."

Chumley flourished a little bow and took Pietro's arm.

"But we should be searching for him. I should be," Pietro explained.

"Yes, yes, and we will," Chumley assured him, and led him away. At any other time, it would have been a comical sight, the tall, thin psychologist being led away by a diminutive fellow in a magician's cloak, but tonight the sight made Phil feel a little *passionato* herself.

"What was that all about?" Bev asked.

Phil shrugged. "The Nash sisters, I think. It seems Rose Nash spurned Ivan's attentions. Ivan, broken-hearted, goes off to war.

And returns like you saw him. Someone said that Rose was encouraged by her sister, Georgina, to turn him down. And now
Georgina's dead."

"Georgina Nash," Bev said. "You know, that name does sound
familiar."

"Really?" Phil said. It would be wonderful if Bev just happened
to know the murder victim. A relief to them all.

"Though I suppose it's a common enough name," Bev added.

"Well, let me know if to comes to you. Detective Sergeant Atkins would probably kiss you."

"Really?"

"No, but he would be grateful."

Bev sighed.

They heard a commotion outside the door, and the little servant entered, followed by three uniformed policemen.

Atkins marched them right back into the foyer.

Phil, naturally, followed. And she was followed by everyone
else.

She turned to Bev. "I think we should go back to Union House."

But Atkins's next statement stopped her cold. "Ivan is profi-
cient with a firearm?"

"He isn't dangerous," Pietro repeated.

"You said he was in the army. What position?"

"What does it matter? He doesn't have a gun."

"A knife?"

Pietro shrugged.

"Does he have access to a gun?"

"He's alone on foot. He's frightened."

"Just answer my question, please."

"I believe," said Erik Vogeler, his usual cheery demeanor fal-
tering, "that he was what is known as a sharpshooter."

"A sniper?"

"He hasn't used a firearm since his return," Pietro said.

"Perhaps," Atkins said. "Does he still have his rifle?"

"Yes, but it's locked away. For years now. We kept no ammu-
nition for it. You must believe me. You just saw him: did you see
a rifle? Where was he hiding it? In his pocket?"

"Pietro," Elisabeth Weiss said, coming up and taking his arm. "You must stay calm. Detective Sergeant Atkins is trying to help."

Perhaps, thought Phil, until he found out that Dr. Salvos did own a pistol, and a pistol would be easy to conceal in a suit jacket or trouser pocket. Or especially in the heavy coat Ivan was wearing the night of Georgina's murder. Phil grasped her purse and its own rather lethal contents a little tighter.

She waited, praying that Pietro would tell Atkins about the pistol he kept in the clinic so that she wouldn't have to. Because she could not in good conscience hold that bit of information back. It might be the difference between someone living or dying. That someone could be Detective Sergeant Atkins.

Things were looking bleak for Ivan. He was the only one of the group who had no alibi. He clearly was unstable. And he'd been a sharpshooter in the army. Now he was on the run and maybe desperate.

"Detective, please," said Pietro. "He's probably just trying to get home right now. At least let me accompany you to look for him. We can take my car. I can drive."

Atkins deliberated, then he nodded, turned to Godfrey. "I've asked that a guard be posted outside Union House. Though I don't know how long it will take to get him in place. Take the Vogelers straight back there and keep them away from windows. Take Lady Dunbridge and Mrs. Reynolds with you. Keep them there until I can find someone to escort them back to the Plaza."

"I have my Daimler," Phil said, making herself look at him. "We'll caravan with Godfrey. We'll be perfectly safe. You go find Ivan before any harm comes to him . . . or anyone else."

"You stay there until I either arrive or send word. Understand?"

"Completely."

"Bennington—"

"I won't let any harm come to any of them."

Atkins looked skeptical, but he didn't argue further. "Dr. Salvos. I'm trusting you. Do not disappoint me."

"Dr. Salvos, please." Phil cast a desperate look to Pietro, but he didn't seem to see.

He and Atkins were already at the door.

It was now or never. "Detective Sergeant!"

He didn't even slow down but went down the steps.

She ran after him. "Detective Sergeant!" Why didn't he stop?

They had reached the Ford. Pietro jumped in the driver's seat.

"John!"

His hand froze on the Ford's door. He didn't turn, but looked back at her over his shoulder.

Their eyes met.

Phil tried to swallow but she couldn't manage it. She'd just called him by his given name. There was no denying it.

"He may have a gun."

Atkins's gaze snapped to Pietro.

"I keep a pistol at the clinic because of thefts. He wouldn't take it."

"Let's hope you're right." He got in and they drove away.

Phil watched until she couldn't see them anymore, then went back inside to find the others taking their leave. Bev had retrieved their driving coats, and Chumley escorted them all to the door.

"Thank you all for coming. I hope you had a mostly pleasant evening." He waved at them from the front door, then went back inside.

Godfrey escorted the Vogelers to his auto, where his driver was waiting, then started to escort Phil to her car.

"Go ahead," Phil said. "Get the Vogelers to safety. We'll be right behind you."

Godfrey watched until they ran across the street.

When Phil started the engine, Godfrey's Daimler pulled out. Phil waved them on and then steered her vehicle in behind them. They were nearly to Fifth Avenue when the hairs on her neck began to lift in wariness. Something was not quite right.

The auto was running fine; the tires seemed to be okay. She looked in the side mirrors, saw nothing following them. And still . . .

"Keep an eye out," she called to Bev over the engine noise.

"I am."

Phil turned onto Fifth Avenue. There was no sign of Ivan.

And then she understood why.

He rose up from behind them like a phantom. His arm slid

around Bev's neck before either of the two women had time to react.

"I don't want to hurt her," he shouted. "I need to see Rose. That's all. Please. I need to save her."

"Phil?" Bev croaked.

Phil nodded. He must have climbed in and pulled the lap blanket off the seat and onto the floor to hide beneath it.

She had expected trouble tonight, had included her derringer in her evening purse.

But she hadn't checked the back of her auto.

Everyone left their autos on the street, and Phil always checked hers to make certain it hadn't been the object of vandalism or unwelcome riders. It was something she prided herself on, to always be on the alert. She was, after all, a detective.

But she hadn't today. Of all days. Once again, they'd all been so worried about Erik Vogeler that they hadn't thought about the other possibilities. And she'd been so eager to get back to Lily that she'd not been thorough. And heaven forbid, Bev might pay the price.

Bev rolled frightened eyes toward Phil. Phil tried to signal that she had a plan, though the prospect of having your windpipe crushed by the muscular arm of a madman might prevent Bev from picking up the nuances.

And besides, Phil didn't have a plan. She just knew she couldn't let Ivan in the house.

She slowed as they neared Union House, searching for a place to stop but also praying that Mr. X, as was his wont, might be hiding in the bushes of the park, ready to spring out and save them.

She saw an empty spot and pulled the Daimler to the curb, but no Mr. X came to save the day. It looked like it was up to her.

She turned off the engine but didn't get out.

"Ivan, you don't want to do this. They're looking for you. No one wants to hurt you."

He adjusted his grip around Bev's neck. "The enemy, they're—"

"They're not coming." Dear Lord. Phil had no idea what he was thinking, if he even remembered being at Chumley's, and certainly no idea how best to calm him down. "You stopped them in time. You saved us."

Bev's eyes widened and she tried to nod her head in agreement. Ivan's grip tightened.

"You're hurting my friend. She's on our side."

"Take me to Rose."

Ahead of them, Godfrey and the Vogelers got out of Godfrey's auto. The Vogelers ran up the steps and into the house. Godfrey turned to wait for Phil and Bev. He saw at once what was happening.

"It's all right, Ivan. Mr. Bennington is a friend, too. He invited Pietro to dinner."

"And Georgie," Ivan growled.

"No," Phil said. "Georgie invited herself. No one knew she or Rose were coming."

Godfrey had stopped, no doubt assaying the situation and deciding how to act.

She shook her head the barest bit, hoping he could see the gesture in the streetlamp. She was afraid to make a sudden move, but more afraid that Godfrey's actions would send Bev to her maker.

"Ivan?" Godfrey's tone was one that Phil could never have imagined coming from the man she knew. "Would you like to come inside and see Rose?"

What was he doing? Maybe the butler and housekeeper were really battle-hardened government agents who could subdue the distraught man.

"Let's go inside, Ivan."

Phil saw just when Ivan's grip lessened. She willed Bev not to make a sudden move. And bless her, as his arm withdrew, she merely exhaled and stayed frozen in place.

"Why don't you come inside?" Godfrey said affably, and slowly stepped forward.

Ivan watched him. Waves of tension rolled off him. "I need to save Rose."

Godfrey didn't blink. "She's safe inside. I promise you."

"No!" Ivan grabbed Bev again.

"Okay, okay," Godfrey said, holding up both hands. "Come inside and see for yourself."

Ivan didn't reach for the door handle but bounded over the side, managing to keep hold of Bev and half dragging her with him.

She somehow got the door opened, and she tumbled out of the car. Ivan pulled her to her feet.

Phil hurried ahead, past Godfrey, and ran up the steps. Collins was at the door, but a look from Phil and he stepped back. Not in surprise, but in readiness. Phil saw the years of military service take over.

She opened the door wider and stood to the side. Godfrey was the first to enter, followed by Ivan and a wary Bev. But she caught Phil's eye as they passed, and Phil knew she was ready to do whatever was needed when the time came.

"Ivan!"

Ivan whirled around, taking Bev with him, as he searched for source of the voice.

Anna Vogeler stood at the top of the stairs, her husband beside her. "I'm coming down to meet you."

Ivan seemed to shrink back. Was he afraid of her? Or was it her husband, who stood above them with a half smile on his face?

The door to the parlor opened and, surprisingly, Rose Nash stepped out. She showed no alarm, but perhaps curiosity?

Lily was right behind, her stiletto at the ready.

"Lily, no!" Phil hissed.

The hand holding the stiletto slid behind her back.

Ivan released Bev, who scrambled away as he lunged for Rose. Erik yelled. Anna ran down the stairs.

"You must come," Ivan said, grabbing at Rose with both hands. "You must get away."

Phil saw, for the first time, that the backs of his hands were crisscrossed with scars.

"Ivan, let go, you're hurting me."

"Come, *mica zana, viata mea.* Now."

Lily's head snapped toward him.

His head swiveled toward her. "You—*didikai!*"

Lily shook her head and shrunk back.

He stepped toward her, pulling Rose along.

"Yes . . ." His next words were rasped out low, so that it wasn't clear whether Lily could even hear them.

The stiletto fell from Lily's trembling hand, a reaction Phil had never seen from her young maid before. And it wasn't something that she would stand for.

"Ivan, leave her alone!" Phil cried. "You're frightening her."

Ivan turned on her, screaming a mix of English and some other language. Phil stumbled back.

Lily and Rose clung to each other.

Without a word, Godfrey and Collins lunged for Ivan at the same time. For a moment, it seemed as if they had him subdued, but Ivan burst from their grip, yelled a last string of garbled words, and thrashed through the doorway.

Collins stumbled back. Godfrey managed to stay upright, but it took a moment for him to recover.

Phil ran for the door, though she had no idea what she thought she could do, except at least see which way he had run.

Where was John Atkins? Where was the patrolman who was supposed to be watching the house? She looked up and down the street but only found a middle-aged gentleman who had stepped out that moment from a brownstone several doors away and started down his front steps.

And Ivan was running straight toward him.

Phil cringed as she realized they were going to collide.

The man reached the bottom of the steps just as Ivan ran past, and he was knocked a little off his feet. But as he regained his balance, he flipped his cane over, and hooked the curved handle around Ivan's ankle.

Ivan whiplashed back. The action rippled through the gentleman's whole body. For a horrifying moment, Phil was afraid Ivan would drag the man down the sidewalk still holding his cane. But Ivan toppled to the ground.

By then, Collins and Godfrey were running down the sidewalk toward him. A policeman blew his whistle and ran across the street.

They all reached Ivan as he struggled to his feet. But the raging Ivan of a few minutes ago was now strangely docile.

The first policeman was joined by two others. "You want us to take him in, sir?"

"Take him back to Union House," Godfrey said. "Collins here

will you show you where to confine him until I can get in touch with Detective Sergeant Atkins."

The first officer sighed. "Oh, him. Figures. We don't have all night. Got rounds to make."

Godfrey didn't bother to respond. "Collins, take them in through the kitchen. No need to upset the ladies any more than they already are."

Phil wondered which ladies he meant, since the only one who appeared upset by the whole incident was Lily. Even Bev, who had been in mortal danger only moments ago, was taking it all in stride.

Collins bowed and said, "This way please."

Which reminded Phil . . . She perused the street. No gentleman with a walking cane was anywhere in sight. Not sitting on a stoop recovering from the excitement. Not making his way down the sidewalk to wherever he'd been going. Just gone. While they had all been focused on the subduing of Ivan Thomas, he'd simply slipped away, leaving only the faintest aroma of exotic pipe tobacco.

Phil wasn't totally surprised. He'd probably been waiting for them all evening.

21

Phil and Godfrey returned to the house, and Godfrey excused himself immediately to disappear down the hall, presumably to check on their prisoner, perhaps to call someone who could relieve them of the prisoner.

Everyone else stood in exactly the same places as they had been when Phil had left to follow Ivan.

Anna was trying to convince Rose to go back to bed. Erik stood just behind his wife, with his hands clasped in front of him, a pose that Phil had noticed men often took when they were trying to appear thoughtful and unthreatening.

Unfortunately, it only brought Adam and his fig leaf being cast out of Eden to Phil's mind.

"Rose," he said, "listen to Anna."

"What are you doing downstairs? You really must rest. I know best, my dear." Anna tried to take Rose's arm, but the girl slipped away. Anna turned to Lily. "What were you thinking to bring her downstairs?"

"Mr. Collins said it would be okay. And . . . and she wanted to come." Lily cut a fearful look to Phil.

"It's quite all right, Lily—" Phil began.

"Yes, yes, of course," Anna said. "I didn't mean to chastise. How were you to know what's best?" She turned back to Rose. "Now, enough of this nonsense, Rose. I'll take you back to your room."

"No, thank you. I'll wait for Georgie to come take me home." Rose turned and went back into the parlor.

Well, thought Phil. Rose Nash might not be compos mentis, but she could be stubborn.

And now Phil wondered about the permanency of her otherworldly state of mind. For a moment tonight, when Rose first saw Ivan, Phil thought there had been a sense of recognition.

That dreamy expression she always wore seemed, for an instant, clear and rational. She'd recognized Ivan. Even said his name. But she'd lost that expression now.

There was probably a scientific name for that, but at the moment, Phil didn't care. She was too concerned about Lily.

She hadn't moved. Only when Rose turned to go back into the parlor did Lily suddenly snap to life, darted a quick look to Phil, then scooped up the stiletto off the floor and followed Rose out of the foyer.

Phil and Bev exchanged looks.

"Are you okay?" Phil asked, perusing her friend's countenance.

"Perfectly," Bev said. "He didn't hurt me at all. I don't think he ever meant to."

"Thank God for that," Phil said.

"Now, you go see about Lily. I'll speak with the butler. I think tea would be in order." Bev huffed a breath. "Though for myself I'd rather something stronger."

"I completely agree on both," Phil said. "But thank you." And she followed the others inside.

Rose sat in a wingback chair that dwarfed her lithe figure. Dressed in the gown she'd worn to Godfrey's dinner, its diaphanous skirts spread over the cushion, she reminded Phil of a fairy tale that she couldn't quite place. *A child on a throne.*

Tonight the gown hung loosely on her. She'd lost weight in the last few days and looked so frail that she might blow away on the slightest breeze.

Lily had taken her place behind the chair, like a servant in waiting.

Phil felt a prickle of unease . . . more than unease. The sooner these "mind" people were gone, the better, and the rest of them could all go back to plain old crime solving. Greed, jealousy, love, revenge. Simple motives. Straightforward investigating. Well, mostly straightforward.

Anna took a step closer to Rose. "Rose, dear . . ."

Her husband hurried past her and dropped to his knee at Rose's feet.

An acolyte to a beloved? Phil wondered.

He took one of Rose's small hands in his. "You don't have to worry about anything. I, Anna and I, will take care of you. You can live with us."

Phil glanced at Anna for a reaction. Got none. Not even surprise. Had husband and wife discussed this already? Not only would they continue to treat Rose, but would support her completely? Would she become a member of their household?

Rose's gaze slid from Erik to Anna. The slightest flicker in her eyes. And there it was again. That sense of awareness. Her expression wary. Distrustful, thought Phil, even conniving. And she wondered, not for the first time, if this could all be an act. That Rose had found a way to murder her sister, and that Atkins wasn't at all wrong to suspect her.

But how would that be possible? It wasn't. She'd sat on that bench without moving.

Phil glanced over to Lily, who was usually alert and on the lookout for clues to whatever they were working on. But Lily was just staring at a spot on the carpet.

Where was Atkins?

The door opened and Phil turned toward it expectantly, but it was Bev and Collins, followed by the cook, who set down a tray of sandwiches and tea.

"Thank you, Collins," Phil said. "We'll serve ourselves."

Collins and the cook left the room.

Bev picked up a plate, piled several of the dainty sandwiches in the center, and handed the plate to Rose.

"Rose, I believe you'll like these."

Rose smiled at the plate, then picked up one of the sandwiches and stuffed it into her mouth.

Phil poured a cup of tea and set it down on the table next to Rose's chair.

Then she and Bev moved away from the group and watched Rose eat.

"Thank you for the brilliant idea of serving sandwiches."

"It was obvious to an outsider," Bev said. "They've been starving that poor girl to death." She lowered her voice. "What exactly is wrong with her?"

"The general consensus seems to be that some experiment that her sister, Georgina, was conducting, and for which Rose served as a test subject, went terribly wrong."

"How awful."

"Yes," Phil said. "But no one knows for certain. At least that they're telling."

"So if no one knew that they were living in Manhattan or nearby, how did they find out about the dinner? Was it announced in the society pages?"

"No, it was just a small party of old friends and colleagues."

"Someone must have told them." Bev dipped her chin toward Erik Vogeler, who had returned to stand with his wife. "Do you think . . ." She left the rest unsaid.

"I'm thinking about a lot of things, and that's one of them."

"Won't be the first time. Get rid of the sister and . . . Should we be concerned about Mrs. Vogeler?"

"I don't know," Phil said. "Right now, I'm concerned about Lily. Whatever Ivan said—or maybe it was just him in general—she's upset. I want to get her home, but I don't think we should leave."

"At least make her sit down, for heaven's sake." Bev didn't wait, but walked over to the tray and carried a cup of tea to Lily. She pushed her down in the closest chair and handed her the cup.

Godfrey returned at that moment and came straight over to Phil. "Collins says that Atkins called a while ago. He had to go to the Orchard Street station to get to a telephone. Evidently Salvos doesn't have one. How can a doctor not have a telephone? Anyway, he's left two local men at the Salvos place and he's on his way here. He should be here soon.

"I'm afraid it will be another long night," he said ruefully. "I didn't take the Vogelers' concerns seriously. Now we're in it up to our eyeballs."

"So what do you want to do now?" Phil asked.

"Wait for Atkins. I think I'll make us all a drink."

"That is just the reason people like Chumley Griswold should not be allowed to use hypnotism as a game," Erik Vogeler pronounced.

He was well into his second scotch, and still there was no At-kins.

"A treatment like that is very dangerous in amateur hands. And even more dangerous if the subject isn't a willing participant."

"But he wasn't a participant," Bev pointed out. "I was."

"Yes, but being the subject of hypnosis before possibly made him more susceptible."

"And that theatrical prop, the gold watch," Anna added. "The spotlight alone would be mesmerizing to someone tenuously balanced on a precipice."

Then why had they invited Ivan in for the evening? Surely they must have known this. Except that Chumley had not told them what he'd planned for the evening. He had said it would be a wake. A coincidence with a terrible outcome? Or a planned distraction?

Anna dabbed a handkerchief to her mouth. "It's so unfortunate to see Ivan now. When he first came back from the army, I tried to help him. And my treatments were succeeding. But after the scandal with the university, Pietro took him out of my care. I guess Pietro failed to continue with his rehabilitation."

"It would be like him to neglect his own assistant as he neglected his patients before," Erik added.

"Did you use hypnosis with Ivan when you were treating him?" Phil asked.

"Oh, yes," said Anna. "As one of several techniques to reconcile the conscious mind with the memory. In the beginning it was quite useless. He was too unresponsive to cooperate. Later, when he was making progress, I was able to help him reach into his memories. We were just on the verge of a breakthrough when Pietro's malfeasance was exposed and he removed Ivan from my care.

"I could have helped him but for that stupid unworthy man. And from his behavior this evening, poor Ivan seems so much worse. I can only say, though it breaks my heart to do so, it appears that he may be past helping."

"I'd like some more sandwiches, please," said Rose.

Bev snatched the plate from her hand and filled it again.

"I'm afraid they'll have to institutionalize him," Anna continued. "Pietro is obviously incapable of caring for him." Her voice broke. "I can't help but feeling a little responsible. And so very disappointed."

"Not nearly so disappointed as Ivan will be when they cart him away," Bev said, coming back to Phil's side.

Phil had been thinking just that. She was getting quite sick of these people. Treating everyone like a case to be solved and bickering over how to do it. She just wanted to take Lily home and wash her hands of the entire situation.

Unfortunately, she still had a murder to solve.

The door opened, and Phil nearly jumped with joy, thinking that Atkins had arrived at last. But the relief was short-lived: Alan Toussaint strode into the room. He was dressed for an evening out, and smelled of brandy.

"What's happened?" he asked, looking from one to the other.

"Where have you been?" demanded Anna.

"At the theater. Dr. Vogeler said I shouldn't bother attending Griswold's nonsense. I'm sorry. Did you need me?"

Phil had to admit she hadn't missed him that evening. And yet he might be a key player in this investigation. She hadn't even had a chance to tell Atkins about seeing him at The Oddity Shop.

But she would make those amends this very night.

"Ivan Thomas attacked Rose this evening," Anna said. "He's being held somewhere in the house. We're waiting for the police to come for him."

"Oh dear." He looked at Erik Vogeler. "You look tired, sir. Why don't you go up to bed? Surely they don't need any of us tonight."

"We're waiting for Detective Sergeant Atkins to arrive," Godfrey said curtly, not bothering to rise from the club chair where he had just sat down. "Though I'm certain he can wait to speak with you all until tomorrow. Except for Miss Nash. I know he'll have a few questions for her."

"Oh, I cannot allow her to be questioned," Anna said. "She is in no state—"

The door opened and Atkins walked in at last. "I'll be the judge of that."

If he'd been Nick Carter himself, he couldn't have made a more timely entrance. Phil wanted to applaud.

"Sorry that you all waited up for my arrival, but it wasn't

necessary. I wish you good night. I'll come round tomorrow to further discuss this business and to escort you to the lecture hall, unless you plan to cancel."

"I certainly will not cancel," Erik said.

"Your choice. Now, I bid you all good night."

No one moved.

Phil glanced at Bev, who snapped her mouth shut.

"Oh, before you go," Atkins continued, unruffled, "I understand you were planning on leaving the country after the lecture."

"Yes, we are," Anna said. "We're booked to sail in two days' time."

"You will most likely have to change your plans."

"We will not. What right have you—"

"Unless we have arrested the murderer of Dr. Nash—"

Anna gasped, cut her eyes at Rose.

"You mean she isn't aware that her sister—You haven't told her?" he said incredulously.

"She is in no state, and I'll thank you not to do more harm."

Phil watched as the color drained from his face. He was the only person she knew who lost color the angrier they became. And he was definitely on the edge with Anna Vogeler.

"I'll take her upstairs now."

"Miss Nash will remain here."

"I can't allow that. She needs constant care. I will not leave her unattended."

"She won't be," Godfrey said, adding himself to the standoff. "I've requisitioned a nurse to take care of Miss Nash until her future is decided. She's waiting to be summoned. She will take Rose to bed after the detective sergeant is finished questioning her and will sit with her during the night."

"You can't question her. She is very fragile."

"And I plan to be very gentle. Good night." Atkins gestured to the door.

Anna didn't move, and Atkins delivered his final coup de grâce. "Perhaps it's time Miss Nash became a ward of the state."

"You can't do this."

"But, of course, I can."

"We'll see what the consulate has to say about this."

"I believe they open at ten tomorrow. Perhaps they can also help you rearrange your travel plans."

"This is an outrage!" Alan Toussaint said. "You can't talk to the Vogelers that way. They are very respected scientists."

"Out," said Atkins.

Godfrey finally stood. Phil half expected him to yell, "Bravo!" and burst into applause. She certainly felt that way.

For a breathless moment, everything hung in the balance, then Erik said, "The detective sergeant is quite right. We need our rest. And I find myself in need of some peace." He tilted his head at the room in general and took Anna's arm, and they left the room, Alan Toussaint following in their wake.

"I suppose Bev and I should take Lily away, too," Phil said.

"No. I'll accompany you back to the Plaza when I'm finished here."

"But what about Ivan?"

"I have no choice but to have him committed to Bellevue for observation. I should have done that the very first night, though I had no cause, and he would have no doubt ended up under psychological commitment. I balk at doing that to any man who isn't a danger to himself or others."

"What changed your mind?" Phil asked.

"I had time to talk to Salvos tonight. And got a very different side of the events that led to this. Which, yes, I will tell you, but not tonight. Secondly, I found the pistol that may well have killed—" He glanced over at Rose. "—the victim. But this is the first time Miss Nash has been accessible, and I need to make good use of it."

"Wait—" Phil began.

"Later."

He walked over to Rose, who was still sitting up in her chair, her second plate of sandwiches empty. Lily, who had seemed to be dozing, jumped up and went to stand beside her.

"It's all right, Lily." He gave her a reassuring smile and knelt down in front of Rose.

"I wish I could get men to kneel at *my* feet," Bev said under her breath.

Phil had just been trying not to think the same thing.

"I'm glad to see you up and about," Atkins said in a gentle tone that he'd never used with Phil. "Tell me what happened the other night at dinner. In the park."

"The ducks weren't there."

"Where do the ducks live?"

"Near the big wheel."

"Is that where you live?"

She didn't reply, just looked confused.

"A water wheel? Do you live in the country?"

No reply.

"Tell me what happened tonight," he said gently.

"Ivan came. Georgie's late. I had sandwiches."

"Where do you live?"

"With Georgie."

"Where is that?" Atkins persisted. "Where do you live with Georgie?"

Rose looked up, not focused on him or anyone else in the room. "Where the ducks are. But they weren't there."

Why did she keep talking about ducks? Phil wondered.

"Can you take us there?"

Rose had returned to her blank expression, and she'd begun to slump slightly in the chair.

"Georgie will take me. I'm tired now. Tell Georgie I'm ready to go home."

"You can stay here for a while longer. You don't have to be afraid." He stood. "And you don't either, Lily."

Lily started. "I am not afraid. I am never afraid." But her words were barely above a whisper and there was not one rolled *r*.

And that's when Phil, herself, became afraid. They'd been in scrapes like this before, some more dangerous. Why was Lily reacting the way she was? What made this different?

Atkins turned to Godfrey. "Could you telephone to Dr. Faneuil and ask him to please come? Assure him that he will receive a better welcome than he did the other night. I would like him to oversee the admittance of Ivan Thomas. That will assure that the man gets better treatment than otherwise."

"Gladly. But with Ivan off the streets, do you expect more trouble?"

"Of course, don't you?"

Godfrey huffed out a long breath. "Yes, I'm afraid I do. I'll telephone directly. But what am I going to do with her?" He gestured toward Rose.

"If there is no family, I expect she'll be headed for the same place as Ivan Thomas."

"No," Lily cried. "You can't send her away."

They all looked at Rose. She hadn't moved, her expression didn't change, but her eyes suddenly welled, then overflowed with tears that slowly ran down her face one by one. There was no other reaction—no sobs, no sniffs, no shudders—just silent, rolling tears.

It was eerily chilling. And Phil wondered if they were for her sister, her lost brilliant future, or from the sheer weariness of being cast adrift.

Godfrey called for Collins, who in turn brought in the new nurse, probably also government issued, who took Rose's hands. She gently pulled the girl to her feet and, murmuring soft assurances, led her from the room.

Godfrey followed them out.

"Take Lily home," Atkins told Phil when they were gone.

"Don't you want to know what happened?" Phil asked.

"Yes, but Lily is exhausted, and I still have to get Ivan situated. Tomorrow will be soon enough." He glanced at his watch. "Perhaps ten?"

"Worried about our beauty rest, Detective Sergeant?" Bev asked.

He smiled wearily. "Never for a moment. I'll walk you out to your car."

"You've apprehended Ivan," Phil said. "Do you think he killed Dr. Nash?"

"For now, everyone is still a suspect. And no one is out of danger. I'll come to the Plaza in the morning. I want to talk with Lily, as well. Where we won't be disturbed."

Phil nodded. They would have to find out what passed between Ivan and Lily, but not tonight.

He did much more than escort them. He checked in the back seat and in the front, searched every inch of the floorboard.

"What are you looking for under there?" Phil asked.

"Not for another unwelcome guest, though you should be more careful."

"Duly noted," Phil said.

"I was hoping that he might have left a clue as to what he was planning to do with Rose once he took her."

"Do you think he really was going to take her?" Phil asked. "He said he had to save her, from the advancing soldiers, presumably, but he didn't seem to have a plan for after that."

"At this point, I have no idea. I'm having him taken to Bellevue because it's heartless to leave him in a cell, even overnight, considering the way he most likely will be treated."

"By the other prisoners?" Bev asked.

"And the guards."

"I suppose there are no alternatives?" Phil asked. "Couldn't Pietro . . . no, I guess not."

"I can't take that responsibility. If he's cleared by the psychiatric division at the hospital, I'll make a request to have him remanded to Dr. Salvos's care. Unless you or Mrs. Reynolds want to press charges."

Bev shook her head.

"No, of course not," Phil said. "He needs help. I really don't think he was intending to hurt anyone."

He put all three of them in the Daimler. "Please go straight home. And you, Mrs. Reynolds . . ."

"Oh, I'll stay at Phil's for the night. I don't want to miss anything—I mean, I'll be ready first thing in the morning to do my part."

"Actually, for once, I think that is a good idea. Just turn around in the street. I'll watch until you get to the Plaza, then go directly inside and stay. Understand?"

"Yes," Phil said. "But I wish I knew what you were worried about."

"Nothing that won't wait until tomorrow."

He stepped back and Phil started the engine. She made the turn and drove straight toward the Plaza.

"Whew," Bev said. "Those psychoanalysts are the weirdest people I've ever met. It can't be healthy mucking about in other people's minds all the time."

"I agree," Phil said. "I hope I never run across another one as long as I live. I'm beginning to see repression and all those other things with everyone I meet."

Bev both eyebrows rose comically. "Not me."

"Not you," Phil assured her. "But I do feel for people like Ivan and Rose. It's like they're trapped in a place that no one understands."

"The way Rose acts . . . ," Bev said. "Did you ever think she might be taking drugs on the sly?"

"They're keeping her sedated." Phil slowed and made the turn on to Fifty-ninth Street.

"I mean before that. You said she acted 'otherworldly' at the dinner. I remember when Lady Sizemore . . . well, better not to remember that. But she acted similarly."

"I've been wondering that myself," Phil said. "After what we saw in Chumley's lab, yes, I think possibly she is."

Phil pulled the Daimler to the curb outside the Plaza and deposited the key with the night porter.

Phil paused just inside the lobby. Her nose gave her the first clue that her evening was not over: that faint aroma of pipe tobacco that she knew so well. He was sitting in a club chair just outside the gentlemen's bar, nursing a glass of sherry.

The same dapper gentleman who had foiled Ivan's getaway.

It looked like she wouldn't be going straight upstairs after all.

22

"Bev, take Lily upstairs," Phil said quickly. "See that she has some hot cocoa and fix yourself a drink. I'll be up in a minute. I need to give the porter directions about some work on the auto."

Bev frowned.

"Please. Lily is dead on her feet and I want her out of this business right away. I'll only be a minute."

Bev nodded and led Lily across the marble floor to the elevators. As soon as the elevator doors closed, Phil made her way over to where the "gentleman" was sitting.

"Have you been waiting here the whole time?" she said, trying not to look at him. Meeting a gentleman in public alone and at this hour was bound to lift eyebrows even at the Plaza, which ordinarily wouldn't concern her. But this particular "gentleman" was another matter altogether.

He tactfully put a finger to his lips.

The gesture shut her up as effectively as an entire hand over her mouth.

"I needed Ivan out of the way, but I couldn't very well jump him when he got out of the Daimler. Your friend Bev would have breathed her last. Besides, I'd hoped that Atkins would arrive with a little more alacrity. Honestly, what's the point of stopping him if there's no one to arrest him?"

"Why did you want him arrested?" Phil asked. "Did you know he was in the back of my auto? He could have killed us."

"I didn't know. I was actually waiting for someone else. I didn't expect you until much later. Must have been a boring party to send you home at that hour."

"Far from it," Phil said. "Ivan was mistakenly hypnotized and thought soldiers were after us. He ran out of the building. It was quite awful."

"Poor sod. Where is he now?"

"At Godfrey's. Atkins is going to have Dr. Faneuil take him to Bellevue."

Mr. X flinched. And some of Phil's anger toward him sloughed away.

"Who were you waiting for?"

"I wasn't sure, and as it turned out . . . I'm still not sure."

"Your lack of confidence in me is not helping this investigation," Phil said. "Can you at least tell me what Rose Nash has to do with all of this?"

"I can make a guess, but I couldn't share it yet. Shall I order you a sherry? Unfortunately, they won't let you into the bar, even accompanied by such a well-heeled gentleman such as myself."

"Certainly not," Phil said. "They might get the wrong idea." She saw the flicker of his usual smile. And felt somewhat mollified.

"Do you think Ivan killed Georgie Nash?"

He shrugged. "I don't know. I'm expecting you to figure it out. I'm after someone else, but I need Ivan subdued for another twenty-four to forty-eight hours."

"Because you expect something to happen?"

"I always expect something to happen."

"Because the Vogelers will be leaving the day after the lecture?"

He tilted his head. "You ask too many questions."

"If I knew more—"

"Then we'd all be in trouble. This is how we work. Accept it."

"Who is we?"

"You and me and . . . ?" He circled his hand in the air, a gesture that reminded Phil of Chumley's conjuring. And then an amazing thought hit her.

"You don't know, do you? That's it. You don't know any more than I do. How can we even be certain we're working for the right side?"

"Look at our track record." He grinned. "Now I must be going. Ah." He lifted his head and looked past her, as if to acknowledge someone he'd been waiting for.

She couldn't help herself; she turned to look.

There was absolutely no one there.

And when she turned back, he was gone, too.

Phil didn't bother going after him. He wasn't meeting anyone, and he wouldn't be anywhere she looked.

She just stood with the cool marble beneath her feet while she steamed inside, then called for the elevator. When it came, she stepped inside.

Could it be true? They were both working without knowing whom they were working for? Some branch of the government, surely. Or some individual, a secret agent, fighting crime anonymously. A very rich secret agent.

Not for the first time, Godfrey Bennington came to mind.

When Phil finally arrived upstairs, she found the others in the kitchen: Bev seated at their small table; Preswick standing, with a steaming pan in one hand; and both watching Lily, who sat next to Bev, slowly sipping a cup of cocoa.

Bev flashed Phil a frown, half "Where have you been?" and half "What are we going to do about Lily?"

Phil sat in the chair on Lily's other side. Lily started to rise, but Phil stopped her.

"You've earned a rest after the excitement of tonight. When you finish your cocoa you're going straight to bed. And I think it isn't necessary that you go back there now that they have engaged a new nurse."

Lily bobbled her cup and a dot of cocoa spilled on the table. She moved quickly to clean it up, but Preswick was there first with a clean cloth.

"Well, we'll discuss it tomorrow," Phil continued. "You were only asked to help Nanny the first night, not be a nurse to Rose, too."

"But she'll wonder where I am. And she likes me to read to her."

Phil couldn't help herself; she asked, "What made the two of you come downstairs tonight?"

"Rose wanted to. It's boring staying in her room all day. If they find her up, they make her get back in bed. They won't even let me keep the draperies open. She's getting very weak."

"She looked like she hadn't been fed in days, poor thing," Bev concurred.

"Broth," Lily said with disgust.

"Does she talk to you?" Phil asked.

"Only when the others aren't around. She's not always like she is. Well, she is, but . . . I don't know . . . Sometimes she knows she's like she is."

Phil nodded. The moments of clarity she'd seen herself.

"She'll get worse if they lock her away."

Phil fought off the urge to promise Lily that it wouldn't happen. It most likely would, unless they could find a family member who would take her in and care for her. "Has she said anything to help us help her?"

"Not really. I tried, but she gets confused about where she lives. As if it were a secret that she's forgotten. She likes when I read to her. Especially the one where Nick Carter goes to Coney Island. But she can take care of herself, mostly. She just can't get home." Lily sniffed. "It must be awful."

"Yes, it must," Phil agreed. For Rose. For Lily. For anyone, even herself. "It must, indeed."

"Perhaps you might continue this discussion in the morning," Preswick suggested.

Lily was nodding over her cocoa.

"Yes, and we must be about early. Detective Sergeant Atkins will be paying us a morning visit."

Not even this roused Lily, and a moment later, she trudged wearily down the hall to bed.

Phil had to fight the urge to follow her, promise her that everything would be okay. It wouldn't be okay until they made it so. At least for Lily. Unfortunately, Phil had no idea of what lay ahead for Rose Nash, or if there was anything to prevent the inevitable.

But they wouldn't solve it tonight. Preswick was right: They all needed their rest. Tomorrow would be soon enough.

"Well, if you ask me," Bev said, buttering a piece of toast the next morning, "Erik Vogeler may be brilliant and passably good-looking, but Lord, what a nondescript, boring man."

Phil, who had not asked her, looked up from the morning paper.

They were sitting at the table in the window alcove that overlooked the park. Preswick had wanted to serve in the dining room, but Phil had nixed the idea. She really must have a dinner party soon, just so he could finally use her grandmother's silver that he'd managed to "confiscate" from the castle before their precipitate departure for America.

In a more enlightened, just world, that silver would still belong to her, not the cousin of her dead husband.

Bev waved her piece of toast at Phil. "Anna Vogeler has more drive and possibly more intelligence than her adored doctor-spouse."

"I can't tell if you admire her or disdain her," Phil said.

"Neither. But I just don't see why women must make themselves subservient to a person who is considered smarter just because he's a man. It makes me tetchy."

"I can see that," Phil said, distractedly. Bev had slept in their guest room, and Lily had dressed her that morning in one of Phil's silk kimonos, after adjusting it for length. She was looking exquisitely rested.

Phil went back to her paper. There was plenty of news: the Republican convention in Chicago, antibetting arrests at the track, a boy saved from choking on a bone, an escalation in the contentious relationship between King Edward and the German chancellor, the upcoming Gran Prix in Paris, the Ladies Kennel Association show. . . . Normally, she would have read it all, but this morning she wasn't interested in any news other than that which might affect her own situation. And so far, the papers remained mum.

"Don't you agree?" asked Bev.

"What? Oh, yes," Phil said, finally putting down the paper and nodding to Preswick to pour more coffee. "It's no secret that the most prominent men owe their success to the hard work and intelligence of their wives. Anna Vogeler is no different."

"The way she dotes on him . . . *euww*."

"I guess this means you *don't* like her."

"Do you?"

"No. She seems smart, decisive, certainly compassionate, but not for herself. Elisabeth Weiss is more to my taste."

Lily came in with more toast, and a chill stole over Phil, one not caused by the central air supply piped in from the basement. The girl was paler even than usual, and drawn. Dark shadows lined her eyes. She'd insisted on dressing them both this morning and serving breakfast, and no amount of persuading could change her mind.

"Thank you, Lily."

Lily curtseyed. "My lady."

Phil sighed.

"You don't have to 'my lady' for my benefit," Bev said. "Though, I must say, your curtseys are top-of-the-line."

Lily barely managed a smile.

"Are you feeling better this morning?" Phil asked.

"Yes, my lady."

Phil's spirits sank even more. Even Bev looked gloomy.

"I really don't think you need to go back to Union House again, now that they've hired a nurse for Rose."

"But I must," Lily blurted, slapped a hand over her mouth, and curtsied at the same time, looking so sadly flustered that Phil wanted to hug her. Of course, she didn't. That would never do. As much as she was beginning to hate the servant-mistress relationship, she knew that the unity of her household depended on it.

How would she ever get them past that awkwardness? She often had fantasies of Preswick sitting in a comfortable chair, smoking his pipe and reading the paper; Lily and Phil playing backgammon or reading dime novels out loud. But it would never happen. Preswick would retire one day, and Lily would—Phil didn't want to contemplate it.

"Phil?"

"Sorry?" She realized Lily was still standing there, looking stricken. "Oh, we'll discuss it later. You may go, Lily."

Lily hurried away.

"What was that all about?" Bev asked.

"I don't have the slightest. Ivan must have really upset her, but I don't understand why she insists on going back. Something is troubling her beyond the danger. I'm certain of it. We've been in dangerous spots before and Lily has more than risen to the occasion. She's worried or frightened or both. There's something she's not telling. But why? Surely she trusts us by now. I would never let any harm come to her."

"Why don't you just ask her?"

Phil blinked. And started laughing. "Why not, indeed?"

But before she could buzz for Preswick, he appeared in the archway. "Detective Sergeant Atkins is downstairs. Shall I tell the concierge to send him up, or shall I have him wait?"

"Send him up," Phil said, taking a last sip of coffee and placing her napkin on the table. Bev bounced up and ran to the mirror to check her teeth and hair.

The table was cleared and Phil and Bev were sitting on the sofa when they heard Preswick answer the door.

A minute later, John Atkins strode into the room, followed by Preswick and Lily.

"I hope you don't mind," Atkins said. "I've asked Lily and Preswick to join us."

"Not at all," Phil said. She knew very well he didn't care if she minded or not. And besides, he knew she always included them in—almost—everything.

Atkins sat in the club chair that Phil had arranged for the occasion. Preswick and Lily sat together on a wide ottoman, a strange choice considering the number of free chairs throughout the room, but Phil thought she understood why. Preswick was doing what he could, in his stoic way, to give Lily support. And Phil couldn't help but feel a rush of affection for them both.

Atkins took out his notebook; Preswick took out his.

Atkins mouth tightened, but he merely said, "Let's start with what happened after you left the wake last evening."

"Gladly, but can you first tell us what happened with Ivan Thomas after we left? We are all concerned for that poor man."

"He was taken to Bellevue. I informed Salvos immediately. He was pretty angry, as I expected."

"What will be Ivan's fate?"

Atkins shrugged. "We'll have to wait until he's evaluated. It will take some time, I imagine, unless Salvos can argue that he is capable of keeping him from violence. My guess is . . ." He glanced at Lily. "He will ultimately be housed in a safe place where he can be treated."

"He is not a cr-r-r-riminal," Lily said, not looking up.

Phil had never been so glad to hear a rolled *r* in her life. And though Preswick had tried to break Lily of the habit, Phil would instruct him to do so no more. She thought he would agree.

"Perhaps not, Lily," Atkins said. "But he may not have the capability to live on his own. And if it's discovered that he killed Georgina Nash, he will be locked away for good."

Lily moved just a little closer to Preswick. It broke Phil's heart.

"But surely, he didn't," Phil said, knowing that if Ivan hadn't killed Georgie, the chief suspect again became the missing aide-de-camp. "What about Alan Toussaint? He doesn't have an alibi, and he makes as much sense as anyone else."

"Like this temporary secretary Francis Kellogg."

Phil forced her heart to slow down. "As you say."

"Or Bennington," He dipped an eyebrow.

She should tell him about seeing Toussaint at The Oddity Shop, but she didn't dare. What if she blew up the whole operation? If there was an operation.

"I suppose it's useless to speculate. Shall we tell you about the events of last night?"

"That's why I'm here."

Put succinctly in her place, Phil began.

She told him just what she remembered about the drive to Union House from Chumley's. "We did exactly what you told us to do. I even noticed that the lap blanket had fallen to the floor. I just didn't think to look beneath it. We were halfway back to Union House when he sprang up and demanded we take him to Rose."

Bev took up the tale. "He didn't hurt me. I don't think he meant to hurt me. I know that sounds strange, but it was like he needed a shield. It was scary and unexpected, but as soon as we reached the house, he seemed to lose interest in both of us."

Phil nodded. "He kept saying—as much as we understood, some of it was just gibberish—" She noticed Lily's change of expression and broke off, began again. "He said that he had to warn Rose. He seemed to think we were all under attack. It was that silly hypnotism bit by Chumley."

"It was," Bev concurred. "And the thing is, it didn't even work on me, but on Ivan who was standing at the back of the room. How is that possible?"

"Hmm," Atkins said.

Phil's eyebrows rose with an idea. "Maybe Chumley intended to hypnotize him all along."

"So he could run amok among his party guests, then kidnap two women and break into a government residence? The motive being?" Atkins poised his pencil above his notebook.

"I don't know," Phil admitted. She was grasping at straws. They all were.

Atkins turned to Lily. "What happened next?"

Lily started. "Rose—Miss Nash—and I were in the parlor. Mr. Collins said it was okay."

Atkins nodded.

"I was reading to her and then we heard yelling and Rose just got up and went to the door." Lily ran her tongue over her lip. "Ivan was in the foyer and he ran for Rose and said she was in trouble, and . . . and . . ."

"It's okay, take your time. What else did he say?"

Lily glanced at Mr. Preswick. Then back to Atkins.

"Think, Lily," Atkins encouraged. "What else did he say?"

"I don't know. How could I know?"

"It's okay, Lily," Phil said. "A lot of it was incoherent. The detective sergeant doesn't expect you to be able to tell him that part. Just what you understood." Phil looked at Atkins, who nodded.

"Just to the best of your ability."

"She was in danger and . . . I can't know. I didn't understand."

"It's all right, Lily, you've done enough," Phil said.

But Atkins didn't dismiss her. "But you know something else, don't you, Lily?"

Lily cowered back into Preswick.

Phil bound from her chair. "Leave her alone!" she cried, as much to take his attention from Lily as to give vent to her state of mind. "Can't you see that she's frightened and doesn't know anything else?"

Atkins stood and looked around the group, lingering on Lily. "I hope that you are not forgetting that anyone—anyone—who withholds information from the police is breaking the law and is subject to punishment."

Phil's mouth dropped open. Why was he acting like this? He'd never threatened them before. But he definitely was now.

"But if you have nothing to add, I'll take my leave . . . for now."

He turned and strode out of the room.

And for the first time in her life, Phil witnessed her impassive butler have to run to get to the door before him.

"What was that about?" Bev said, breaking into the stunned silence. "I didn't think I'd ever live to see the day when John Atkins lost his temper. And certainly not like that. It was quite . . . amazing."

"It was," Phil said, walking to the window. And it was something she never wanted to see again. Because she understood what it meant. Unless she missed her guess, he was getting pressure from more than just the Vogelers and Godfrey Bennington to get the case wrapped up and put to rest. And he didn't have an idea of whom to arrest.

She turned back to the room. Lily hadn't moved. So Phil came to sit beside her.

"You know you are always safe with me and Preswick."

"And me," Bev interjected.

Lily nodded.

"So can you tell me what is bothering you?"

She shook her head.

"Because you're afraid that it will get you in trouble?"

Another shake of her head.

Phil took a slow breath. "Because you're afraid something bad will happen?"

A shrug.

"Nothing bad will happen." Phil would see to it. "You don't have to be afraid."

A vigorous shake of her head.

"Was it something you heard that the rest of us didn't?" Phil continued, grasping at anything that might help her get through to Lily.

"I didn't," Lily mumbled. "I couldn't."

"Couldn't what?"

"Couldn't understand what he said."

Phil let out her breath. "It's all right; none of us could understand. Most of what he said didn't make any sense."

Lily looked up then. There were tears in her eyes, which completely unnerved Phil. This was not the feisty, brave young woman that she knew and, yes, had grown to love.

"I did. I couldn't, but I did."

"Did what?"

"Understood," Lily cried. "He didn't make any sense, but I understood what he was saying. I understood! I must be mad, too. They'll lock me up like Ivan and Rose."

23

For a moment, Phil could only stare, nonplussed.

"They'll send me to Bedlam," Lily said in a defeated voice.

"Nobody is going to send anyone to Bedlam," Bev said. "The only place you're going, young lady, is to wash your face."

Phil looked at Bev; she sounded just like someone's nanny.

"Mrs. Reynolds is right," Phil said.

"But they committed poor Ivan . . ."

"He hasn't been committed yet, he's just under observation. Detective Sergeant Atkins was being kind to send him for an evaluation instead of subjecting him to ill treatment in jail. Dr. Faneuil will make certain he is cared for until they can determine what to do with him."

"But he grabbed Mrs. Reynolds," Lily said.

"Well, don't you worry about me," Bev said. "I'm certainly not going to insist he be charged. Poor man."

"But Detective Sergeant Atkins might."

"We'll convince him to be lenient, won't we, Phil?"

"Yes."

"However," Preswick said with a stern look, "it is not your decision. It is one thing to fight off custom men out of desperation, but it not permissible to flout the law."

"What if the law is wrong?" Lily said.

"It often is," Preswick agreed. "But it's still the law."

Phil wondered if they'd had this conversation before. Was he afraid that Lily might abet Ivan to steal Rose away?

She dismissed the thought. Lily was brave, and perhaps impetuous, but . . .

Lily hung her head. "It wasn't gibberish. At least, not all of it. I could understand some of what he said. And Rose understood him, too." She looked up, her eyes beseeching. "How could he make sense to me?"

"Well, if you understood it, it must be a foreign language," Phil said matter-of-factly.

"It wasn't French or Italian," Bev said. "Didn't someone say he was from Romania?"

Phil nodded, but it wasn't like any Romanian or any other language she'd ever heard.

"That must be it," said Bev, unconvincingly. "Romanian."

"Well, regardless of the language, Lily understood it. Which is very helpful," Phil added hastily.

"So, no more of this nonsense about Bedlam," Preswick said. "It is obviously a language you have heard somewhere before. Tell Lady Dunbridge exactly what Mr. Thomas said."

His words and tone brought all of them tumbling back to normalcy.

Lily lifted her head. "Yes, Mr. Preswick. He said 'danger' and 'home,' and he called her his little flower." She took a stuttering breath. "Then he looked at me and said 'gypsy.' At least, that's what I think he said. But I'm not a gypsy. I'm not. That's all I understood. Really, I swear."

"Very well, Lily," Preswick said. "Now, go tidy yourself."

"Yes, Mr. Preswick."

"And when you come back," Phil added, "we're going to convene a serious council of investigation. I'm growing weary of these self-involved scientists with their egos and repressions."

"Well, in that case," Bev said, "let me telephone home for a change of clothes. I can't think rationally dressed in all this flowered silk. Though it is divine." Lily curtseyed. Bev bobbed one, too, then gave Preswick a saucy grin before they both went off down the hall.

"Pardon my intrusion, my lady."

"Not at all, Preswick. I was out of my depth, I'm afraid." Phil clasped her hands together. "But what do you think it all means?"

"Merely that Lily must have understood the language. And no, my lady. She has told me no more about herself than I suspect she has told you. But I think we can agree that she led a colorful life before she came to us. She must have picked up all sorts of knowledge."

"Yes." Phil sighed. There was still so much she didn't know

about her young protégée, and she was loathe to pry. "Do you think she's afraid of what we would think of her? Or maybe her past is so awful that she can't bear to remember it. What if she's in danger? Good heavens, Preswick. What if she can't remember it at all?"

"I'm certain she will tell us in good time."

"But she must be so afraid."

"She knows she is safe with us."

Phil took a deep breath. It wasn't like her to be so . . . so . . . overanxious. "You're right, as always, Preswick. I just want her to be happy."

"Yes, my lady." Preswick bowed and left the room.

By the time Bev's clothes arrived, Lily had changed Phil into a day dress and coifed her hair. Neither one spoke of Ivan Thomas or the Nashes, but once Lily left to help Bev with her toilette, Phil's anxiety about Lily returned.

She'd needed to solve this case so things could go back to the way they should be. She went straight to the study to refresh herself with what they had learned so far. She was standing before the investigation board when Bev strode in, wearing one of her split skirts and a tailored shirtwaist.

"My investigator outfit," she exclaimed. "Now, where do we begin?"

Preswick entered next and took up a position next to the board. Lily came last, carrying her stack of dime novels and her notepad and pencil.

Phil began. "We're up to date on what we know of the investigation so far. We also know that Anna Vogeler could not have seen the Met's exhibit of German Expressionists, because according to the *Times*, it has been postponed until winter. So either she was mistaken about what she saw or she's wasn't at the museum at all. It's unlikely she would mistake English landscapes for the Expressionists. Which brings us to . . . Why would she say she saw it when she didn't?"

"Because she was doing something else," Lily said.

"Exactly," Phil said.

"Meeting someone," Bev said. "What about that Alan Toussaint? He's manly . . . enough. Do you think maybe Mrs. Vogeler might be having an *affair de coeur*?"

"A possibility," Phil said.

Preswick wrote it on the board, while Lily entered it into the notebook.

"Toussaint was in Manhattan at least a day before any of us knew it," Phil continued. "And the hotel isn't sure when he left. Where was he in between? And how does Chumley Griswold fit into all of this? We know he owns The Oddity Shop. He met Anna at the zoo in the morning. She handed him a flat parcel; he put it in his jacket and left. Rather furtively, I thought."

"Perhaps payment for sedatives for Miss Nash?" Preswick said.

"Dr. Faneuil had prescribed laudanum. There was practically a full bottle."

"But the others," Lily reminded her.

"Yes," Phil said. "Perhaps she needed drugs for Rose's treatment. Is it possible that Chumley might have access to those kinds of drugs? He isn't a doctor. Though . . ." She stopped suddenly. She had to be careful with her speculations about Chumley and give Mr. X time to do whatever he had to do. She just wished he would hurry.

"Or concoct them, along with his virility and love potions," Bev said. "Maybe that was why Alan Toussaint went to The Oddity Shop. To procure them."

"Why not just ask Dr. Faneuil?" Phil said. "Or Salvos or Lutz. They're all doctors."

Lily leaned forward in her chair. "Coney Island."

"What about it?" Phil asked.

Lily pulled over her stack of novels and tapped the cover of Nick Carter's "Four Scraps of Paper." She opened it to the title page. "Or 'Coney Island Search.' Mr. Kellogg left me this story on purpose. Mr. Griswold has a shop in Coney Island. And he's a magician." She pushed the Nick Carter aside to reveal another cover. "Mr. Magic. And the girl on the poster I saw looked just like Rose. And Rose had his card hidden in her purse."

She crossed her arms and jutted out her chin.

"You think Rose works for a magic act in Coney Island?" Bev asked.

Lily shrugged. "No, but she knows a magician. And there's a lot of Coney Island."

Phil was thinking the same thing. After all, Mr. Kellogg was actually her mysterious colleague. She'd thought earlier that he might have left her a clue or at least some information in the novels. She'd found nothing.

She turned the covers around to see them better. "Lily's right, there *is* a lot of Coney Island in this case."

And nobody was talking. Not one person mentioned Chumley's shop, not even Chumley. Mr. X was definitely after Chumley, but he didn't say why. Fraud? Selling potions that didn't work might lead to lawsuits. Blackmail? Getting old ladies to divulge their innermost secrets under hypnosis and making them pay for his silence? He wouldn't last long with those kind of recommendations.

Lily sighed. "I just keep thinking about that girl on the poster. It looked so much like her."

Preswick cleared his throat. "Pardon me, my lady, but shall I telephone Detective Sergeant Atkins and ask him to have someone look into it?"

"We probably should, but I don't want to push his patience. He's under a lot of pressure and doesn't need any half-cocked theories."

"And we can't very well tell him you broke into Chumley's shop," Bev added.

"No," Phil agreed, but not for the same reasons.

Lily lowered her head.

"I've got a better idea," Phil said brightly, more brightly than she actually felt at the prospect of what she was about to suggest. "What do you say to taking another trip to Coney Island? Get another look at that poster, before we bother Detective Sergeant Atkins."

Lily's face lit up. It would be worth the drive to set her mind at ease.

"And we can take another look at The Oddity Shop in the daylight," added Bev.

"True," said Phil.

"In that case, I'll call the Pabst while you all are getting ready and tell them to leave word for Bobby that we'll be needing him again."

Within the hour they were back in Bev's Packard, headed for Coney Island.

As soon as they pulled up in front of the Pabst hotel, Bev jumped out and snatched the driving hat from her head. "Watch my car, we'll only be here a minute," she told the bellboy who ran out to meet them.

They found Bobby sitting in the dance hall. It was dark and not too crowded, being still early in the day, though several men were playing cards at one table. Bobby was indulging in another activity at the next table.

Bev shrieked his name. Bobby jumped up; his drink toppled over; the showgirl who had been balanced on his knee rolled to the floor.

"Miz Reynolds," he squeaked. "They just told me you was coming, but I didn't expect you so soon."

"No matter, but we need you now." She looked down at the showgirl. "Sorry to interrupt. Have a drink on me; in fact, all of you have a drink. We won't be long."

Bobby grabbed his bowler, slammed it on his head, and followed her out. Phil, Preswick, and Lily hurried out behind them.

Bobby flicked his head at the bellhop, who disappeared back into the hotel. "Now, before we go anywhere, what are you up to? You're not gonna break into that shop again, are you?"

"No. We're just going to drive by on our way to somewhere else."

"I'm gonna regret this," he said, mostly to himself. He climbed in the back with Preswick and Lily. And they took off.

By day, Mermaid Avenue was a different world. Shoppers and workmen went about their business. Women in kerchiefs haggled over fish with the fishmonger. Carriers hauled furniture out of an apartment building. Children lined up to get into the candy store. Laundresses and florists, butchers and hardware stores were all open and doing business.

The Oddity Shop was the only store that was closed. Bobby jumped out. Went over to the door and cupped his hands to his face to peer inside.

After a long minute, he turned back and shook his head. Held up a finger and walked across the street to a butcher shop.

He came back almost immediately.

"He only opens at night," he informed them. "If you want to talk to him, we'll have to come back."

"We don't," Phil said. "I just wanted to see, though there is one other thing. Lily, do you think you can find the poster you saw?"

"If we go the same way as before, I can," Lily said, and leaned out toward the street to be ready to spot it. Bev drove down Seventeenth to the end of the block, where it ended at the entrance to Steeplechase Park, and turned left onto Surf Avenue.

They passed the ads from the night before, except overnight, new ones had been added, merely covering up old ones. Phil mentally crossed her fingers that the poster would still be there.

Bev drove slowly, giving Lily a chance to find that one poster among the multitude. Phil was about to give up hope when Lily cried. "Stop!"

Bev screeched to a halt, setting off a cacophony of yells, honks, and grinding brakes. Bev merely waved at the dissenters and pulled to the side of the street. As soon as the Packard came to a stop, Lily jumped out. "See? There it is."

The poster she pointed out was almost five feet tall and nearly as wide, with THE AMAZING MADAME ZHORA written in white, black-lined letters across the top. At the bottom, a lithesome creature floated in a graceful curve above the words CLAIRVOYANCE, FORTUNE TELLING, HYPNOTISM, TELEPATHY. At the center of the poster a larger-than-life torso of Zhora, wearing a green-and-yellow turban and purple robe, conjured over a crystal ball. This was not Rose Nash.

Lily rushed over to the wall of advertisements. The rest of them piled out of the auto after her and crowded around the poster.

"See? It is!" She pointed not to the fortune-teller but to the bottom of the poster, where the other, smaller figure, THE ENCHANTING ZHARINA, danced, fairy-like, on billowy clouds. A beautiful young woman in a diaphanous gown, with light, flowing hair—and looking just like Rose Nash.

Phil stared at Rose, then stood on tiptoe until she came come nose to nose with the larger depiction of Madame Zhora. And with closer scrutiny, she had to admit, Madame Zhora could certainly be Georgie Nash.

But what were the odds? How on earth would a psychologist become a fortune-teller in a sideshow?

Bobby scratched his head. "This is what you're looking for? What's so interesting about Madame Zhora?"

"We have good reason to believe that Madame Zhora is dead," Phil told him.

"Naw, how? I saw her at the track just last week. She looked fine." He stopped, his eyes rounding. "You don't mean—Naw, please tell me that wasn't why we were at that Oddity Shop? Aw, your-ness, you don't want to get involved with any kind of murder down here."

"Too late," Bev said.

"It was not my fault," Phil said. "And it was not down here. I was asked to be hostess at a small dinner party at the Arsenal in Central Park. One of the guests was shot after dinner."

"Well, that wouldn't be Georgie, if it was one of your guests. People like her don't get invited to flash dinners. She's a cheap entertainer. Nice woman, but just an entertainer."

Suddenly the surrounding sounds muted to silence.

"Did you say Georgie?" Phil asked.

"Yeah, Madame Zhora, her real name's Georgie Nash."

"I knew it!" exclaimed Lily.

They had collected a few curious pedestrians as they stood there. Phil moved them away from the newcomers. "Georgina Nash was at a party the other night with a group of fellow psychologists."

"Psy-what?"

"Doctors of psychology," Preswick informed him. "They scientifically study the intricate machinations of the mind and emotions."

"Then that really can't be Georgie. She was a pip, but she weren't no scientist."

"She has a sister named Rose," Lily said.

"Rose? Well, I'll be dam—danged." He moved them a little closer together to let a larger group pass. "Zharina. *Her* name is Rose. But she's a little . . . you know. She don't make much sense, but she's a sweet thing. Dances to get people's attention and they follow her inside to get their fortunes read. But it don't make sense. What was Georgie doin' at an uptown dinner?"

"It's hard to explain. Can you take us to her place of business?"

"Sure. She was practicing from a joint on the street until Steeplechase reopened. And that was this season. They gave her a stall inside while they're rebuilding along the street. She just moved in not too long ago.

"Georgie Nash, a scientist? Don't that just beat the Dutch? Guess maybe all those potions she sells might really work." Bobby chewed on his lip. "Wait a minute, are you sure Georgie's dead?"

"I'm afraid so," Phil said. "These look like the same people who were at the dinner. Same names."

"Wait a minute. Where's Rose? I don't think she can take care of herself too well."

"She's being cared for on the Upper East Side for now. But she wants to go home, only she doesn't seem to know where home is, and none of the other guests knew, either. Do you know where they lived?"

"Nah, I can't help you there, but I can show you where Madame Zhora has her setup in Steeplechase."

"Then let's go," Bev said. They all piled back into the car, and Bev turned the Packard around, causing an uproar from vehicles and pedestrians alike. A few blocks later she pulled to the curb and stopped.

Bobby jumped out. He looked around the street, put his fingers to his lips, and whistled so shrilly that Lily covered her ears, and Phil was tempted to.

A young man came running from down the sidewalk, jostling passersby in his haste.

He skid to a stop in front of Bobby and dragged his cap from his head. "Yessir, Mr. Mullins."

"See this yellow Packard here?"

"Do I," said the boy with admiration.

"See this dime?" Bobby said, retrieving said coin from his pocket.

"Sure do."

Bobby flipped the dime in the air, the boy snatched it and

shoved it into his pocket. "Watch this Packard like it belonged to your granny."

The young man's eyes widened and he nodded slowly.

"Make sure nothing happens to it. No touching, no joyrides, no trying it out for size. If it's fine when I get back, you'll get another. Abscond with my dime, and I'll come looking for you."

The boy nodded, a little less enthusiastically.

"After I tell your granny."

"Ain't nothin' gonna happen to that automobile, Mr. Mullins."

"See that it doesn't." He turned from the boy. "This way, ladies, Mr. Preswick."

They turned in the direction Bobby pointed, Phil and Bev leading the way. Lily followed close behind. Bobby and Preswick brought up the rear. Preswick, Phil didn't doubt, was keeping an eye out for any potential botherations, but Bobby was as comfortable as a cow in clover.

"Honestly, Mr. Preswick," Bobby said in an undervoice pitched to carry, "I don't know how you can keep track with these ladies."

"I do my best," Preswick said.

They stopped at the entrance to Steeplechase Park.

"Just stand here," Bobby ordered. "And from now on let me do the talking . . . Miz Reynolds and your lady-ness. Understand?"

"Understood," Phil said. And Bev and Lily nodded vigorously.

They waited in the shade of the entrance while Bobby walked over to the ticket kiosk and stuck his head close to the money-exchange grill. A few words, a few gesticulations, and the seller handed Bobby five tickets.

Bobby flicked his head toward them and they all hurried after him. "It's not far, right down the fairway a bit. Stay close."

Once inside, they joined the throngs of amusement seekers, some veering off to the Bump the Bumps ride, others turning left to the wooden Steeplechase racing ride, the rest pressing forward to other amusements: the carousel, the Ferris wheel, the tearoom.

They nearly lost Lily twice, and Phil made a note to bring her and Preswick back to enjoy the fun when they were clear of this murder investigation. Maybe they could invite Just a Friend to come along.

Bobby suddenly moved crosswise against the crowd. Phil grabbed Lily by the elbow and hustled them across. When they were spit out onto the far side of the fairway, they were standing in front of a little house whose façade was painted in the same bright colors of the poster. Purple siding, white stars, and a yellow moon holding up a bridge of letters that spelled out MADAME ZHORA. On a white board near the door was a list of the amazing things that awaited them inside.

But no one was entering or leaving.

Madame Zhora's was locked tight.

24

"Now what do we do?" Bev said.

Phil and Bev looked at Lily, who reached for her purse and certain tools she kept there that were helpful in getting into locked doors.

"Oh, no," Bobby said.

Phil, Lily, and Bev turned as one to look at Bobby.

"Nuh-uh. Not in broad daylight. We'll all end up in the Tombs." He pulled off his cap and scratched his head while he looked around the fairway. "I got a better idea. You three just stand here with Mr. Preswick and don't do nothin' till I get back."

He sauntered off into the crowd. Phil stretched to keep sight of his beacon-red hair. He stopped at a booth nearby. Chatted for a few minutes, scratched his head again. And walked back into the crowd.

Across the way, the wooden horses of the Steeplechase ride sped down the track, carrying their riders, women and men alike, astride. The Giant See Saw rose and fell behind them. Ahead, the Ferris wheel made its circle of passengers, and all the while, Phil searched the bobbing pedestrian heads for where Bobby would turn up next.

When she found him again, he had reversed his course and now appeared near something called the Upside Down House.

Then he was hidden from view by a sudden surge of people. When he popped up right next to them, he was holding a key.

"Brilliant," Phil said.

"I thought she might leave it with someone in case of emergency. They're just building back from the big fire last year. Started in the Cave of Winds. Burned just about everything down to the ground. Just like that." Bobby snapped his fingers He shook himself, as if dispelling the memory; squeezed in between them; and went to work on the door.

"The fire took out a few hotels and the concert hall," he continued as he worked the lock. "It woulda taken out the whole town if hadn't been for Stauch's dance hall. Made of brick. Stopped it cold. Everyone is still a little jumpy."

The lock clicked open and they all pushed inside.

He quickly shut the door and they were plunged into dark.

"Bobby, can you find a light switch?" Bev's disembodied voice asked.

"No, ma'am. We don't want to attract any attention. What if a customer saw us and wanted his fortune read?"

"Perhaps this will suffice." Phil opened her bag and pulled out her Ever Ready torch. Between her pistol and her torch, Phil was thinking she needed to buy a larger purse.

She shone the torch around, picking out drapery-covered walls, niches, and pedestals, all holding strange statues and symbols.

She could feel the others crowding behind her as she continued moving the beam of light around the room. The room was larger than it had appeared from the outside; the back wall was covered in thick drapes. A square table was placed at the back of the space, covered with a dark cloth. Two chairs faced each other across the top, with a settee and several padded chairs off to one side.

The torchlight went out. Phil groped her way to the back wall of drapes, felt along until she found a door, and prayed it wasn't locked as she turned the handle. It was locked.

"Lily?"

Lily scurried over. Phil turned on the torch again and shone it on the lock. Without a word, Lily reached in her bag and pulled out her tools. In a few moments, the door was open and they were all crowding inside another room, this one a narrow rectangle that stretched across the back.

Preswick pulled a pair of white butler's gloves from his pocket and moved away from the others. Then, with a click, a pool of light from a Tiffany-style lamp shone down on a small writing desk, illuminating the rest of the room enough to see where they were going.

This room was the opposite of the first, clean and ordered. A room, Phil suspected, Madame Zhora's customers never saw. A tall cabinet held rows of dark vials. Phil clicked on the Ever Ready to read the labels. LOVE, COURAGE, NERVES, STOMACH AILMENTS, STUTTER-ING. Vials that looked uncannily familiar. The same shapes, sizes, and even labels as the ones at Chumley's.

Madame Zhora had been buying her potions from Chumley Griswold. Which must mean she had been in some kind of contact with him. He might not know where she lived, but *she* at least knew where *he* worked. And if the card in Rose's purse didn't prove that, these certainly did.

It must have been Chumley who told her about the dinner. But had it been done in innocence, or had he been setting her up, and if so, who was his partner in crime?

Preswick tested the knee drawer of the desk. It opened easily, and he almost immediately pulled out a small, blue ledger.

Phil's first thought was, *Why leave something like that here, where someone might break in?* Unless it was safer here than where she and Rose actually lived.

Preswick held it to the lamplight. "It appears to be daily financial transactions. Nothing unusually large, at first glance."

Bev stretched up to read the entries. "No names, only initials," she said, disheartened. "We've been here before."

They had indeed, when Bev's husband had been murdered.

"Customers," Bobby said. He reached over to point out the entries. "These here are customers. Most of what's inside the park is free after you pay for your ticket, but there's a few independents still. Zhora is one of them. "See, these three here are the boys from Holly Farms. I've seen her write these down and initial them. Probably so she can keep track of the repeaters. So she doesn't give 'em the same fortune all the time. These bigger ones. Dunno. Don't look like any crooks I kn—may have heard of."

He bounced on his toes impatiently—or anxiously?—watching the door.

"No address or clue as to their living quarters?" Phil asked.

"No, my lady. Shall we leave it here or take it to turn over to Detective Sergeant Atkins?"

They would have to tell him, of course. He would be furious with her for disturbing the scene, and she still didn't know how far Mr. X's investigation had spread. She didn't dare take something that might be needed as evidence. If they would only tell her what was out of bounds and what wasn't, she would be vastly more efficient.

"We'd better leave it; we'll call him immediately when we return to the city and apprise him of what we found."

"There's a makeup table over here," Bev said. "What's this?" She reached for something, her features warped by the standing mirror.

"No!" they all cried.

"Fingerprints," Preswick said. "The detective sergeant will most likely look for prints. Not that it will be admissible if it gets to court."

Since he was the only one wearing gloves, he picked up the object. It was a heavy gold necklace, and at the end, a large, round pendant, the same symbol as Chumley's store.

They peered down at the other items on the vanity table: greasepaint and kohl and colorful creams to paint eyelids and cheeks and lips.

"Theater makeup," Bobby informed them. "All the actresses wear that kind of paint." Bobby, as they all knew, had a particular liking for the theater.

"Preswick?" Phil made a suggestive nod to the vanity.

Preswick searched the top, unscrewed jars and bottles. Smelled the contents. He opened the small drawer, swept his hand inside. Felt beneath it, shook his head. He straightened up and looked around, pulled out the table, and slipped between it and the wall.

"Ah," he said, as the mirror wobbled back and forth. A minute later, he slipped out again, holding a small, flat notebook.

"A diary," Phil said.

"Taped to the mirror backing," Preswick replied, in a voice that clearly said that he didn't think much of Zhora's hiding place.

"What does it say?" Bev asked.

"We'll need a closer look. I think we have no choice but to take this with us," Phil said. "At least get a good look before we turn it in." After all, Mr. X had said the murder investigation was her bailiwick. She'd rather not think what Atkins would say.

"Well, not here," Bobby said. "I told the Upside Down boys that we weren't gonna to take anything, just make sure everything was all right and tight, because we were friends and we were worried about Madame Zhora. But they're gonna get suspicious pretty quick."

"And none of them knew where she and Rose lived?" Phil asked.

"No. Said there was no call to since they only knew her here."

"Should we ask some more people?" asked Lily.

"No. We should get outta here before the park security folks—or worse—get suspicious."

Preswick took the diary and slipped it into his breast pocket. "For safekeeping until we turn it over to the detective sergeant."

"Then I think we're finished here," Phil said. "Shall we?"

Preswick waited until they had returned to the front room, then turned off the light and followed.

Lily relocked the door, and they all groped their way to where Bobby waited at the front door. "Now, just look like concerned friends of the family," he said, and opened the door.

The sun and heat glared back at them, and they all had to stand for a minute to blink in the sudden light. Then Bobby ran off to return the key.

Soon they were headed back to the entrance. Once there, Bobby saluted the ticket taker, and they hurried across the street.

The Packard was still parked where they'd left it, unscathed. The boy Bobby had paid to watch it had been leaning back against the hood, but when he saw Bobby, he jumped to attention. He took his second dime, doffed his cap to Bobby, and walked jauntily down the sidewalk.

"It'll be gone in ten minutes," Bobby said.

"Candy?" Phil asked.

"Naw, he'll save one for his granny. It'll get back to her if he don't. He'll probably lose the other one in a quick pitch."

"A baseball game?" Phil asked.

"Street gambling."

"It seems a shame that Mr. Preswick and Lily have come twice to Coney Island without experiencing any of the fun," said Bev. "I know, we could at least stop at Feltman's for a frankfurter."

Phil shook her head. They had just dropped off Bobby at the Pabst, where Phil had no doubt his dance-hall girl would be waiting. "We'll come back when this is all over. Spend days sea bathing and riding the most revolting rides. Is that all right with you two?" Phil leaned back to see her two servants looking very serious in the back seat.

"Though it's awfully hot. Perhaps some lemonade or root beer from one of the sidewalk carts," Phil suggested.

Bev stopped at the first pushcart they came to, where even Preswick agreed to a refreshing drink. Then they started back to Manhattan.

They sped through the hot air, the kind of heat that snatched your breath away. And it only got hotter the farther they traveled from the water.

"Are you going to tell Detective Sergeant Atkins about what we did?" Bev shouted over the noise of the Packard's engine as they sped up the highway.

"Yes, but not all of it." Phil considered. "Though perhaps we should 'come clean,' I believe is the expression, about discovering the identity of Georgina Nash and finding Madame Zhora's place of business." Phil turned around to the back seat, but her two servants were busy looking out opposite sides of the road.

"It was really Lily's insistence that led us to the poster, and Bobby who led us to Steeplechase. Though I imagine Bobby would rather be left out of it." Phil sighed. "And there's a chance that Atkins already knows all this and didn't see his way into sharing the information with me."

"Us," Bev corrected.

"Us," Phil agreed.

"He's going to be angry."

"I know," Phil said.

"He becomes quite spectacularly quiet when he's angry."

"True, but I rather not be the brunt of it."

Bev left them off at the Plaza. "I'm going home to take a long, cool bath and change clothes. Then I'm taking a taxi back to read the diary. Don't start without me."

"Then hurry. We're going to have to turn over what we know

to Atkins. It can't wait much longer. We could be jeopardizing the case by withholding evidence. And with Atkins not sharing anything, how are we to know?"

The first thing Phil did when they were upstairs was to ask Preswick to telephone the nineteenth precinct and inform Atkins that they had information that he might be interested in. Then she glanced at her purse, where the diary had joined her pistol and her Ever Ready. "On second thought, perhaps I should tell him myself . . . after a bath . . . perhaps after dinner."

That would give them time to peruse Georgina's notes, before Atkins demanded that she relinquish it to the police. Hopefully, he would be feeling generous and not cart her directly to jail for breaking and entering and theft.

He didn't seem to be making much progress. Someone had to do something. And Phil was happy to oblige. She just didn't want to serve time because of it.

Bev arrived in a timely fashion, and they dined on tomato aspic, sole almandine, and asparagus, accompanied by crisp French rolls and a bottle of excellent Chardonnay, consumed rather too quickly in their anticipation of reading the diary.

When the dishes were cleared and only the Chardonnay remained, Preswick and Lily joined them and Phil opened the diary.

"Well?" Bev said, when Phil didn't begin reading right away.

Phil turned a few pages, turned back to the beginning. "Not your ordinary daily diary," she said. "It looks more like a cross between her thoughts on some kind of treatment interspersed with chemical formulas."

"Well, that won't help us." Bev cast a hopeful look at Preswick, who did have a diverse knowledge of various subjects. "Any chemistry?"

"Rudimentary, I'm afraid," he replied.

Phil ran her finger down the page, turned to the next. "Here's something."

"'Fourth February, 1902. R's treatments are going well.' That must be Rose. 'She hardly ever displays . . .' Something I can't decipher. Latin, I think. Then some more that I can't read. She must be talking about whatever Rose suffers from. The next page is mainly symbols and abbreviations." She turned past them; they did her absolutely no good. Atkins would surely have a chemist who could make sense of it.

She continued to turn pages. More symbols and Latin. It seemed to be a log for medicinal applications. Strange, since Phil was under the impression Georgie had been a psychologist, not a chemist.

"Just formulas and comments and . . ." She turned the page and nearly dropped the book. "Good God. Look at this." She turned the diary so the others could see the large, thick "X" scratched across the page and obscuring the words beneath.

"It looks angry," Lily ventured.

"It does, indeed," Phil agreed. *Angry and desperate and final.*

"But what does it mean?"

Phil peered at the partially visible words. "'All is lost. All . . .' something . . . 'work.'"

"'All that work'?" Bev suggested.

"'All that work,'" Phil repeated. "'I have destroyed a bright future.'"

Preswick was the first to find his voice. "Is there a date?"

"'Twenty-third October, 1902.'" Phil sat back. Looked at the others. "But what happened between February, when R was doing well, and October, when all is lost?"

Phil thought back to the conversations she had heard. Salvos blaming Rose's condition on the Vogelers. Salvos blaming it on Georgina. These doctors were always so dramatic, it was hard to know what was factual and what was mere emoting.

And into her thoughts, Preswick said, "The end of the Boer War."

"And Ivan came back from the war." Phil turned the page, hoping to find some elucidation; found nothing but blank pages.

"Georgie stopped writing after that." Phil fanned through the remaining pages, caught a flash of black ink near the back. "Wait. Here is something. Dated only a few weeks ago." She riffled back through the pages, found nothing more. "Six years go by without her writing even one entry. Then she starts up again?

"'Tenth May, 1908. C. today. It's more than I can pay, will have to depend on the ponies this month.'"

"C.," said Bev. "That must be Chumley Griswold. Bobby said she was always broke. Maybe she couldn't pay him for the tonics he sold her."

"Perhaps," Phil said, "but listen to this.

"'C. slipped, said too much, and it all fell into place. Even though now I finally know the truth, still, I blame myself. I should have protected her from *le petit mal*. I knew what they were. Now, I know what they did. I will make them pay.'"

"Unfortunately, it looks like Georgina was the one who paid," Bev said.

Phil looked ahead, but all the remaining pages were blank. "I don't think we can wait to call Atkins. He needs to know this. Maybe it will make sense to him."

"Shall I make the call, my lady?"

"Thank you, but I'd better deal with this myself. It is my responsibility, after all."

Phil went out to the telephone, gave the telephone girl the precinct exchange, and waited.

As expected, the desk sergeant answered. "Hello, this is Mrs. Dalrymple. I need to speak with Detective Sergeant Atkins immediately."

As expected, he knew the name. She'd once jokingly told Atkins that in order not to sully his reputation that she would identify herself as Mrs. Dalrymple if ever she needed to contact him at the precinct. And in spite of the frivolity, it seemed to work. They all thought he was keeping a secret lover. And strangely enough, it upped his reputation in their eyes. It made the honorable policeman a little more human. A little less honest.

How wrong they were.

His voice came on the line minutes later. "Mrs. Dalrymple, how can I help you?"

His voice was tight. She just hoped he could hang onto his temper and not give her subterfuge away.

"Now, stay calm. Have you found where Georgina Nash lives—lived?"

"Unfortunately, not as yet."

"Well, we have. Well, not exactly, but we found her place of business."

"Wha—"

"Temper."

"Which is where?"

"Ears," she reminded him. Someone might be listening to their conversation.

"No one here is interested. Go ahead."

"Steeplechase, Coney Island. She has a booth there, and goes by the name of Madame Zhora. She's—was a fortune-teller."

An under-the-breath expletive was his response.

"I'll check it out. I don't suppose that you, uh, went in to have your fortune read?"

"Of course I did. It was an opportunity not to be missed. I know. How droll—" She stopped. Strange that those words echoed in her mind. Anna Vogeler's last words to Georgina before Georgina was killed. Not droll at all. Tragic. "I may have learned something, but perhaps you should see it for yourself. A stroll through the park? Tomorrow morning? Shall we say ten o'clock?"

"As you wish. Until then." He rang off.

Phil cringed and returned to the others. At least he'd have time to cool off before they met in person. "Tomorrow morning I will turn over Georgina's notes and tell him all."

Except perhaps Chumley's involvement. Atkins would have no trouble figuring that out from the diary. And Phil wouldn't have to involve the others. She just hoped Mr. X had finished whatever he needed to do before his part in this affair was blown to high heaven.

25

But the next morning, when it came to telling Atkins everything, Phil lost her nerve. Not because she was afraid of his reaction, or even of going to jail, though she'd rather not have either happen. But as usual, Mr. X had given her no instructions, and she didn't know exactly how much she could tell without exposing Mr. X's investigation and possibly leading him into a trap.

Atkins was standing by their usual park bench, staring across the pond, now tinged green by the lack of rain. The morning already promised to bring more heat, and Phil had dressed in her lightest lawn frock. Atkins was wearing a full summer suit, and suddenly Phil had an overwhelming desire to see him in his shirtsleeves.

Beyond that, she refused to go. Ever the gentleman, even in her imagination, he refused to overstep. Ah, but what a temptation.

He turned on that last thought, and Phil smiled. She hadn't meant to, but it would out. She snuffed it right away. This was serious business and she had a field of mines to tiptoe through.

Pay attention, she warned herself, and went to meet him halfway. Both literally and figuratively.

"Well, Mrs. Dalrymple. What are you going to astound me with this morning?"

She didn't like his mood. She wasn't quite as glad to see him now.

"Some things have come to light that I thought you should know."

"Shall we sit or walk?" he said, so polite and disinterested that she wanted to smack him. Which sent a dangerous image into her mind. She shoved it away.

"Walk, if you don't mind."

"Not at all." He offered her his arm and she took it. Walking would definitely be better, even though she had to admit her knees were shaking slightly. Still, if they were side by side she wouldn't have to look him in the eye as often.

"Actually, it was Lily who made the discovery."

"Ah, I thought she knew something she wasn't telling. She should learn to trust me."

Now she did make eye contact.

"Not all policeman are what she thinks they are," he said.

"She has utmost respect for you, as do we all," Phil added, in case he had any doubt. "But she just made the connection. Actually, we didn't quite believe her—"

"Perhaps you could get to the point."

"We were out at Coney Island the other day."

"Was this before or after you found Chumley's business card in Rose's purse?"

"After. Please don't groan."

"That wasn't a groan, more the gritting of teeth."

She looked up quickly at that. There was a definite twinkle in his eye. It was quickly gone.

Time for a little prevarication. "As you must know, Bev had horses running this past week at Brighton, and again in a couple of days in Sheepshead, so she asked if we would like to drive out with her."

"And The Oddity Shop just happened to be on your way. I know you were there, so why this elaborate—"

"I was just prefacing my information to give you some background."

"Of course you were."

She frowned at him and continued. "When we were driving to the track, Lily saw a poster advertising a fortune-teller named Madame Zhora." Phil risked a peek at his face to see if this was information he already knew. And was pleased to see that he looked quite oblivious.

"And?"

"And there was a picture of a woman in a turban and a young woman dancing. Lily thought it looked like Rose Nash."

"In a fortune-teller's ad?"

"Yes. Bev—Mrs. Reynolds and I had the same reaction, but Lily was insistent, and since no one seemed to be getting any closer to finding their address, at least not that they were telling, we decided to take a second look at the poster."

He stopped and turned toward her, causing a cyclist to swerve out of the way.

"I don't know why you think you should be involved in these cases. The first one I could take as a coincidence and a heightened sense of duty to help your friend when her husband died. Maybe even a second coincidence, when you were a guest at Godfrey Bennington's party for his godchild. But that even pushed the bounds of reason. But you just keep at it. It's gone way beyond being an infuriating, bossy—" He stopped abruptly. Took a breath.

Unfortunately, she was beginning to enjoy his loss of composure.

"I don't know how you fit into this. Did Godfrey ask you to look into the Vogeler situation? Is that why you were there when Dr. Nash was murdered? What is your relationship? Does he pay you to meddle? Then why bother to call me? He knows I'll get no support except what he dictates."

"Don't be absurd. And don't ask so many questions without giving the object of your questions a chance to answer. Basic interrogation technique."

"You're not under suspicion."

"That is gratifying to know," Phil said. She retook his arm and they started walking again. "Godfrey asked me to be his hostess. I agreed. Then, when I was a witness to Dr. Nash's murder, I felt compelled to help. And now that Lily is so affected by this young woman, Rose, I feel it imperative."

"Are you in his employ?"

"Don't be insulting. I may be a dowager, but I'm still a countess."

"You are that."

And it might have been her imagination, but it seemed as if he tightened his hold ever so slightly.

They walked along for a few moments in silence, the sounds of children and friends enjoying the day surrounding them. But between the two of them there was only business.

It was time to "come clean." *Well, cleanish.*

"We returned to Coney Island yesterday." She glanced over to him. "Now, that was a groan."

"Go on."

"We found Madame Zhora's stall in Steeplechase. It was closed, as you might expect."

"Please tell me you didn't break in."

"We didn't. Madame Zhora, who is indeed Georgie Nash, had left her key with a neighboring business, and they loaned it to us."

"And 'us' would be?"

"Myself, Bev, Preswick, and Lily, both of whom I'm responsible for." She hesitated. "And Bobby Mullins. But do not blame him. We just took him to watch our backs and facilitate things if there was trouble, which there wasn't."

"You should have turned that information over to the police and let us deal with it."

"Well, considering you were over an hour away if I could even find you, and the local police would no doubt ignore us, that didn't seem feasible."

"So you took a look around."

"Of course we did. When opportunity knocks, and all that. There was ledger of daily income and expenditures. We left that for you."

"Many thanks."

"Sarcasm doesn't become you, Detective Sergeant."

"You called me John a few days ago."

Phil stopped. "I never did. I wouldn't presume."

"Well, you did."

"If I did, I beg your pardon."

"Please don't."

Not being able to think of any acceptable reply, Phil continued with her story. "We found something else. A little notebook with what appears to be notes on chemical formulas, a running description of Rose's 'condition,' and several personal diary entries."

"And you have this?"

"Yes, in my purse. And since none of us has a knowledge of chemistry, perhaps one of your people will?"

"And Bennington's people don't?"

"I have no idea. Godfrey and I are friends, perhaps, though I wouldn't exactly call us that. I rather think that Godfrey never stoops to friendships. But if you're not interested . . ."

"You know I am. And you will turn it over."

"I have every intention of doing so. 'Little evil.'"

"What is?"

"Dr. Nash mentions it in the diary. *Petit mal.* Little evil. Do you think she was talking about Rose? Anna Vogeler is small, but Elisabeth Weiss is as tall as I am." And there were two women on the cover of "Nick Carter and A Dangerous Woman."

Atkins slowed. He was obviously thinking of something. Phil hoped he was about to impart something useful.

"I wonder," he said, after some moments of walking in silence.

Phil had been hoping for a little more than that.

"Let me see the diary."

"Here?"

"Yes."

She extracted it from her purse and handed it to him. Watched him read as pedestrians passed by and cyclists sped around them.

"Not an evil person. A thing. A condition. Petit mal seizures. I remember them from my Studies in Pathology course."

"Rose?" Phil asked. "I would say what Rose is suffering from is more than a seizure. She hasn't changed for days."

"So it would seem. Something else must be at work here."

"Georgie said in the diary that she blamed herself . . . even now that she knew the truth. The passage is there somewhere."

"I see it."

A boy on roller skates whizzed past, adjuring them to get the heck out of the way. Atkins pulled her to the side of the path without looking up.

"If Dr. Nash was treating her sister, perhaps gave her something that was responsible for the current state of Rose's mind." He turned the page. "See, these formulas are just variable enough to—" He broke off, suddenly remembering who was whom. "I'll take this and have someone I know look more closely."

Phil resisted the urge to stamp her foot, even though the toe of his polished boot was awfully close and tempting.

"That's the tragedy everyone speaks of, but no one names?" Phil said. "I wonder if anyone even knows?"

"You realize that this makes even a stronger case for the killer being Ivan Thomas."

"Because he blames Georgie for Rose's condition? That doesn't wash. Rose evidently wasn't like this until after he returned from the war, after Rose had turned him down."

"The first time she turned him down. Who is to say he didn't try again after he returned? Regardless, he had the most to lose, and he was the only one of their immediate group who was not in attendance at the scene."

"True." Phil had to admit that it was looking very bad for Ivan. And they already had him in custody at Bellevue. And yet . . . "There just seems to be a missing thread. Things that don't fall into place."

Atkins took her arm and he began to retrace their steps, suddenly in a hurry to end the meeting. Phil shouldn't have told him about the notebook so soon.

"So, now you don't think the intended victim was Dr. Vogeler?"

Receiving no answer, she continued. "But there had been one attempt on Vogeler's life in Washington," Phil argued, lengthening her stride to keep up with him. "And the only person that we know of in Washington at that time was his assistant, Alan Toussaint. And he—" She'd almost slipped about Toussaint's visit to The Oddity Shop.

"I'm keeping an open mind," he countered.

They were practically jogging toward the park entrance.

"There is the aide-de-camp secretary—"

Phil's breath caught. "Who had, as yet, not been assigned to him."

"So says Godfrey Bennington. And there's Bennington himself."

"Oh, really. You don't suspect Godfrey of attempting to have the man murdered?"

"I haven't ruled it out. He sees the future of war in one way, and Vogeler in another."

"War seems like such a stupid thing to haggle over."

Atkins laughed. "An interesting way to look at it."

"Whether Dr. Vogeler was the intended victim or not, Georgie Nash is dead," Phil reminded him.

"All the more reason for me to have the contents of her notebook analyzed."

"I agree. Dr. Vogeler's lecture is this evening. Godfrey wants to see the back of them, and I confess, so do I."

"So do we all," Atkins agreed.

"Then I suggest you cooperate with me and we see this to a quick end."

Well, her last suggestion hadn't gone well, Phil thought after they had parted at the park entrance. Rather than agreeing to cooperate, Atkins had told her in no uncertain terms to "back off." A rather strong way of putting it, she thought. And a suggestion she had no intention of following.

If you asked her, she had been doing an awful lot of legwork not to get any thanks for it.

But her fate had been sealed the moment she'd turned over the notebook. No matter; she and Preswick and Lily had taken copious notes.

And she hadn't told Atkins about the vials of potions Georgina had in her fortune-teller's stall. Well, he could just find that out for himself.

There was a link between Chumley and Georgina. Chumley would be at the lecture tonight. But did she dare give him cause to think he was being investigated?

Here she was again, Phil thought as she waited for the Plaza elevator. Staying away from a promising lead because she was afraid of stepping on Mr. X's investigation. And there was no way she could ask, since she never knew where he was. At least she could telephone the detective sergeant. Not that confiding in him gained her one little thing.

She stamped her foot in frustration just as the elevator door opened.

"Is something wrong, Lady Dunbridge?" asked Egbert as she stepped inside.

Phil sighed. "Nothing at all, Egbert, nothing at all."

She was just walking in the door when the telephone rang.

Preswick answered it. "Dr. Weiss is downstairs asking if you are at home."

"Interesting. By all means, I'd be delighted to see her."

Phil quickly took off her hat and barely had time to toss it on a chair before the buzzer rang and Elisabeth Weiss entered.

"Good morning, Lady Dunbridge," Elisabeth said brightly. Evidently without the inducement of whiskey, they were back on formal terms.

She was wearing her teaching uniform of skirt and shirtwaist. "I snagged Dietrich as he was pulling out of his garage. He was on his way downtown to make a house call. How wonderful it must be to have so many ladies with neuroses. Even if he has to help them imagine them so he can treat them.

"I coerced him into giving me a ride. He let me off at Columbus Circle, and since I was in the neighborhood, I thought I would pay a morning call."

Phil doubted very seriously if Elisabeth had just happened to be in the neighborhood. And the twinkle in the professor's eye showed that she didn't expect Phil to believe her, nor did she care.

So why had she come? Phil wondered. Not to make innuendos about Dr. Lutz. Georgie had made pretty much the same accusations just before she was killed.

"I came to see how your investigation is going."

"My investigation? I'm merely—"

"Investigating. Let's skip the façade, shall we? I just saw you leaving the park with the detective sergeant. And though he's a fine specimen, I don't believe you're being courted."

"Indeed not," Phil said. "And I'm glad you came."

"You are?"

"Yes. I wonder if you could give me some background on the Nashes. Fix some points in the time line that I'm not clear on."

"If I can."

"When Ivan came back from the war, was Rose already the way she is now?"

Elisabeth's eyebrows knitted. "Let me see. No, not at first, now that I think about it. She was quite normal—as normal as brilliant people ever are. Occasionally, she seemed to be somewhere else.

But that is also common in higher thinkers. . . . Though there were times I did think . . . But I never pursued it."

"What?" Phil asked.

"That she might be . . ."

"Having petit mal seizures?" Phil finished.

"It had crossed my mind. But what makes *you* think that?"

"Just a bit of information I came across. But she was not like she is now?"

"Oh, no. The times I saw only lasted seconds, so I was never sure. Of course, I would never say anything. It's hard enough for women to make it in this world without giving men reason not to advance her."

"Did it affect her work?"

"I don't see how it would."

"Unless they became worse," Phil said.

"They wouldn't, not like this. Something else is at play here. Something with a tragic outcome."

"Drugs?"

"My, you are being blunt today."

"Time is running out."

Elisabeth's eyebrows rose. "For you or for someone else? Surely you don't think there will be another murder?"

Phil hadn't even considered that. Well, not out loud, anyway.

"I'd just like to bring this to a close."

"And you think Rose's condition has something to do with Georgie's murder?"

"Do you think there could be another reason?" Phil asked.

"I was under the assumption that it was Erik's life that was in danger. He mentioned it often enough at dinner."

"I'm just looking at all possibilities," Phil told her.

"I don't think Georgie was an innocent bystander, if that's what you're trying to find out. I have to wonder why she even came to dinner, except to make accusations. All that talk of dark omens and lurking danger? That was pure Georgie. She was putting on an act. But for what reason? That's what I can't figure out. And why bring poor Rose?"

"To make a point?"

"To whom, about what? It doesn't make sense."

Phil thought of the diary entry about making them pay. But she held her tongue. She liked Elisabeth, but she was quite capable of making a morning call to divert suspicion from herself.

There were four women in that circle: Georgie, Rose, Elisabeth, and Anna. Georgie was dead. The other three had been in plain sight when Georgie was killed. Elisabeth and Anna were both capable of planning a murder, but Phil didn't think Rose could imagine such a deed.

"For what it's worth, I had no part in planning or conducting the murder," Elisabeth said. "I had no idea of Georgie and Rose's whereabouts. I don't expect you to take me at my word. And though it stings my pride, I would be disappointed if you did. Just know that I will be willing to help in any way I can." Dr. Weiss rose. She'd been there less than fifteen minutes. "I'll let you get back to it. Thank you for seeing me."

"Wait," Phil said, standing. "If Georgie had not been warning Dr. Vogeler, but instead was threatening him, what would be her reason?"

Elisabeth frowned; sat back down. "Is that what you think?"

"It's possible."

"I know that Erik and Anna discouraged Rose from becoming involved with Ivan. They considered him unsuitable. Not that they should have a say in it, except that they hold certain views."

"What views?"

"Ivan wasn't actually Romanian but . . . Roma."

"Roma?"

"A gypsy. Orphaned, educated, employed, yet still what Erik would call inferior. Though I've sometimes thought . . ." She shook her head.

"What? Now is not the time to let sensibilities strike you mute," said Phil.

Elisabeth laughed. "I doubt if yours ever do."

"Rarely," Phil agreed.

"I've wondered if perhaps Erik had interests there himself. Not that I think he ever stepped over the line, but you can tell from a glance, a pause. Those little things that give men away when they're being oh-so-careful."

Phil thought of Erik at Rose's bedside, his eye red-rimmed. "Do you think Anna knew?"

"If she didn't, it's because she chose not to."

Phil nodded. "The English way of life."

"Oh, please. England doesn't have the corner on that market."

"Do you think Georgie suspected?"

"I have no idea. She was against the match herself. Or would have been if Rose had pressed the issue. Rose wasn't about to marry anyone. In fact, we all thought she would be accepted into advanced theoretics, before whatever happened and she became what you see today. She liked Ivan but she wasn't in love with him.

"Now, I must go. I have an afternoon seminar. I'll see you at Erik's lecture this evening?"

Phil nodded.

"Good. Then after that, we can say goodbye to the Vogelers and their games of the mind. I find that I quite prefer the petty jealousies of women's college."

26

Phil spent the rest of the afternoon in contemplation of what she'd learned that day, which had only made the investigation more complicated and their next move unclear. There was something more surrounding this murder that she hadn't, as yet, plumbed. There usually was when Mr. X was on the case.

She knew her part of the investigation was to expose the killer and see him or her brought to justice. Mr. X's job was to do whatever would be the domino effect that was dependent on her success.

It put an enormous amount of pressure on her, especially since she didn't understand it completely . . . ever.

Once the lecture was over, time would be of the essence. Though if Atkins wanted the Vogelers held for longer, she had no doubt Godfrey would see that it was done.

Maybe tonight would be the night when it would fall into place. She imagined all members of the original dinner party would be in attendance. Except Ivan, of course, who, as far as Phil knew, was still being observed at Bellevue. Salvos said he wouldn't attend, but could he really stay away?

By the time Lily came in to dress her for the lecture, Phil's patience was stretched beyond enduring and she had no interest in choosing an evening wardrobe.

"A countess must always strive to look her best," Lily reminded her. Something she must have heard in the maids' withdrawing room at some function they'd attended. And her slightly ironic tone went a long way to settling Phil's nerves.

Phil decided on a gown of deep amethyst with an aqua soutache border, simple enough for serious listening but with a little panache in case there were more formal activities afterward—and, if she was lucky, utilitarian enough for bringing a murderer to justice.

Bev arrived at five for a prelecture cocktail, and soon they all set off for an evening walk, Phil and Bev to the Pantheon Club on East Sixtieth Street, and Preswick and Lily to Union House farther up Fifth Avenue.

They passed Just a Friend on the way. He still had several papers to sell and was holding out for the stragglers hurrying home from a day at work.

He fell in step with them until they crossed the street, then ran back to his post. Phil stopped at the corner. "Lily, if you feel at all threatened, tell Collins. I'm certain things will be secured very efficiently tonight."

"I will be fine," Lily said. "And hopefully I will learn something." She and Preswick waited until Phil and Bev had traversed the half block to the Pantheon Club, then continued on their way.

"You know, I've never been here," Bev said, as they passed between the four columns of the Beaux Arts building that housed the private social club. "I suppose that means I've been remiss on lectures on arts, humanities, society, and political theories."

"You've been busy with other things," Phil said.

They were welcomed at the door by a uniformed porter, who directed them to the lecture hall, where gold spindle chairs were set up facing a stage and podium.

A number of people waiting to hear the lecture had gathered at the back of the room. Phil spotted Chumley Griswold immediately. He was talking seriously with two bearded men. He handed them both what appeared to be business cards, but Phil doubted if they were ones from The Oddity Shop. So, was he drumming up trade for his party entertainments? Though she wouldn't put it past him to drum up a little business for his potions, either.

There was a smattering of women, dressed from severe to frivolous, determined, Phil imagined, by their plans for after the lecture. But the majority were men.

"Psychoanalysts must have an inordinate number of weak chins," Bev said under her breath. "I don't think I've seen so many styles of beard in one room ever. A veritable Sears catalog of facial hair."

It was true. There were Vandykes and goatees; straggly and full; long, short, and close to the jaw. A few lone mustaches rode above an occasional clean chin.

"Perhaps it makes them look more erudite." For Phil's part, she preferred a clean-shaven cheek.

Godfrey Bennington, sporting neither mustache nor beard, was talking with several men whose sashes identified them as members of the New York Psychology Society.

He saw Phil and Bev and came to greet them.

"Any news?" Phil asked.

Godfrey shook his head. "Atkins is here somewhere. He assigned extra details to the building."

"Are you expecting trouble?" Bev asked.

"Not really. I'm beginning to think my assessment was correct at the outset."

Phil nodded. *That no one was out to kill Erik Vogeler at all.*

Elisabeth Weiss and Dietrich Lutz entered, nodded at Phil and the others, and walked down the center aisle to take seats in the front row.

Erik and Anna Vogeler were already standing on a raised stage at the far end of the lecture hall, talking to one man who appeared to be the presenter. Alan Toussaint stood just behind Erik Vogeler's shoulder, looking more like the proud owner of a clever poodle than a lowly assistant.

Anna stood a little apart from the others, either ignored or willfully ignoring them, looking over the crowd. And Phil wondered what she was thinking. Was she proud of her husband's success, content to be a wife and a mother? The woman behind the man?

How many women were stuck in just that position? And how many had grown resentful?

Phil turned back to Erik, who was, at the moment, speaking with one of the members who was dressed in a conservatively fashioned black suit and sporting an unwieldy beard. He practically hovered over the shorter Vogeler. Whatever he had just said made Vogeler frown.

The sheer sight of him made Phil's heart stutter with panic.

The former Francis Kellogg. What was he doing? He'd lived for several days under the same roof as Vogeler's personal assistant, the army aide-de-camp and never-who-he-seemed Mr. X. She was amazed that Erik didn't recognize him. Phil certainly did, even with the beard, and she was at the opposite end of the room.

What bravado and sheer deviltry. He might be recognized by any number of people attending. Godfrey, especially.

And if Godfrey did suddenly recognize him, he would warn Atkins that his best suspect was here. Phil searched the room and found the detective sergeant standing off to one side, conveniently equidistant between two wall sconces and looking rather menacing in the shadows.

He caught her eye, and Phil's expression went blank. Then he turned his gaze toward the stage. Had he seen her reaction to Mr. X in that one moment of recognition? Did he have any idea of the man's involvement with all the cases they'd been involved in?

Phil ordered herself not to look at either of them.

At last, the Vogelers and other dignitaries on the stage sat down. The master of ceremonies took his place at the podium.

"Good evening, ladies, gentlemen, and esteemed colleagues. The New York Psychology Society is privileged to present Dr. Erik Vogeler, world-renowned psychoanalyst and Jungian psychologist." He continued on with biographical details and introduced Erik to enthusiastic applause.

Phil quickly took her seat at the back with Godfrey and Bev, and noticed that her ersatz psychologist had left the stage.

"As you are aware," Erik began, "there have been amazing strides . . ."

Phil quickly scanned the rows of guests, looking for her illusive comrade. It was impossible to see among the other seated audience members.

". . . strict, rigorous scientific method, but not enough. Some mental phenomenon have been inexplicable until now . . ."

Vogeler spoke animatedly, but Phil was only half listening. Where was Atkins? She didn't dare turn around. Had he spotted his quarry and was in pursuit while she sat here?

". . . every weak or broken link can be modified for maximum utility. No longer will fear, anxiety, indecision hamper the decision-making process."

"Here, here," someone called out.

"Nonsense," called another.

Vogeler talked on, and Phil kept looking for Mr. X. When

she returned to listening, she realized that the atmosphere had gradually grown tense. Those who had been merely listening to an interesting lecture before now sat on the edges of their chairs. Others leaned back with their arms crossed in obvious dissension.

Beside her, Godfrey stiffened with barely suppressed feelings. Surely Vogeler wasn't going to spill the governmental beans.

"Are you actually claiming to make a person more functional than his fellow beings?" This was a voice Phil recognized. Dietrich Lutz.

"Ridiculous," someone echoed.

"If the means are present, it would be criminal not to," Vogeler answered.

"Hogwash!" Dietrich shot back.

Now Phil understood why Dietrich had taken a seat at the front.

"Not to those who keep up with the times," Vogeler countered.

"Immoral," another audience member cried. "You dare to toy with God's creation?"

"Absolutely not, merely finely tuning it."

Beside her, Godfrey was practically rumbling. "Immoral and seditious. You see where this is going."

Phil was afraid, in light of what Godfrey had already told her, that she did.

"You're not trying to help people, you're daring to make automatons."

"Not automatons," Vogeler said. "Superior men. Stronger men. It's the future. The future will belong to those who have the courage to grasp it. And whoever refuses to keep up will be left behind."

"Insupportable."

"You're talking about manipulating the species, man."

"I'm talking about man achieving his full potential," Vogeler countered.

"Blasphemy!"

"Fools!"

"Scoundrel!"

The director jumped to his feet and hurried to the podium. "I'd like to thank Dr. Vogeler for his splendid talk this evening," he called out over the noise. "Now, if you'll all join us for some refreshments at the back."

There was polite applause by some, but the heckling continued.

As Vogeler descended the steps from the dais, he was immediately surrounded by a group asking questions and arguing their own theories.

Bev leaned over. "At this rate we'll be here all night. I'm going to need more than punch."

"Pompous ass," Godfrey said under his breath.

"Come, let us join the others," Phil said, and rose. Godfrey belatedly remembered Phil and Bev, and gestured them ahead. They walked to the back of the room, where a crowd had gathered around the punch bowl.

By the door, Atkins was ramrod stiff.

Of the hirsute psychologist there was not a sign.

And finally, she saw why. Another one who had been present was no longer among the crowd: Chumley Griswold.

Phil had to fight the impulse to run out to the front door and search the streets for the two missing men, but she didn't dare.

Then all choice of what to do was taken completely out of her hands. The porter entered the room and headed directly and swiftly toward Godfrey.

"Mr. Bennington," the porter said. "A Mr. Collins just telephoned to say that you are needed immediately at Union House. That the bird had gotten out of its cage and no one can get it back in."

Godfrey didn't even blink. "My daughter's parakeet, tiresome bird." He turned and quickly scanned the room. "Ah, Lutz, could you tell the Vogelers I'll send the car for them, but I have another pressing appointment?"

"You can be assured I will, but no need. I'll drive them myself," Dietrich said, and strode away, a satisfied smile on his lips.

Bev, like a homing pigeon, was at Phil's side. "What's happening?"

"I don't know for certain, but it appears Rose has made her escape."

Godfrey was heading, seemingly unhurried, toward the door. Atkins just happened to arrive before him, and opened it for him. They walked out apparently separately, but Phil knew better.

"And Lily?"

"I don't know, but let's find out." They headed for the door.

They caught up to Godfrey and Atkins on the sidewalk.

"What did Collins say? Is Rose gone? What about Lily?" Phil demanded.

"He didn't say," Godfrey said. "We'll know more soon enough."

"I have the station's auto. Do you need a lift?" Atkins asked.

"It will be faster walking. But the ladies might—"

"The ladies would not," Phil said, and set off toward Fifth Avenue without waiting.

"Fine. I'm going back inside to organize a search, but don't do anything until I get there." Atkins was already running back inside, leaving the end of his sentence trailing behind him.

Godfrey and Bev caught up to Phil as she'd reached the corner. The three of them practically ran the two blocks to Union House.

And came to a dead stop when they saw Collins standing on the stoop and Preswick sitting below him on the steps, holding a towel to the head of a small boy.

"Don't get up!" Phil ordered when she saw Preswick start to his feet. "What happened?"

"I let 'em get away," Just a Friend said, his bottom lip quivering below a blackening eye.

"You did no such thing," Preswick said sternly. "You took on a very powerful man. It was a brave thing to do."

And something a boy shouldn't be doing. Ever. Even if he was a street urchin and was perfectly capable of taking care of himself. Even if he had decided he was their protector.

Phil didn't know what to say, and before she could frame her most pressing question, Just a Friend said, "They took Miss Lily."

Phil shot a frightened look toward Preswick.

"Mr. Collins telephoned me right after it happened and I came straight over. I took the liberty of ordering the Daimler, my lady. I thought we might need it."

"Indeed, we will, Preswick."

The Panhard et Levassor pulled to a stop at the curb, and Atkins jumped out.

"Now that the detective sergeant is here," Godfrey said, "Collins, can you tell us exactly what happened?"

"Sir." Collins stood at attention. "The staff and I were having
our supper when we heard a crash. We ran out to see what it was,
expecting there might be some trouble. He had broken the glass
in the parlor window and let himself inside by the time we arrived. He held a pistol, army-issue Mauser, I believe. Miss Nash
had run down the stairs by then.

"I think he and Miss Nash had somehow planned it. She was
carrying a bundle with her, and the books Lady Dunbridge's Lily
brought to read. Lily ran after her and pleaded with Miss Nash
not to go with him, but he grabbed Lily, held the pistol to her head.
I don't think he intended to hurt her, but he was as jumpy as a
wet cat. We didn't dare take the chance."

"Rightly so," Godfrey said.

"They made Lily go with them. She wasn't a part of the scheme,"
Collins assured Phil.

"And the nurse?" Godfrey asked.

"Drugged. We found her afterward in the dressing room. Cook
is looking after her now."

Godfrey turned on Atkins. "I thought you locked the poor bastard up."

"He was transported to Bellevue. I wasn't advised that he'd
been released."

"I followed them outside," Collins added. "They were in an old
auto—"

"Dr. Salvos's Ford," Atkins said. "Of course. He wasn't at the
lecture; now we know why."

"There appeared to be only the man, Ivan Thomas, besides the
two young ladies. Miss Nash got into the auto willingly, but he
had to push Lily into the back. That's when this brave lad sprang
from behind the car. Thomas knocked him down and jumped in
the car. They were traveling south."

Just a Friend hung his head. "I shoulda stopped 'em."

"You were a brave soldier, young man," Collins said. "If you ever decide you'd like to join the services, you just come to me and I'll fix it all right and tight."

Phil smiled at the butler, so full of gratitude that her eyes welled up. She forced them back. This was the time for action, not sentiment.

Bev, the dear, didn't bother. She choked out. "You were so brave. We're all proud of you." She finished with a loud sniff.

"I've requested several officers to go round to Salvos's clinic in case they turn up there," Atkins said. "Collins, do you think the nurse might be able to help us with what transpired upstairs?"

Collins shook his head. "I doubt if she'll be lucid for another hour or so."

"By then it might be too late," Phil snapped.

Atkins cut her a sharp look. "Calm yourself. I don't think there is immediate cause for alarm."

"I will not calm myself. I will do something," Phil snapped back. "And here's how I will do it," she added, as her blue Daimler pulled up behind Atkins's Panhard et Levassor.

"You will go back to the Plaza and wait until you hear from me."

"Fat chance," Bev mumbled.

The standoff was interrupted by the sight of a taxi screeching to a stop and Pietro Salvos jumping out. The driver immediately started yelling.

"I don't have the fare," Salvos explained.

Collins went over to pay the driver.

"I came as soon as I discovered it gone."

"The automobile," Atkins said.

"Yes."

"How did Thomas get out of Bellevue? Did he escape?"

"No, they ran their tests, and he passed them all. Dr. Pullman, head of the division, and I discussed his prognosis and agreed for him to take medication that Dr. Pullman prescribed. There are certain drugs that sedate and calm but leave the body functional. The doctor agreed that under this medication he would not be a threat to himself or others and released him to my care."

"Then why has he kidnapped Miss Nash and Lady's Dunbridge's maid?"

Salvos dropped to the steps and cradled his head in his hands. Finally looked up.

"This is not the act of a demented man. He is doing what any lover would do. Saving his sweetheart from a dastardly conniver. I would have done it myself, if I had only understood."

"And just what didn't you understand?" Atkins asked.

"The Vogelers treated Ivan when he returned from the war. I believe they may be treating him again. He hadn't had any serious episodes for a long while. Not until they came to New York. I didn't realize until dinner that they had been here for a number of days earlier. That's exactly the time that Ivan began to disappear for long stretches of time, and acting distant and agitated.

"I couldn't imagine what caused this sudden change. Now I know he must have been meeting them and getting treatments. I don't know how they found us and lured him away, but whatever they were doing to him caused him to relapse. He felt it, though he was helpless against it. He was afraid they would to the same thing to Rose. It was dangerous for either of them to be around Erik and Anna. He had no choice but to try and save her."

Having heard some of Erik Vogeler's theories tonight, Phil was inclined to believe him. "Where *are* the Vogelers?" she asked. "Shouldn't they be back by now?"

"Lutz is bringing them home," Godfrey said. "It's better that we deal with this before they return."

Atkins took Pietro aside. "Do you have any idea of where they might have gone?"

Pietro shook his head. "Not to the clinic. Ivan knows that would be the first place you would look. Indeed, your men were there when I left, ransacking the place. It will take who knows how long to set things to rights. But I knew I had to choose."

"Anywhere else?"

"I have no idea."

"How about Madame Zhora's?" Atkins pressed.

"Madame . . . who? I don't know of this person."

Atkins huffed a sigh. "No, I don't think you do."

Collins pulled something from his back pocket. "Lily dropped this in the scuffle as they were leaving. I don't know if it was by accident or on purpose. Does it mean anything?"

Akins took it. "It's one of Lily's dime novels."

Phil and Bev both pressed close to see, but Phil already knew what it would be: "Nick Carter's Coney Island Search."

"They've gone to Coney Island."

"Wonderful," Godfrey said. "Do you know how many people live in Coney Island or how many thousands of tourists are there this time of year?"

"Does Ivan know where Rose lives?" Atkins asked.

"I don't see how. He was shocked to see her that night at the Arsenal."

"Do you know where they live?"

Pietro shook his head. "I would have told you, and so would Ivan."

"Do you think Miss Nash capable of finding her own way home?"

"From what little I've seen of her, I doubt it."

"No," Phil added. "But maybe we can."

27

"How?" Atkins demanded.

"The only thing we found among Rose's possessions was the Oddity Shop card," Phil said. "Why?"

She was met with blank stares, and one angry one.

"She's lost, she can't find her way home . . ."

"But if someone directed her or took her to The Oddity Shop, they would know how to get her home," said Atkins. "Which means Chumley has been lying all along."

"And he'll probably be there now. It's the only lead we have."

"*My* lead. I'll telephone the Coney Island precinct and ask them to get someone over there. You go to the Plaza and wait to hear from me."

"There's no time. We have to find her—them."

"No," cried Pietro. "I need to see Ivan first. Calm him down."

"I'm afraid it's too late for that," Atkins said. "I'm truly sorry, Salvos. Lady Dunbridge, stay out of this. Bennington, the telephone?"

"Certainly, come inside." Godfrey hurried up the stairs, with Collins running ahead and Atkins following behind with Pietro.

"The precinct," Phil said. "By the time they get find someone to take the call, organize a party, God only knows how long that will take."

"Why wait?" Bev said. "Come on. You drive. I'll navigate."

Without another word, Phil, Bev, and Preswick hurried toward Phil's Daimler.

But when Just a Friend tried to climb in behind Preswick, the butler stopped him. "You've done your duty. You stay here with Mr. Collins and keep an eye on things."

Just a Friend shook his head.

"Mr. Preswick is correct," Phil said, and started the car. "Thank

heavens for this key apparatus, so much faster than the crank."
The auto fired up.

"No sir-ree, *my* lady. I'm coming, too." Just A Friend threw
himself under Preswick's barring arm and landed on the seat beside him.

"Aw, let him come," Bev said. "He deserves to be in on the
chase." She leaned out the door to check traffic just as the house
door opened and Godfrey stepped onto the stoop. "Traffic's clear.
Take Fifth down to Broadway. To the bridge. Whoo-hoo! Hang
on, Lily, we're coming!"

Phil turned the Daimler into the street and sped away, accompanied by a horse breeder, a butler, and a newsboy. The best
irregulars a detectival countess could wish for.

Bev turned around, smiled, and waved. "I do believe we're being followed," she called over to Phil.

"Good. The more the merrier. Let them try to stop us." Phil
swerved around a slow-moving lorry, squeezed the Daimler in between two opposing wagons, and shot forward.

There was traffic, but that didn't bother Phil. She wove in and out
of the other vehicles like she was running the French Grand Prix.

They passed over the Brooklyn Bridge in record time, hair flying, dirt-and dust-speckled, and for one small passenger, eyes
wide with amazement and perhaps just a little unease as the lights
of Manhattan receded behind them—except for two headlights
that mirrored their every move.

"I have to hand it to John Atkins," Bev said. "He's keeping up
very neatly. Interesting."

Phil, for once, was glad of the escort. Even if she was bound to
suffer for it once he caught up. She didn't care. She'd do whatever
she had to do to save Lily, even go to jail, if that's what he wanted.

And with him following her, she could go about getting Lily
back without worrying about flat tires or running out of gas or
the hundreds of other things that went wrong with these machines
when one was desperate to get somewhere.

Atkins didn't try to overtake her. Just followed close behind,
close enough now that she could see Godfrey and Dr. Salvos ac-
companying him.

Even at the outrageous speed they were going, it seemed to take forever before they pulled to a stop in front of The Oddity Shop. The lights were off. Had Chumley not come here after all? She'd been so sure that he was the key to Lily's whereabouts.

"Everyone stay where you are," Preswick commanded. "I'll check the door."

They were all so shocked at Preswick's order that they didn't move.

The Panhard et Levassor pulled up behind them, and Atkins, Godfrey, and Salvos got out and hurried across the dark street. Their arrival broke the spell, and Phil, Bev, and Just a Friend followed them, Phil pausing only long enough to grab her purse and the pistol inside.

Preswick was just trying the handle. The door opened.

"Stand back," Atkins said, and reached inside his jacket pocket.

Phil froze. Mainly out of sheer surprise, as she realized she'd never actually seen the detective sergeant with a firearm. Perhaps it was merely a handkerchief. But as she watched, he indeed pulled out a long-nosed Colt .38. Phil recognized it from the Sears catalog.

He slipped inside. The others waited, barely breathing, until a light came on and they all squeezed through the door.

The shop was empty.

Phil started immediately for the stairs to the second floor. Atkins was there before her. He didn't bother to give her orders. She had no intention of standing down for him—or anyone.

"Good God!" Atkins exclaimed at the top of the stairs. Chumley's lab had been ransacked. Vials lay on the floor, beakers were broken, and chemicals dripped from the table edges. But no Chumley.

Phil hurried to open the closet door. It, too, had been ransacked. But no one had been stuffed inside.

Atkins gave her a sharp look, but he said, "We'll find her."

They went back downstairs to find Godfrey and Preswick studying the bookshelves. Just as Phil opened her mouth to ask what they were doing, the case sprang open to reveal a second set of stairs, this time going down.

"A basement," Phil said. "I didn't think of that."

Atkins moved her aside, none too gently, but she followed right behind him. Once again, he stopped at the bottom and the others had to squeeze around him. Atkins rummaged in his jacket and brought out a torch, much smaller than Phil's. And brighter, she noticed as the beam shone through the darkness.

For a moment, she could only stare as the light swept over beakers, bottles, large glass containers, tubes, and Bunsen burners.

A light came on. Someone had found the light switch. They were surrounded by a large and very ordered laboratory that put the little one upstairs to shame.

Godfrey let out an expletive.

"Drugs," Pietro said. He strode over and opened a bottle of crystals, took a minute amount on his finger, and touched his tongue to it. He flicked the rest away. "So, that's it. No wonder he lives so well."

"Black market for cocaine and morphine because of the new law?" Bev asked.

"No," Pietro said sharply. "Well, perhaps that, too, but these are . . ." He took the cap off another, sniffed, and recapped it. He turned to Godfrey. "If I'm not mistaken, they are mixtures of medicine to treat different forms of neuroses and psychosis." He picked up another glass vial, which held hard, yellow grains. "Experimental preparations that aren't available to most practitioners. Or beyond their ability to pay." His hand closed around the vial so tightly that it began to shake. "Here is the future of psychology—if used correctly. And most certainly the future of the military programs that Vogeler is espousing."

"What?" Godfrey's disbelief and ire exploded into the room. "He would drug our soldiers?"

"He would do anything to further his cause."

"Psychoanalysis?" Bev asked.

"A mere means to his end."

"What end?"

"Eugenics, by God," Godfrey said. "I should have guessed. Warfare training was just the beginning. I thought there was something unsavory about the man."

Phil was surprised that she wasn't as shocked as she should be. She'd gotten an inkling from her conversations with Anna.

All her talk about broken men and making them even better than before. The exchange in the park with Chumley. Toussaint at his shop that night. He must be supplying them with drugs. They were all in on it.

"An army of supermen," Phil said.

"Good heavens," exclaimed Bev.

"What are they talking about?" Just a Friend whispered to Preswick.

"Something bad."

"Have they done something bad to Lily?"

"Not if we get to them first," Atkins said. "Everyone upstairs and outside. Do not touch a thing on your way."

No one argued.

Once outside, Atkins dispatched Preswick to summon a patrolman to guard the shop, then came over to Phil, who was perusing the street.

"I was sure I was right," Phil said. "It was the only thing she had with her. Maybe all her talk about ducks and wheels led them to the country and not here at all."

"Or maybe . . ." He turned her to look down Seventeenth Street.

The street formed a tunnel straight to the bright lights of Surf Avenue and the Steeplechase entrance. And beyond, rising above the landscape was . . .

"The Ferris wheel," Phil exclaimed. "Not a water wheel, but a Ferris wheel. It's not about The Oddity Shop except as a starting point. Georgina must have drilled that into Rose's head, in case she ever got lost. That's why she had the card. Someone could always direct her here. Go to The Oddity Shop. She'd see the Ferris wheel. And she'd go toward that. They must live somewhere close."

Phil started off down the street.

"Wait," Atkins said. "We'll all go. Here comes Preswick now."

Preswick and two patrolmen. Atkins quickly gave them orders, then they all started down the street en masse.

Phil tried not to imagine what they might find when they finally did get to Lily and the others. She concentrated on *ducks*.

There were no ducks around here. No ponds. Just bricks and paving stones and lots of people. She didn't remember seeing any ponds in Steeplechase when they'd gone to Madame Zhora's. And as far as she knew, no one actually lived in the amusement park. So where were the ducks?

They reached Surf Avenue, where the lights of oncoming autos sped toward them like a new and dangerous thrill ride. Phil stepped into the street, stopping traffic by the expedient of sticking out her arm. Accompanied by screeching brakes, yells, and horns, Phil led the others across the street.

Right into the entrance of Steeplechase Park.

Phil stared at it in disbelief. She hadn't made that connection. The stone in her stomach was suddenly wedged in her throat.

Bev slipped up beside her, and put her arm in Phil's. "We'll find her."

"Of course we will," Phil returned, but looked at Atkins for an answer. "The Ferris wheel is inside the park. She had no money, how could she get in?"

"I doubt if they live in the park, even secretly. There are strict fire laws." He turned away to peruse the street. "Ducks," he said thoughtfully.

"The shooting gallery," Just a Friend said.

"What?"

"Over there, the shooting gallery. They're ducks."

Ducks, thought Phil. They'd stood across the street from this very gallery while waiting for Bobby to get tickets to the park, passed by it without even looking, because they hadn't thought beyond the most obvious. *Not ducks in a pond, but ducks in a shooting gallery.*

"Dammit, Ji—Just a Friend. They're ducks," Atkins said.

"That's what I said," Just a Friend said, running behind him as Atkins crossed the street again, Phil at his heels.

Once more, traffic screeched to a halt as they all recrossed the street.

Atkins checked at the shooting gallery. The barker pointed to a door just to the right of the gallery. "First landing, apartment A. We don't want no trouble."

Atkins led the way inside. The pistol came out again. "Will you please stay here?"

Phil shook her head.

"Let's just get on with it, Atkins," Godfrey said.

Atkins blew out a breath. And headed up the stairs.

Once at the top, he held up his hand, stopping them all, listened, then went to the door on his right.

The door was ajar. Atkins slipped inside.

28

He came out a minute later. "Empty. But they were here." He held up another of Lily's novels. "Nick Carter and A Dangerous Woman."

"Dangerous woman?" Bev said. "You're looking at two of them. But what is Lily trying to tell us?"

"That she's running out of novels to leave," Atkins said drily. "Come on."

"Where to now?" Godfrey demanded.

"To Madame Zhora's. It's the only other place they would go."

For the third time, they stopped traffic and crossed the street. Atkins flashed his badge at the ticket seller, then motioned to two of the park's green-uniformed guards. "You two, I'll need your assistance." They followed him into the park. Godfrey slid a silver dollar over to the ticket seller, and they all hurried through the entrance arch.

Atkins seemed to have forgotten the rest of them as he plunged through the crowds that even at the late hour showed no sign of dwindling. He must have come to search Madame Zhora's stall himself, because he seemed to know exactly where to go.

He stopped several feet from the little house. "Stay back. That's an order."

He stole silently toward the door, but when he stepped inside, the others broke rank and they all followed him inside. And stopped cold.

"It's just like a scene from 'Flight from the Seraglio,'" Bev whispered.

It was, Phil thought. Lily, Rose and Ivan, Anna and Erik, Elisabeth and Dietrich were posed against the wall of drapery like a dumb show. What were they doing here? And how did they know where to come? Were they all involved in Georgina's murder? A group plot?

"How very dashing of you, Detective Sergeant," said the cool voice of Anna Vogeler. "But you arrived rather too late."

Ivan held his pistol in a shaking hand.

"Ivan," moaned Pietro. "Dear boy."

Ivan looked up, then down at the pistol, and then back to Pietro. Shook his head slightly.

"I know you didn't mean to do it. It's the war talking."

Phil slipped in behind Atkins. She could just see Lily's eyes blazing from where she stood between Rose and Elisabeth Weiss.

Elisabeth caught Phil's eye, shrugged. "Kidnapped," she said drily, and Phil admired her sangfroid.

"I offered to drive them to Union House, not all the way out here, merely to retrieve this silly girl," Dietrich groused.

"We had to find her," Erik explained.

"And look at what a fix we're in," added Anna, in the first reproof Phil had ever heard her make of her husband.

From across the floor, Lily's eyes flashed. And Phil knew she was trying to relay something. She cut her eyes to the left.

Chumley Griswold lay crumpled on the floor. Atkins saw him at the same time.

"What happened to Griswold?"

"Who knows?" Dietrich said. "He was here with Ivan and the girls when we barged in like a gaggle of unsuspecting geese. Next thing we know, he's lying on the ground."

"Ivan?" Pietro asked.

"No." Ivan shook his head, rubbed his free arm across his eyes. "I didn't hurt him. I . . ." He trailed off, lifted his pistol but didn't seem to know where to point it.

No one else moved.

"Maybe he fainted," Bev suggested.

"From fright?" Dietrich said.

Atkins stood where he was, his revolver still trained on Ivan, but his eyes taking in the whole room and all the people in it.

Anna moved closer to Erik.

"Please, no one move." Atkins voice was low, calm but firm. "Dr. Salvos, would you see to Mr. Griswold?"

One last agonized look toward Ivan, and Pietro hurried over to examine the fallen man. He checked for his pulse, lifted his eyelids, and finally turned him onto his back. Ran his fingers over the man's neck, his bald head, took his hands, checked his fingers.

"What's he doing?" Bev whispered to Phil.

Phil had no idea.

Finally, he looked over his shoulder to Atkins. "He's been poisoned."

"Is he still alive?"

"Yes. If this is what it appears to be, it is slow-acting, but deadly. First, it cripples the mind, then the respiratory system, then death."

Godfrey stepped forward. "He should be gotten to hospital. Is there an antidote?"

"Yes, but it is not a well-known drug. I don't know if there would be any antidote available."

"Well, we can try. I want to know exactly what this man has been up to. Is there a telephone here?"

No one seemed to know.

"This is insanity. I'll go out to the street."

Ivan didn't attempt to stop him. For a killer, he wasn't very vigilant; the pistol had begun to slump in his hand.

"If I'm correct," Pietro continued, "it was delivered through this pinprick on his palm, very faint, very small, devious. Brings the Borgias to mind." He stood suddenly, his gaze sweeping the room. "This is not the work of Ivan."

"Self-inflicted?" Atkins asked.

"Perhaps."

"Oh, my dear Lord," Elisabeth said. "She shook his hand." She slowly turned her head to look at Anna. "Anna, you shook his hand. You poisoned him with a pinprick." Her voice held a profound disbelief.

"One of his own formulas?" Pietro demanded. "Have you no regard for human life?"

"Don't be absurd," Anna said. "I came for Rose. Detective Sergeant, can you please arrest this poor man and let us get Rose back to Union House. I'm truly afraid this evening has been too much for her. I shudder to think what will happen if she goes further into her mind."

Ivan lifted the pistol, but Phil could tell he wasn't aiming at anyone. He wasn't even attempting to get away. It was like all the spirit had drained out of him.

And Atkins made no move to disarm him.

Lily was glaring at Phil, blinking furiously. Trying to signal something? Phil wished they had paid more attention to Morse code in their studies. It would make an excellent communication in times like these.

Lily's eyes widened and glanced to her right. Phil followed the gaze. Erik's hands were hanging free beside him. Anna's were clasped in front of her in a beseeching gesture.

Phil blinked back. She was beginning to understand, but only part.

"It's all just too much," said Anna, imploringly. "May we please take Rose away from this horrible situation?"

Atkins didn't answer.

What a muddle. He wasn't sure whom to arrest. And he couldn't very well take them all on by himself. And if he arrested one, the others would get away. And surely, they weren't all innocent.

Phil thought of her own pistol inside the purse she clutched in her hand. But it might as well be in China. Ivan was a trained sniper.

"Ivan, please," Anna said. "Let Rose go. She doesn't belong to you. You can't take care of her."

"Georgie takes care of me," Rose said.

Erik Vogeler stepped toward her. "My dear girl. Georgie is dead. You're going to live with us now."

He reached toward her, but Anna cried, "Erik, don't."

Still Ivan didn't move. Just watched the three of them with an eerily detached calm.

"I live with Georgie," Rose repeated. "I will wait until Georgie gets here." She looked at Ivan. "That's what I'm supposed to do."

And suddenly the vapidness in his eyes was replaced with an expression so full of love that it was painful to watch. Because Phil knew that this love story had no happy ending. For either of them.

"Rose, you can't stay here," Anna said. "Mr. Bennington will take us back to Union House. We leave for Europe tomorrow. We'll have some lovely sandwiches. You like sandwiches."

Rose bit her lip and, strangely enough, looked at Lily.

Then her head snapped back to Anna. "You gave me drugs."

Anna stepped back. "To help you sleep after Georgie left."

"No, the ones to help Ivan. You said it would help Ivan, but it didn't. They didn't, did they, Ivan?"

Ivan looked at Pietro.

Pietro looked at Anna. "You gave him drugs?"

"Standard treatment for patients suffering from trauma," Erik said. "He made great strides while we were treating him. You're the one who took him from our care."

"Because you cheated me out of my job and my future. And Ivan's, too."

"Both of you, stop," Elisabeth said. "It's past time for recriminations. Let bygones go."

"No!" Ivan suddenly brandished the gun around the room. Erik stepped in front of Anna.

"Easy, easy," Atkins said.

"No one is taking Rose."

"Fine, Ivan. I will send everyone away and we'll have a talk, just you and me and Rose. Okay?"

Ivan shook his head.

"It was a secret," Rose said.

"What was a secret?" Atkins asked gently.

"She said not to tell."

"Georgie said? It's okay to tell. Georgie said it is okay to tell me."

Rose shook her head.

Phil wanted to shake her until the truth fell out. The girl did seem to have moments of clarity.

"It's okay," Atkins assured her.

Rose just shook her head. "It will ruin everything. Georgie says."

"Oh, for heaven's sake." Pietro rose from the unconscious Chumley. "Rose has petit mal seizures."

Rose clapped both hands to her mouth.

"What?" exclaimed Erik.

"That isn't possible," Anna said.

"She never told us," Elisabeth said, glancing at Phil.

Pietro turned on them. "Because she didn't trust any of you not to tell. She was afraid you might use it to keep Rose from advancement. Anyone might. The competition in our profession isn't always honest. Is it, Erik?"

"Is that the secret, Rose?" Atkins asked.

"No," Anna said. "It can't be true."

"It's true," Pietro said. "Georgie was treating her with potassium bromide, and she must have had a reaction to it. She's been like this ever since."

"You lie," Erik cried.

A nasty suspicion popped into Phil's mind. "Rose just said you gave her drugs. Not just now, but then. You were treating Rose with drugs, too. Weren't you? You told her she could help Ivan." Phil saw the sudden understanding in Erik's face. Understanding and fear. "You gave her drugs, too."

Erik dropped his face to his hands. "Oh my God, my God."

"Please, love," Anna said, touching his bowed head. "How were we to know?" She fairly spit the question into the room.

"You might have asked," Dietrich said. "I suppose it was something experimental that Chumley whipped up for you. Is he still supplying you with his wonder drugs? Oh, yes, he tried to touch me, too. An exorbitant charge for a bunch of nonsense."

"Dietrich, please," Anna said. "You should really try not to let your ignorance show. Drugs will be the path to greatness."

"Hogwash," snapped Dietrich. "Come, Elisabeth, if you want a ride back to town. I'm leaving."

"No one is leaving," Atkins ordered.

"You monster!" Pietro cried. "You dosed Rose and it reacted with Georgie's treatments. All these years, she thought it was her fault. It wasn't; it was you. You bastard." He lunged at Erik.

Erik merely stepped away. "You pitiful excuse for a man. You and your less-than-a-man over there."

"And you were party to this, Anna?" Elisabeth's voice was hard.

"Of course. My husband is a great man. He will lead the way into the understanding of the human mind. Create better men because of it. Men who will rule the world."

"Holy smoke," whispered Bev. "What are they talking about?"

"Superior men. Not in a good sense."

"Now I definitely don't like her."

"When Ivan first returned from the war, Rose came to me, riddled with guilt for sending him away. I told her there was a way she could help. By taking the drug I was treating Ivan with, so that I could compare its effectiveness. She volunteered readily. She didn't love him, just wanted to clear her pathetic little conscience. Besides, she needed the money. And I needed her superior mind and body. She was oh-so easy to convince." Anna's eyes gleamed with unseen success. "Ivan showed potential. In spite of his mental damage, he was strong and bright and fierce. But she was perfect. Beautiful, brilliant, and healthy, or so I thought.

"I was having great success with Ivan, He was stronger than ever, his reflexes quicker, his ability to act . . . it was truly amazing. If he was like this, imagine what Rose could be. But Rose didn't react to the drugs as Ivan did. Instead of getting stronger, she got weaker. Instead of quicker, she became slow and unfocused. And then one day . . ." Anna threw an offhanded gesture in Rose's direction. "This. How was I to know that her moments of complete, intense thought were, instead, merely the effects of petit mal seizures? She was already damaged. If I had known . . . But they kept it a secret while her sister, a mediocre physician, at best, treated her with potassium bromide. It interacted adversely. She destroyed everything I'd strived for. Stupid, stupid, stupid woman."

"You're a lunatic," Dietrich said.

"How dare you," Erik said. "Anna and I are the future. You will be left behind in the chaff of humanity."

"Not in this country, you won't be," Godfrey said, striding into the room. "By God, I knew there was something off about the two of you. You can take your superior soldier and sail tomorrow and I'll be glad to see you go."

"The more fool you," Erik scoffed. "And now, Anna and I must leave you."

And Phil suddenly realized that Alan Toussaint was not with them. Was he waiting for them outside, or were they meaning to take Dietrich's car to leave the scene?

"Where is your assistant?" Phil asked. "Waiting to scuttle you away?"

"Alas, he nearly made a cock-up of this whole affair. We won't be needing his services anymore."

"You fired him?"

"In a manner of speaking," Erik said. "But first, Anna, a little demonstration?"

Phil's blood ran cold.

"A small parting example that may change your mind about bidding on our program."

"Of course, my dear. Ivan? It's time." Anna said his name conversationally, but Ivan turned slowly to face Rose.

"No," cried Pietro. "How are doing this to him?"

"All those hours I was supposed to be spending in the museums of Manhattan were really meetings with Ivan. Didn't you ever wonder where he was these last two weeks? He was with me, regaining the skills he'd acquired under my treatment and that were withering under your lack of imagination. And now, behold the fruits of my labor."

"Ours, dear," Erik said, and came to stand by her side.

"Yes, dear, ours," she agreed. "And none of you once questioned why we invited you to dinner. Where are your minds, such that they are?"

"Georgie knew," Elisabeth said.

"Georgie. She knew nothing. Though I admit she did have me fooled for a moment. I thought she had figured out what had happened. Someone was blackmailing me. A minor annoyance. My family is very rich, but as it turns out, it wasn't Georgie at all." Slowly, she looked over to where Chumley lay so still; Phil thought he must be dead. That would not please Mr. X or the powers that be. Of course, if they didn't get out of here alive, he might never know what happened.

"Alas, it was Chumley after all. Funny old Chumley figured it out, while the rest of you . . ." She waved them away like so many flies. "Damn him, he'd been supplying one of the versions of hallucinates I was using. Actually, it was his drug that pushed poor Rose over the edge of sanity.

"Poor chump, Chumley, I would gladly have continued paying his exorbitant prices for the drugs. Would have helped him distribute them in Europe. But it wasn't enough. Greed was his undoing. At what point does mutual understanding turn to manipulation? Do any of you great men of science know? Or you, Elisabeth, forced to sequester yourself in a women's college?"

Elisabeth smiled. "You're the one to be pitied, Anna. You must be taking too many of your own drugs if you think your experiments will take you anywhere but to the gallows."

Ivan looked from Rose to Anna. "You told me Georgie made Rose the way she is." He looked to Pietro. "*You* said Georgie did it."

"I thought she did. I was wrong." Pietro buried his face in his hands. "What have I done?"

Anna let out an exasperated breath. "Pietro, ever the melodramatic. You should have gone on the stage, not the laboratory. But we're running late, so please observe. A repeat performance. First the sister, and now Ivan will kill Rose Nash, once the love of his life." She paused; a slight smile spread across her lips. "And the unrequited love of my own husband."

Erik stared at her. "No," he said, in almost a whisper. "Must we?"

"Yes, my dear. If you want to continue your research, sacrifices must be made. I've made mine—and now you must make yours."

Rose just smiled vapidly over the scene. It was impossible to tell how much she really understood.

Suddenly, without warning, Anna laughed delightedly. "Brilliant, Rose, you're always so droll!"

"Huh?" Bev blurted.

But Phil was remembering Anna's last words that night, right before Georgie was killed. *Brilliant, Georgie, you're always so droll.*

She started forward, but Atkins held her back.

Ivan turned toward Rose, his pistol directed at her heart.

Rose just smiled blankly back at him.

"No," cried Lily and Phil at the same time Ivan raised the pistol.

The next moment lasted an eternity as everyone's reflexes seemed to slow down, leaving them helpless to stop the inevitable.

Anna laughed again. "Brilliant, Rose, you're—"

Ivan lifted the pistol a little higher, then he lowered his arm and dropped the pistol at his feet.

"Ivan . . ."

But he backed away to stand with the others.

"Another man who has failed the test." Anna snatched the pistol from the floor and took aim at Rose. The pistol trembled in her hand.

"Anna, no!" Phil cried, helpless to stop her.

Anna's finger tightened spasmodically.

Ivan threw himself between her and Rose.

Anna's scream of rage and Pietro's cry of "Nooooo!" were drowned in the report of the gun, and blood sprayed in the air.

For a moment, no one moved. Even Anna seemed shocked.

When the reverberations finally died away, it was Ivan who lay dead at Rose's feet.

Pietro dropped to his knees. Felt for a pulse, then sat back on his heels, shaking his head.

For the first time, Erik seemed confused. "Are we going to leave them here?"

"No need for you to worry about it, my dear. Dietrich, I'm sure you won't mind if we borrow your automobile?"

Anna grabbed Rose and pushed her into Erik's arms. He dragged her toward the door, while Anna aimed Ivan's pistol at the others. "You will stay in place or Rose will no longer be an asset."

"For God's sake," Godfrey shouted. "What about your children?"

"Our people know what to do."

And they were gone.

29

Phil and Atkins reached the door just in time to see the Vogelers dragging Rose between them. They were racing toward the street only to be swallowed up by a surge of people as the Giant See Saw expelled its passengers onto the midway.

"Where are they?" Phil cried. "Can you see them?"

Atkins was stretched to his toes. "There."

Phil just caught sight of them, jostled by the crowd and fighting against the tide. And suddenly the crowd churned as they all hurried toward different destinations, toward the next thrill, driving the trio apart, leaving Erik alone and pushing Anna and Rose back the way they had come.

Erik, after a frantic look around, headed for the street.

"Watch the women," Atkins ordered, and ran after him.

Phil was so shocked that he actually included her that she lost sight of Anna and Rose. But only for a second.

She found them again, being forced back toward Phil only to be engulfed again by a sea of people.

Damn. Phil started in the direction she'd seen them, only by chance glimpsing their two heads bobbing slowly through the crowd.

"Rose!" Phil called, but Rose didn't appear to hear her.

Phil shoved her way into the crowd. And realized Rose had stopped moving. Alert, Phil scanned the nearby crowd for Anna. She was gone. Rose just stood there as people hurried past. She showed no surprise or fear at Phil's sudden appearance, merely said, "She left me."

"Anna? Did you see which way she went?"

"She's gone. I'm glad. I want Georgie to make lunch."

Lunch? It had to be close to midnight. Which could account for the frenzy of the crowd, to squeeze in the last few moments of fun or get to the exits before everyone else.

"Can you get to Madame Zhora's by yourself?" Phil asked, still searching the crowd for Anna. Found her threading her way in the opposite direction.

"I'll take her." Bev appeared miraculously by Phil's side. "Well, you didn't expect me to let you down, did you?"

"No, indeed." Phil caught sight of Anna, farther away now. "If Atkins returns, tell him she's headed for the boardwalk."

Bev nodded. "Come, Rose. Are you hungry?" Rose went docilely, and Phil let the crowd sweep her forward until she could see Anna, running now, heading straight down the fairway to the boardwalk entrance.

Phil hiked up her skirts and ran full tilt after her.

Anna, for all her superbeing intentions, was not in the best of shape. As she passed the Ferris wheel, its lights circling dizzily, she stumbled. She managed to keep her feet, but she'd lost valuable time, and Phil closed in on her.

To their left, the wooden horses of the Steeplechase raced past them. Screams rose above them as the airships hurtling to earth met them ahead. They ran past the carousel, its menagerie turning to the music of the calliope, every movement reflected in hundreds of mirrored pieces as they passed. All the while, lights exploded around them, making it hard for Phil to keep her eye on her target.

Phil was mere feet away when Anna reached the exit and ran onto the boardwalk. There, she hesitated, seemed to deliberate on which way to go. Did she mean to catch up to Erik and the auto? Had they preplanned a secondary escape route?

Anna turned for a moment and saw Phil, the expression on her face so feral that it took Phil aback. Then she turned and ran straight ahead, not down the boardwalk, where she might be able to meet up with Erik or lose herself in the attractions, but straight ahead onto the pier—and a dead end.

Phil paused to take a deep breath, then heard the steam whistle. Not a dead end. The steam ferry was moored at the end. It must be about to leave for the city, where its passengers would change to trains or taxis or automobiles that would take them in all directions.

Phil didn't dare wait, but ran ahead.

Anna slowed, doubled over, and grabbed her side, and Phil recognized the sign of cramp. She'd had one herself on one of the Newport health hikes that were so popular this summer.

Here was her chance. With a burst of speed, she closed in on the villain.

Anna saw her coming and swung away toward the ferry, back toward Phil. And in what Phil had to admit might be considered a superhuman effort, Anna leapt toward the rails of the pier.

In a burst of energy born of sheer terror that she might escape into the sea, Phil lunged to stop her, grabbing her around the waist and pulling with all her might. Anna wrenched away, but instead of freeing herself, she just pulled Phil over the side.

And they fell. Phil's only thought was to keep hold of Anna as blackness rose to meet them.

For a moment, time stopped. Then they hit the biting-cold water, and the fabric of Anna's skirt was torn from Phil's fingers. She came up sputtering—thanking heaven the tide was in and the water had broken their fall—and searching for Anna.

She was several feet away. They were both wet but undamaged, sputtering in breast-deep water, while the waves pushed them toward the shore and the undertow tried to pull them out to sea.

The ferry blew its final whistle and chugged away from the pier.

Anna screamed—from rage, Phil suspected—and threw herself forward in the water. Did she really think she could outswim the boat and be taken aboard?

Her desire for superiority had instead driven her around the bend.

Phil dove after her; managed to grab a handful of fabric long enough to drag her back. She kicked Phil away; Phil fell back into the water, only to scramble up again. Her skirts were heavy and holding her down, but so were Anna's.

They might have drowned each other but for the late-night revelers on the beach who came to the rescue and pulled them both onto the shore.

Anna fought, scratched, and screamed like a madwoman.

Phil merely thanked her rescuers and cried, "That woman is a thief, don't let her escape!"

There was no hesitation on the part of her rescuers. Anna Vogeler's fate was sealed.

One did not steal at Steeplechase Park.

Someone slipped his jacket over Phil's shoulders.

"Thank you," she began.

"My pleasure," he said, leaning so close his breath warmed her salty cheek. "Rather late for a swim, no?"

"You were here this whole time, and you let me—" She started to turn around. He held her in place. "I just got here and I have to leave. Tell Atkins I had to borrow Chumley. And Salvos, since he may hold the key to this whole business, if he can find an antidote to save the chemist. I need Chumley to name names. They've both been removed to a secure hospital. "We'll return Salvos when we're finished with him, but you might not see Chumley again. Give my apologies to Atkins, but we were after him first."

"We were? Can I tell him about you?"

"God, no. Just say that Griswold is in the hands of the proper authorities. He can have Louie the Lump."

"I suppose I'll have to read about unexpected arrests in the newspaper."

"Most likely, though not as quickly as usual. It's rather a large operation."

"You know Atkins will—"

"Of course he will, but you can handle him." A soft laugh. "You handle me."

She'd just stopped a killer from escaping, nearly drowned, and they were surrounded by gawkers, and he was flirting? The man was insufferable.

A commotion at the back of the group got everyone's attention, including Phil's. The police had arrived at last. They were accompanied by several uniformed park attendants.

She didn't bother to even glance over her shoulder; she'd felt him leave.

He'd left his jacket draped over her shoulders. Of course, he wouldn't have if there were any clues as to its owner. She checked the pockets anyway. Empty.

"Which one of you is Lady Dunbridge?"

"I am Lady Dunbridge," Phil said, giving the officer her full attention. "Detective Sergeant Atkins is waiting to arrest this woman."

"Yes, ma'am. We've received orders to meet him."

They all trudged through the sand toward the park, Anna still fighting the two policemen who accompanied her. One of the park attendants attempted to help Phil but merely managed to get in the way. Her skirts were heavy and cumbersome enough without trying not to trip over the man's rather large feet.

Once, she thought she saw *him* walking calmly away with the crowd as it began to disperse. But though she never let her focus waver, he eventually just disappeared.

No superman. Just a man very good at his job; trained, inventive in so many ways, and as elusive as a wisp of smoke.

Atkins was waiting for her at Madame Zhora's.

One look at her, and he turned away, not from any sense of modesty but to keep from laughing.

"Oh, madam," Lily said, moving toward her, looking worried.

"Oh, Phil," Bev echoed, and burst out laughing.

"I could have drowned," Phil groused. "But oh, I'm happy to see you all sound and safe." She frowned. "But where is Preswick and Just a Friend?"

"At the shooting gallery, killing ducks," Lily said.

"I granted them leave," Atkins said, still not turning around. "As soon as we learned you had been fished safely out of the ocean, Preswick thought . . . thought you would want a little privacy."

"I know you're laughing," Phil said. "I think I prefer you groaning."

"Phil!" Bev said.

"Ugh, I give up. Lily, perhaps Madame Zhora would have something suitable to clothe a bedraggled countess."

Lily took her into the back room, where together they rummaged Georgina's wardrobe for something appropriate.

"Is Mr. Griswold going to die?" asked Lily.

"I don't know; I hope not," Phil said, her hand arrested on a shimmery robe made of one of the new synthetic fabrics. "But if he doesn't, he will most certainly go to jail."

"Then what will Rose do?"

"Rose? Mr. Bennington will see that she gets the best of care."

"And they'll hypnotize her?"

"Possibly." Phil shoved the garish robe back into the wardrobe. "Why do you ask?"

"That's what Mr. Chumley did. He hypnotized Rose and made her know things."

Phil's attention totally arrested, she turned to Lily, who was looking decidedly young and incredibly vulnerable.

"What things?"

Lily shrugged and withdrew into the hanging garments. "Things that happened to her," she said into the clothing.

"How do you know this?"

"Rose told me. She said he made her see things that she'd forgotten. She made me promise not to tell."

Phil swallowed. She could sense they had wandered into new territory, and she didn't want to move too precipitately, lest she break this moment when she could feel that Lily was about to confide in her.

But Lily said no more, just pulled one of the garments out and held it up to Phil.

Phil pretended to consider the robe, a pink confection with a feathered hem. Usually they would both laugh at such a horrid design, but Lily wasn't laughing. Her eyes were wary, and Phil decided to jump in. It couldn't be worse than her recent swim in the Atlantic.

"Have you ever gotten hypnotized?" she asked, inspecting the feathers so she wouldn't look too closely at Lily.

"No."

"Would you like to?" Phil asked, still fingering the feathers.

"No. It doesn't matter."

Phil's heart fell with disappointment. She wanted to say, *No, it doesn't matter. Whatever we find out, you will always be ours.* Should she push? Or should she be patient? The answer forced its way out.

"Well, if you ever want to get hypnotized, we'll all get hypnotized."

Lily finally looked at her. Hopeful, and with just a flash of her usual wit. "Mr. Preswick, too?"

Phil gulped at the sheer audacity of that idea, but said, "Of course, Mr. Preswick, too. Shall we make an appointment with Dr. Salvos? I'm certain he is quite as good as Chumley Griswold."

Lily shook her head, but she looked happier. "Maybe one day." And a second later, she pulled the perfect robe from the wardrobe.

The moment had passed, but Phil had hope for the future. And the robe Lily had chosen was bound to dazzle. Which would help to distract Detective Sergeant Atkins while she imparted the message from Mr. X.

Phil returned to the others several minutes later, wrapped in a flowing, jeweled kaftan in orange and yellow fire motifs. The swath of fabric was held in place by a dazzling ersatz-diamond sash, and at the last moment, she had pressed a turban to her head.

She got more than the reaction she had expected.

Atkins's expression changed from mirth to something Phil couldn't quite make out. It might have been horror. Bev clapped her hands in delight. Dietrich continued to sit to the side, grumbling like he had done most of the evening. And Elisabeth just shook her head.

But the best was Just a Friend, who, with Preswick, was just returning. "You shoulda seen Mr. Preswick! He—Wow," he breathed, and pulled his cap from his head in wonder.

Godfrey returned moments later. "Vogeler has been apprehended and the ambulance is on their way. I told them it was a matter of national security. I don't think it did any good."

Atkins stared at him. Turned on the attendant he'd left in charge.

"They already came. Just a few minutes ago. Took that tall fellow with them," the attendant said.

Atkins's steely frown moved from the attendant to Godfrey. "What are you playing at?"

Godfrey said nothing. Slowly both men turned their attention to Phil.

She swallowed. "There's something I need to tell you."

30

Atkins was not amused. He wasn't even civil when Phil delivered her message. He was angry enough when he learned that Chumley had been stolen from him, but when Phil refused to give up the name of the person or persons who had usurped his case, he was so furious that he turned a shade of white that even the colorful lights of the park couldn't erase.

"I should have you jailed for obstructing an investigation."

"Atkins," Godfrey said, "she just caught your killer. One would think that thanks were in order."

"Thank you, Godfrey," Phil said demurely.

Without a word, Atkins walked outside. He didn't return for several minutes.

Through it all, Rose never looked up. Someone had found her an apple, and she sat quietly munching it while the world changed around her.

"What's going to happen to her?" Phil asked Godfrey.

"We'll see to it that she's given the best of care. You can assure Lily that it will be a lovely place where they are kind, and may be able to give her proper treatment. And where Lily can visit her if she likes."

"Thank you," Phil said.

"Not at all. It's the least we can do."

We? Who was the "we" this time? He hadn't seemed surprised that someone had taken Chumley and Pietro away.

"And the children?"

"If they're still there, which I somehow doubt, they'll be returned to some family member who is willing to take them in. Anna Vogeler has a very rich, very large family in England. Surely one of them will see fit, considering. Preferably someone who won't encourage them to follow in their parents' footsteps."

"That's good to know," Phil said. "They were annoying, but

even annoying children deserve a good home." Which drew her eye to Just a Friend, who was standing close to Preswick and listening to every word of the adult conversation.

Soon she and Preswick and Lily would have to have a serious conversation about the boy's future. Which might conceivably include a real trip to Coney Island for them all.

When the rest of them left Madame Zhora's, Atkins stayed behind to instruct the mortuary truck about the handling of Ivan's body. He would have a long night ahead of him, and there was nothing Phil could do but get in his way.

The Vogelers were on their way to the Tombs to wait proper sentencing, and the detective sergeant's mood seemed to have improved. Maybe he was actually relieved to have Chumley taken off his hands. He would have plenty to keep him busy with charging the Vogelers.

They said good night to Dietrich and Elisabeth and watched them walk down the street to Dietrich's automobile.

Then they made their way up Seventeenth Street to The Oddity Shop, where the other two autos were parked.

Godfrey bowed over her hand. "I promise our next dinner will not include murder on the menu."

"I hope that is an invitation," Phil said. "I'd be delighted."

"Excellent. I'll ring you when I'm next in the city. First, I must arrange for Miss Nash and the Vogeler children, and report that the Vogeler program has been found flawed. About time I got back to my aeroplanes. Preswick, see your mistress home."

Preswick bowed crisply.

Bev offered to drive, and Phil chose to sit in the back with Lily and Just a Friend, while Preswick sat beside Bev. Phil was tired, exhilarated with the chase, and more than anything, happy to have her little family safe and sound and together.

It was almost dawn before her bedroom door clicked open and Mr. X slipped into the room. Morning was nigh and the room light enough to see that he'd managed to find another suit jacket, which made her think that perhaps he had come in by the foyer and elevator. With him, one never knew.

He immediately began to take it off.

Phil held up her hand.

"Before you go any farther, I have a couple of things to say."

He shrugged the jacket back over his shoulders and came to sit on the edge of the bed.

"First, Atkins is very upset with me."

"I heard."

"From who? Ah, from Godfrey."

"From Preswick, just now."

"You talked to Preswick?"

"I didn't have much choice. He was up. Doesn't the man ever sleep? He had a few choice words for me, then offered me coffee."

"Does he know who you are?" Phil asked, feeling suddenly like one of those wives who is always the last to know that her husband is carrying on with every demimondaine in London.

"He could guess. I let myself into your apartment."

"He'll think I gave you the key."

"Shall I go back to scaling buildings for the pleasure of your company?"

"No, but you need to know something. Something I maybe should have withheld from Atkins. But I didn't because . . ." She glared at him. "I didn't know who knew what, because I'm never told anything."

"But you do it so well," he said, not fazed at all. "What didn't you withhold from Atkins that you should have? Not your favors, I hope. Though, hell, Countess, the man is a Puritan."

"I do not want to discuss Detective Sergeant Atkins with you. It was Georgina's diary."

"I've already seen it."

"You knew about her?"

"Yes, she was an informant."

"I'd never have guessed."

"That's the point with an informant. She was paid well, of course. She was always strapped for money, that one."

"Little good it does her now."

"True, but for the record, we didn't know she was going to get herself killed, or that she even knew about the Arsenal dinner. Or that you were going to be there. Imagine my surprise. For what it's worth, I don't think we could have stopped it."

"I might have if I'd known about it," Phil argued.

He stood, pulled off his jacket. "We're on separate branches of the same tree, Countess. Tangle the branches and the tree dies."

Phil blinked. "I've never heard *that* old saw."

He shrugged.

Those shoulders told her more than he'd ever said. It was the first time she'd seen him express anything but cool precision. Except perhaps when they weren't discussing business.

"Even if you and I had both known in advance, we would have never put it together before that dinner." He pulled his shirt over his head. "Murder by proxy. I wonder if they can make that stick."

Though Phil felt much better after Mr. X's visit, especially knowing that she hadn't been responsible for not stopping Georgie's murder, she did feel a certain trepidation when the telephone rang the next morning and the porter announced that Detective Sergeant Atkins was downstairs.

She doubted if he felt any better after most likely spending the night tying up loose ends and explaining to his superiors how he lost two of the prime actors.

She picked up the newspaper she'd been perusing and waited with fluttering stomach for him to make the trip upstairs.

Preswick showed him in. As usual, he was impeccably dressed.

"I owe you an apology," he said without preamble.

"Not at all," Phil said, setting her paper aside.

"Is Chumley still alive?" Atkins asked.

"I have no idea. I certainly hope so."

"Who has him?" His questions were precise, clipped, and not at all friendly.

"I don't know," Phil said. "Truly, I don't."

"An investigation by a higher authority than the New York Police Department?"

"If I were to guess. Are Nanny Cole and the maid in custody?" she asked quickly, before he could interrogate her further.

"Yes, and harping about the embassy and immunity."

"And Alan Toussaint?"

"Flown or dead."

"Atkins—" she began.

"Was it Bennington?"

"I promise you, I don't know."

"How do you fit into all this?"

She didn't know that, either, but she wasn't going to give him the satisfaction of knowing that she was also somewhat in the dark. "As you've said, I'm just a meddlesome countess. It seems that I must have been put on earth to annoy you."

She saw his face and relented.

"Oh, come now, Atkins, it's not so bad. You have your murderers. You've solved the case and have none of the tedious cleanup of things beyond your jurisdiction."

"I suppose this means I'll be seeing you on another one of my cases in the future."

"Indubitably, Detective Sergeant. It seems to be a habit with us."

She wasn't sure if the sound Atkins made was a groan, a growl, or his way of saying, "Welcome aboard."

She let it pass.

A few days later, the headline she'd been expecting caught her eye. Not a banner across the front page but four inches of one column, several pages in, reporting on the arrest of Chumley Griswold—which must mean Salvos had been successful in finding an antidote—leading to the arrest of several members of an illegal network of experimental drugs used in the treatment of psychological pathologies, not readily available to medical practitioners at this time. Some that were said to have deadly side effects.

No other names were listed, and Phil wondered if Dietrich Lutz had been one of those apprehended. She hoped that Elisabeth was really unassociated with them. She liked the college professor. She reminded herself to telephone Marty about doing an article on Barnard College for the *Times*.

Phil turned the page, glad to be rid of all of them at last, and her eye caught an article on the new styles in bathing attire. Now, here was something she could get her teeth into.

The next time she took a dip in the Atlantic, she would be wearing an appropriate bathing costume: one of the new one-piece bathing tights that were rumored to be the next big fashion revolution in Europe.

Now, that was her kind of revolution. They would need brave women not to go mindlessly into war but to blaze the bathing-costume future.

And for that, Lady Dunbridge was happy to oblige.

AUTHOR'S NOTE

History is interesting, but it is, alas, ephemeral. Fortunately, the early 1900s are awash with primary materials: newspapers, photographs, books, memoirs, as well as edifices that survived fires, dilapidations, and demolitions.

In 1908, when Phil first visits Coney Island, there were three major amusement parks: Steeplechase Park, Luna Park, and Dreamland, as well as blocks and blocks of independent amusements, thrill rides, eateries, saloons, theaters, music pavilions, and some of the largest hotels in the county. These were all packed tightly together and constructed largely of wood. The possibility of fire was a constant worry, and when it was ignited it would quickly spread throughout the area, taking everything in its path. Among the many fires that swept through the area was the Steeplechase fire of 1907, destroying the majority of the park. Only momentarily daunted, the owner, George C. Tilyou, quickly posted a sign with this promise.

> To enquiring friends: I have troubles today that I had not yesterday. I had troubles yesterday which I have not today. On this site will be built a bigger, better, Steeplechase Park. Admission to the burning ruins—Ten cents.

As he promised, the new Steeplechase Park opened in May 1908, just in time for Bev and Phil's visit to the races and Coney Island.

There were three Coney Island horse-racing tracks in 1908: Brighton Beach Race Course, Sheepshead Bay Race Track, and Gravesend Race Track. Brighton Beach was forced to close at the end of that summer due to the new antibetting laws; the other two soon followed.

The Manhattan Beach Hotel was built in 1877. Constructed of wood, it rose three to four stories high and sat a mere 400 feet from the surf on 660 feet of beach frontage. There was elevator service to each floor, and its 300 guest rooms all were equipped with private baths, and several with their own verandas. The two main restaurants and a wide veranda could accommodate up to 4,000 diners at a time. With its own bandstand and bathing pavilion, the Manhattan was just one of several large luxury hotels in Coney Island, and a member of the Jockey Club.

The Pabst Loop Hotel, where Bobby and the jockeys stayed for the races, burned down completely the following month, on July 9, 1908. It was not rebuilt.

Louis "Louis the Lump" Pioggi was actually arrested in May for the murders of Max "Kid Twist" Zwerbach and Vach "Cyclone Louie" Lewis, but with a name like that, I couldn't resist bending history a few weeks in order to give him a cameo appearance.

I love the dime novels of the day, a time when reading became a national pastime, though they were not what was considered by the upper classes to be edifying, and there were movements to suppress their distribution. I think those stories, printed on cheap paper and sold at every newsstand, captured the hopes and dreams of the modern person of the times. They were certainly an inspiration to Phil, Lily, and Preswick, and to me. I included four of them in *Resolution,* though I did have to stretch history a bit to include "Four Scraps of Paper, Or, Nick Carter's Coney Island Search." It was actually published the following year, in September 1909, but it was just so perfect I had to use it.

A word about motoring in 1908. It was no easy feat. One didn't jump in the car and take off. Most still required cranks, push starters, and open throttles. Gas tanks typically held ten gallons, and generally got ten to twenty-one miles to the gallon, depending on the auto. An extra can of gasoline would usually be carried in the auto, since refill stations were still few and far between. Coney Island is a good twenty miles from the Plaza, and with the inconsistent quality of the roads, trips there would be subject to flat tires, overheating, and breakdowns, all of which were common occurrences. I chose to spare Phil and Bev these inconveniences for the sake of moving the story along.

And yes, in 1908, most avenues and streets in Manhattan still carried two-way traffic, including Fifth Avenue.

Black Diamond was a North American bull bison given to the Central Park menagerie by the Barnum & Bailey Circus; he resided there for over twenty years. He was said to be very calm, and was a favorite of children and adults alike. A popular rumor had it that he was the inspiration for the buffalo-head nickel. Black Diamond met an ignoble end when, too old and sickly to remain at the zoo, he was put up for auction. When no bids materialized, he was sold to a local butcher. Steaks bearing the name "Black Diamond Steaks" sold for two dollars per pound.

To learn more about Coney Island's history, I recommend two of my favorite sites: www.heartofconeyisland.com and www.westland.net/coneyisland/articles/earlyhistory.htm, as well as many other books and websites.

I hope you enjoy Phil, Bev, Lily, and Preswick's trips to Coney Island as much as I did.

Enjoy,
Shelley

ACKNOWLEDGMENTS

This book was unusual in many ways, but particularly because it was written mostly in isolation as the Covid virus swept through our New York Tri-state area. So no in-person interviews, no trips to see things for myself. This novel was researched nearly exclusively online or over the wires. Thanks to the many lovers of history and especially Coney Island history who continued to share their expertise with me personally and with the world via podcasts, blogs, and webinars, some of which I list in my author's note.

Also thanks to the Bowery Boys (boweryboyshistory.com) and New York Adventure Club (nyadventureclub.com), who made history almost like being there and sometimes better.

I've been to Coney Island many times, but seeing it through the eyes of history gave me a much bigger appreciation of its amazing adaptability.

Much appreciation to Kristin Sevick, Patrick Canfield, Libby Collins, my agent Kevan Lyon, and my entire Forge Team. And special thanks to the amazing cover artist, Andrew Davidson, who captured just what I imagined Coney Island would be in 1908.

ABOUT THE AUTHOR

SHELLEY NOBLE is the *New York Times* bestselling author of *Lighthouse Beach, The Beach at Painter's Cove, Whisper Beach,* and the Lady Dunbridge series, which started with *Ask Me No Questions.* A former professional dancer and choreographer for stage, television, and film, she's a member of Sisters in Crime, Mystery Writers of America, and the Women's Fiction Writers Association. Noble lives in New Jersey.

EC

April 14